THE STORY OF US

Barbara Elsborg

COPYRIGHT

The Story of Us is a work of fiction but the events and locations used are a mix of real and fictional.

Copyright © 2018 Barbara Elsborg

Cover design by B4Jay

Edited by Deco

THE STORY OF US

Two boys. One love. Ten summers.

Are you okay?

The first words Zed says to Caspian, and the first time someone has cared about the answer. On a hot summer's day, the lives of two boys are changed forever. A rebel and a risk taker, Caspian doesn't give a damn for the consequences. Studious and obedient, Zed is the good boy who is never good enough.

The two couldn't be more different, but there's one thing they share, a need to belong to someone who understands them, someone who cares. Their friendship goes deeper than either can possibly imagine. They're young, in love, and planning their future when an act of betrayal tears them apart.

Fate deals its hand. Seasons pass. Zed's words follow Caspian through pain, fear and into the darkest of places. Friendships can last a lifetime, even when the world conspires to crush them. But this is more than friendship. This is love and they're not going to let it slip through their fingers.

The Story of Us is a tale of love and survival, and the triumph of good over evil against the odds.

Acknowledgements

Thanks to Rita, Katerina, HL, Ali, Dawn, Laurie and Claire for all the advice and encouragement I received while writing this book. I should thank Google too! There was a lot to check when covering a period of ten years!

SUMMER ONE

Chapter One

2010

Zed handed over his school report, then fidgeted as his father read it.

"Stand still, boy."

He curled his toes inside his shoes. Would he ever be something more than *boy* to his father? Their family name was Zadeh—hence his nickname Zed, though his father never called him that. Nor did he use Zed's proper name, and although it was a mouthful, Zed doubted that was the explanation for his father's reluctance.

Does he dislike me that much?

Zed's name was Hvarechaeshman, which meant having eyes like the sun, but who had yellow eyes? His were blue which was unusual for someone who was half Iranian. Instead of inheriting his father's brown eyes, Zed had his mother's blue ones, though the rim of brown around the blue was probably from his father. His mother had chosen his name and she'd used it, calling him Hari for short. No one else ever had. He'd never wanted anyone to call him Hari after she died.

"Forty-three percent in religious studies?" his father bellowed. "Did you make no effort at all?"

He'd not been well that day due to his father having beaten him the night before, but it was pointless offering any excuses.

"Hardly better in history." His father shook the report in Zed's face. "*Needs to learn to answer the question.*"

Seventy percent and he'd come fourth. One question he'd slipped up on, misunderstanding the meaning of aberration. His teacher pointed out he'd explained the word in class only a week before but hadn't remembered Zed had been absent that day. Zed had bunked off school because of the bruises on his arms which would have been seen when he changed for football. Zed wondered if his father would make any comment about his attendance record, wondered what to say if he did. *It's your fault.* Yeah, well he could imagine how that would go down.

His father picked fault with everything, ignoring all the praise and concentrating on the negatives, though Zed was hoping his music teacher's comments would be passed over. *Talented. Confidence beyond his years when performing. Hard-working. A pleasure to teach.* He'd come top of the class, but this was the final year he could study music. Not just because it was *haram*, forbidden in Islam according to some, but also because his father considered it a waste of time.

Sometimes Zed felt his father was Muslim when it suited him, which made it difficult for Zed to gauge how to behave, to work out how much he could get away with. His father believed wine was *haram* but the verse in the Quran that forbade it only talked about drinks made with dates or grapes, so whisky was okay. Not all Muslims believed that, but Zed had seen his father drinking whisky in his study. The bottle was hidden in a cupboard which suggested he didn't want anyone to know he drank it.

Once, when his father had said not to disturb him because he was praying, Zed had been passing the study window and caught a glimpse of him watching naked women on his laptop. But then his older brother Tamaz did that too. Not the whisky, Zed didn't think, but the women.

Their mother had converted to Islam before she and his father had married, and Zed presumed they'd loved each other at some point, but once he was old enough to notice, he hadn't seen much affection between them. Sometimes he'd thought his mother was frightened of his father. He knew the feeling.

His father had been a Sunni Muslim in Iran, a country where almost everyone was a Shi'i Muslim. The reason his father had left. Zed had been brought up as a follower of Islam, but he didn't believe anymore. He just pretended. There was a lot he pretended to be. Happy, when he wasn't. Obedient when he wasn't. Straight when he wasn't. He didn't want to get sent abroad or maybe killed, either of which was a possibility if his father found out he was gay.

Two more years until he was sixteen and could leave home and not be forced to return. Two more years putting up with physical and mental hell. If he could survive that long.

"*Doesn't always hand his homework in on time.* Why not?"

Zed bit his lip.

"I asked you a question."

"Sometimes I fall asleep before I've finished my schoolwork." *Because you've made me do the ironing or washing or cleaning.*

His father's face fractured with anger. "Then set your alarm to wake early and do your homework in the morning."

Zed nodded.

"*Doesn't mix well with other pupils.*"

That was true.

"Why not?" his father snapped.

What was the point trying to make friends when Zed would never be allowed to go to their house or go out with them? He was never

2

permitted to go bowling, or to parties, or the cinema, or visit a theme park.

"I work hard. They mess around." Not a complete lie.

His father grunted. *"Is reluctant to speak out in class or volunteer."*

Safer to stay under the radar of teachers and pupils. He was already bullied. He didn't want to do anything to make that worse.

"His woodwork projects rarely resemble his designs."

The design and technology teacher had also said that Zed tried hard, was a delight to have in his class and his ambition was admirable.

"He is easily distracted, often by nothing more than himself."

Read on Zed wanted to shout. *I'm good at English.*

His father glared and threw the report on his desk. "Not good enough. I'm more than disappointed."

Oh fuck this. Sometimes Zed had to fight back even though he knew the consequences. "It's not a bad report. There are nice comments too. Mr Carter said I was—"

"You have let me down." His father's eyes hardened into glittering pebbles. "Your brother works much harder. He will get four A grades this summer. Your marks are not acceptable. How can you expect to be an accountant?"

I don't want to be an accountant. He wanted to be a musician. He'd said that once to his father and would never say it again. Zed had locked up his hopes and dreams tight in his heart and maybe they'd have to stay there forever, but at least they were his and no one would make fun of him or deride him or condemn him for them.

His music teacher had been shocked Zed wouldn't be taking a GCSE in music, and he'd asked Zed to try and persuade his father. The idea of persuading his father to do anything might have made Zed smile but disappointment swamped any chance of that. He picked his battles carefully and one over music was doomed to fail. Most of his battles failed. The war would only be won when he left home.

"You're lazy."

I am not! "I came seventh in the class."

"To be first is better."

Zed bristled. He took a deep breath and looked his father in the face. "I'm not lazy. That's not fair. Seventh is good."

"Do not dare to argue with me."

Zed gulped when he caught the deepening anger in his father's gaze, the set of his jaw, the narrowing of his eyes. "I did my best."

"Not good enough."

3

His brother popped his head around the door. "Dinner's ready. Time to get cleaned up."

Zed waited for his father to let him go. When he nodded, Zed fled.

Since his mother had died three years ago, the three of them took it in turns to cook, though much of what they ate was from the freezer, bulk-bought from an Asian supermarket, defrosted overnight and stuck in the oven the following evening. Only if his father was working late could Zed eat what he liked. Tamaz sometimes drove to get fish and chips. Zed's mouth watered at the thought of hot chips smothered in salt and vinegar.

But last week, Tamaz had moved out. He'd gone to live in a student house in Canterbury and had only come back today to pick up more of his things. He'd landed a summer job taking tourists for trips on the River Stour, and in September, he'd be studying biochemistry at Canterbury University. Zed was going to miss him. He had the feeling Tamaz wouldn't come home much, which would leave Zed doing even more around the house, more cleaning, more washing and ironing, more gardening and preparing more meals, including food his father liked but he didn't.

Tamaz had made a cucumber, pomegranate and tomato salad that Zed loved, but the other dish on the table was *zaban* with carrots and potatoes. *Beef tongue.*

"Sorry," Tamaz whispered. "Dad wanted it tonight."

Last time Zed had tried to eat *zaban*, he'd thrown up. His stomach was already churning at the smell of it. He didn't much like meat although he wasn't vegetarian. But he particularly didn't like anything that looked like the original animal, nor anything with a name like tongue or cheek or heart, and he had a pathological hatred of eating anything on a bone.

Once the bowls of food were on the table and they were seated, his father's and brother's lips moved in silent prayer. The *du'a* was a way of feeling a connection to God at any time of the day and because it could be done silently, it was one of the easier things Zed could pretend to do. If he was ever challenged over anything, he claimed to be talking privately to Allah.

Though that didn't always work.

"So…last day of school," Tamaz said.

"Yes."

"What are you going to do for the next six weeks?" his brother asked. "Apart from redecorating the living room and my bedroom?"

Zed looked at him in shock. "What?"

4

"Joking. There'd be more paint on the carpet than the walls. Hey, maybe you could move into my room. It's bigger and—"

"He can stay where he is," his father said. "You'll be coming home sometimes. You should keep your room."

Tamaz shrugged. "It was just a thought. So what are your plans for the holidays?"

Zed opened his mouth but his father spoke first. "His school report was terrible."

"It wasn't," Zed whispered.

His father reached out and smacked the back of his head so hard it brought tears to Zed's eyes. He screwed his hands into fists wondering if he'd ever dare hit him back.

Tamaz kicked him under the table, warning him to be careful. "What did you come in the class?"

That question wasn't going to help. "They didn't tell us, but a couple of boys worked it out. I was seventh."

Tamaz turned to their father. "That's good, particularly when he's not yet doing subjects he's chosen."

"He was only seventh because he did well in subjects that are irrelevant and have no use."

"Such as?" Tamaz asked.

"Music." His father spat the word out as if it didn't deserve to be said.

"He's still young," Tamaz said.

"He only came third in maths!"

Four percent had separated him from first place and Zed still thought he was right and the teacher wrong about one of the answers which would have given him extra marks and put him equal first. He helped himself to more salad because he wasn't going to be eating any tongue if he could possibly avoid it. He just had to put up with his father's sharp tongue instead. He started to smile, then looked at his plate and gulped. *How am I going to eat this?*

"I've ordered workbooks for you to do this summer," his father said. "You can get ahead of the class."

Zed chewed the inside of his cheeks. He needed a rest, not more schoolwork.

"There's a place in Canterbury running a course over the holiday for Muslim teenagers," Tamaz said. "I'll look into whether they have a space."

What? No! "I don't want to go on a course. I'll be too busy with the workbooks."

His father patted Tamaz on the shoulder. "You're a kind brother."

5

Sometimes. Zed kept his mouth shut and his gaze down. The one good thing about moving to this small village four years ago had been that it was no longer possible to go to the London madrasa he and Tamaz had attended each day after school. His father still went to the mosque every Friday but Zed and Tamaz were only able to go in the school holidays. Though Tamaz had been going a lot since he'd finished his A levels. But Zed wondered if he was actually going or doing something else.

"Say thank you," his father snapped.

"Thank you," Zed mumbled.

His father spooned more *zaban* onto Zed's plate and passed the dish to Tamaz.

Oh God, I can't eat it. One sniff and he gagged.

"It only runs a couple of days a week." Tamaz helped himself to the *zaban*. "If I can get you in, you can stay with me overnight and I'll bring you back the next day."

Zed slumped, then reared back when it brought him closer to his plate.

Tamaz laughed. "Don't look as if you're being sent to work in a sewer."

Zed would rather have worked in a sewer *and* done the workbooks.

He did his best with the food, tried to bring a piece of the meat to his mouth and failed.

By the time his father and Tamaz had finished eating, it looked as though Zed hadn't started.

"Oh Allah! Bless the food You have provided us and save us from the punishment of the hellfire. *Bismillah.*" His father smiled at Tamaz. "It was delicious. Thank you."

Zed tried one more time and heaved before the *zaban* met his lips.

"What was that noise?" His father's smile had vanished. "Clear your plate."

"I can't eat it." Zed's heart pounded, and he kept his gaze fixed on his lap as his father pushed to his feet.

"Eat it." His father loomed over him like a big black crow.

Don't bring up the starving people who'd love to be fortunate enough to be able to refuse perfectly good food.

"You ungrateful, selfish boy," his father hissed. "There are people around the world who are starving and—"

"I can't eat it."

Damned if he did, damned if he didn't. If he continued to refuse, he'd be beaten. If he ate it—which would be a miracle—he'd vomit and

6

he'd be beaten for vomiting. He thought he might as well choose not to eat.

His father smacked the side of Zed's head again, made his ears ring and his hand fluttered to where he'd been struck.

"This is your last chance."

"I can't."

His father took down the riding crop he kept on the top of the door trim. He'd never ridden a horse. It had been purchased specifically to hit his sons. One son.

"You're not sorry at all, you *antikke*."

Farsi for a piece of shit. *That's all I am to you?* It was hard to have a father who seemed to hate him no matter what he did.

His brother picked up the plates and cleared the table. Tamaz knew better than to intervene, though Zed could count on the fingers of one hand how many times Tamaz had been beaten.

"You ungrateful…" His father rolled up his sleeves.

Zed didn't have much to be grateful for since his mother's death. A roof over his head. A bed. Clothes, though never the ones he wanted, and mostly Tamaz's hand-me-downs so by the time they fit Zed, they were never the latest fashion. Some food he could eat. That was about it. No kind words. No hugs. No gentle touch. Ever. If he was touched, it was only to be beaten.

His father dragged him out of his seat by the scruff of his neck and hauled him into his study. Zed sometimes felt as if he were living in a different world to everyone else. His was dark and lonely, full of pain, disappointment and sadness. Whenever anyone at school complained about their parents, it was because they hadn't bought them the latest mobile phone, or allowed them to stay out late, or up late, or because their computer time had been limited or their phone confiscated. Zed couldn't even tell anyone what his father did to him. Shame and fear kept his lips sealed. If he was asked about his bruises, he lied.

"You know what to do." His father's eyes had the glassy look that scared Zed.

Zed took off his T-shirt, pulled his shorts and boxers down to his ankles and leaned against the back of the chair. The first strike was always a surprise, because for a brief moment, it didn't hurt. Then it did. Zed buried his face in his forearms and clenched his teeth. With each blow, his skin became more tender and the burn increased until he felt as if he were being licked by flames.

7

His father struck his back, bottom, and the top of his legs. Zed couldn't help crying. Tears rolled down his cheeks, but he didn't utter a sound. He'd have bitten through his arm before he did that.

"Pull up your clothes."

Even doing that hurt. Zed clutched his T-shirt hard to hide his shaking fingers.

"I forgive you." What his father always said, as if it made the beating excusable.

"Thank you, father. I'm sorry I disappointed you." Zed forced out the words his father expected to hear. If he hadn't, he'd have been hit again. He wished he was brave enough to keep quiet, to take another beating and another until he passed out, but he wasn't.

He went straight to his room, each step on the stairs sending searing pain down his legs and up his back. He cleaned his teeth, tried to piss and failed because he was so tense, then lay face down on his bed. He heard a faint knock at the door and turned his head to see Tamaz. His brother came over and put a packet of crisps on the pillow.

Tamaz sighed. "I'm sorry he beats you. You should try harder not to aggravate him. All he wants is for you to be a good Muslim."

That wasn't it. Zed didn't have the energy to speak or to open the crisps. He closed his eyes and heard Tamaz leave.

Twice in the last year, his father had beaten Zed so hard, he'd lost consciousness. This time hadn't been too bad. No blood for a start. No tell-tale warm trickle down his skin. Part of him wished his father would go too far and he'd have to be taken to the hospital, assuming the bastard cared whether he lived or died. If his father really went too far and killed him, then it would all stop.

The glimmer of hope that one day it *would* stop was the only ray of light in Zed's darkness. Maybe a little bit of him wished he was dead. He didn't know anything other than unhappiness and it was only going to get worse. Two more years at home with no Tamaz to comfort him. He'd count down the days.

He reached for his alarm clock and set it for five thirty. Zed wanted to be out of the house before his father left because he'd insist Zed went with him. It was what always happened in the holidays. On Fridays, Zed would be expected to work in the pharmacy. All day spent moving products so he could dust shelves only to be told to do it again and again. Following that, he and his father would go to the mosque. *No thank you.*

The next morning, Zed sneaked out at twenty to six and silently closed the door behind him. He'd removed two slices of bread from the middle of a new loaf, resealed the packaging so no one would notice and put the folded bread in his pocket, along with a bottle of water. It was likely all he'd get to eat that day because he'd be in trouble when he returned home. It was more than likely the tongue would be served up again, because he suspected it lurked under foil on the top shelf of the fridge.

His father hadn't bothered closing the electric gates but there was a way through the hedge at the side anyway. The village was quiet. Still early for the commute to Canterbury or London, though there was plenty of traffic on the bypass. Zed hurried across the road, heading for the grassy field on the north side of the village. He squeezed through a gap in the hedge and made his way up a long slope to a wooded ridge.

He usually ran up the hill, pretending he was escaping from aliens or big cats or an axe-wielding father. Running fast set him free, let him forget, but his body hurt too much to do that today. It had said on his report that he'd won the school cross-country race, beating runners a lot older than him, but his father had either not noticed, or probably not cared. The cup had been presented in assembly and Zed was entitled to take it home for the year, but he'd left it in the school trophy cabinet.

Once he climbed over a wire fence and moved into the wood, he was hidden and felt safer. Not that his father was likely to come after him, neither he nor Tamaz had any idea where he went when he had the chance, but he was on private land now. Whoever owned it might get pissed off even though Zed was doing no harm. He made his way to the rocky outcrop he'd come across a couple of years ago, and gingerly sat down.

Unfortunately, there was no book to retrieve today. He usually put one in a plastic bag and tucked it under the front of the rock so he had something to read when he was up here. But he'd had to take the one he'd been hiding back to school. It was about an assassin in a fantasy world and it was good, but he hadn't had a chance to finish it.

He often spent hours there reading or composing, even when the weather was cold, but for six weeks, he'd have no access to books, and no access to music, no way to practise the instruments he loved, the piano and the cello. He could only listen to music at school. Only play an instrument there. But music was always in his head. He hummed when he was alone, kept the sound inside him when he wasn't. He often ran to the rhythm of a song though he was too out of breath to hum at the same time.

His music teacher let him practise at lunchtimes and after school and had said as long as the room was free, Zed could continue doing that in September. There was no library in the village. No book in the house except for the Quran. It wasn't forbidden in Islam to read novels, but the type allowed wasn't what Zed wanted to read.

His mother had had lots of books but after she'd died, his father had given them all to charity. Even his baby ones and Zed had really wanted to keep some of them, particularly the one she used to read to him about a little bear and his mum. The bear got into all sorts of trouble, but his mum was always there to keep him safe. Zed didn't even have a photograph of her. Photographs weren't forbidden but couldn't be on display. Maybe his father had some in an album but whenever Zed asked, he'd been told there were none.

Below where he sat, the land fell away down a green, treeless expanse into a wide valley patterned with fields of every shade of yellow, green and brown. It looked like a massive, neatly arranged plate of salad. Beyond that was another ridge, and in the distance, out of sight but not too far away, was the sea. He hadn't been to the sea for years. Could he walk there and back in a day? Maybe if he set off very early.

The village in the valley below was called Lower Barton. The one he'd come from was Upper Barton. Zed had been surprised when his parents said they were moving from Lewisham, but the house in Kent was much nicer. His mother said it was a better environment for all of them. She'd been a primary school teacher and had landed a job in the village school. His father stayed as a pharmacist in Maidstone and now commuted in a different direction.

Tamaz told Zed that the house in Upper Barton had been bought with money left to their mother after her parents had died. Zed missed his English grandparents. He'd loved going to see them. He'd never met any Iranian relations. His father sent money to his parents in Iran but he'd never been back. Any questions about his father's homeland were met with silence.

Zed sat on his rock imagining he was a successful king overlooking his domain. He hummed *Morning* by Grieg as he watched his world come alive. Cars pulled out of neat gravelled driveways onto the road, people crisscrossed the village on bikes and on foot, a delivery van stopped outside a shop and a removals lorry reversed to the door of a big house. He could see people walking their dogs, stopping to talk. While he watched, the express raced through the station on the way to Sandiford, the closest place to catch a fast train to London.

London. I could disappear there.

But while he was underage, if he was caught, the police would bring him home. Desperate as Zed was, he would never admit his father

10

beat him because no good could come of that. His worst fear was that he'd be sent to Iran to live with his grandparents and he'd never escape. Even if he was put into care, not an alternative that appealed, he'd always be scared his father would find a way to destroy him. So when he went, he had to go for good, make sure he disappeared completely.

Zed ate one of the slices of bread, taking small bites and chewing each mouthful slowly to try and trick himself he'd eaten more than he had. He had two pounds in his pocket, but he didn't want to waste it on food. He needed to save as much as he could to start his new life.

Though when would he ever have enough? The money he'd collected, hidden in a box under the bottom of his wardrobe, was made up of what he didn't spend on school lunches, loose change Tamaz sometimes slipped him and odd coins he'd picked up that his father had left lying around in the house. He knew it was stealing but he never took much.

He pushed to his feet and headed down the field toward the wood at the bottom. He'd never bothered exploring there before but today he wanted to be as far from home as he could get.

Chapter Two

Caspian watched the boy walking down the field. The wood he'd emerged from at the top of the slope belonged to Caspian's father, as did the field he was tramping through, and the wood he was heading towards. He was a similar build to Caspian, tall and skinny, and wearing light grey cargo shorts and a plain pale blue T-shirt that looked too big for him. A bottle of water dangled from his fingers.

As the trespasser drew nearer, Caspian leaned out of the window of his treehouse to get a better look. The boy seemed sad, not just miserable but bowed down with the weight of unhappiness, his whole body screaming with it.

Sad boy in blue
You cry with white loneliness
For technicolour hopes and dreams
Your future grey
Unless you find the sun

Worth the effort of writing that down? *No.* It was rarely worth the effort.

Caspian climbed down the ladder and moved closer to where the strange boy would enter the wood. When Caspian spotted him about twenty metres ahead, he slipped behind a sycamore tree and watched.

The dark-haired boy put the water bottle in the pocket of his shorts, then dragged a fallen branch to a clearing. He dropped it and went for another one. *What's he doing? What's he humming?* Caspian's father would be furious if anyone lit a fire on his property, especially in the middle of a wood when there'd been no rain for weeks. But the branches the boy was collecting were too big for a fire. Though maybe he didn't know that. Or maybe he wanted to burn the wood down. That wasn't going to happen. Caspian wouldn't let him. He loved these trees.

He waited until the boy was heading away from him, then shinned up the tree he'd hidden behind. As the boy came back, he headed straight for Caspian's hiding place. Realising he might have been seen, Caspian reached for a higher branch. As he tried to pull himself up, the branch broke, and he crashed back to a fork in the trunk with a gasp of pain as he scraped his knee.

"Are you okay?" the boy called from below him.

"Too-wit too-woo."

The response was a laugh. "That was a really good impression of a flamingo. But flamingos don't live up trees."

12

Caspian grinned and looked down at him. "How do you know?"

"Well, that's true. I'm not an expert on flamingos, but you're obviously rare because you're not pink."

"I'm extremely rare. One of a kind."

"Ah, right."

"What are you doing with those logs?"

"Building a den."

"Why?" Caspian asked.

"To hide from flamingos, obviously."

Caspian's smile widened. "Now I know about it, you're doomed."

There was a pause before the boy spoke again. "Want to help me make it?"

"I think I might be stuck."

"Will the fire brigade come out for a flamingo?"

You're funny.

The boy started to climb. A moment later, he was standing on a limb close to Caspian, steadying himself by holding onto an overhead branch. His eyes… *Wow.* Blue with a dark line around the iris. Caspian had never seen eyes like that before.

"There's a branch just behind you. You need to reach out with your left hand, grab it, and push yourself up so you can untwist, and you'll free your foot."

Caspian leaned back and looked up. "I can't stretch that far." He probably could but he was interested to see what the boy did.

"You're disappointingly unbendy."

"What! My flamingo knees bend backwards. You can't get more bendy than that."

"That's not your knee, that's your ankle, flamingo."

Caspian gasped when the boy swung round and ended up straddling a branch above him. He leaned down and looked so exotic surrounded by leaves, as if he were some strange woodland creature, that Caspian froze, not wanting to spoil the moment.

"I'll pull you up, but you need to hug the trunk the moment you're upright or we'll both fall."

He reached down and Caspian grabbed his hand. A moment later, Caspian was on his feet clutching the trunk. A moment after that, the two of them were on the ground. Same height. Same build. But this boy had smooth olive skin, hair darker than his, and those amazing eyes. Then he smiled and Caspian was lost. Not just lost but lost forever. Something inside him opened up, burst into life and the breath caught in his throat.

This is the boy I want.

"You okay?" the boy asked for the second time.

I am now. "Yes. Thanks for rescuing me. I could have been there forever."

"You weren't that stuck."

Oh, you noticed? "What's your name?"

"Zed."

Caspian widened his eyes. "Didn't your parents know what to call you? Archibald, Bertram, Cuthbert, Desmond, Eustace… Did they get to the end of the alphabet and stop?"

Zed rolled his eyes. "My family name is Zadeh."

"So what's your real name?"

"Zed."

Caspian tsked. "Okay. I'm Caspian Ulysses Octavian Nathaniel Tarleton."

Zed gaped at him.

"I'm not making it up. My brother is Lachlan Josiah Mortimer Nash and my sisters are Araminta Eugenia Persephone and Cressida Beatrice Juliana. Our parents clearly think we're still living in the nineteenth century. And I'll say it before you do, once you register my initials. I'm almost a cunt. Thank fuck for the Octavian. I must be one of the few people in the world who's grateful to have that as one of his names. Your actual name can't be worse than any of mine."

"Caspian's good. I like it."

"Unless you get called Ass or Pee, or Aspie." Though no one usually did that twice, except for his pain-in-the-neck brother. Caspian might be dyslexic, but he didn't have Asperger's. It wasn't fair to make fun of anyone who did, though Lachlan didn't care.

"My real name is Hvarechaesham."

Don't laugh. "Right, yeah, Zed is easier. Does Hvare… mean something?"

"Having eyes like the sun."

Caspian stared at him. "You do."

"They're golden yellow orbs that blind you when you look at them?"

Part of that is true. "They shine. They're b…beautiful."

For a moment neither of them spoke. Caspian waited to be hit for telling a boy his eyes were beautiful, but Zed shrugged and looked both embarrassed and maybe a little pleased.

14

"I suppose I should be grateful I wasn't called Frashaoshtra. That means having useful camels. Or Spityur, one who possesses white lambs."

Caspian laughed. "What country are they from?"

"Iran. Persian names. I'm half Iranian, half English. English mother. Iranian father. I was born here though. So you want to help me build a den?"

That was a swift change of subject, but Caspian went with it. "Okay."

Zed smiled at him again and Caspian's heart lurched. *Shit.*

"Let's lean these pieces of wood either side of this low branch to make an A-frame, like a tent," Zed said. "Then we can weave in the smaller twigs."

The two of them worked together, dragging larger logs from all over the wood though Caspian was careful not to lead him toward the treehouse. They levered up the branches and propped them against the horizontal living branch until they'd made something big enough to sit inside. A couple of times he noticed Zed wince as if he were in pain.

"You all right?" Caspian asked. "Have you hurt yourself?"

"No. Like some water?" Zed offered Caspian his bottle.

Caspian took a slug and passed it back. "Thanks. Where do you go to school?"

"Middleton Academy. What about you?"

"Shelton. Well, I *was* at school there."

"Where's that?"

"Boarding school. Miles away in Hampshire. How old are you?"

"Fourteen."

"I'm fifteen. Brothers and sisters?"

"One brother who's four years older than me."

Caspian gave a short laugh. "Snap. I have ten-year-old sisters as well. The terrible twins."

Zed laughed. "Do you get on with your brother?"

"Yes. He hates me and I hate him. Perfect relationship. What about you?"

"Tamaz is okay, but he moved out last week to live in Canterbury. He starts university in September."

"My brother is heading for Cambridge if he gets good enough grades. He probably will." Though Caspian had wondered how much influence his father had on his brother's acceptance since he'd had to

15

repeat a year and take two A levels again. "So how do we make it more den-like?" He knew but wondered what Zed would suggest.

"We need to twist in bendy branches to make the sides. Maybe we could weave a door. We can put leafy branches on the ground to make it more comfortable. Then we're all set to hide from predators: bears, wolves, and terrifyingly evil flamingos that want to destroy any of their kind who are different."

"You're trying to protect me?"

"I rescued you. You're mine now." A look of horror flashed across Zed's face. "Sorry. I'm letting my imagination escape from my mouth. Which way do you prefer to rest your head?"

Caspian blinked. That had been a fast change of subject. "Why?"

"Most flamingos prefer to rest their head to the right. The ones that prefer to rest their heads on the other side are more likely to be involved in violent clashes with other birds."

"How do you know that?"

"I just remember stuff. I like spotting signs of danger."

"You could be useful."

Zed laughed and they both went in search of branches. Caspian broke slender stems from a shrub, ripped off more of the same growing from the stump of a tree felled a couple of years ago, then threaded them through the log sides. He used to make dens until he'd inherited his brother's treehouse, but he wondered how long it would be before the twins invaded and forced him out. Though they were into clothes and shoes and tormenting him, not dirt and fun.

Finally, he and Zed crawled inside the structure. There was just about enough room to sit up side by side.

"This is cool," Caspian said. "Definitely safe from terrifyingly evil flamingos. Not sure about bears or wolves."

He dropped onto his back, but as Zed did the same, Caspian heard the catch in his breath. As Zed twisted onto his front, Caspian caught sight of a long, raised red welt above the waist of Zed's shorts. Zed saw him looking and yanked his T-shirt down.

"What happened to your back? Was it when you rescued me, when I didn't need to be rescued?"

"No." Zed lay with his head on his arms and stared at him.

Caspian didn't push. He didn't want him to leave. "Are you going away this summer?"

"You mean on holiday? No. I was told last night I might have to do some sort of summer school thing in Canterbury. I'd prefer not to."

16

"It might be fun. Kayaking, abseiling, making rafts, playing sport, learning how to break open safes or hotwire cars."

"It's for Muslims. And don't say then it must be about building bombs, or how to make suicide vests."

"I wouldn't." Though it had briefly crossed his mind.

"And I don't consider myself to be Muslim but don't ever tell anyone I said that."

"What are you then?"

Zed shrugged.

"An unbeliever like me?" Caspian asked. "We had church every Sunday at school. I kept thinking I'd get hit by a thunderbolt because I didn't listen."

"But being Muslim is a way of life. It's a lot stricter than other religions. But I can't be Muslim and be..."

Caspian wondered what he'd been going to say. "We can go to hell together. Assuming they don't have individual hells for each religion."

Zed smiled. "This is the first time I've said more than a sentence to anyone but a teacher or my father and brother for a long time."

"No friends around here?" Caspian hoped the question didn't piss him off.

"Not really. What about you?"

"Not here, no. I had friends at Shelton but since I was expelled, I doubt I'll see them again."

Zed's eyes widened. "Expelled? What did you do?"

"Didn't conform to their high standards of behaviour, according to the Head. The way he reacted it was as if I'd destroyed the fabric of society and it was only that I got caught smoking."

"You got expelled for that?"

"Well I might have accidentally set fire to some paper in the science lab which caused a bit of a fire. My first cigarette and I didn't even like it, which was why I chucked it in the bin but it mustn't have been completely out. The alarm went off and the fire brigade came."

Zed winced.

"There were a few other incidents too. I sneaked off to town when I wasn't supposed to. I told a few white lies to teachers and apparently I swear too fucking much."

Zed laughed and then frowned. "Was your father furious? What did he do?"

17

"He yelled a lot. I've been expelled before and had to repeat a year. But he's called another school and convinced them to take me. Blackstones has a rep for being military strict. It's in the middle of nowhere in Scotland. I'll have to be up at some godawful hour for a freezing cold shower, go cross-country running in wind, rain and snow, and be served thin porridge for breakfast. And more fucking church on Sundays. I can't wait. Not." Caspian shredded a leaf that poked through the side of the den. "I really don't want to go, but my father won't budge."

"I have a father like that too. Do you live in Lower Barton?"

"Yep, do you?"

"Upper Barton." Zed pulled a crushed slice of bread from his pocket. "Want some?"

"To eat?"

"I'm feeding my pet flamingo."

Caspian snorted. He didn't really want the bread, but he broke off a small piece and ate it.

"Are you going on holiday this summer?" Zed asked.

"Probably. But not yet." He didn't want to tell Zed they had a home in France as well as here. He was enjoying just being a normal boy, not getting picked on for being stupid. "What sort of things do you do in the holidays?"

"Nothing much."

"Except hide from bears, wolves and flamingos. Do you have a bike? We could go off for the day."

Zed shook his head. "I don't have one."

"Give me your phone number and we can plan something. Maybe I can convince my brother to lend me his bike and you can have mine."

"I don't have a phone."

Caspian clapped his hands to his face in mock-horror. "No phone? How do you survive?"

"It's a terrible struggle." Zed gave an exaggerated sigh.

"But it's safer to have a phone. I mean what if you were attacked by a murderous flamingo? You couldn't call for help. You might get pecked to death. Shit, look, my head's leaning left."

Zed sniggered.

"Seriously, how do you manage without a phone?"

"I just do."

Caspian thought about it. "Would you want one?"

18

"'Course I would. I'm just not allowed. Maybe when I'm sixteen. That was when my brother got one."

"What else aren't you allowed? Can you watch TV?"

"So long as it doesn't contain any nude scenes, extreme violence or vulgar music. Of course, that's exactly what I want to watch."

Caspian laughed.

"But I abide by the rules. The no vulgar music one is hard."

"Are you allowed a computer?"

"No. Nor books that are inappropriate which are mostly the only sort of books worth reading."

"Your father wants to suck all the fun out of life." Though Caspian's wasn't much different.

Zed sighed. "He does but it's not that. If you're a believer you're happy to respect and follow the rules. There's nothing wrong with being Muslim. The vast majority of Muslims are good, kind people, though not all of them, which is true in any religion. Partly it's just down to the way everything is interpreted. Vulgar music being an example. What the hell is that? Words in a song that are offensive or suggestive? All popular music? Schubert and Tchaikovsky were reputed to be gay so did they write vulgar music?"

Gay? Caspian stared at Zed. "Your parents sound strict." *Is that how you got the marks on your back?*

"My dad is. My mum's dead. She had cancer."

"Oh, that sucks. I'm sorry."

"She died three years ago. She'd just started a job teaching at the village school when she was diagnosed. We'd only been here a year when she died. I miss her."

"What does your father do?"

"He's a pharmacist in Maidstone. What about your parents?"

"My mum doesn't work. She does *good* things when she can fit them in between her tennis lessons and shopping. She volunteers and stuff. Campaigns on behalf of various organisations. Throws dinner parties and lunches to persuade people to donate to causes she feels are worthy. That sounds mean because she *is* sincere, but in a way, it feels like she's doing no more than picking up one piece of litter and putting it in a bin."

"But doing that is better than nothing."

"I suppose. My dad's a senior civil servant. He works for the government. He's always busy."

19

"Do you like him?"

"He's okay. Unless I've done something bad. Which is a lot of the time." He grinned. "Can't you convince your father you need a computer for schoolwork?"

"Not when I can just use a school computer."

"Can't you use your father's while he's at work?" Caspian asked. "Or does he take it with him? You can delete the history. If you don't know how, I can explain how to do it."

"You're an expert in that?" Zed smiled. "What have you been watching?"

I wish I dare tell you. Caspian sighed. "*Bob the Builder.* The shame…"

"I should think so. I thought I knew how to hide having used his computer but somehow, he still knew. I got into a lot of trouble. I didn't do it again."

The Adam's apple rising and falling in Zed's throat made Caspian think the trouble might have been physical.

"I've got an old laptop you can have." Caspian shocked himself by offering but the laptop was just sitting there doing nothing. He got a new one every year. One upside of having a learning difficulty. As if his father buying him a new laptop would make any difference. He didn't try to understand Caspian's dyslexia.

"That's really kind but if my father found it, he'd take it off me and he *would* find it."

What an arsehole! For a moment, Caspian wondered if he was being spun a line, a picture being painted of a father who sounded worse than his. But for what reason?

"What's your favourite thing to do?" Zed asked.

Caspian thought about saying—jerking off—though not to *Bob the Builder*, then changed his mind. "My father would say—making trouble, but I like taking things apart and putting them back together, not always back to the way they were. I like making models of things." *And writing poetry.*

"You mean models that you buy and construct?"

"No. Just thinking up designs and constructing them. I try to repair stuff too. Most of my inventions I don't have the equipment or knowledge to make so they just stay as ideas."

"What's your favourite invention?"

20

"A doll that falls apart when you squeeze it, and it's full of plastic insects."

Zed gaped at him. "How old were you when you did that?"

"Nine. I kept unfastening the joints in my sister's dolls and stuffing plastic bugs inside. They freaked out and I got into trouble. I had to make a stable for a herd of *My Little Pony* because I'd been so mean. But it was the twins who'd started it. They'd— Well, they're vicious little monsters."

"What's the best thing you've come up with?"

"A way to stop one of our dogs chewing its damaged tail. I cut out a hole in an old baby ball that was made of a strong plastic mesh and figured out a way to harness it to Monty so he couldn't lick the wound or bite the ball off. The vet was impressed. My father less so when Monty wagged his tail-ball so hard, he knocked a glass of red wine onto a cream carpet. So I managed two in one there. Making trouble and making something. What about you? What do you like?"

"Music. Running. Reading. Peanut butter. But music above everything."

Caspian pushed himself up on his elbow. "Me too. I lurrrrve vulgar music. What sort of music do you like?"

Zed laughed. "Everything. Almost."

"Do you play an instrument?"

"Piano and cello. But only at school. I'm not allowed..." Zed gave a heavy sigh. "My dad says music is forbidden in Islam, so in my house I have to be careful. Do you play anything?"

"Not really. I tried recorder, trumpet, piano and saxophone—in that order because you had to play something at school. I was terrible at all of them."

"Did you have a favourite?"

"The guitar. I haven't ruined that for me yet."

"You play the guitar?"

"*Play* is a strong word. I look at my guitar and imagine myself playing it. Then I try and I'm crap." Caspian smiled. "Come with me." He crawled out of the shelter and headed toward his treehouse, Zed on his heels.

When he stopped at the foot of the ladder, Zed looked up and gave a short laugh. "This is yours? We spent all that time making a hovel and you had a mansion?"

21

"Making the den was fun and I didn't make this. It was made for my brother."

Zed walked around the tree looking up at the treehouse. "Wow. It looks amazing. Is that glass in the window?"

"Perspex. And there's music up there."

"A piano in your treehouse?"

Caspian grinned. "Climb up and see."

Zed went up fast but Caspian didn't miss the marks on his lower back and the top of his legs. Someone had hit him. His father. *Shit.*

By the time he'd clambered up through the trapdoor, Caspian's smile was back on his face. His father never used physical force, just mental cruelty. Once he'd finished yelling about Caspian's expulsion, he'd ignored him for days, walked right past him as if he wasn't there.

Caspian dropped the trapdoor in place.

"Wow," Zed sighed. "All you need is a water supply and you could live up here."

There was a single foam mattress piled with cushions along one wall, a shelf holding a few books he hadn't read and wasn't likely to, piles of drawing pads filled with his designs and a box of pencils. Battery powered fairy lights hung all over the ceiling, though Caspian rarely came here at night.

"What's that wire for?"

"Burglar alarm. Flip that switch to turn it on and off."

"What noise does it make?"

"Try it."

Zed flipped the switch, a lion roared and he laughed. "This is brilliant. Does your brother still come here?"

"No. I'll probably have to fight the Terrible Twins for possession at some point, but they don't like spiders or any sort of insect or getting dirty so maybe it'll stay mine."

Zed looked out of the window. "Bird boxes. Did you make them? Have birds been in them? Wow, this is like living in a giant nest."

"With a roof. Yep, I did make them but I don't know whether they were used because I was away at school in May and June."

"You could build a walkway between here and that tree. Construct a platform to sit on."

"I'd thought that too. I made a pulley system to haul myself from one tree to another, but my father made me dismantle it after I fell and cut my head. I'm always breaking something. Both arms, a wrist, a leg, ribs. Not all at the same time."

"I've never broken a bone."

"Don't. It hurts. Maybe we can make a zip wire."

"Okay. You can have the first go if you're accident prone."

Caspian smiled and picked up earphones and an MP3 player from the shelf before he dropped onto the mattress. "Music. We can share." He offered Zed one of the earpieces.

Zed sat next to him.

"So what music do you want to listen to?" Caspian asked. "Kaiser Chiefs? Green Day? Take That? Beethoven?"

"Do you have Beethoven on there?"

"No." Caspian grinned. "It's a mix but not Beethoven."

"Play the music you like." Zed put the earpiece in, leaned against the wall then jerked forward with a grimace of pain.

"What have you done to your back?"

"Nothing."

Caspian stared at him and even though Zed met his gaze, he knew he wasn't telling the truth.

"We can lie down," Caspian said.

They settled on their stomachs and Caspian switched on his music player. The first song was by Robbie Williams. *Something Beautiful* from *Escapology.* How apt was that? Zed was beautiful. This place was their escape. Caspian was in love.

He wasn't. Not really. But if he'd ever doubted his attraction to guys, he now knew the truth. Zed had kickstarted his heart. *That* had been the feeling in his chest.

Zed closed his eyes and Caspian stared at him. His eyelashes were insanely long and thick, and Caspian wanted to run his tongue along them. When Zed licked his lips, Caspian swallowed hard. He had no idea whether Zed was into boys or not. He was too afraid to test it out or ask, in case the answer was a thump in the stomach or a plain *no*. More than someone to crush on, Caspian liked the idea of having a friend nearby, someone to talk to and do things with. He thought Zed might like that too.

When Caspian's stomach rumbled, he tugged out their earpieces and sat up. "I'm going to go and get us something to eat. What do you want?"

Zed rolled onto his side. "From your house?"

23

Caspian nodded.

"Whatever you're having would be great. Thanks. Er…as long as it's not on a bone."

"Peanut butter sandwich and I'll take the bones?"

"Great."

As Caspian made his way home, he wondered if Zed would be there when he got back. Or his MP3 player.

Both were exactly where he'd left them and Zed looked so pleased to see him, Caspian felt a pang of guilt for distrusting him, followed by a pleasurable quiver in his groin. *Do not get a boner.* He'd made the sandwiches himself, not asked Betsy, their housekeeper, and grabbed packets of crisps, bottles of water and a couple of chocolate biscuits without anyone seeing him. He should have gone for a haircut with Lachlan at two, but stuff that.

Caspian and Zed sat on the mattress to eat.

"Thanks for feeding me," Zed said.

"What were you intending to eat? That piece of bread?" He started to laugh then stopped when he realised that was exactly what Zed had been going to eat.

"I could have gone home for something."

Caspian heard the defensive tone in Zed's voice and knew he'd offended him.

"My house is nearer. You can get us both something next time." *Is there going to be a next time?*

"Okay."

Please mean that. "What hours does your father work?"

"He leaves at around eight and doesn't get back most days until at least six-thirty. Sometimes later if he's the dispensing chemist. He does the occasional night shift and Saturdays are shared between him and three others."

"So you're home alone for the whole summer? What are you going to do?"

"Unless that course in Canterbury is going to be about hotwiring cars, probably nothing exciting."

"Why the hell not?"

Zed stared at him a moment, then grinned. "Got any suggestions?"

None that Caspian thought Zed was quite ready to hear, but he had plenty of others.

24

Chapter Three

Zed was relieved to be home before his father. Mostly because he didn't want to be caught red-handed with the book Caspian had lent him, but also because it was Zed's turn to cook. He doubted he was going to get away with having sneaked off this morning after his father had expected him to go with him to work, then to the mosque. Another beating seemed possible. He could try to convince his father he'd forgotten. One advantage of having no phone.

Though now he wished he did have one. He hadn't cared much when the only people likely to call him were his brother and father, but today, that had changed.

I made a friend!

He hid the book under his shoes at the bottom of his wardrobe and hurried down again. Since he'd forgotten to take anything from the freezer, he decided on a cheese omelette and salad for dinner. Once the salad was prepared, he tidied up, made beds, wiped down work surfaces, hoovered, cleaned the kitchen floor, started a load of laundry, made the house look as neat and smart as he could, and sprayed a lot of polish so everything smelt of lemons. While he did all that, he reran the day because it had been the best of his life for as long as he could remember, so good he'd stopped thinking about how much he ached, so good it was worth the beating he might get.

That sounded wet, but it was true. Everything had been perfect. Building the den. The treehouse. The music. Talking. Laughing. He really liked Caspian with his untidy jet-black hair and his crooked smile. Zed couldn't remember ever smiling so much. And he'd made Caspian laugh. The pleasure in that brought a lump to his throat. Had Caspian noticed how often he'd looked at him? Zed had found it hard to drag his gaze away, and sometimes, he'd caught Caspian staring at him too.

Maybe he'd discovered the secret to making friends. One to one. No one else around. A physical project to work on. No distractions. No school. It gave them chance to get to know one another without interference. Whatever Caspian came up with that was fun to do, Zed was going to do it. Being good hadn't made him happy. He wasn't going to back off from an opportunity to have fun, regardless of the consequences.

When Caspian had gone to get them lunch, Zed had looked at his books and drawings. There were some wacky ideas, but a lot of them sounded as though they could be developed into something. Pencils, pencil case and a school bag all made from recycled materials. Edible dinosaur eggs with a dinosaur inside made from vegetables. Lego men made of melted crayons. Themed craft kits for kids of different ages. Snowflakes made of pieces of jigsaw glued together and sprayed silver.

Caspian wasn't short of ideas. His drawings were really good though his spelling and handwriting were terrible. Zed was okay at spelling and his handwriting was probably the best in his class, but he couldn't draw at all. Well, not for anyone to recognise what he'd drawn.

This was the happiest he'd been since his mother had died. His life had spiralled down after her death. No more treats brought home for him. No more jam doughnuts or iced buns. He'd used to make her a cup of tea every afternoon. It was the first thing she wanted when she got back from work. He missed her so much.

The front door slammed and Zed flinched. His father came into the kitchen carrying an Amazon package, headed straight for him, and it was all Zed could do not to back away.

"Cheese omelette and salad for dinner," Zed blurted. "Is that okay? Shall I start the omelette now?"

"Where were you today?"

"I went for a walk."

"You were supposed to come to Maidstone with me and go to the mosque."

"I forgot." *Oh shit, what a lie.* "I'm sorry." *Another lie.*

"I called the house several times. Who were you out with?"

"No one."

"A girl?"

"No one." Zed met his father's gaze. The less that came out of Zed's mouth the better. It was so easy to talk himself into trouble. "If you'd have reminded me about going with you…" *Why did I even say that? Shut up.*

His father narrowed his eyes. "You're saying it's my fault? A good Muslim does not forget about Friday prayers."

Zed shuffled his feet.

"What were you doing all day?"

"Walking, exploring. I wasn't out all day. I've cleaned and tidied. I washed the floor."

His father looked around the room. "Make the omelette."

Zed put a knob of butter into the pan and turned on the heat. His father opened the package and placed two thick workbooks on the work surface.

"Maths and physics. You'll do a section of each every day." He pulled a knife from the block, turned to the back of the maths book and sliced out the answers, then did the same with the physics book. "What do you say?"

"Thank you, father." Which wasn't what he wanted to say.

Zed tipped the cheese and egg mixture into the pan then set the table.

"Tamaz called to say there *is* a place on the course in Canterbury. He'll collect you on Monday night and bring you back on Wednesday evening."

I'm not saying thank you for that.

But the blow to the back of his head changed his mind. *Ouch!* "Thank you, father."

"He has a sleeping bag you can use. Don't expect him to share his bed. You can manage on the floor. You will behave perfectly in front of strangers. I do not want to hear you don't mix well with others or that you've not volunteered or tried your hardest. Since you've not been attending a madrasa for the past four years, you'll have to work hard to catch up on your study of the Quran and the history of Islam. They also give tuition in Arabic writing. Sign up for that."

That sounds like fun. "Yes, father."

When his father took the foil-wrapped plate from the fridge, Zed's heart and stomach sank in unison. "You will eat this. I'll have the omelette."

He scraped it onto Zed's plate and carried it to the table.

I'm going to run away now. Not this minute because I wouldn't get out of the house, but this summer. I'm not waiting two years. I can't live like this. Zed swallowed his sob, turned the perfect, fluffy omelette out onto his father's plate and put it in front of him.

He tried not to look at the congealed mess on his own plate. There was barely room for salad without the *zaban* contaminating it. He ought to have eaten before his father came home and then he wouldn't be going to bed hungry.

After prayers, his father started to eat. "Are we going to have the same problem tonight?"

"I can't eat it."

"Won't or can't?"

"I can't. I'll throw up if I try."

27

"Then get out of my sight."

Zed pushed back from the table and fled upstairs. It was too early to go to bed, but it wasn't as if there was anything else he could do. He heard the sound of the TV and hoped his father became absorbed in watching it. Zed got ready for bed and cleaned his teeth but instead of getting into bed, he sat at his desk. He took a sheet of plain paper from his drawer and cut it into a square. He wanted to make an origami flamingo but with no pattern to follow, it wasn't going to be easy.

When the piece of paper he was working with became too creased from being folded, unfolded and refolded, he threw it away and started another. Forty minutes later, he had something that really did look like a flamingo and he smiled. He gave it yellow eyes and a half-black beak, then coloured it pink before hiding it at the bottom of his wardrobe with Caspian's book.

The book was too tempting. *Northern Lights* by Philip Pullman. Zed wasn't tired. He wanted to read it now. He figured he'd hear his father coming up the stairs and would have time to shove it under his pillow. There was no need to put on his bedside lamp. It would be light for ages outside.

He took the book to bed and curled up under the covers. He'd told Caspian he'd see him tomorrow, and that might be the last time if he ran. He sighed. He was already back to *if*. But he wasn't stupid. He was a kid. His chances of disappearing into any place good were small. Maybe he ought to talk to Tamaz on Monday. Zed knew he couldn't live with his brother, but he might have some advice. Then again, Tamaz might just tell their father. It hadn't escaped Zed's attention that Tamaz had become more religious lately. The two of them used to laugh about some Islamic extremes but that had stopped. He couldn't count on Tamaz being on his side.

Zed pulled a sheet up over the book so it would be easier to hide and began to read. He quickly became enthralled by the story of Lyra and her daemon. So enthralled, he missed the sound of his father's footsteps on the stairs and only reacted when the door opened. Zed pushed the book down the bed and sat up.

"You didn't do any work today." His father threw the maths and physics books onto the place the other book was hidden. "Do a section of each tonight or do double tomorrow."

"Okay."

"I'm working tomorrow and I'll be back late. Make sure the door is locked before you go to bed."

Zed nodded, then breathed a silent sigh of relief when his father left the room. That had been close.

28

He didn't feel like doing maths or physics but if he wanted to spend the day with Caspian, he ought to do two sections of each book tonight not one. Hopefully, they wouldn't be too difficult. Once he'd hidden Caspian's novel in the wardrobe, he sat at his desk and started with maths. When he realised it was all new stuff he had no idea how to do, he groaned.

It took him so long to work through two sections that his father had come to bed before he'd finished. He'd opened the door of Zed's room, seen him working, huffed and closed the door again.

As soon as Zed thought his father must be asleep, he sneaked downstairs and helped himself to a chunk of cheese from the fridge and some crackers from the box in the cupboard, crept back to his room and ate while he worked. Tomorrow he'd have to be out of the house early in case his father stopped him. He hadn't told him he couldn't go out, but Zed wasn't going to risk it.

Caspian sat at the dinner table with his family and thought how much he'd enjoyed eating a simple lunch with Zed compared to this torture. The Terrible Twins sat either side of him kicking his legs. His brother and mother sat opposite and his father was at the head of the table. They didn't always have formal meals like this because his father often stayed overnight in London, but when he was home, family dinner was compulsory.

"I thought you were getting a haircut today," his father said to him. "Did I pay a fortune for a millimetre of hair to be removed?"

"I forgot," Caspian said.

"Why? What were you doing?" his mother asked.

"Working on something." *Someone.*

"And I suppose it's a secret." His mother raised her perfectly manicured eyebrows.

"For the time being."

"There'll be no more of that nonsense when you're at Blackstones. You won't have time." His father topped up his wine glass and passed the bottle to Lachlan. "You'll be up at six thirty. The school day starts at eight in the morning, ends at nine in the evening and they have lessons on Saturday morning too."

Caspian didn't even try to keep the horror from his face. "But not on Saturday afternoon and Sunday as well? That's so disappointing."

His father gave him one of his looks. "After lunch on Saturday there are team games and organised activities. Church attendance is compulsory on Sundays, morning and evening, as is participation in the Combined Cadet Force."

This was sounding worse and worse.

"You can choose between the Army, Royal Navy or Air Force."

Fucking great.

"Don't pull a face like that. You'll learn to be adventurous and team-spirited."

I am *adventurous and no one wants me on their team.* "Do I get to fire a gun?" Caspian snapped.

"Don't take that tone, either. Yes, you will. Learning marksmanship skills requires concentration, focus, determination and self-discipline. All of which you lack."

"Training me to be a killer. Great."

Lachlan let out a quiet snigger which earned him a glare from his father.

"You *will* behave, Caspian. This school does not tolerate disobedience. Break the rules and the punishment is some form of physical activity. Long hikes whether it's raining or not. Digging in the school garden. Collecting litter."

"Fuck," Caspian muttered.

"What was that?" his father snapped.

"I said just my luck," Caspian mumbled.

"Caspian said a bad word." Araminta widened her eyes.

His father let out an exasperated sigh. "Don't think you'll get yourself expelled. That's not going to happen. The school has a no-expulsion policy with special measures to deal with disruptive influences."

"Special measures?" Caspian asked.

"Let's hope you don't find out what they are."

Fuck, fuck, fuck.

"Did you hear me, Caspian? You will not get expelled from this school."

Don't bet on it. "Not even if I set fire to the science lab?"

His father glared. "That stunt cost me a lot of money. Don't do it again. Don't let me down. Don't let the family down. Don't let yourself down."

Don't, don't, don't. Fuck off.

"I do hope we have to wear shorts whatever the season, sleep on hard bunks in huge unheated dormitories and lick the senior boys'… shoes clean."

Oh God. He'd nearly said something different then.

"Don't be facetious," his father snapped.

30

"What does that mean, Daddy?" Cressida asked.

"Caspian is being silly." His father smiled at her.

"Caspian's always silly," chimed in Araminta. "I'm better at reading than him, aren't I, Mummy?"

"Don't be unkind. You know Caspian suffers from dyslexia." His mother sent him a patronising smile.

Caspian concentrated on his food. His mother said it like it was a disease, though the suffering bit was right. For years he'd struggled with reading, writing and remembering facts unless it was something that fascinated him. He had poor organisational skills and the concentration of a fruit fly, which was worse than a goldfish, according to the internet.

His father thought he was lazy but no matter how hard Caspian tried, there were some things he just couldn't grasp. Tests were a nightmare. Exams enough to cause depression. Even if he worked hard, he came close to the bottom in almost every subject, so he'd stopped trying. There was no point stressing about schoolwork when the result would be the same whether he worked hard or not. He still got stressed.

"Does dyslexia mean he's stupid?" Cressida asked.

Lachlan laughed. "No, he's stupid anyway."

"That's enough." His father rapped on the table.

Caspian's school had brought in a psychologist who'd put him through a barrage of tests and to Caspian's horror, he hadn't even been able to remember five numbers in the right order, let alone repeat them in reverse. The lady testing him was kind but as he kept getting things wrong, he pulled his real self deep inside him and turned into a joker. She'd seen through him. The first one ever to do that.

But the dyslexic label had at least stopped most of his teachers thinking he was stupid or not trying, though it hadn't stopped the bullying or mocking. Caspian read very slowly, finger under each word, and if he had to read out loud, he sounded terrible—like a five-year-old or a robot. He still fooled around more than he should and made jokes, so at least he felt the laughter was not all at his expense.

"Are you listening?" his father barked.

"Sorry?" Caspian looked up.

"I've engaged a tutor to help you catch up. He's starting on Monday. Nine to five. Four days a week."

A black cloud formed over Caspian's head. "But it's the holidays."

"It's for your own good. He'll work with you until we go away to France."

31

I hate you. Caspian put his cutlery neatly on his plate. "Please may I be excused?"

"You don't want dessert?" his mother asked.

"No thank you." *I want to run away.*

"It's Eton mess." She smiled at him.

It was his favourite. "No thank you."

"You may leave the table," she said.

Caspian made sure he didn't scrape the chair legs on the wooden floor though he really wanted to. Once he was in his room, he threw himself on his bed. He didn't want to spend weeks on more schoolwork. There was no point. He wasn't going to get better at it. He wanted to spend time with Zed.

The next morning, when Caspian climbed into the treehouse, Zed was already there, sitting on the mattress with a book on his lap and a pencil in his mouth. He looked up, took out the pencil and smiled, and suddenly Caspian's heart seemed too big for his chest. He couldn't remember when he'd been so glad to see anyone or when anyone had been glad to see him.

Zed set aside whatever he was working on. "Where've you been?"

"Escaping from sadistic flamingos. Family dinner last night. Family breakfast this morning." Caspian dropped down next to him and looked at the book Zed had been holding. "Physics? Why are you doing school stuff?" He gave an exaggerated gasp of horror and held up crossed index fingers. "Are you a swot?"

Zed raised his eyebrows. "Yes, but not voluntarily. My father says I have to do a section of maths and physics every day. I'm catching up on what I should have done yesterday. I did all the maths last night and the first section of the physics, but I have to finish this by the time he gets home. I thought I'd do it while I was waiting for you."

Caspian picked up the book and looked at it. "GCSE level?"

"I know. It's hard. Are you any good at physics?"

"I'm not good at anything."

"What? That's not true. Your inventions are brilliant. I could never come up with anything like that."

"I…" Caspian hesitated. He didn't tell people he was dyslexic but… "I'm dyslexic."

Zed blinked. "Okay. So reading and writing are difficult?"

"And other stuff. I can read, but I'm slow."

"I read too fast. I don't remember half of what I've read."

"Reading slow doesn't mean I remember it."

They looked at each other and smiled.

"By the time I was eleven, teachers didn't know what to do with me apart from give me word puzzles or stick me in front of a computer." Caspian sighed. "That was another thing I got expelled for, looking at porn when I was supposed to be working on a history project."

Zed clapped a hand over his mouth as he laughed. "They didn't have a way to stop pupils doing that?"

"I bypassed it."

Zed grinned. "See, there *is* stuff you're really good at. I've never even had the chance to look at porn."

"They ought to show it in sex ed lessons. I've learnt more from watching sex on the internet than from listening to a teacher."

"Now you're making me jealous."

Caspian's heart gave a loud thump but he shied away from saying more. He didn't want to frighten Zed off.

Zed shoved the physics book to one side. "I had to thank my father for giving me the workbooks and I wanted to shove them up his…"

"Arse."

Zed's face lit up and a wave of joy crashed over Caspian. "Yeah, arse."

"You're not the only one whose father thinks holidays are perfect for catching up on schoolwork. Mine's hired a tutor to come Monday to Thursday, nine to five."

"Well that sucks."

"Yeah, it does."

"In our final school assembly, the head told us we should focus on ourselves in the summer, relaxing and having fun. That if we did more studying, it'd turn into a monotonous grind of having to get stuff done, and when we came back next term, we wouldn't have our minds in the right place." Zed sighed. "I can't think of anyone who'd *want* to study in the holidays. Most of the school were sniggering at the thought of it. I was too. Until last night."

"My father thinks having a tutor will help me catch up. It won't. Unless the guy brings an actual magic wand, it isn't going to make much difference."

"I thought there were things that could help if you're dyslexic."

Caspian shrugged. "The tutor will probably suggest working on phonics. Sounding out the words. And lots of handwriting practice which is fucking torture. Maybe I should call Childline." He wished

Zed had been facing him when he'd said that because it had reminded him about those marks on his back.

"I think their definition of torture might be a bit different," Zed said.

"Yeah." He bit his lip. "It isn't that I don't understand stuff at school, it's more that I can't write quickly or clearly enough and by the time I've copied things down, the teacher is talking about something entirely different. Certain types of information doesn't stick in my head for long. People think I'm dumb, but I'm not."

"No, you're not."

"It's as though as soon as I work out what I want to say, my brain shuts off at the thought of moving a pen across a sheet of paper."

"You labelled your plans okay."

"A few words. That's easy and I know it's barely legible. The prospect of writing an essay on *Who is more evil? Macbeth or his wife?* makes me want to throw up. Even using the computer is hard because I still have to look at the keys and I get muddled."

"Maybe you could invent your own shorthand."

"If I could remember it. I've got a voice programme too, but I speak too fast because I have to get everything out before I lose track so it doesn't show exactly what I say and then I have to go back and correct it." He flung himself on his back. "It's not fair. The only thing I wanted to do this summer with paper and pencils was invent things. Now I'm going to be made to sit for hours practising joined-up writing like a seven-year-old. It's going to be shit."

"I have to do that course in Canterbury on Tuesdays and Wednesdays but compared to you, I've got off lightly."

"It might not be so bad."

"Study of the Quran, the history of Islam and Arabic writing. It'll be shit."

"Fucking shit."

Zed looked at him.

"Say it." Caspian grinned. "Fucking shit."

"Fucking shit."

They both laughed.

"Being dyslexic won't stop you being a great inventor. One day people will be lining up to buy things you've created. I'll be one of them. I mean I'll be lining up, not that I'll be one of the things you created. I'll say—I knew him when he was a flamingo."

There was a tinge of colour in Zed's cheeks and warmth spread through Caspian's body. *You have to be gay. Please be gay.*

34

"The bad news is we're not going to be able to get together as much as I'd hoped," Caspian said. "But we can meet on Fridays."

"No we can't. I'm going to be made to go to Maidstone with my father and work for nothing all day in his pharmacy, then go to the mosque afterwards for prayers."

Zed's obvious disappointment made Caspian happy and sad at the same time.

"We can meet at the weekend if you're not busy?" Caspian said. "Or in the evenings? We should have some sort of system for letting each other know." He bit his nail. "Leave a message in here? On the bookshelf?"

"Yep, we can do that. Or…" Zed released a shaky breath, "do you want to run away with me right now?"

Caspian knew Zed wasn't joking. But much as the idea had appealed last night, the will to do it was weaker this morning. How far could they get? Where could they go? How would they survive? All Caspian would do was piss off his father even more. Same for Zed who was staring straight at him.

But Caspian didn't want to make light of the idea of running, not when his heart was yelling at him to say *yes*. "We'd not get very far. We're tall but we look fourteen. Or fifteen in my case. We'd be picked up, brought home and not allowed out at all then. Probably not allowed to see each other anymore. I don't want that to happen."

Zed opened his mouth as if he were going to say something, then closed it.

Caspian pulled at a thread on one of the cushions. "I remember when I was little and jealous of the twins, I packed my teddy and PJs in a bag and walked away from the house. I'd gone about 200 metres before I felt hungry and went back. I should have taken biscuits. I'd have got further. Maybe another 100 metres. Not sure Teddy ever forgave me for going home."

"If we were sixteen," Zed whispered.

Caspian stared straight at him. "If we were sixteen I'd pack right now."

He pulled a piece of paper from his pocket. "My list of fun things to do, not all bad but I have nothing to be good for so why not be bad? It's more fun. So do you want to be bad with me? Yes or no?"

"Before I look at this piece of paper?"

Caspian grinned. "Be brave. Decide before you look."

"Okay. I'll be bad with you. Maybe we'd better try and fit in as many bad things as we can." He read the list. "*Dye our hair red, green or blue. Or all three.*" Zed gaped at him. "My father would explode."

"I should have put that first on the list. Make our fathers explode. Life would be so much simpler. Want to dye your hair or not?"

"Definitely. Er…as long as it washes out because if my father does explode, I'd get caught in the blast."

"It said it washes out on the can. Mum bought them for the twins to use last Halloween, but they decided to dress as angels. The irony."

Zed looked back at the paper. "I like the idea of making a crop circle, but we'd have to do that at night, wouldn't we?"

"Can you sneak out?"

Zed chewed his lip. "I can try. Tonight?"

"Here at midnight."

"Deal." They bumped fists.

"We'll wait for my mother to take the Terrible Twins out shopping and then we can go my house and use the hair dye."

"Okay." Zed checked the list again. "Bike ride? Did you ask your brother?"

"He said no, but he's out all day. He won't know. I'll wear his helmet and you can have mine. You *can* ride a bike?"

"Yep." Zed ran his finger down the sheet. "Make a zip line. Go grass sledging. Do a treasure hunt. That sounds good, but it would take a bit of organising. If we're doing one for each other, we'd have to set them up separately."

"Next weekend?"

"Okay."

"Want me to help you with the physics while we're waiting for my family to leave the house?"

He thought Zed would say no but he budged up on the mattress to let Caspian sit closer. Caspian wished he was brave enough to press right up against Zed, allow their legs touch, but he wasn't.

As Zed read, he ran his finger under the words. *For my benefit?* "*An object dropped near the Earth's surface will accelerate downwards at 9.8 metres per second squared due to the force of gravity, and regardless of size, if air resistance is minimal.*"

"What does near the earth's surface mean?"

"I guess it means from a point where gravity is normal. I remember my mum showing me that if you simultaneously drop a cricket ball and a scrunched up ball of paper, they'll hit the ground at the same time. We tried with lots of things. A book and a packet of rice. A toy car and a bag of sugar."

36

"If I dropped my brother and sisters from a skyscraper?"

Zed chuckled. "So you *are* the murderous flamingo? They'd hit the ground at the same time, assuming minimal air resistance. If your sisters wore very floaty dresses that acted a bit like parachutes, they might be slightly slower to reach the ground, but it wouldn't be enough to save them."

Zed read on. "*If you throw a rock downward from Mount Everest with negligible air resistance, after it leaves your hand, the rock accelerates at a. less than 9.8 ms^2 b. 9.8 ms^2 c. more than 9.8 ms^2 d. depends on the speed of the rock.*" He turned to Caspian. "What do you think?"

"Is it a trick question?"

Zed grinned. "Sort of."

"9.8 ms^2?"

"Yay! Negligible air resistance was the clue. All objects fall at the same velocity until the lighter object reaches its terminal velocity. The trick was the word *throw* because that implied it'd go faster but it will only travel at 9.8 ms^2."

Caspian felt a small thrill in getting it right. "So what's terminal velocity?"

"That's the next bit in the book. *Objects fall at the same rate, depending on wind resistance, until the moment the lighter object reaches its terminal velocity.* A *person would reach terminal velocity after falling around two thousand feet. They'd be travelling around 53 metres a second or 122 miles per hour* before splat."

"Is says *splat* in the book?"

Zed nodded and grinned.

"Some people have survived falling without a parachute."

"They have. They were lucky. Hitting the ground at 122 miles an hour? Even if they landed in the sea, it'd be like hitting concrete."

"I'll stop interrupting. You'll work faster." Caspian lay on his side and watched Zed. While Zed was concentrating, it gave him chance to stare.

I'm falling for you.

What happens if I reach terminal velocity?

Will I survive?

Chapter Four

When Zed saw Caspian's house, he stopped in his tracks. "Whoa. You live here?"

"No, in a stable at the back. Of course, here."

The house was huge and old and…awesome. "Was it built by the Romans?" Zed widened his eyes.

"Ha ha. It was constructed in the 18th century, but bits have been added."

"Electricity and indoor plumbing?"

Caspian grinned. "No, we still use candles and crap in a shed at the bottom of the garden."

"Your house looks like the sort people pay to come and visit."

"They do, a few times a year. They can tour some rooms, visit the gardens, crap in the shed. I think my father gets money to help with the upkeep if he opens the place to the public."

Caspian used a key to unlock the front door and Zed followed him in. It was as impressive inside, and a world away from his own modern, sleek-lined, sterile home. The touches his mother had added were long gone. His father didn't like clutter, didn't like anything that had no purpose. No flatpack Ikea products had ever been assembled in this place. The furniture was hundreds of years old. The chairs didn't look safe to sit on.

All sorts of stuff just waited to get broken—vases, clocks, ornaments. The walls were covered with oil paintings of animals, landscapes, flowers and stern-looking people. Persian rugs covered an old wooden floor. Real ones. It was more like a museum than a home and yet more of a home than Zed's house. There were shoes piled up near the door, mail thrown onto a table, an empty wine glass sitting on the stairs next to a pair of high-heeled sparkly shoes.

Zed followed Caspian up a curving staircase to a bedroom three times the size of his, equipped with everything Zed didn't have—an electric guitar, computer, TV, telescope, stacks of films and a games console. *Oh and a—*

Caspian dived onto the bed and stuffed a battered looking teddy under the duvet. Zed felt a pang in his chest at the thought of Caspian keeping his bear close.

"Tell me you didn't see that." Caspian's face flushed.

"I have a bear too." Zed hesitated, then continued. "I feel too guilty to put him aside. A friend who's listened to everything I had to say without a word of complaint or criticism? A friend who's never let me down? I can't not have him near me."

Caspian let out a shaky breath. "Does yours have a name?"

"Teddy Robinson."

"Mine's Charlie Bear."

They smiled at each other.

"We never tell anyone, right?" Caspian said.

"No. Is that an iPod?" Zed changed the subject.

"Yep. I like my MP3 player though."

Zed's walls were blank, Caspian's were covered with sketches, more of his inventions. Caspian's duvet was plain grey, the only thing that looked like Zed's. The long dark blue curtains were covered in constellations and planets.

"Is your room like this?"

"No. Well, it has a bed and curtains."

Caspian sighed. "I'll get the hair dye."

When he'd gone, Zed pulled the bear from down the side of the bed and brushed his fingers against its face. "Nice to meet you, Charlie Bear."

Caspian came back with three cans. "Red, green or blue? Or all three?"

"Surprise me."

"Shall I do you first? Let's go into the bathroom."

The bathroom was three times the size of Zed's with a bath *and* a shower.

"Take your T-shirt off," Caspian said.

I can't. "It's an old one. It doesn't matter if it gets spoiled." Except it did.

"Then put this round your shoulders." Caspian handed him a dark blue towel. "Sit on the edge of the bath and close your eyes."

The sensation of Caspian running his fingers through his hair as he sprayed it, sent Zed's cock hard. *Shit.* He crossed his legs and clutched the towel to his stomach.

When the spraying stopped, and Caspian was no longer touching him, he opened his eyes.

"Wow," Caspian whispered. "You look great."

Zed pushed to his feet, but Caspian stepped between him and the mirror.

"Do mine first and we'll look together. Blue." He held out the can, then grabbed Zed's towel and draped it around his own shoulders.

Zed scuttled behind him and sprayed the bright blue dye all over Caspian's head, threading his fingers through his hair to spread it, just as Caspian had done to him, which made his cock even harder. Fortunately, it was hidden by his cargo shorts and baggy T-shirt.

39

"Okay. Done," Zed said.

They stood side by side in front of the mirror, their faces creasing as they smiled at their spiky-haired reflections.

"You think we look older, Red Boy?" Caspian asked.

"Maybe, Blue Boy. We're a bit like freaky twins."

Caspian turned his head to one side, then the other. "I don't know why I didn't do this before. I like it."

You have to be gay.

"My school has rules about hair colour," Zed said. "They sent a boy home who'd only bleached the tips of his hair. He had to dye it brown before they'd let him come back."

"I like the idea of doing just the tips."

"Me too."

As they washed their hands in the basin, Caspian sucked in a breath. "The colour's not coming off as easily as I thought it would. It said on the can it washes out."

Zed used a nail brush on his hands and eventually they were almost clean. While Caspian was working on his, Zed picked up one of the cans and read the instructions. Something he probably should have done earlier.

"Ah," Zed muttered.

"What?" Caspian dried his hands and came to his side.

"It does wash out, but it says after a few weeks. *Avoid getting onto skin.*"

"Fuck. Good thing we're not at school."

Zed's dad was going to kill him.

"Oh shit. Your dad." Caspian winced. "Is he going to explode?"

Zed made himself shrug but he felt sick. He'd get beaten again.

"Want to make sandwiches and go for a bike ride?"

Zed really wanted to stand under the shower until the red had gone, but he followed Caspian downstairs and into a large kitchen.

"Hi Betsy, this is my friend Zed."

The middle-aged woman gasped when she saw them, then laughed. "Master Caspian, whatever have you done!"

"It washes out," Caspian said.

"Good thing it does."

Zed held out his hand. "Hello."

She shook it. "Nice to meet you, Zed."

"We need a picnic," Caspian said. "We're going exploring."

"Want me to make it for you?" she asked.

"Please." Caspian smiled at her. "We like peanut butter."

40

"Ah so you were the one who left the jar out and the top off yesterday lunchtime. Go on, be off with you. Come back in ten minutes."

It took that long for Zed to get the hang of Caspian's bike. He could ride, he wasn't lying, but after he'd grown out of the first two-wheeler he'd had when he was eight, there hadn't been another one bought for him. He was glad he was wearing a helmet because he fell off twice. He kept practising while Caspian went to get their lunch and though he improved, he wasn't sure he was safe enough to share a road with cars and lorries.

But fifteen minutes later, he was cycling out of the village behind Caspian who carried their lunch in a backpack. There was a dedicated cycle lane but every time something overtook him, Zed wobbled.

He was relieved when Caspian pulled off the main road onto a smaller track and even more relieved when he dismounted.

"We'll hide the bikes behind this wall and go on foot," Caspian said.

"Where are we?"

"Didn't you look at the signs?"

"I was too busy looking for bumps in the road."

"Not my backside?"

Zed gaped at him. "Obviously…and your backside."

Caspian grinned. "We're going to watch the gliders. Come on."

They lifted the bikes over a wall, left their helmets with them, then headed up the side of a field. At the top the view opened out over the Kent downs. Zed could already see a glider in the sky.

Caspian lay on his back with his arms crossed under his head. "I'm happy," he said quietly.

Zed joined him, and when their fingers briefly touched, and Caspian didn't move his hand, Zed was happy too.

Zed wasn't so happy later that afternoon after he'd washed his hair over and over, using half a bottle of shampoo, to find it was still red. Not such a vivid red but still more than enough to get him into trouble. Good thing his father wasn't home until late so Zed thought he probably wouldn't notice tonight, even if he looked in on him, but he would tomorrow.

Being home alone was an opportunity to make himself chips for dinner and watch what he wanted on TV, but anxiety churned his stomach and he didn't feel like eating anything. The village shop was now shut or he'd have gone to see if he could buy hair dye.

41

He took a flashlight from a kitchen drawer and hid it in his room. He'd need it to get back to the treehouse, though Caspian said they couldn't use lights in the field in case they were seen. The two of them were both going to design a crop circle and then they'd decide which to make. Zed didn't draw anything too complicated. A spiral that turned into a snail. They'd talked about how to flatten the wheat while they were watching the gliders. Zed had come up with the idea of dragging planks behind them and Caspian was going to find two and some rope.

Zed worried about going to sleep in case he slept through his alarm, because he'd need to keep it in bed with him to muffle the sound. He decided he might as well do more maths. It would be nice to think his father wouldn't expect him to work over the weekend, but Zed knew he would. Probably on Tuesday and Wednesday too, even though he'd be at the camp.

Despite his current anxiety, he'd had a brilliant time today. He wished he was brave enough to kiss Caspian, but he wasn't. He was too afraid of losing him as a friend.

When he heard the door open downstairs, he put his book and pencil on the floor and slid down the bed, covering his head with the sheet. *Please, please, please. Don't come into my room.* He was desperate his father not see him. Tonight, he'd ask Caspian if he could dye his hair back to normal at his house because tomorrow his father would be at home all day.

The more Zed thought about it, it was a better idea not to come home tonight at all. After they'd made the crop circle, he'd sleep in the treehouse and buy dye first thing in the morning. Then he thought how wimpy that made him look. Caspian didn't seem to care what his father thought, but then Zed doubted Caspian's father beat him.

He heard voices downstairs and froze. TV? Or someone with his father? He listened but he couldn't make out what was being said. What he did make out was that his father was with a woman. He knew his father had started to go on dates. Zed had no problem with that. Anything that kept his father happy was a good thing.

Caspian was waiting at the foot of the treehouse when Zed came through the trees.

"Am I late?"

"Perfect timing. We're lucky the moon's out. It'll make it easier to see what we're doing. What's your design?"

Zed pulled the piece of paper out of his pocket. "A snail."

Caspian nodded. "Okay. Well this is mine."

Zed's jaw dropped when he saw what Caspian had drawn. An erect cock and balls with cum spurting from the top of the cock. He turned the paper round and frowned. "What is it?"

Caspian groaned. "It's obvious. It's... Ah, very funny. We'll do the snail if you want."

"Yours is more fun."

"Is it? Why?"

"Everyone likes rockets."

Caspian handed him one of the planks. "The field's not far but we won't use the road in case we're seen."

They set off through the trees.

"Is it okay if I spend the night in the treehouse? I've brought some money with me for hair dye. I daren't let my father see me like this."

"Mine almost exploded. He told me I wasn't allowed out of the house until it was back to its normal colour. The twins were angry I'd used their stuff. My brother said I looked like a Smurf. My mother is buying dye tomorrow. You can stay in the treehouse and I'll come and get you so we can both use it."

They had to cross the main road to reach the field but there was little traffic. Once they'd climbed over the gate, they looked up at the expanse of bright yellow wheat rising up into the distance.

"A field of gold," Zed said.

"It's perfect. Everyone driving along this road will see our grand design."

"You want it to be that big?"

"The bigger the better, right?"

"I guess so."

After a few minutes discussion about how to actually make the shape, and a few more minutes attaching rope to each end of the planks, they set off parallel to each other, walking along tractor lines until Caspian told him to stop. "We can do the balls on the way back. But start the cock here. Stay parallel with me."

Zed looped the rope over his shoulders, made sure the plank was level and set off. It wasn't as easy as he'd thought to drag a piece of wood up the field and when he glanced back, the wheat had been only partially flattened.

"I'll do the cum," Caspian told him and Zed laughed as Caspian accompanied each line he stamped out with a loud grunt or groan culminating in a breathless gurgle as he finished.

He picked his way back to Zed's side. "Was it good for you?"

Zed chuckled. "Are you that noisy?"

"Aren't you?"

43

"I'm silent as a ghost."

"Christ, aren't you supposed to jack off either?"

"It's *haram*—forbidden in Islam. Well, not everyone agrees about that but my father's on the—*you're not allowed to wank*—side. Not sure how he could stop me apart from tying up my hands when I'm in bed. He might if he thought of it."

"I've mastered the handless wank. Rub against the mattress. It works fine."

Zed sniggered.

They walked back down the tractor lines, stamped out the balls and then went over the outline again. Back at the bottom of the field, they dropped down into a patch of wheat well away from their design.

"I should have brought water," Caspian said. "That was hard work."

"We can't even see if we've done it right."

"I was going to pay for us to go up in a glider tomorrow to take pictures of our cock circle."

Zed looked at him. "Don't you think they might guess it was us then?"

"That's true."

Zed closed his eyes. His heart was pounding with fear and exhilaration rather than exertion. Dyeing his hair was one thing, but this night's work could get them into a lot of trouble. It was worth it. It had been fun.

He felt a tickle on his cheek, and guessed Caspian was teasing him with a piece of dried grass. Caspian trailed it over Zed's nose, his eyes, his chin, his lips. Zed couldn't open his eyes. He nearly did when he felt the sensation of Caspian's warm breath wash over his cheek, but the moment was too precious to spoil. For as long as he could, he'd pretend Caspian was his boyfriend and about to kiss him, rather than a friend who was teasing him.

But when he heard the catch in Caspian's breathing, he opened his eyes to find Caspian's face inches from his.

"Shit, now you've opened your eyes I don't know if I dare," Caspian whispered.

"We just drew a huge cock and balls in a field. We dyed our hair red and blue. We dare do anything."

Zed reached for Caspian's hand and their fingers threaded together.

"What's going through your head?" Caspian whispered.

"I'm supposed to think as well?"

"As well as what?"

"Breathe. Talk… Want."

Caspian released a shaky breath as he laughed and tentatively moved his mouth closer to Zed's. He was moving so slowly it was like watching the minute hand on a clock. *Oh God, oh God. Do it. Do it. Do it.*

Their lips met, the barest touch, though they weren't really kissing. Then Caspian let go of his hand, slipped his fingers to the back of Zed's neck and pulled him in close. Zed's heart raced. He didn't know how to kiss. He'd never kissed anyone—not like this. Not someone he fancied. Just kisses on the cheek for his mother. Never on the mouth.

"Are you thinking about punching me?" Caspian whispered.

"No. Kicking."

Caspian laughed. "I've practised this. But my arm is crap at kissing me back."

"I'm not sure I'll be any better than your arm."

Caspian smiled. "Yeah you will."

Zed wanted to be the one to make the next move. He put his arm around Caspian, spread his fingers on his back and held him tight but didn't pull him close. His cock was pressing against his zip. The slightest touch and… Then Caspian gently brushed his lips against Zed's, over and over until Zed couldn't breathe, forgot how to breathe, forgot how to do anything.

"You're so beautiful," Caspian whispered.

His fingers slid into Zed's hair, then drifted across his face and when they touched his lips, Zed kissed them, licked them, sucked them and dragged a groan from Caspian's throat. Knowing he had the power to do that made his head spin. Caspian held Zed's face in his palms and stared into his eyes. Zed wormed his other hand under Caspian so that both hands were on his back. Not just on his back, under his T-shirt, his hot skin burning Zed's hands.

"This is why I can't be a Muslim," Zed whispered.

Caspian whimpered and pressed his lips back to Zed's. Zed opened his mouth and Caspian's tongue slipped inside, warm and slick and tasting of…chocolate, and Zed sucked on it.

Oh fuck he's kissing me he tastes so good he tastes like chocolate and his breathing is as shaky as mine and my cock is hurting but a good hurt and he likes this as much as me.

They explored, they tested, they tried to do everything with their tongues, with their mouths, licking, nipping, sucking. Caspian yanked him closer and Zed felt the ridge of Caspian's erection pressed against his own.

45

This is why I can't be a Muslim. Caspian had to know what he meant. *Oh fuck.*

This was so good.

It was great.

It was perfect.

They lay in each other's arms, wrapped around each other, kissing as if it were the most natural thing in the world, as if it was the only thing in the world, and Zed still couldn't breathe properly, he was so excited, so terrified, so turned on.

But the sound of a car pulling up on the other side of the hedge jerked them apart.

"What the fuck?" Caspian whispered. "Keep still, don't move."

A car door slammed. Then another door and the beam of a flashlight came over the top of the hedge. A moment later it landed on them.

"Hello, boys," said a policeman.

Zed pushed to his feet, Caspian at his side.

"Run," Caspian whispered.

But when Caspian stayed where he was, so did Zed.

A policeman climbed over the gate and shone a powerful flashlight over the field. "You two are in so much trouble."

"Run," Caspian murmured. "You'll be in more trouble than me."

Zed shook his head and brushed his hand against Caspian's. He wasn't running and leaving a friend to face this alone. But when they were put in the police car, Zed felt as if he were falling into a deep hole.

"How old are you?" the driver asked.

"He's fourteen, I'm fifteen." Caspian squeezed his fingers. "Can't you just tell us off and let us go? Please?"

"You've caused hundreds of pounds worth of damage. A flattened wheat crop can't be harvested. Names."

"Caspian Tarleton."

Zed saw the way the policeman reacted.

"Your father is going to be furious with you, young man."

Caspian's shoulders slumped.

"And you?" the policeman asked.

"Hvarechaeshman Zadeh."

"Address?"

"Larch Cottage, Middleham Road, Upper Barton."

"I doubt your father will be pleased either."

Zed wanted not to care what his father would say, but he did care because he knew he'd pay heavily for tonight. It would still be worth it.

"How did you know we were there?" Caspian asked.

"A passing motorist called it in. Whose idea was it?"

"Mine," Caspian and Zed said together.

Caspian held tighter to Zed's hand.

The policemen drove Caspian home first. They left Zed in the car when they walked up to the door. Zed assumed it was Caspian's brother who eventually answered. He looked like an older version of Caspian but not as good-looking. Then his father appeared, a dark silk robe over pyjamas. The police talked to him and Caspian's father turned to look at the car—at Zed. Much as Zed wanted to curl up out of sight, he didn't, though he dropped his gaze.

When the policemen got back into the car, the one in the passenger seat turned to look at him. "Whose idea was it really?"

"Mine," Zed said. "All of it was my idea. I had to push Caspian into helping me."

The guy laughed and turned round. It was all Zed could do not to either throw up or wet himself as they drove him home. By the time they pulled up outside his house, Zed was shaking. They took him to the door and rang the bell. It took his father ages to appear. He'd put on trousers and a shirt. When he saw Zed, he did a double take.

"What's happened?" he asked.

"Your son has been caught with another boy making an obscene diagram in a wheat field on the edge of Lower Barton. Fortunately, the other boy's father owns the land and has offered to compensate the tenant farmer for the lost crop. I doubt there'll be action taken against the boys, but I trust you'll ensure your son never does anything like this again."

"Of course. I'm horrified by his behaviour. I had no idea he'd crept out of the house. Thank you for bringing him home." He turned to Zed. "Go to bed."

Zed hurried into the house. If he'd had his money, he might have gone straight out of the kitchen door but all he had was the couple of pounds he'd intended to use to buy hair dye, so he went up the stairs and sat on the floor in his room. He listened to the police car pull away, heard the door slam and flinched. A moment later, his father came up the stairs. His steps were heavy. Zed didn't even bother wishing they'd continue past his room because he knew they wouldn't.

47

The door swung open and his father stood there holding the crop. "Get to your feet."

Zed pushed himself up.

"How dare you?" His father gripped the crop so hard, his knuckles turned white. "You not only dye your hair a ridiculous colour, but you sneak off in the night, damage a farmer's field and leave a disgusting image for everyone to see."

And I kissed a boy. You don't know about that. And I liked it.

His father slapped his cheek so hard, Zed's face whipped round and he bit his tongue. A coppery tang filled his mouth.

"After all I do for you, and you shame me like this," his father shouted.

He shoved Zed onto the bed. The first strike had Zed writhing in agony. He curled up, trying to present as small a target as he could but his father hit him everywhere, including his face. Zed fell off the bed as he tried to escape the blows, only to be hauled to his feet for his father to hit him again and again.

"You disgust me," his father hissed. "The sight of you disgusts me. You will not leave this house without my express permission."

I hate you. I hate you. I hate you. Each time the crop made contact, it was like being struck by lightning. As if the crop wasn't bad enough, he was kicked, slapped, punched, and thrown around until blood pooled in his mouth and seeped down his chin. There was blood in his eyes and he couldn't see. Everywhere hurt and he was too weak to even fend off the blows.

He repeated in his mind—*this will stop, this will stop.*

Finally, it did.

"You are not my son," his father snarled. "You are not a brother. You are nothing."

After his father had gone, Zed managed to get onto his bed but no further. He couldn't run away because he doubted he'd manage more than a few steps without collapsing. But the moment he was strong enough, he was leaving.

Chapter Five

After the police left, Caspian was sent straight to bed with instructions to go to his father's study the next morning at nine. He was worried about Zed but what could he do? He'd told him to run, tried to take the blame but Zed had stayed at his side. Caspian wished he'd never suggested the crop circle, wished he'd not persuaded Zed to have his hair dyed, but he didn't wish the kiss hadn't happened.

At least he knew now that Zed was into boys too, and the kiss had been magical. It was hard to wipe the smile from his face when he thought about it except the price might be too high. Not for him. He was already being exiled to Siberia. How much more could his father do? But Zed's father... *Oh fuck.*

No one spoke to him at breakfast, not even the Terrible Twins. He managed a slice of toast but that was all. He knocked on the study door as the clock in the hall struck nine.

"Enter," his father called.

Caspian walked in with his back straight, his head up. His father sat behind his desk and Caspian stopped a few feet away.

"Who's the boy you were with?"

"Someone I met from Upper Barton."

"Name?"

"I'm not giving you his name. It was all my idea."

"You and he worked together. He has to take responsibility as well. You do realise I can find out his name?"

"I know but I won't give it to you."

His father nodded. "I admire loyalty though I think it's misplaced on this occasion."

"My idea. My design. Not his fault."

"Yet he worked with you."

"Because I persuaded him to."

"You're never to see him again."

Caspian pressed his lips together.

"I mean it. You're grounded until I say otherwise. You will not leave this house without permission. Give me your phone."

Caspian put it on the desk.

"You'll get this back when I feel you deserve it. You will pay me back out of your allowance for what I have to pay Giles Forman for the damage to his crop. What were you thinking? Well, you weren't thinking, were you? Same with your hair. I don't want to even see you again until that ridiculous colour has gone. Do you understand?"

"Yes."

49

"Do you have anything to say?"

"Sorry." *I'm not.*

"You could try to sound as if you meant it."

"Sorry." *I'm really not.*

"Get out of my sight."

Caspian fled.

He didn't dare leave the house that day. From the way Lachlan was behaving, Caspian suspected his brother had been instructed to keep an eye on him. The twins knew Caspian was in trouble but didn't know why and kept tormenting him.

Once Caspian's hair had been returned to its normal shade, he followed a delicious aroma to the kitchen. Betsy was making biscuits. She tsked when she saw him.

"Why couldn't you have made one of those lovely concentric designs?" she asked.

Caspian cringed. "Have you seen it?"

"I have. Very impressive. Straight as a die. It's the talk of both villages according to Doreen in the post office. There's been a plane up taking photographs. Not sure if they can put something like that in the paper though. Giles Forman is talking about charging people to view it but that won't work. All you have to do is drive past and look up the hill."

"My father's going to pay him compensation. Then I'll have to pay my father. I didn't realise it would damage the crop. I thought it could just be harvested as usual."

"Your idea, I take it?"

"Yes."

"So what about your friend?"

"You know how persuasive I can be." He pinched a bit of the biscuit dough and Betsy rapped his fingers.

"I want to go and see Zed, but I'm not allowed to leave the house."

"As if that would stop you."

She was right. It wouldn't stop him, but he'd wait until tomorrow when his father was at work. If he made sure he got back before the tutor arrived, no one would know.

He was perfectly behaved all day, but in bed he reran that kiss and their embrace so many times he ended up spurting all over his stomach.

The first place Caspian headed for early in the morning was the treehouse, in case Zed had left a message. He found an origami flamingo on the shelf and smiled. So Zed was okay, but when had he

50

left that? Maybe not yesterday. Caspian felt a knot of anxiety tighten in his stomach. He moved the flamingo to the mattress, wrote Zed a note saying he was on his way to see him, in case they missed each other, then headed to Upper Barton.

After he'd heard Zed give his address to the policeman, Caspian had repeated it in his head until he was sure he could remember it. Middleham Road ran straight through Upper Barton and out the other side. He'd just have to walk until he found Larch Cottage, then make sure Zed's father wasn't home before he knocked on the door.

He found the house on the outskirts of the village. There were no close neighbours and a thick hedge ran along the front. Caspian couldn't see any cars parked on the drive but that didn't mean there wasn't a vehicle in the garage. The moment he left the shelter of the hedge, he'd be seen from the house. While he hesitated, there was a loud creak followed by the hum of a rising garage door which sent him scurrying into bushes on the other side of the road. He ducked out of sight and waited. A guy with a beard pulled out onto the road in a silver BMW and turned left. Zed's father? Caspian waited a few minutes before he crossed the road and walked up the drive.

There was no answer when he banged on the door. He lifted the letter box and yelled, "Zed. It's me. Are you okay?"

When there was still no answer, Caspian walked around the house. The back was a wall of glass doors. Everything was neat and tidy inside. No pool of blood. He grimaced. No sign of Zed, though Caspian was convinced he was there. He banged on every sheet of glass all the way around the house until he was back at the front door, then pushed open the letter box and yelled, "Zed!"

"Wait."

The voice was faint but unmistakable. Caspian sighed and stood up. When the door opened, he sucked in a breath. "Fucking hell. What…?"

It was Zed but it wasn't. He was wearing the same clothes as he had in the field. His hair was still red and his face was too pale. One eye was swollen shut. Every piece of Zed's skin that Caspian could see was bruised, scratched or marked by dark red lines. His left arm…hung at an odd angle.

"Your father?" Caspian whispered.

"Yes."

"Your arm looks broken."

"It might be. I can't move it. It really hurts."

"Why hasn't he taken you to hospital?"

"Why do you think?"

51

Caspian sagged. "Shit. I'm sorry. This is all my fault."

"No, it's not. What did your father say?"

"Told me off. Said I have to pay for the damage, but he didn't hit me. Jesus, Zed, your father's nuts. He's not allowed to do this."

"I'm going to run away. Today. Now he's gone to work. I've started to pack my bag. I can't stay here any longer."

Caspian's heart pounded. "Where are we running to?"

"Don't know."

"I'm coming with you."

Zed let out a deep sigh that Caspian felt in his bones.

"You don't need to do that."

"I want to. I've got money. I can buy us rail tickets. We can get to London. Then we'll go to a hospital. We can lie about who we are and how old we are. We can be together."

Oh no, I've made you cry.

Caspian reached out and touched Zed's cheek. "I'll go get my things and my money and I'll come back. I promise."

He ran. He needed to get in and out before the tutor arrived. Caspian thought about retrieving his phone from his father's study but maybe it was better that he couldn't be contacted.

He burst into the house and ran straight into his mother who grabbed his arm and brought him to a halt.

"Your father told me you're not allowed out. Where've you been?"

"To see if I'd left my French book in the treehouse. I hadn't."

"Your tutor's in the dining room."

Caspian gasped. "What? It's not nine yet."

"He's come early to get to know you."

"I need...the bathroom. I need to wash."

"Hurry up."

Caspian bolted up the stairs. *Where to fucking start?* He grabbed a sports bag from the back of his closet and rammed clothes into it. After a moment's hesitation, he put Charlie Bear in too. He had about seventy pounds in his money box and he took that. Then he went down the backstairs to the kitchen, intending to leave by the rear door.

Betsy emerged from the laundry room, looked at him and then at his bag. "What are you up to? Running away?"

Caspian pressed his lips together.

She sighed. "How far do you think you'll get? This isn't the end of the world. Things will go back to normal. Your father doesn't hold grudges."

"Zed's been beaten," he whispered. "His face... There are bruises and marks all over him. His arm's broken but his father didn't take him to hospital. He's gone off to work and left him alone."

Her face paled. "His father's hit him?"

Caspian nodded. "He's done it before."

"Oh my goodness."

"He needs to go to hospital. I'm going to take him."

She sighed. "Caspian, you're just a boy. You can't handle this."

"Yes, I can."

"You need to tell your father or your mother. Running away isn't going to solve anything. You're only fifteen years old. Where can you go? How can you support yourselves? How can you stay safe?"

"I have to help him."

"You can but not by running away with him."

He sagged. "Then what can I do?"

It was hard to do anything with just one arm. Unfastening his shorts so he could pee took so long he thought he was going to wet himself. And it hurt. Yesterday, he'd seen blood in the toilet bowl but not today. Zed didn't pack much. For months he'd planned exactly what he wanted to take but now his head ached too much to concentrate on anything. He put in a few items of clothing, his bear, Caspian's book and all his money.

He dragged the bag down to the front door, then sat on the stairs to wait, cradling his arm. Zed had no idea how long it would take Caspian to go home, pack and come back, but he guessed no more than an hour. Hopefully less. He didn't allow himself to feel relief that this would soon be over. Until he and Caspian were in London, he wouldn't feel safe.

When Zed heard a car pull up on the drive, his heart rate shot up. He assumed it was his father and he struggled to his feet, grabbed his bag and threw it in the downstairs cloakroom. An action that resulted in him biting back a cry of pain when he jolted his injured arm. But the bell rang, so it wasn't his father. Maybe Caspian had ordered a taxi to take them to the station. Zed opened the door and blinked when he saw a policeman and a lady in a flowered dress standing next to him.

"Hvare...chaesh...man? Do I have that right?" the woman asked. "My name's Susan Reeves. I'm a social worker. This is Constable Garrett. Can we come in?"

"Is this about the wheat field?" Zed asked.

"No, it's about you." The woman gave him a kind smile and Zed's world began to crumble.

"Can we come in?" the policeman asked. "Is your dad home?"

"No. He's at work." *Go away. I don't want to talk to you.*

"What's happened to you?" the woman asked. "You don't look very well."

"Why are you here?" Zed whispered, his heart cramping in pain.

She took a step forward. "We've had a report that you've been beaten, that your arm might be broken."

Zed understood then that Caspian wouldn't be coming, and he wanted the world to end right at that moment. The future Zed had hoped for had been taken from him in an instant. He had to be careful now. If he told the truth, he'd get put into care. Not a foster family because who would want a fourteen-year-old boy, a Muslim who wasn't, except for the wrong sort of family? His father would be so angry Zed would never feel safe.

But he wasn't safe now. "I should call my father." He tried to close the door but the policeman's foot was in the way.

"I think you need to go to hospital, get that arm looked at," the policeman said. "We'll take you and contact your father."

Zed's arm hurt. And his ribs. All of him hurt. He didn't even know if his father intended to let a doctor look at his arm, whether making him wait was part of the punishment. But it hurt so much. "Okay, but I have to do something first."

"What?" asked the policeman.

"There's a bag in the downstairs cloakroom. It needs to go back into my wardrobe."

"I'll do that." The woman stepped into the house. "Which is your room?"

"First on the left up the stairs."

Zed knew she was spying but there was nothing to see and hiding the bag was more important. She took the bag up and came back down a few moments later.

"Running away isn't the answer," she said.

So she'd looked inside, and running *was* the answer just not right this minute.

"Do you have a key?" the policeman asked.

"In my pocket. The door locks when you pull it closed."

It hurt getting into the car. Hurt when the woman helped him put on the seatbelt. Hurt when he saw the looks the pair exchanged. She kept talking to him in a quiet, calm voice, telling him not to be frightened, to tell them the truth. Zed knew they were convinced his father had done this and he wasn't sure how to make them believe otherwise, but maybe the longer he stayed silent the worse it looked.

"Some boys attacked me," he whispered.

"Boys? What boys?" the policeman asked.

"Don't know them."

"Describe them."

"Four boys. Older than me. It all happened so fast."

"You go to Middleton Academy?" he asked.

"Yes."

"And the boys who attacked you don't go there?" The policeman glanced at him through the mirror.

Zed knew they trying to trick him. "I've never seen them before." The huff told him he wasn't believed.

"Where were you when it happened?" the woman asked.

"My father grounded me but I sneaked out yesterday. On the way into the village, I was attacked. I lost consciousness and woke to find myself in the bushes. I walked home."

She raised her eyebrows. "Your father didn't notice the state you were in?"

"He was out. When he came back, I was in bed. He didn't see me. He left this morning before I was up. My friend came this morning and saw me and... I guess he called you."

He released a shaky sigh and closed his eyes. It was done. He wouldn't say anything else. He knew Caspian thought he'd done the right thing in telling the authorities, but he'd made everything worse.

Zed's arm *was* broken. He was given an anaesthetic so it could be reset. When he woke, his arm was encased in blue plaster and his father and brother were at his bedside.

"Finally, you're awake." Tamaz smiled at him. "How are you feeling?"

"Okay."

"The police want to talk to you again. See if you can remember any details about the fucking scum who attacked you." Tamaz stroked his fingers. "Did you do anything to provoke them?"

Can't you guess who did this to me? Maybe he could. Maybe Tamaz was trying to help him or protect their father. "No. I was just walking along the side of the road."

"Were they white boys?" his father asked.

"I don't know." Anger surged at the thought of his father hijacking the lie to make it a racist thing.

"Maybe it would be a good idea if Zed came to live with me for a while. You work such long hours, *Bâbâ*. One of the guys who's sharing the house won't be coming until mid-August, so Zed could have his room."

Even with the thought of the Muslim summer school, Zed wanted to go.

"No, it's not fair on you. He'll be fine on his own. He has plenty of work to do. When he's better, he can come with me to Maidstone."

The tiny shoot of hope that had sprung in Zed's chest shrivelled and died. He already knew Tamaz wouldn't push this. Though it gave Zed the chance to go and see Caspian, so maybe it wasn't such bad news.

But it was. When his father brought him home a day later and showed him his room, Zed let out a little cry. The bag had been taken from the wardrobe, all the clothes thrown on the floor, Teddy Robinson pulled apart and Caspian's book ripped to shreds.

"I have what you seem to think was your money. I imagine you stole it. It will go to the mosque."

Zed kept quiet. Nothing he said would make this any better.

"Sit on the bed," his father snapped.

Where was the guy who'd spoken so kindly to the nurses, thanked them for looking after his son, thanked the police for their care, smiled at Zed as they'd left the ward?

He'd never existed.

A metal chain had been fastened to the headboard. His father fastened the other end around Zed's ankle with a padlock.

"There's plenty of length for you to get to the bathroom and your desk. There's hair dye in the bathroom. Use it. Until I can trust you, you'll stay in your room. You've plenty to do."

When he'd gone, Zed gathered up the pieces of his bear and hugged them to his chest.

Caspian's tutor was a guy in his fifties and he was a pain in the arse. Nothing Caspian did was right. His handwriting had improved but if it took him thirty minutes to write four lines beautifully, what was the fucking point? He wanted to go and see Zed but his parents wouldn't let him. They accused him of lying about Zed's father, as if the short item on the local news about a boy being attacked in Upper Barton by some unidentified young men proved that Caspian hadn't told the truth. *Fuck that.*

It was three days before he managed to sneak away to Zed's. Three days with no messages from Zed left in the treehouse, so either he couldn't get away from his father or he didn't want to. Caspian needed to talk to him.

The BMW was on the drive. Caspian took a deep breath as he knocked on the door. He was hoping Zed would answer, but it was his father.

"Hello, can I speak to...Hv...Hvare..." *Oh shit.* "Please?"

"He's gone to stay with his brother for the summer."

"Oh. Okay."

Caspian turned to go.

"Are you the boy who enticed him into making that obscene image in the wheat field?"

He turned. "Yes."

"I don't want you anywhere near him ever again. You understand?"

Caspian nodded, then yelled at the top of his voice, "Zed. I'm sorry. Forgive me." He wasn't sure if he wanted Zed to have heard him or not. Because if he had, he was trapped in the house.

SUMMER TWO

Chapter Six

2011

Caspian's father gave a heavy sigh, then dropped the report card onto his desk. "This was a chance to start again, away from anyone with preconceptions about you. You're predicted mostly Ds for your exams next year. Was there a subject you didn't come bottom in?"

Fuck you. "Design and technology."

His father snorted. "A subject that counts for something?"

Physics as well but stuff you. "I'm trying. I've done everything you wanted. I stayed after the end of term for the summer school." Though it wasn't as if he'd had a choice.

"You were asked to leave the army section of Combined Cadet Force, then the navy. How long before the air force gets fed up of you too?" His father consulted the sheet in front of him. "*Not good at doing as he's told. Insufficient respect for authority. Poor concentration.*" He gave a short laugh. "Nothing new there. While I admire an independence of spirit, a willingness to test boundaries, you have to learn when it's appropriate to do so."

Caspian bit his lip. He'd never be the golden boy, never make his father proud or happy. He wouldn't even marry well and have kids. Well, he might marry and he might have kids but he doubted his father would be happy at his choice of partner. Thank fuck Lachlan had made it into Cambridge, *and* he'd got a first in his Part One exams, *and* he was going out with a pretty medical student. *He's probably got a bloody halo.*

"What am I going to do with you?" His father shook his head.

Just accept me for what I am. Recognise the things I'm good at. Praise me sometimes.

"Is there any point me employing another tutor this summer?"

Please no! Caspian shook his head, wondering if it was worth repeating what the psychologist had said. *Fuck it, why not?* "I need a break from schoolwork. My brain is wired wrong. When I read, the letters jump around on the page. It takes me longer to sort things out. I'm never going to be able to do well in exams. It isn't that I don't try, I do, but I get frustrated and then I get angry and…"

"Then you mess around and get into trouble."

Imperfection wasn't allowed in the Tarleton family. "I'm sorry."

"All right. No tutor. But you will read at least one book a week this summer."

Find Spot at the Zoo? Meg and Mog? The Gruffalo?
"I'll be choosing them."
Fuck.
"Steinbeck, Salinger, Dickens."
You have to be kidding!
"There's no need for you to delay going on holiday if I'm not employing a tutor. You can leave with your mother and sisters on Friday."
"Can my friend come too?"
"Which friend would that be?"
"Zed."
"No."
"Can I stay here and go with you in August?" He crossed his fingers behind his back.
"So you can get up to more mischief with that boy? I think not."
Double fuck. Caspian stamped off.
"Don't slam the door."
Too late. Well it wasn't but too bad.

Caspian had arrived home from Scotland late last night. His father had sent his driver to collect him and his things. A nine-hour journey to get home, though he'd slept for a few of them. No point asking if his father would let him go to a local school, preferably Zed's school. Now Caspian was halfway toward taking his GCSEs, he had to stay where he was, even if he wasn't going to pass any of the fucking things. A Grade D wasn't a fail but in his father's eyes it was.

It had been a year since he'd seen Zed, but only a week since he'd heard from him. Caspian had saved every letter Zed sent to Scotland. The first had been waiting for him when he'd arrived at Blackstones last September. When he'd scanned to the bottom to see who the letter was from, he'd almost cried. He'd shoved it in his pocket, found a place where he couldn't be seen and taken a deep breath before he'd plucked up the courage to read what Zed had put. The first thing he'd ever been eager to read. He still struggled to decipher it.

Hi Caspian,
I'm okay. I hope you are too and that school won't be as bad as you think. I heard you shouting through the door. You can yell really loud! There's nothing to forgive. You did what you thought was right. I think I'd have done the same if you were hurt. We might have made it to London, but we'd have struggled to survive. I get that.

59

I told the police four boys attacked me. I wasn't brave enough to tell the truth. I'm still not. You're the only one I can tell and I'm sorry for that as well because it's not fair, but to know you're on my side, to have someone believe me, means more than I can say. I'm proud to call you my friend. I hope you still are my friend.

I really wanted to come and see you after I left hospital or at least leave you a message but by the time I was allowed out of the house, you'd gone on holiday to France. I worried someone might find any note I left so I hung flamingos from the ceiling whenever I went to the treehouse. You have a flock now! Did you know a group of flamingos is called a flamboyance?

I wish you could write back, even though I know you hate writing, but my father might intercept your letters. Not might, he would. I'm going to ask one of my teachers—there's one who likes me!—if he'll let you send letters to me via him. That's assuming you want to. I'll write again next week and hopefully give you Mr Carter's address.

I don't regret anything we did. It was all brilliant. Every second of it.

Your friend Zed

The letter took him a long while to read even though Zed had beautiful handwriting. The relief that Zed hadn't been angry brought a lump to Caspian's throat. He knew how he'd have felt if he'd sat waiting with his bag and Zed hadn't appeared. He'd have assumed all sorts of things. None good. He'd wanted to write straight back and the thought made him laugh. He never wanted to write and now he was desperate. If Zed's teacher said no, was there another way of getting a letter to him without Zed's father finding out?

He'd thought for a long time but come up with nothing.

Caspian had practically torn open the next letter.

Hi Caspian,

Mr Carter said no. He was worried if my father found out, he'd get into trouble and lose his job. I said I'd read your letter and destroy it, never even take it home, but he won't change his mind. So I'm going to take the risk of keeping on writing to you and hope you want to hear from me. If you don't, leave me a message in the treehouse at Christmas. I'm guessing you won't be home at half-term. If you don't want to hear from me anymore, I suppose you'll throw these letters away.

I looked up your school on the internet in my school's library. It sounds like a prison camp, but I still wish I was there with you. I hope you've made some friends. I haven't. I only need one friend. Shit. Too much pressure, right?

I had a question come up in physics about terminal velocity and for once, I put my hand up and answered! And I was right!! I hated doing those workbooks, but it's made this term easier.

My father doesn't know but I'm doing music GCSE as well in my free time. I forged his signature on the form. At least I have some lessons that I love. I'm going to do exams in piano and cello next year and Mr Carter's going to buy the music and pay the entrance fee himself. I think he felt bad about saying no to the letters.

My dad has a girlfriend! She's someone who works in his pharmacy. It means he's out a couple of nights a week so I get to eat what I want and watch Doctor Who. I don't know what my father's told her about me, but she hardly speaks to me when she comes round.

I miss you.

Zed

He read the last few words over and over. Caspian missed him too. He'd written back. A painstaking effort to ensure his handwriting was legible, and that he had something interesting and funny to say. He wrote a poem but was too much of a coward to send it so he didn't. He sent the letter in an envelope addressed to Middleton Academy with a note inside asking them to give it to Zed because he'd lost his address. The next letter from Zed said although the school secretary had given him the letter, he'd been told it wasn't to happen again. *Wanker* Zed had put.

They didn't get to meet at Christmas because Caspian went skiing in North America, but he'd left a note for Zed asking him to keep writing because his letters were the only things he looked forward to. He thought he'd see Zed at Easter, but he was taken to the house in France and when he came back, it was time to return to school. It had crossed his mind that his father had made sure the pair of them didn't get the chance to see each other.

But now it was the summer holidays, Caspian would find a way to speak to Zed. He went straight from his father's study to the treehouse, hoping to find Zed or at least a message. No Zed but there was a small yellow square of paper on the shelf.

My first is in garden, my second in track, my third in place, my fourth in trove, my fifth in pride. Poor Matthew. Only twenty-two.

It took Caspian a while to get it but when he did, he grinned, headed for the graveyard and checked his ancestors' graves. The treasure hunt took him all over the villages of Upper Barton and Lower Barton. Some of the clues had been pictures. They were easier. The whole thing took him ninety minutes before a clue stuck behind a lamppost led him back to the start. *A nesting site for rare flamingos.*

He raced to the treehouse. When he pushed up the trapdoor and saw Zed sitting on the mattress, he almost slipped down the ladder in his haste to get onto the platform. Caspian wanted to throw himself into Zed's arms but held back. Wanted to ask him to run away with him but stayed silent.

"Hi." Zed smiled at him. "You've changed."

"I'm even *better* looking?"

Zed laughed. "You're taller. Taller than me now. But thinner."

Caspian dropped onto the mattress. "I've had a stressful year. How did you know I was back?"

"I went to your house last Monday and Betsy told me you were due back yesterday." Zed held out his hand. On his palm was a small object wrapped in tissue paper.

"What's that?" Caspian asked.

"Your prize for getting to the end of the treasure hunt."

"I thought you were the prize."

Zed's head jerked up and Caspian tried hard not to swallow and failed. He took the prize from Zed's hand and opened it. It was a small clear blue marble with a frosted map of the world etched on the outside.

"I've had it a long time," Zed said quietly. "My mother bought it for me, but I want you to have it."

"It's beautiful." Caspian looked straight at him and his heart lurched. *You're beautiful.* He put the marble in his pocket. "I'll keep it safe." *Run away with me! I'll keep you safe.*

"I have more work to do this summer," Zed said. "Maths, physics and chemistry. A tiny part of me wants to leave now before I even sit an exam. The whole year has been test after test."

Caspian held his breath. "All of which I failed."

"Oh shit. Did you?"

Caspian shrugged. "Not Design and Technology or physics. I did okay in those. How did you do?"

"I did okay."

"Liar. I bet you aced them all."

Zed smiled. "Most of them."

"You can't leave now." Caspian's heart sank but he knew he was right.

"I'll be sixteen next May. By the end of June the exams will be over and with GCSEs, it'll be easier to get a job in an office."

"If you had A levels…"

Zed shook his head. "No. Next summer I'm leaving. I won't stay longer."

"I'll come with you." Caspian's mouth was dry.

"See how you feel next year."

"I won't change my mind. If you wanted to go now, I'd go with you." He slid his fingers over Zed's and Zed turned his hand over to hold Caspian's. For a long moment Caspian couldn't speak and he wondered if Zed felt the same.

"A year on and I'm less reckless, more sensible." Zed gave a wry grin.

"Shit, my influence has worn off fast."

"I've always been a good boy. My father thinks I'm a bad boy and I'm not. But I liked being bad with you. I want to do more…bad things with you, but all the hard work I've done this year will be wasted if I leave now."

"How's your father been? You never said in your letters if he was still hitting you."

"Sometimes he lashes out. But him having a girlfriend has made my life easier. He lets me leave the house. He likes me out of the house when she's there."

"He *lets* you leave the house?"

"I didn't tell you before but after I came out of hospital, he chained me up in my room for three weeks."

"He what?" Caspian stared at him in horror.

"He didn't trust me. He knew someone had reported him to Social Services. Even though I lied to protect him and said some boys had attacked me, he still didn't trust me. He was right not to, because the lie wasn't really to protect him. I was trying to protect myself. But those chains… It was horrible. Stuck in my room with a broken arm and a chain around my ankle. Nothing to do except dye my hair again, which was not easy one-handed, do schoolwork and think of you. Guess which I liked best."

"I worried you'd be angry with me."

Zed shook his head. "Maybe at first but not after."

"It was Betsy who made me see the police needed to be involved."

"I'm not mad at her either. If we'd run, we'd have been in more trouble."

"I can't believe he chained you."

"And he ripped my bear apart, and your book. I was angrier about him doing that to my bear than the chaining up. It was mean. I've sewn the bear back together but I didn't make a very good job of it. I'll buy you a new book if you want. I didn't want to leave one in here over the winter because I knew it would get damp."

"Forget the book."

"I think my father wanted me to beg to be released from the chain. I didn't because he wouldn't have let me go. Though maybe he kept me imprisoned longer to make a point." Zed sagged. "I should have just begged."

"I'm sorry."

"It's not your fault."

"Yeah, it is. If I'd run with you…"

"And when we had to go to a hospital because of my arm? What then? I'd have given a fake name, fake address. If they'd discovered it was fake, they'd have called the police. They might have called them anyway because I looked like I'd been beaten up. He lost control that night. He knows he went too far though he'd never admit it."

Caspian squeezed his fingers.

"So how much of this summer do we get to spend together?" Zed asked, rubbing his thumb over Caspian's palm.

"I have to go to fucking France on Friday."

Zed's shoulders dropped and the rubbing stopped. Caspian held back his whine of disappointment.

"But I've been thinking. My father isn't leaving for a few weeks. He has work commitments. I could do something that stops me getting sent with my mother and sisters, then go later with him."

"Do what?"

"Tell him I'm gay."

Zed sucked in a breath. "You're gay?"

Caspian laughed.

"You're braver than me," Zed said. "I'm never going to tell my father. He'd kill me. If you tell yours, maybe he'll definitely send you to France on Friday."

"He won't want me out of his sight until he's talked sense into me."

Zed raised his eyebrows. "Seriously? He'd think he could talk you into being straight?"

Caspian shrugged. "He'd try. I've never tried to hide what I am, but no one's ever guessed. Well, maybe Lachlan but he's a dickhead. Maybe he doesn't realise his name calling is accurate. I'm sixteen. It's time I stood up for myself. I've never cared what people think about me. I don't care that they know I'm gay."

"Except if you come out, you'll probably drag me out too. You might not care what people think, what your family thinks but I can't afford not to. When I said my father would kill me, I meant it. I remember seeing on the news about someone who killed his son for being gay, he pushed him down the stairs, and my father said, "I'd do the same." He'd rather spend the rest of his life in prison than be shamed by what his peers and community would think of him having a gay son."

"I'll stay quiet for another year then." Caspian saw the relief spread through Zed.

"My father has no idea about me but maybe some people have guessed," Zed said. "Mr Carter, my music teacher, for a start. Just something about the way he treats me that makes me wonder. Not in a pervy way but a concerned one. Though he knows my father is difficult and anti-music. Maybe that's all it is. I get called names at school but like with your brother, I don't know whether they're just going for anything that might hurt rather than calling me an arse licker because they think I lick arses."

"Are you an arse licker?"

"No. Not yet."

Caspian laughed. "Want to add that to the list of things to do before Friday?"

"I'd rather start with lips." Zed pushed him over onto his back and stared down at him.

"That's fine by me." Caspian pulled him down until their foreheads were pressed together. Their noses nudged, then Zed's eyes fluttered closed as he pressed his mouth to Caspian's.

They both moaned, the soft sounds barely audible, as their open mouths brushed back and forth, over and over, not quite kissing, more teasing, but fucking hot. And when Zed's weight settled on him, Caspian's cock shot to attention. Zed's was the same. He threaded his fingers in Zed's hair as Zed slid his tongue deeper into his mouth. Caspian sucked on it and heat flooded his body, made his balls tingle. *Oh hell. Do not fucking come. Not yet.*

Zed moved from gentle nibbles to full-on consumption and Caspian loved it. It was all fantastic. They broke only for air before claiming each other again. Their moans grew louder and Caspian wanted to yell out for the sheer joy of it. Their tongues tangled and played in endless ways, and when Zed thrust his tongue in and out of Caspian's mouth as if he were fucking him, Caspian felt like he was a space shuttle on countdown.

"Oh, oh, oh, I'm going to come," Zed whispered.

65

"Not yet." Caspian wriggled from beneath him and lay on his side facing him. "Undo your shorts."

They looked down at their hands and Caspian held his breath as their fingers swapped places, Zed's hand shoving down the waist of his boxers, his doing the same with Zed's. Then for the first time in Caspian's life, a hand that wasn't his wrapped around his cock. And for the first time in his life, he wrapped his hand around another guy's cock. It wasn't just his cock that threatened to explode, but his heart.

"We try…for ten minutes…right," Caspian gasped.

"Be realistic. Ten seconds."

A few moments later, and Caspian hadn't counted, they were coming all over each other's fingers and his heart was beating hard enough to break and he didn't care if it did because this was the best thing that had ever happened to him, probably forever. They dropped onto their backs, chests heaving, sticky fingers threaded together and Caspian knew there was no way to stop this fall. That was fine by him.

For the few days they had left, from nine in the morning to six in the evening, they were inseparable. They played together and worked together. To his amazement, Caspian began to grasp concepts of maths and physics that had so far eluded him. Zed made it fun, made the rewards for getting it right a lot more than fun. It was hard to keep their hands off each other.

Caspian discovered that happiness came when he least expected it. Like when they were walking three miles to buy chips, came back eating them, then slipped into a field to exchange salty kisses—and gentle caresses. Happiness came when Zed sneaked out one night and they lay on their backs, invisible to the world, looking up into a star splattered sky. Caspian was thrilled that he could teach Zed a few constellations: Cassiopeia, Cepheus, Draco, Ursa Major, Ursa Minor. Zed taught him about declination and ascension.

They made a rope swing in the woods. They tried to make a go kart. They made an unsteady zip line. They made each other happy. That feeling in the chest when everything fell into place and you felt at your most alive, that was what Caspian felt and it was the greatest thing of all.

He took Zed to his house when everyone was out and Zed discovered the piano that everyone but Caspian had mastered. When he saw Zed's face, heard him play, he knew he'd always have to share Zed with music. Zed played from the heart, played with his entire body, better than anyone Caspian had ever heard before. He stood mesmerised as the world stopped turning for a while.

Zed made him feel different, made him want to be different, better, made him want to bring out the best in himself and in Zed. When he was with Zed everything fit, everything.

"You are the most important person in my world," Caspian whispered.

"You are all that I have," Zed told him.

Caspian felt the weight of it and embraced it. "I will never let you down."

The rest of Zed's summer could only be a disappointment. Caspian had told him the chances of seeing him in October were small. Christmas was to be spent in Aspen. Easter in France. *How will you revise?* Zed had asked and Caspian had laughed.

But the following summer and every summer after that would be theirs because they were going to run.

Even the news that Zed's father and his girlfriend were going on holiday to Italy for two weeks didn't make up for the disappointment of not having Caspian around. His father told him he had to go and stay with Tamaz and Zed hadn't minded because there was nothing to keep him in Upper Barton when Caspian wasn't there.

Tamaz collected him and his small bag on Saturday night.

"Sorry you got lumbered with me," Zed muttered.

"I'm looking forward to having you around, little brother. We're going to London for the weekend and back to Canterbury on Monday morning."

"Where are we going to stay?"

"With friends."

When Zed followed his brother into the house in Islington, he had feeling of foreboding. Tamaz had a key and he wondered why. A broad-shouldered, bearded man wearing a shalwar kameez, loose trousers and a long shirt, his big muscles straining the material around his arms and shoulders came out of a room on the right. He smiled when he saw them. "*Asalaamu alaikum.*"

"*Wa alaikum assalam,*" Tamaz replied. "This is my brother Hvarechaeshman. Everyone calls him Zed. Zed meet Fahid."

"Zed." Fahid drew Zed into a cologne-scented embrace that sucked the air from his lungs, and Zed instantly disliked him.

"Just in time for prayers," Fahid said.

67

Now he *really* disliked him. Zed hoped it was a joke, but it wasn't. He went with them to the mosque because he didn't want to let his brother down, but he stumbled his way through everything. He heard Tamaz sigh, felt Fahid's disapproval and tried harder, pretending to believe.

"Has it been a long time since you attended a mosque?" Fahid asked when prayers were over.

"There isn't one anywhere near where I live," Zed said.

"So you pray at home." Fahid nodded and Zed kept quiet.

Two other guys returned with them to Fahid's place. One who looked to be in his late twenties who wore a shalwar kameez, the other a little older than Zed, who wore jeans. Fahid ordered *lahmacun*, Turkish pizza, for them all and after it arrived, he sat next to Zed to eat and hardly stopped talking.

Fahid tackled everything—the situation in Syria, Pakistan, Afghanistan, Egypt, Jordan, Uzbekistan. The others joined in. Well, Tamaz and the older guy, Wasim, but the younger one, Parwez, was as quiet as Zed. Though it didn't appear to be through lack of interest. Parwez stared at Fahid as if he was the answer to everything as well as *having* the answer. Zed tried to sound interested, but he wasn't. Well, not beyond wishing people could just let other people live their lives without interfering.

Fahid painted everything black and white and Zed knew life wasn't that simple. When he attempted any sort of disagreement, Fahid just talked more at him and louder, and eventually Zed gave up and let it all wash over him. He was an expert at *in one ear and out the other.*

"Your little brother is very quiet," Fahid said.

"And you're not." Tamaz laughed and Fahid grinned, though his smile looked a bit tight.

When Tamaz showed him where he was sleeping, a small storage room with a pull-out bed, Zed said he was tired and he'd stay up there. He didn't like these men with their religious talk. He didn't like that Tamaz seemed to enjoy their company. For the first time in as long as he could remember, he wanted to go home.

But the next day, Tamaz took him on the London Eye. Zed thought it looked as if it was about to lift into the air and spin away like some UFO. But it brought them safely back to earth. They went to the aquarium and ate at Borough Market and Tamaz bought him new jeans and they laughed and had fun and everything was all right again. Zed's world wasn't complete but next summer it would be. He and Caspian would be together.

SUMMER THREE

Chapter Seven

2012

Every exam was over. The continual tests and constant revising had taken their toll and left Zed drained. He never wanted to take another exam as long as he lived. He was almost glad he didn't have a burning desire to be a lawyer or a doctor or anything that required A levels and a degree. He didn't try to fool himself into thinking he could earn a living through music. He was more likely to get a job in retail, but music would always be part of his life.

He thought he'd done okay. Maybe more than okay but he'd never say that out loud. He was neither someone who boasted questions were easy—though they sometimes were, nor someone who whined and moaned about not finishing—because he always did. He hadn't emerged from any exam thinking he'd messed up, though he couldn't be sure of that until the results were out. Hopefully by then, he and Caspian would have a place of their own, somewhere school could send his certificates.

It had been a long, difficult year. He was always on edge with his father, trying not to draw his attention, trying to be good even though Zed knew he'd never be the perfect son his father wanted. Zed and Tamaz had grown further apart. Tamaz came home less and less frequently and when he did, he talked too much about Islam with their father. Zed missed Caspian. It hurt to think about him and yet that pain made Zed feel alive, kept him hoping.

Would he have felt the same about Caspian if he'd had a normal family? A father who loved him, supported him? A father who didn't hit him? *Yes, I would.* Caspian meant everything to him. The whole of the past two years thinking about Caspian had been what kept him going until his sixteenth birthday.

Is it love?

How can I tell?

Zed was a sensible boy. Words that appeared on his report time after time. He'd rarely thought about love unless it was to feel the lack of it. He'd loved his mother and he missed her, but what he felt now was something different. A kind of madness. A sort of craziness. Every time he thought about Caspian, his heart beat faster. Knowing he'd soon see him made his heart jump and his cock twitch.

But love?

Was it?

Did he?

Could he?

Was he confusing friendship with love?

Probably. Possibly.

Zed had scored distinctions at grade eight in both cello and piano. Five marks short of a perfect score in both instruments. The best anyone had ever done at his school. Mr Carter had been more excited than Zed. He'd had to beg his teacher not to tell anyone, not to let it be announced in assembly because if his father had found out, there would have been so much trouble. Mr Carter was the only teacher Zed would miss. He'd told Zed he was the best pupil he'd ever had and he was under the impression that Zed was going to do A level music in his spare time. Zed felt bad he couldn't even say goodbye to him.

Over the year, Zed had saved over two hundred pounds by not having school lunches and by spending less than his father gave him to buy things he needed. He'd peeled the reduced stickers off food and clothes to make it look as though he'd paid more. Deliberately lost a few receipts that would have betrayed him. His money, which he'd changed into notes at the post office, was hidden in the garage under a pyramid of paint cans. Every time he went to check it was still there, his gaze landed on the chain his father had used to keep him in his room. As if he needed a reminder.

Zed hadn't packed a bag. Safer to wait until the last minute, though he had put everything together so he'd be ready to leave the moment Caspian was too. He fretted because he hadn't been able to find his birth certificate. No sign of it in his father's study, though Tamaz's was there along with their father's and their mother's and her death certificate. It didn't make sense that Zed's wasn't there too. He'd even looked in his father's clothes and in the bathroom cupboard.

The pack of condoms he'd found there—*ribbed for her pleasure*—had shocked him. Apart from the fact that devout Muslims didn't agree with their use, the idea of his father having sex with anyone made him feel ill. His father was such a hypocrite. He went on and on about being a good Muslim and he wasn't. Sex before marriage was *haram*.

Zed eventually gave up hunting for the birth certificate. He'd looked online at school and found he could order a replacement and pay by postal order, since he didn't have a credit or debit card, but he needed an address so he had to wait until he and Caspian had found somewhere to live. But without proof of his identity, he couldn't get a National Insurance number and without that he couldn't work—well, not legally and without a job, finding a place to live would be hard.

His stomach and heart lurched between excitement and worry. He and Caspian had to find work as soon as they could. Zed hoped they could work together. In a café? A shop? Zed could have busked if had an instrument. He had enough money to buy a cheap cello though the sound wouldn't be good and having a place to live and food was more important.

He was counting down the days until Caspian returned home. Zed had written to tell him he'd be in the treehouse on the twenty-fifth of June, the day after his last exam, but instead he'd been forced to go to Maidstone to work for his father then accompany him to the mosque.

Today his father had taken his girlfriend to Brighton, so Zed went straight to the treehouse. There was no message from Caspian but there were new books on the shelf since the last time he'd been there. He laid on the mattress and read *The Hunger Games,* but Caspian didn't turn up. Zed left a message saying he'd come every day that he could and took *Catching Fire* home. Caspian had left his phone number and Zed memorised it, but he had no way to call him. It was too much of a risk to do it from home. There was no longer a public phone in Upper or Lower Barton.

Zed was surprised to find Tamaz's car parked outside the house when he got home. He slipped the book into the pocket of his winter jacket that hung by the door before he went into the kitchen.

"Hi," Zed said.

"Hi, not so little brother."

Tamaz hugged him and once Zed had overcome his shock, he melted into his brother's embrace.

"You're too thin." Tamaz let him go and turned to the stove.

He was cooking the meal Zed was supposed to have prepared. *Kotlets*—potato and mince rissoles, a yoghurt dip, and *Shirazi* salad made from onions, cucumbers and tomatoes. Zed's mouth watered.

"Does he starve you as well as beat you? He's a cruel man. Not a good Muslim."

Zed froze.

"I should have done more to help you," Tamaz said quietly.

"He'd have beaten you too."

"Even so."

Zed swallowed hard. "Why do you think he hates me so much?"

"I don't know." Tamaz set the salad aside.

Zed wasn't sure he wanted to know anyway. He'd had a thought when he'd been unable to find his birth certificate that maybe he wasn't his father's son, though it was probably wishful thinking.

"What have you been up to?" Tamaz asked.

"Exams, exams and more exams. I worked in the pharmacy yesterday and went to the mosque."

Tamaz nodded. "A good Muslim should try to gather in a congregation to worship on as many days of the week as he can."

Zed frowned. Since when did Tamaz spout religion at him without a little smile? "I am *not* going to work in the pharmacy every day. There's only so many times a shelf can be dusted. Anyway, since I seem to annoy Dad by even breathing in his vicinity, I think it'll be a once a week thing." But it wouldn't be because he was leaving.

"Fancy a job in Canterbury over the summer?"

No! "Doing what?"

"Walking up and down the high street touting for tourists to go on the river tours. You'd hand out leaflets and show people where to go. You'd get paid. Not a lot but better than nothing. And you can stay with me for the whole summer. We can go to the mosque together."

Zed stood and stared at him.

"Well, what do you say?"

No. "Have you talked to Dad about it?"

"Not yet. I'm sure he'd be okay with it though."

"When would I start?"

"Next week."

"Can I think about it?" He knew Tamaz expected him to leap at the chance.

His brother gave a puzzled chuckle. "Waiting for a better offer?"

"It's just that there's someone who asked me to coach his son in maths and physics over the summer and I sort of said yes."

His brother shrugged. "I just thought you might like to spend some time with me. We could go to London again. We had fun last summer, didn't we? Fahid would like to see you."

What the hell for?

"He was very taken with you. He doesn't very often get people who argue with him."

I hardly did.

Zed turned when he heard a car pulling up on the drive. "Thanks for cooking," he said quickly.

"No *zaban* today." Tamaz grinned and Zed shuddered.

"Tamaz!" His father strode into the kitchen, hugged his brother and ignored Zed. "This is a surprise."

"I came for dinner but I can't stay overnight."

"You work so hard."

Why Zed deserved the glare his father shot him, he did not know.

He washed up after the meal and put the kitchen to rights while his father and Tamaz talked. Zed wondered if his brother would mention the job. He hoped he didn't because that would mean more lies to make up about a fictitious tutoring role. Zed went to bed while the pair were still talking. He retrieved the book on the way and slid it under his pillow. His father rarely looked in on him but he was still ultra-careful, lying curled up in a way that would hide the book from view.

When he heard the front door slam hard, he jumped. He'd shoved the book under his pillow before his door burst open, but he still jerked upright.

"You will not be working in Canterbury this summer," his father snapped.

"Okay."

When his father frowned, Zed realised he should have sounded more upset.

"What's that?" his father asked.

Oh fuck. He didn't look at where his father's attention was fixed but he realised the book must be visible. His father dragged him out of bed by his hair and pulled him onto the floor.

"Where did this come from?" His father held up the book.

"I borrowed it." Zed stayed where he was. *Be good. Don't upset him. Don't let him get angry enough to hurt you.*

His father opened the book and looked through the first few pages. "Not from school. There's no stamp to say it's their property."

Shit. "From a boy at school."

73

"A new book? Why would he lend you a brand-new book? Who is this boy?"

No way would Zed give him Caspian's name. But in his terrified struggle to think of another, he was far too slow.

"Br—"

"Don't even think about lying." His father yanked him to his feet. "You stole it."

"No, I—"

The smack across his face sent him sprawling across the bed.

"I'll give it back," Zed cried. "I'm sorry. It just looked like a fun story. It's set in the future. There's nothing *haram* in it."

His father pulled his belt from his trousers.

"Please don't." Zed couldn't get another broken arm, any injury that stopped him leaving with Caspian.

"I am sick of you." The belt slashed across his ribs. "The sight of you disgusts me."

Zed curled up as his father kept hitting him. Each strike made him cry out even as he tried not to. *This is the last time. The last time you strike me.* He squeezed his eyes shut and imagined himself fighting back, the shock on his father's face when Zed hit him.

Eventually the belt stopped falling, his father left the room, and Zed let out a shaky exhalation. He bit his lip as he uncurled, pain radiating through his entire body. He felt as if he'd fallen into a snake pit and been repeatedly bitten. He hurt but there was no blood, no broken bones and as long as his father didn't come back with that chain, he could survive.

But if he did get the chain, Zed would have to fight. Whatever happened, he was leaving tonight.

He lay and waited and waited. Once he was sure his father was asleep, he silently filled his backpack and went down to the kitchen. He picked up a bottle of water and an apple. He saw his father's wallet and phone sitting on the counter and stared at them for a long time.

Zed wasn't a thief. He'd been tempted sometimes when he was hungry or wanted something sweet like a chocolate bar or when he'd spotted a book he'd like to read but he'd never helped himself to anything apart from his father's loose change and he hadn't done that for a long while. Almost everyone he knew at school was given pocket money. Those who didn't just asked for what they wanted and got it.

He opened the wallet. Six twenties and three tens. He could have taken a twenty and maybe his father wouldn't have noticed but what did it matter? He took the lot along with the phone. Once he'd retrieved his money from the garage, he walked away. He didn't hurt so much now. Adrenaline had overpowered his pain.

One look back when he reached the road and Zed grimaced. He promised himself he'd never come back, even if everything turned to shit.

Once he was in the field and heading up to the ridge, he called Caspian. It was gone midnight and he didn't expect Caspian to answer but he did.

"Hello?"

His voice made Zed smile. "It's me."

"You got a phone?"

"Not exactly. I took a phone. It's my father's."

"Are you okay?"

Zed stumbled and pain flared. "No. I'm on my way to the treehouse. I'm not going back. I have my backpack and money."

"You need to get rid of the phone. They can trace you. Switch it off. Take the battery out. Dump it. I'll meet you at the treehouse."

"You're at home?"

"Got back late yesterday. See you soon."

"See you soon."

Zed dropped the battery into the soil and stamped on it, then threw the phone into the bottom of the hedge before he carried on walking. He imagined his father coming downstairs in the morning, and not seeing his phone. Would he be certain of where he left it? Would he look for it? How long before he stormed up to Zed's room? At what point would he realise what Zed had done?

Now he regretted taking the phone and the money. His father would know he'd run before he'd managed to get away from the village. It was small consolation that now he was sixteen, he couldn't be made to return home.

Caspian was waiting for him in the treehouse, sitting below a halo of starry lights. He pushed to his feet as Zed lowered the hatch. When Zed eased his backpack from his shoulders, Caspian sighed.

"What's he done? Fucking hell. I can see what the bastard's done." He reached for Zed's face but pulled his fingers back before he touched him.

Zed sank onto the mattress. "At least he didn't use the buckle end of his belt."

"Had you forgotten to stir his tea?"

Zed managed a small laugh. "I stirred it clockwise instead of anticlockwise."

Caspian settled at his side. "I want to hurt him. I should have told you to keep his phone and we could have ordered a ton of stuff off Amazon. Bondage gear, a cock ring, a thousand condoms, a gallon of lube, a butt plug, a *How to have sex with Dummies* book."

Zed smiled.

"What had you done?"

"He found me with one of your books, *Catching Fire* but I don't think he needed an excuse. Maybe he's even trying to force me to run."

"We're not running. We're leaving home. There's a difference. Tomorrow we'll go to Sandiford Station, buy tickets and catch a train to London. We'll find a place to live and we'll get jobs."

Caspian sounded so confident, Zed felt better. "We need National Insurance numbers. I couldn't find my birth certificate. I can apply for a replacement but I need an address."

"I was sent a National Insurance number just before my birthday last year."

Zed sighed. "My father will have intercepted mine."

"We can sort it out. Let's get some sleep. Everything's going to be fine. This time, I won't let you down, I promise."

Zed lay on the foam mattress and Caspian curled around him. It hurt but he'd rather put up with the pain than lose Caspian's touch. Caspian slipped into sleep quicker than him. Zed's mind was racing, worrying. How were they going to find somewhere to live? What if they ended up sleeping rough?

What if…? What if…? What if…?

When Zed woke, Caspian was still curled around him like a squirrel except the zip was open on Zed's jeans and Caspian had his hand inside and it felt good. Really good. Caspian gently jacked him off and Zed moaned.

"What the fuck?"

The loud voice coming from the open hatch made both Zed and Caspian lurch.

"What the hell are you two doing?"

"Get the fuck out of here, Lachlan," Caspian snapped and pulled his hand out of Zed's jeans.

His brother. Zed zipped up.

"Father's looking for you. He's pissed off. You better hurry." Lachlan gave Zed a long look and then went back down the ladder.

Zed turned to face Caspian. "He's going to tell your father what he's seen."

"I don't care."

Zed's heart pounded. "What if he locks you up? What if he sends you away? I have to go today. I can't let my father find me."

"We *are* going today." Caspian chewed his lip. "I need clothes and my money. But I need to sneak out." He dragged his fingers through his hair. "Go to Sandiford Station. Buy tickets that will let us catch any train today and wait for me. If you don't want to stay on the platform, go over the bridge to the park. I'll come as soon as I can. No more than ninety minutes."

"Promise?"

Caspian pressed his lips to Zed's, gave him the sweetest kiss, then pulled back. "I promise."

Caspian disappeared down the ladder and Zed leaned over to watch him as he headed through the trees. When he'd vanished from view, Zed picked up his backpack and climbed down. He'd go across fields to get to the station just in case his father was driving around looking for him. No way was anything going to wreck this.

Chapter Eight

Caspian didn't bother hurrying back to the house. He wouldn't beat Lachlan who was no doubt desperate to tell their father just what he'd seen. *Bastard.* Didn't matter. Tonight, he and Zed would be in London. Together. Caspian had enough money to pay for a couple of nights in a hotel while they sorted themselves out.

He'd told Zed there was a difference between running and leaving home, though it wasn't as simple as that. He couldn't just pack a bag, wave goodbye and walk out. His father would find a way to stop him. Not by force but maybe by a threat.

Or yes, by force if he's desperate enough. Caspian sighed.

He went straight to his father's study and knocked on the door.

"Come in," his father called.

Of course Lachlan was there. He smirked as he passed Caspian, but he looked odd. Spaced out. The door closed and for once, Caspian kept his mouth shut and waited to see what his father was going to say.

"You are never to see that boy again."

There was nothing more guaranteed to make Caspian do the exact opposite than being forbidden to do something, but he simply didn't care what his father thought or said. Zed was his. He was Zed's.

"Whatever you were doing, you will never do it again. Are we clear?"

As a fucking bell. I won't be gay anymore. No problemo. He sucked in his cheeks.

"His father rang this morning and asked if I'd seen him."

Caspian's heart did a small skip of distress.

"I said no but I'd check."

Oh God. Run fast, Zed. Be careful.

"He stole his father's mobile and took money from his wallet. What were you two planning?"

Not were—are.

"Zed's father hit him last night with a belt. Repeatedly. After Zed and I made that crop circle, his father beat him so hard that he broke Zed's arm. Zed's had enough. He's leaving."

"And you intended to leave with him?"

Caspian knew from his father's tone of voice he'd guessed that was the plan.

"You're only seventeen. How the hell could you support yourself? Because there would be no money from me. No flat in London for you to live in. You're not likely to pass any GCSEs. You have no skills.

78

You can't even cook for yourself. You can barely read. Christ, Caspian, you're not stupid but you're behaving like it. Think! Think."

His voice had grown louder and louder, but it softened on that last word.

"I understand you feel sorry for this boy, but this ends here. You are not going anywhere with him. You are not leaving home. Go upstairs and pack for France. Stay in your room until your mother is ready to leave."

Fuck you, fuck you, fuck you.

"I can see you thinking, Caspian. This is quite simple. Do as you're told, and I won't call the boy's father and tell him what you and his son were doing in the treehouse."

Caspian shrugged. "Tell him. I don't care." Better that Zed's father wasted time looking here rather than checking the train stations.

"So he's not in the treehouse?"

Damn. Caspian kept quiet.

"I could report the man for assaulting his son," his father said.

"You've already seen that didn't work."

"Why did he lie?"

"He knew what his father would do if he told the truth."

"How do you know he's not lying now?"

"He's not."

"Hitting your child in a way that causes actual bodily harm is against the law. Zed can be helped. There's no need for him to run. He can be looked after in a safe place away from here."

Away from me. That wasn't what either of them wanted.

"Shall I report his father? Call the police?"

"No," Caspian said quickly.

"Give me your phone."

"Why?"

"Because I don't want you contacting him."

Caspian handed it over. He'd been going to get rid of it anyway.

"Now go to your room. Pack and wait."

Caspian walked out to find Lachlan at the foot of the stairs. His pupils were huge.

"Been a naughty boy?" Lachlan asked.

Caspian ignored him but Lachlan followed him up the stairs.

"What did Pa say about you being into guys?"

"That I wasn't to do it again."

Lachlan laughed. His hand settled on Caspian's shoulder and he squeezed. "It's okay. He'll come around."

79

Caspian shrugged him off, then turned and glared. "It wasn't up to you to out me. You don't get to decide when that happens. I'm supposed to be the one who says it. I choose when and how. My choice not yours. You should have kept your fucking mouth shut. It's my life, my sexuality. It has nothing to do with you."

Lachlan sighed. "All I said was that you were cuddled up to a boy. I didn't tell him you had your hand in his jeans fondling his cock."

Caspian went into his room. When he tried to close the door, Lachlan's foot was in the way.

"I've been instructed to keep an eye on you so don't get any ideas."

Caspian kicked him in the shin, slammed the door and locked it. *Shit.*

It didn't take him long to pack a small bag. Not a backpack but a sports bag. He gathered all his money together and zipped it into a side pocket. Then he wasn't sure what to do. It briefly crossed his mind that he could tie his sheets together and lower the bag to the ground before climbing down himself, but when he tried to open the window, it would only rise six inches and the tool to unfasten the locking mechanism had gone. *Fuck.*

He retrieved the money from his bag and stuffed it into the pocket of his jacket. When he unlocked the door and opened it, Lachlan sat on the floor opposite the door, messing around on his phone. Caspian headed for the stairs.

"Where do you think you're going?" Lachlan pushed himself to his feet.

"To get something to eat. I missed breakfast."

"Have you packed?"

"Yes. Take a look if you don't believe me."

Lachlan clattered down the stairs behind him and followed him to the kitchen.

"Good morning, Betsy. I'm sorry I missed breakfast. Could I have something to eat please?"

"What would you like?"

"One of your delicious waffles?" Caspian blinked his eyes and tried to look like a sad puppy.

She laughed. "All right. You too, Lachlan? Do you have your appetite back yet?"

"No thanks. I'll stick to coffee." He poured himself one and sat at the table, tapping away on his phone.

"Shall I get the maple syrup?" Caspian asked.

Betsy smiled at him. "Yes please."

He made his way down the corridor but hurried past the pantry and headed straight for the back door. He was through it and gone in seconds. He knew every inch of the gardens around the house, every shortcut, every hiding place and he was fast. No way was he letting Zed down again. By the time Caspian heard his brother calling, he was already in the wood. He couldn't risk going anywhere near a road. If Zed had any sense, he'd have avoided roads too. He took off his jacket and carried it as he ran.

There was no way Caspian could get to the station inside the ninety minutes he'd promised, but Zed would wait. He took a route to keep him in woodland for as long as he could before he had to cross a road. Lachlan didn't look in a fit shape to be running anywhere so hopefully it wouldn't be difficult to shake him off. He'd been out at a party last night so he might be hungover or maybe he'd taken drugs. Why hadn't their father noticed Lachlan wasn't...right?

Caspian panted heavily as he ran. This wasn't the way he'd envisaged leaving home. Just as well he wasn't carrying his bag. He would have liked his clothes, but he could buy more. He'd been saving for ages, taking small amounts from his bank account in case his father found a way of blocking his access. He and Zed needed to disappear and leave no trace.

As he approached the first road, he was careful. He waited and listened before he bolted across. The second road was more of a problem. He could see a man in a tractor in the field he needed to cross. It just so happened to be Giles Forman, the one whose crop he and Zed had...re-arranged. Caspian decided to head down the road and cut in a few fields down.

But he'd hardly run more than a few metres before he heard the familiar throaty purr of a car coming up behind him. He groaned and slowed down. When Lachlan pulled in ahead of him in their father's classic Jaguar, Caspian stopped.

Lachlan opened his door and leaned out. "Get in."

Caspian walked up to the car. "Take me to Sandiford station. Please. Let me at least talk to him." He was going to do more than talk. He was going to get on the train.

"Get the fuck in the car."

"Please, Lachlan." There was more chance if he pleaded than if he argued.

"Get in."

"Take me to the station."

"Okay, but get the fuck in."

81

Caspian climbed in, dropped his jacket in the footwell, and clicked on the seatbelt. Lachlan accelerated down the road and Caspian gripped the sides of his seat.

"Does Dad know you've taken his car?"

"I've no idea."

"Sure you're not over the limit?"

Lachlan glanced at him. "What?"

"You're either still drunk or stoned from whatever you were doing last night. I'll tell him unless you take me to the station."

"You little shit." Lachlan glared at him.

"Yes I am. You owe this to me after outing me. Take me to the station."

"Don't you fucking tell me what to do, you retard."

Lachlan took the corner far too fast and the car skidded.

"Slow down, you idiot!"

But Lachlan accelerated and there was another bend ahead. As Caspian registered people in the road he shouted, "Look out!"

It was too late. There was a sickening crunch as the vehicle hit them. Caspian was thrown against the door and his world blinked out.

Zed bought two open singles to London, then waited on the platform. He'd thought Caspian would make the next train but he didn't. Nor did he arrive in time for the one after, much to Zed's disappointment. He followed Caspian's instructions and stayed in the park between trains, but when it got to lunchtime and Caspian still hadn't appeared, Zed grew increasingly worried.

Why hadn't he come? Had his father stopped him? His mother? Had he suddenly realised just what he'd be leaving behind? Had he never meant to come? Had he fallen ill? Had an accident? Zed's brain was on a Möbius loop going over and over everything before coming back to the same point. Caspian wasn't coming. No matter how long Zed waited, he wasn't going to come, and Zed couldn't go back.

He waited because a flicker of hope was still alight. Caspian *might* come. The guy in the ticket office had noticed Zed coming and going but hadn't said anything, but Zed was petrified the police would arrive or his father. But he still waited and hoped.

Hope turned to despair. Despair turned to worry. Was Caspian okay? In trouble?

But everything had been fine. What could have gone wrong in such a short period of time?

Worry turned to anger. Caspian didn't care. He'd lied. This was all a game to him. Rage changed to sorrow. Zed was on his own. He had no choice. He couldn't go home. He had to get on a train.

Late afternoon, he asked a woman who was waiting if he could make a call from her phone. He offered her a pound, but she waved it away.

"As long as you're not calling abroad," she said with a smile.

"Local. Thank you."

Zed's mouth dried as he pressed in Caspian's number. All he wanted to know was why. But when the phone was answered, it wasn't Caspian who was speaking but a man.

"Hello?"

"Can I talk to Caspian, please?"

"Zed?"

"Yes."

"Caspian is no longer your friend. Don't call him again."

"Can I speak to him, please?"

There was a pause and then the man said, "He doesn't want to speak to you. He said he made a mistake and he was too ashamed to tell you to your face. He doesn't want to leave home."

Zed ended the call and handed the phone back to the woman, his heart hammering.

He'd still wait. Just in case. How could he not? His own father would have lied. Maybe Caspian's father was lying too.

He'll come.

He *will* come.

He *will*.

He *will*.

But he didn't.

Zed waited until the last train. It was almost ten. Even when it pulled into the station, he hesitated, thinking he'd turn and see Caspian running towards him, and he *did* turn and look but the platform was empty. Zed was the only one catching the train. He climbed on board, found an empty seat and sat with his face pressed to the window. All day, he'd not given in to the tight feeling in his chest but when the train pulled out, he started to cry.

He cried because he was feeling sorry for himself. He'd thought with Caspian at his side, he could face anything. London wasn't going to be a city paved with gold. He wasn't stupid. But he was a kid. Now a homeless kid.

He cried because this was the day he'd lost his last connection to love. He'd loved Caspian. He knew others wouldn't see that, would call

83

him childish and naive, but Zed knew what was in his heart. Caspian had meant everything to him.

His tears eventually ran out, but the pain went on.

Arriving at St Pancras station late at night meant Zed's choices of what to do were limited. From the moment he'd got on the train, he'd felt as if he were falling with no parachute. He had nowhere to go, no idea of where to go. He put his backpack on, winced when it rubbed his sore back, and headed down the platform.

There were transport police everywhere. Zed doubted he'd be allowed to sleep on a bench even if he said he was waiting for a train. But he couldn't see any benches. Nor did he have a ticket to prove he was a waiting passenger. He had nothing to show who he was. He was hungry but there were no cafés open. He'd already eaten the few things he'd taken from the fridge and finished his water, though he'd topped up the bottle, so at least he had something to drink.

How long could he keep walking through the station, looping in circles, before he was challenged, or collapsed? Every time he thought about Caspian he wanted to lie down and sob. Caspian had promised not to let him down. Promises meant nothing. He'd never believe anyone ever again.

All the plans they had, all Zed's dreams of lying next to Caspian in bed, touching him, being touched, it was all gone. Over before it had begun. Zed would never see him again. He'd lost him and the sooner he accepted that the better because he was on his own now, and if he was going to survive, he had to be smart.

Yet even after all that, he struggled to let Caspian go. If he'd really changed his mind, Zed wanted to know why. He walked slowly through the concourse, hunger gnawing at him, spots dancing in front of tired eyes. He was drawn towards a public phone and before he could change his mind, he called Caspian.

"The number you have called is not in service."

Zed groaned. He wished now that he'd not left without talking to Caspian. He could have slept in the treehouse. He'd let Caspian down as much as Caspian had let him down. Zed knew he ought to call his brother and tell him he was okay though he worried about making things difficult for him with their father. Still, Tamaz was all the family he had left, and he didn't want to lose him too.

"Tamaz? It's me."

"Oh thank God. *Alhamdulillah.* Where are you?"

"London."

"What happened?"

"You're not with *him*, are you?" Zed had no father now.

"No. He called to say you'd stolen his phone and his money and run off. Wanted to know if you'd come to me. Though he seems to think you'll be back when you realise you've made a mistake. Are you safe? You want me to come and get you?"

Yes. "No, I'm fine."

"Why did you run?"

"Because he hit me again and I can't take his hatred anymore."

An announcement came over the loud speakers and Zed winced.

"Let me call Fahid. He'll come and get you. You don't have to go back home."

"I've a hostel sorted out. I'm fine. Really. I'll be in touch again. Don't worry about me. Bye."

Zed put the phone back the hook. No way was he going anywhere with Fahid. He'd longed to ask Tamaz to help him but he didn't want to come between his brother and his father. That didn't seem fair.

As he wandered through the station concourse he heard someone playing the piano and followed the sound. An old guy was belting out a jazz number on an upright painted in rainbow colours. Zed stood and listened. The music was lively and fun, but it didn't improve his mood. Still, listening to a slow sombre piece wouldn't help either.

There was a notice near the piano saying it was a gift and open to everyone. Zed wanted to play. His fingers twitched in anticipation. He'd wait for the guy to finish.

When he had, Zed waited a little longer until no one was watching. He sat on the stool and kept his backpack on. He couldn't afford to lose it and he tended to get distracted when he played. But when he lifted his hands, he didn't know what to play. He let his mind run and somehow his fingers worked without him telling them what to do. Liszt's *La Campanella*.

The rhythm of the bell kept him grounded, steadied his heart. Playing allowed him to stop thinking. Playing let him escape. The world blurred until it was just him and the piano.

He moved to the next piece by Chopin, also in G# minor where his right hand had to race through fast moving semi-quavers. Followed that with more Liszt, a series of *Transcendental Etudes* that lasted almost forty minutes. He didn't want to stop but before he started another piece, he looked round to see if anyone was waiting for a chance, as he had. He was alone.

He played Beethoven, Bach, Debussy, a couple of Liszt's Hungarian Rhapsodies before he stood up and walked away. He was feeling more content, until he saw Fahid.

85

Chapter Nine

Caspian opened his eyes long enough to take in that he wasn't dead, at least he didn't think he was, and closed them again.

The next time he opened them, he realised he was in hospital. Machines were bleeping, his body felt sluggish and his head ached. His closed his eyes, remembered everything and panic surged. Was Lachlan all right? Those girls? His heart flipped and flipped again. How could they be?

A whimper slipped from his mouth. *Zed!* Even if only a few hours had passed, and he guessed it was more than that, Zed would have gone. But he'd call. He was good with numbers. He knew Caspian's and he'd call.

"Caspian? Are you awake? You're in the hospital."

The voice whispering in his ear was his father's. He struggled to open his eyes, then decided not to.

"You're going to be okay."

Am I? How would you know? He slid back into darkness where he felt safe.

When he came around again, his father was still there, sitting at his bedside, Lachlan beside him, who didn't look injured. Caspian had hoped to see Zed even though he'd known that wasn't likely.

"Accident," he rasped. "Girls?"

"Listen carefully." His father leaned over so that his mouth was against Caspian's ear. "You are going to do something for the family. The best thing you will ever do in your life, but the hardest."

What is he talking about? Then Caspian looked at his brother who wasn't looking at him and he guessed. *Oh fuck, no. Don't ask me to do this.* His father had told him he'd be okay and now Caspian knew that to be a lie.

"You were driving," his father whispered. "You were late to meet your friend for a day trip to London so you took my car. You were alone. You lost control on a sharp bend and hit the girls."

Caspian groaned. "Badly...hurt?"

Lachlan sucked in a breath and Caspian felt as if he'd plunged into icy water.

"They died," his father said quietly.

Caspian made a sound then that for a moment he didn't think had come from him. The howl of an animal in pain. *No. No. No.*

"Shhh," his father whispered. "Listen. If the police discover Lachlan was driving, he won't be able to finish his degree. He'll go to prison. That will be the end of any chance of his working in the law, of ever becoming a politician. His life will be destroyed. You're too young to go to prison. You'll probably get a slap on the wrist and that will be that."

Caspian clenched his fists, then unclenched them because it hurt. *A fucking slap on the wrist? Is that all those girls were worth?* "I was...a passenger."

His father glanced at Lachlan, then turned back to Caspian. "Your fingerprints are on the steering wheel. You were found behind the wheel."

Caspian's breathing faltered. "He moved...me?"

"Yes," Lachlan whispered.

Caspian groaned. *You fucking bastard.*

"To make the offence even worse as far as Lachlan is concerned, your idiotic brother was probably still over the limit for alcohol consumption and he'd taken drugs at the party. If he admits he was driving, he will not recover from this. You are the only one who can save him. Do something decent for once. Take the blame."

Lachlan leaned to whisper in Caspian's other ear. "For the rest of my life, I will do everything I can to make this up to you."

Fuck you. "I want...my phone."

"I destroyed it," his father said. "We thought it safer. When you're well, I'll get you another. A new number."

Why? Oh... Zed. "Did he call?" Caspian's voice broke. "Does he know?"

"No, he didn't call," his father said. "You understand what you have to say to the police?"

"Lachlan killed three girls... Going too fast... Not looking at the road."

His father stared at him. "Lachlan was with me all morning."

And Caspian knew then that pain didn't only come through being beaten. He closed his eyes and wished he was dead.

But he didn't die. Wishing didn't work. If it had, Zed would be with him. He tried to figure out what to do, as if there was a choice. He hadn't been driving. He hadn't killed anyone. But the truth didn't matter.

87

He heard someone come into the room but he kept his eyes closed.

"Has he regained consciousness?" a woman asked.

"Not yet," his father said.

"You've been at his side for days. You need to rest."

At my side? Not because they were worried about his health. Only because they were worried he'd say the wrong thing.

No one would be rushing to prove he hadn't been behind the wheel when he'd been found alone in the car, in the driver's seat, and his father had given Lachlan an alibi. He shouldn't even be surprised his father wanted to save his brother, the golden child. Caspian slipped into darkness.

When he next opened his eyes, his father and Lachlan were still there.

"What about Mum?" Caspian asked. "Does she know the truth?"

He saw his father and brother exchange a glance and knew they'd already spun their lies. This had all been decided before he'd woken up. Maybe they'd hoped he wouldn't wake up. If he refused to do what they wanted, they'd paint him as a liar.

His father cleared his throat. "She believes you were driving."

Lachlan's future had been saved at the expense of his.

"I want to talk to Lachlan," Caspian said.

His father left the room.

Caspian stared at his brother. "Tell me exactly what happened."

Lachlan let out a shuddering breath. "I got out of the car. One girl lay pinned underneath, the other two sprawled like…broken dolls several metres away. There was blood everywhere. All I could think was if I was caught, it was the end of everything. I'd go to prison."

He swallowed hard. "It was a quiet road. No other cars around. I went back to the Jaguar. You were covered in blood. I unclipped your seat belt and hauled you… not out but onto the driver's side. I fastened the seatbelt around you, dragged your hands up and down the wheel, onto the gear stick and the door handle. I closed the door and ran."

"You fucking bastard."

"You're right. I am. All the way back to the house I knew I'd not done the right thing. I knew Father would be furious. No one saw me. I went straight to his study, didn't knock, walked in and said I'd done something stupid. That you'd given me the slip. I followed in the Jag.

Picked you up. You distracted me and I hit three girls and killed them."
He gulped. "Oh Jesus, I'm sorry. I'm sorry."

"Did he ask about me?"

Lachlan nodded. "I said you'd hit your head and were unconscious when I left you. I didn't know how badly hurt you were. I panicked. If I'd stayed, the police would have tested me and that would be the end of my life."

Instead, it was the end of Caspian's.

"I told Father I'd moved you into the driver's seat. I thought we could say you took the car. If you'd died…I mean there was no point me taking the blame if you were dead. And if you weren't, you're a kid. You won't go to prison."

Caspian's chest ached. He couldn't believe Lachlan had done that.

"I'm sorry. I wasn't thinking."

"Yeah, you were." That was the most terrible thing. Lachlan had known exactly what he was doing. "What did Father say?"

"That what's done is done. Told me to go upstairs, shower, put my clothes in the washing machine, hide my shoes in the woodpile. Take two of Mum's sleeping tablets and go to bed. Try not to be seen. He said he'd report you'd taken the car without permission."

"I hate you."

"I'm sorry."

Caspian closed his eyes. *What the fuck am I going to do?*

Caspian wasn't surprised by the speed with which his father brought a lawyer to the hospital to talk to him. Except Caspian wasn't talking. He listened to Robert Appleby, a tall thin guy with a prominent Adam's apple, explain everything. Caspian would be charged with causing death by dangerous driving, driving without a licence and insurance, taking a car without the owner's consent, and Caspian said nothing. His father didn't know but Caspian had taken his test while he was at school in Scotland. He'd passed first time. He'd been going to surprise everyone to distract them from his inevitably poor CGSE results.

His father patted his shoulder and Caspian turned away.

"Are you going to speak?" his father asked.

Caspian didn't respond.

"I suppose it shows he's in shock," his father said.

Appleby sighed. "He'd be better to show remorse."

"He's sorry. Aren't you, Caspian?" his father asked.

Caspian wished he was deaf.

Then the police came in, their faces hard. He could see what they thought of him in their eyes and how could he blame them? As they outlined what had happened, tears rolled down Caspian's cheeks. The girls were eleven years old, about to go to secondary school. The one under the car had died instantly—decapitated by the impact. The daughter of a policeman. *Fuck.* One died on the way to hospital. She'd lost a leg. The other died in surgery without regaining consciousness. The lawyer had objected when the police described their injuries, but Caspian wanted to know.

Tears continued to roll down his cheeks. They were dead and he was still alive. He didn't think he could speak even if he'd wanted to.

"He's in shock," the lawyer said. "These questions have to wait."

There would never be any answers. Caspian wasn't going to speak, ever again. Let them say what they wanted, he'd admit nothing.

But he'd also deny nothing. Three girls were dead. His brother's life would be saved and Caspian's was over.

That night, he pulled all the tubes from his arms, tried to get out of bed and fell. He had time to register relief that the world was fading before he lost consciousness.

Fahid wrapped his arm around Zed and hugged him. "Little brother. You play like an angel."

Zed tried to pull away and Fahid tightened his hold. "Let me take you to my home. You can sleep. When you wake, have breakfast, then decide what you want to do."

It was three in the morning and Zed was exhausted. Easier to start a new life at the beginning of the day, but he didn't like Fahid.

"Tamaz begged me to look after you." Fahid held him by the shoulders, frowning as Zed winced. He let him go, then reached to touch the mark on Zed's face. "Did your father take a belt to you?"

Zed nodded.

"There is no excuse for striking a child in this way. Islam teaches us to be gentle with our children. Prophet Muhammad—peace be upon Him—advises us to fight our emotions and hold back our anger. Your father is failing in his duty as a parent and as a Muslim. Come, stay with me for a while. Find your feet. London is not a place to be alone."

Zed wished he could say no, but to turn down help when he stood at the foot of a vertical cliff with a wild sea behind him would be stupid. He was so tired, so disappointed Caspian wasn't with him. He followed Fahid out of the station and accepted the coffee Fahid went to buy him. He had no concern that Fahid would chain him up or hit him, but he was worried he'd be challenged about Islam. This was not a man Zed wanted to tell that he was gay and that he no longer had a religion.

Fahid drove him to Islington and Zed dozed on the way. By the time Fahid had shown him to the room he'd slept in before, with the bathroom next door, Zed could hardly keep his eyes open. It might not be what he'd hoped for, but it was better than sleeping in a shop doorway or on a park bench. He washed, cleaned his teeth, undressed, crawled into bed in his boxers and fell asleep longing for Caspian.

When Zed came out of his room the next morning, showered and dressed, with his bag packed, he bumped into a guy emerging from a room opposite. Zed had the impression Wasim had timed his exit to intercept him.

"*Al-salaamu 'alaikum wa rahmat-Allaah wa barakaatuhu.*" Wasim smiled.

Oh shit. "*Sabaah al-khayral…salaamu alaikum.*" Zed hoped he had the greeting right. *Some* Arabic had stuck.

He glanced at Zed's bag. "Leaving already? Come and have breakfast first."

Wasim took the bag from Zed's hand and put it back in the room. Zed was cross with himself for letting that happen but felt awkward about retrieving it when the guy was being hospitable. Plus he was hungry.

Fahid and Parvez, the other person he'd met when he'd been here with Tamaz, were sitting in the kitchen. Fahid jumped to his feet and pulled Zed into his arms. "*As-salaamu alaikum.*"

Zed repeated the greeting, trying hard not to wince or pull away.

"A new day. A sunny day. Sit. Eat. There are plenty of cereals. You're not the only guest with a sweet tooth." Fahid winked at Wasim.

Wasim laughed. "And you don't?"

Fahid pulled out a chair for Zed to sit down. Zed tipped Sugar Puffs into a bowl and Parvez passed him the milk.

91

"Thank you."

"You're welcome."

Zed could feel the others watching him and he put his hands on his lap and dropped his head, pretending to complete a *du'a*, a personal supplication, before he began to eat. *What am I doing? Am I so scared of upsetting them?* Yeah, he was.

"So what are your plans?" Fahid asked.

"Go to the council, tell them I can't go home and need somewhere to stay. Then I'll look for a job."

"What sort of job do you want?" Wasim poured himself a coffee. *Playing in an orchestra? Selling tickets for an orchestra? Working in a music shop?* "I don't mind."

"It's not going to be easy. If you had your GCSEs… But Tamaz says you're clever, that you'll pass all of them." Fahid stroked his beard like some cartoon villain, and Zed had the urge to laugh. He managed to rein it back and spooned Sugar Puffs into his mouth.

"I tell you what." Fahid beamed as if the idea had just occurred to him, though Zed suspected this had been decided earlier. "Stay here with me for a few weeks. With a stable base, you'll be in a better position to find a job. A better position to find a place of your own when you have a job."

Zed opened his mouth but Fahid continued without letting him speak. "It's my duty as a Muslim to help a Muslim brother in need. I'd be letting Tamaz down if I allowed you to walk away from a place of safety. There are many bad people in London. You can stay here as long as you like."

"I—"

"Because of your age, the council will probably put you with a family and you have no idea what they'll be like, what their beliefs will be. You're much better off here. Or you can go and stay with Parwez and Wasim, though I think they only have a lumpy sofa bed. Parwez works part-time in a convenience store on the Holloway Road. He can ask if there's a job for you." Fahid smiled at Parwez, then at Zed. "We also have just two weeks to go before the start of Ramadan."

By which time Zed wanted to be nowhere near here. He didn't intend to fast between dawn and sunset. Children weren't supposed to fast until they reached puberty but as soon as his mother had died, Zed had been made to join in with his father and brother. Though when his brother was out and his father at work, Zed had raided the pantry.

92

"I would be honoured if you would spend the period of Ramadan here. It's the perfect time to reflect on life and how we should become better people. A chance to reconnect with faith and religious practices." Fahid beamed at him. "We will be your family."

"Not sure I can refrain from alcohol and sex," Zed said and wanted the words back the moment they'd come from his mouth.

But Fahid and Wasim roared with laughter.

"Funny boy," Fahid said.

Parwez was the one who shot him a look of disgust.

"Tamaz is going to come as soon as he can," Fahid said. "Wasim, don't you have a friend who works for Islington Council? Perhaps you could have a word on Zed's behalf. See what accommodation is available."

"I'd be pleased to."

The final turn of the key. Zed got what they were doing, being too kind and considerate for him to refuse their help. He wanted to run but knowing the price of a bed and food and safety was little more than mosque attendance and religious compliance inside the house, he'd have been stupid to walk out. He could cope for a few days. It gave him chance to find out what had happened to Caspian.

Tamaz came in time for *Zuhr* prayers. He hugged Zed and kissed the welt on his face.

"No more," he said. "He won't touch you again."

They walked to the mosque together with the others a few paces ahead.

"Did you tell him you know where I am?" Zed whispered.

"He didn't ask. I won't tell him. He was pissed off about his phone, though."

Zed gave a short laugh. "So apart from the fact that I stole his phone and took money from his wallet, he doesn't care about me." He took a deep breath. "You think I might not be his son?"

Tamaz frowned. "Why would you say that?"

"I looked for my birth certificate before I left. Yours was there, along with his and our mother's birth and death certificates. But mine wasn't. I searched everywhere. Why hide it?"

"It might not be hidden. He could have put it somewhere you hadn't looked."

"But why not with the others?"

93

"Maybe he needed it for something and just put it somewhere else."

"I thought he might not want me to see he wasn't named as my father. He… He treated me so badly."

"You really think Mum would have had an affair? Dared to put another man's name on your birth certificate?"

Zed sagged. "No. But you were only four when I was born. You don't know what she was like then. Braver, maybe. Or perhaps Dad insisted because he wasn't my father. The other thing is a letter should have arrived telling me my National Insurance number, but I never saw it. I looked for that too. I can't work without it."

"I'm sure there'll be a way to have it reissued. I'll look into it, okay?"

"Thank you."

Zed coped with the mosque. He was used to going through the motions and if he was being honest with himself, the familiarity and routine were soothing. He knelt between Fahid and his brother, their shoulders touching his and for a short while he wished this was his life, that he wasn't different, that he could conform. Muslims were kind, honest, generous people, but he was gay and that would never be accepted.

At the end of the last cycle, Zed turned his head to his brother and said, "*Assalam alaykum wa rahmatullah.*" Peace and God's Mercy be on you. Then said the same to Fahid.

Zed coped less well with the discussion in the café that followed prayers. He stayed quiet and listened in case he was asked a question. He thought he'd got away with his lack of involvement until Fahid tapped him on the shoulder. "Are we boring you?"

"No. I'm tired. I'm sorry."

"Tiredness is a state of mind. The great warrior Muhammad Mukhtar once stayed awake for three days in order to lead his people to safety when they were under attack. He risked his life to carry supplies to a village cut off by an earthquake. He dug with his bare hands to free a trapped child. He fought in Kandahar until his bullets ran out and then he used the butt of his gun to strike his enemies. It took four to restrain him."

"A brave man," Zed said because he thought he needed to say something.

94

Fahid nodded. "A man we should aspire to emulate."

Day after day, Zed told himself to pick up his bag and leave. It seemed simple and yet it wasn't. He was rarely left alone except in the bathroom. A succession of guys came and went. Fahid was popular. He liked talking, he could hold people's attention, though Zed didn't like what he was talking about. Mistreatment and misunderstanding of Muslims. Public attitude and how to deal with it. Ongoing prejudice. Muslim duty, according to the Quran, which went far beyond anything Zed understood or agreed with. Peace across the Arab world, which of course Zed wanted to see but at what cost?

He thought he was brave when he dared to condemn terrorism, but Fahid merely smiled and told him terrorism was the wrong word. But he didn't suggest another.

Fahid bought him jeans, toiletries, a towel, a shalwar kameez to wear to the mosque. Wasim was waiting to hear about accommodation. There turned out to be no job with Parwez, but Fahid always had promises of another coming up soon, the next day, the one after, perhaps next week. *Be patient. Thanks be to Allah. He will provide.*

Zed was extravagantly praised when he cooked meals or cleaned up. There were always guests in the house, many staying the night though he and Fahid were the only two permanently there. He was applauded when he showed any independent effort to be a good Muslim scholar. Anything he did, was done to deceive, his prayers focused on hope they didn't guess how little interest he had, how much he despised the way he was forced to behave, how much he longed for Caspian. He'd had no chance to try and find out if he was okay. If he tried to go out, there was always something found for him to do.

Then it was Ramadan and he and Fahid rose well before dawn to eat and drink as much water as they could because not even water was allowed once the sun was up. Nothing could pass the lips until the sun went down. Zed had never fasted so strictly before. Over the last couple of years, he *should* have but he'd figured his father wouldn't find out if he had a glass of water or the odd biscuit. It didn't help that the weather was warm. Fahid was full of praise for Zed's abstinence but Zed was always hungry.

Fahid had others in the house quite often. Zed had never known anyone who loved to talk so much. It wasn't difficult to listen when the subject was history, even if it was about the glorious rise of Islam.

95

Fahid wove tales around how in the early 600s, a religion began in Arabia and inspired by the new faith, Arabs set out on journeys east and west to conquer and convert. He seemed a different person when he spoke like a teacher. He described how Christendom had been horrified by the rise of Islam, a threat which grew in strength until the Ottomans and Mughals made mistakes and lost sight of the true faith. Fahid knew everything. Zed felt as if there was no question the man couldn't answer.

Though discussions of what was *halal*—permissible under Islam, and *haram*—forbidden, brought out Zed's argumentative spirit even as he told himself to be careful. The old way of thinking—ironically Zed's way of thinking once upon a time when he'd believed—had been that everything was permissible unless it was expressly forbidden. The new way, the extreme way, was that everything was prohibited unless there was evidence in the scriptures to the contrary. What joy did that leave in that world?

Zed had argued for music, after all Fahid had himself said he played like an angel, but Zed now saw those words for what they were—flattery to get Zed to trust him.

"There must be no more piano playing." Fahid patted Zed's shoulder. "The opinion of scholars is that all musical instruments apart from the tambourine are not permitted."

The fucking tambourine? Zed's knowledge of the scriptures wasn't good enough to fight his corner. He'd given a dramatically heavy sigh and nodded. *"Allahu a'alam bis Sawaab."* Allah knows best. The most useful phrase he knew. He stayed quiet. He nodded and smiled and tried not to let his hands shake. There was no talk of bombs or acts of vengeance but Zed thought he was being tested. He hoped he failed but he hoped the price of failing wasn't death.

I need to leave. He thought it all the time. He woke up thinking it, went to bed thinking it. He thought about Caspian too. When Zed had managed to slip his leash, he'd bought paper, envelope and stamp and written to him. *What happened? Are you okay? Send a letter to my brother.* He wrote down Tamaz's address and posted the letter.

He still couldn't quite let go of that small molecule of hope, though it was buried deep inside him. Maybe he never would let it go. Caspian's father might not use force but there were other ways of getting your son to do what you wanted. He could have threatened Caspian to keep him compliant.

But what threat? *What would Caspian have put before me? Who?* Perhaps his mother. That made sense, but Zed needed to know. He needed to understand so that he could forgive because along with that sliver of hope, sat a sharp dagger of bitterness.

Fahid was clever. He knew just how far to push Zed, just when to pull back. Zed thought he was smarter than Fahid because he'd seen through the friendship to what it actually was, but he wasn't smart enough to leave. When Fahid sensed he was losing Zed's attention, he'd change focus to talk about the Olympics, in which Zed *was* interested, or football, in which he was not.

"You don't support a team?" Fahid had exclaimed in shock. "Then support my team. Manchester City."

Tamaz came and took Zed out to the Tower of London and the Science Museum. Zed felt as if he were being fed treats while the teaching waited in the wings ready to resume. He was old enough to realise this was in part indoctrination. He was being enticed, encouraged, flattered and dragged back to the faith. Belief was the only way for him to learn how to be a better man. Fahid didn't see any alternative.

Zed did. He hoped that knowing he was being subjected to brainwashing was enough to keep him safe. Fahid couldn't see inside his head. No one could. They didn't know his thoughts. They didn't know that he longed to be loved but not by them, that he longed to love but didn't want to love them.

He didn't need Islam to show him how to be a good person. He'd been a good boy—mostly—but after his mother died he'd been beaten, never praised, always pushed to do better. He was scared of what Fahid would do if he found out he was gay. Zed didn't dare tell his brother. If his secret was uncovered, he was dead. He wished he was just exaggerating but he wasn't.

How sad that he felt relieved not to be flamboyant, that he didn't gesture or speak or walk in a camp way, that he didn't want to wear bright clothes, or wave rainbow flags, or shout out his gayness as something to be proud of. There were many shades of gay and Zed had to avoid them all. Guilt settled in his heart. One day, he promised himself. One day his life would be a true one.

Then Zed caught snippets of conversation that worried him. Discussions where doors were closed but walls were thin, or when talk abruptly ceased as he entered a room. When he was given money to go and buy something he knew was already in the house, he wondered what they were discussing that they didn't want him to know about.

Perhaps his wariness showed on his face because Fahid came to him and said all this secrecy was because they were planning a party for one of his old friends from Syria. Zed smiled. He knew a lie when he heard it. He listened when he could though he didn't know what he was listening for or what he'd do if he heard something he couldn't keep quiet about.

He'd fled from one snake and jumped into a pit of them. He almost didn't want Tamaz to come and see him because he didn't want him to be involved with whatever was going on. Zed didn't think his brother *was* involved, though he wasn't sure. Yet he had a key to the house. Why? There was a fever of excitement in the house, a sense of anticipation that seemed to centre on Parwez, and that worried Zed because for Parwez, Fahid and Islam were everything.

Zed's search for a job was fruitless. Tamaz told him he'd sent for Zed's National Insurance number, but it hadn't yet arrived. Even those places who were willing to take on employees who worked for cash in hand, doing nothing more than washing dishes in restaurants and kebab shops required someone other than him. Someone older, stronger, more experienced, not olive skinned, not an immigrant. Pointless protesting he was born here. He grew despondent when every job possibility Wasim or Fahid told him about sooner or later turned to ashes. Zed began to suspect they knew before he went for an interview that there would be no job. And yet he asked himself, did he want a job they'd found for him?

The answer was no.

Zed sneaked off to London and searched on his own, wandered up and down streets looking for adverts in windows, scouring the Metro and Evening Standard newspapers, asking in the markets. He found nothing. To cheer himself up he went to the piano in St Pancras and played Grieg, flushing with embarrassment when he was applauded by a crowd who'd gathered around him.

Back at the house, Fahid showed his displeasure with him for the first time. Zed saw a different man. Maybe the real Fahid. A harsh, rigid, unforgiving man. He called Zed ungrateful, wanted to know exactly where he'd been and what he'd done. Zed told him. Just not about the piano.

Fahid shook his head. "You must learn patience. There may be a job cleaning the house of the imam."

Zed knew his jaw had dropped and he snapped it back into place. *Shit. Cleaning?* "*Alhamdulillah.*" Praise be to Allah.

Fahid had friends over for dinner that night. Zed helped prepare the meal and for dessert made *Ranginak*, a date and walnut pie that had been his mother's favourite. He wasn't invited to the meal so he went up to his room which sat right over the kitchen. The mumble of conversation, the lack of laughter, intrigued him.

Maybe he shouldn't have lain on the floor and pressed his ear to the floorboards, but he did. When he realised what they were talking about, his heart stopped.

99

Chapter Ten

When Caspian opened his eyes, his mother was at his side. She clung to his hand and cried, and all he could think was that he felt wrong. Had something else happened? She called the doctor who told him he'd nearly died. He'd been put in a medically induced coma because he'd had a bleed on the brain. Two weeks spent in intensive care, though he didn't remember any of it.

He didn't speak to his mother. He was afraid he'd blurt out the truth. *She believes you were driving.* He wondered now if that meant she knew the truth or not? If he told her he hadn't been driving, would she believe him? If she didn't, he'd have destroyed the family for nothing because once those words were said, once he'd suggested Lachlan had been behind the wheel, and he and his father were lying, she'd have to wonder. Wouldn't she? Or did she know the truth and this was all pretence? *Fuck it.*

On the day he was due to leave hospital, physio having brought him back close to his normal self, though he still had occasional dizzy spells, Caspian reconsidered his decision to never talk again. That afternoon he was due to appear in the Magistrates' Court and if he was to have any control over what happened to him, he had to speak.

A nurse helped him put on the clothes brought in for him to wear. Caspian had assumed his father would bring him a suit, but instead it was his school uniform, he guessed to make him look as young as possible. The sleeve of his blazer only just went over his cast.

He was sitting in a chair waiting when Appleby arrived.

"Hello," Caspian said.

"He speaks! At last. Remember whatever you say to me is confidential, okay?"

"What's going to happen today?" Caspian asked.

"You'll appear at two this afternoon. That's where we'll enter a guilty plea. Because you're only seventeen, it's your first offence and you're unlikely to abscond, plus you've been in hospital recovering from life-threatening injuries, you'll be allowed to go home until you're called to the Crown Court for sentencing. I doubt very much that you'll get a custodial sentence, though it's possible. Three girls died."

I fucking know. "I'm not pleading guilty."

Appleby gaped at him. "But…"

"I didn't kill anyone. I'm not going to plead guilty to something I didn't do."

"You were driving without a licence or insurance."

"I have a driver's licence."

The lawyer drew in a breath. "Ah, that changes things."

"I didn't kill anyone."

"If you weren't driving, who was?"

Caspian didn't answer.

"If you're trying to protect someone, would he or she really want you to take the blame?"

If only you knew.

"Look, Caspian. If you plead guilty you'll get a lesser sentence, though not the reduced sentence you'd get if you didn't have a licence. A guilty plea saves time and expense, and in particular, it saves the families of those girls from the harrowing experience of coming to court to both hear and give evidence. Do you want them to sit there and listen to how their children's lives ended?"

No, but...

"The earlier the guilty plea is entered, the more credit the court will award for it. If you plead not guilty and are found guilty, your sentence will be longer and almost definitely custodial. Think carefully."

"I want to plead not guilty, but that's all I'll say. My name and not guilty. I won't talk when we're in court. Not a word."

The lawyer clenched his jaw. "You don't have to do anything other than that in this first hearing."

"I won't talk in the trial."

Appleby groaned. "Please discuss this with your father. He's expecting you to plead guilty this afternoon."

"That's the other thing." He swallowed hard but the lump in his throat stayed put. "I don't want to go home. I want to be remanded in custody. Tell them I'm a flight risk, that I ran away from boarding school twice—I did. If they send me home, I *will* run. I'll go abroad. Tell them that. If you don't, I will, and I'll run from the court."

Appleby gaped at him. "You do realise the sort of place you'll be sent to? It could be six months to a year before the case comes to trial."

"I don't care. I won't go home."

The lawyer left and Caspian braced himself for the visit from his father.

101

The majority of the nursing staff and doctors had been kind, but Caspian tensed every time someone new came into his room. He'd wondered if any of the fathers of the girls would find a way in, what he'd do if they did. *Not press the button for the nurse. Let them say and do whatever they wanted.*

In everyone's mind but his, his father's and Lachlan's, Caspian was a spoilt privileged boy who'd taken his father's car without permission and as a result of his reckless, dangerous driving three lives had been cut short, the happiness of three families destroyed. Four if they counted his own. Caspian felt guilty even though he wasn't.

Yet in a way hadn't it been partly his fault? If he hadn't run from the house, then Lachlan wouldn't have come after him. If Caspian had never met Zed? If he hadn't been born? He would always feel guilty even though he hadn't been behind the wheel. He wondered what his father would do to help the girls' families. Scholarships for the other children? Holidays? He'd have to be careful not to look as though he was trying to buy their forgiveness, but he'd do something, wouldn't he?

Caspian nervously rocked back and forth on the chair in his room. In his hand, he clutched a bag of drugs issued by the hospital pharmacy. Painkillers and antibiotics. Not enough painkillers to stop all pain forever. He'd never thought of himself as being capable of suicide but… But…

When he started to slide, and he'd found himself sliding a lot since he'd come out of the coma, he'd thought about Zed and let the memory of their kisses warm his broken heart. He wondered where Zed was, what he was doing, if he was safe, if he'd found someone to be with. As much as it hurt, Caspian hoped he had.

Had Zed thought about him? Tried to find out why he hadn't turned up at the station? He should have. *Why did he just accept my non-appearance?* Then Caspian's throat filled with bitter anger at having been betrayed twice. He'd once thought he was as lonely as he could get and he'd been wrong.

His father blasted into the room like a thunderstorm, the doors flung wide, his face twisted in anger. "We're leaving now."

As Caspian pushed wearily to his feet, the door opened again and a porter came in with a wheelchair. Caspian was propelled in silence to the hospital exit and from there, he and his father strode to the car. Well, his father strode, Caspian shuffled.

The car was empty and he assumed his father had dispensed with his driver because he didn't want anyone to hear what he was going to say.

Once they were both buckled in, it started.

What the hell was he thinking?

This had all been decided.

Why hadn't he told them he'd passed his test?

Was he trying to destroy the family?

Ruin his brother?

Devastate his mother?

What did he mean he wanted to be remanded in custody?

Was he insane?

His father gasped after he'd said that and gave a short laugh. "That's it. We need to tell Appleby. You're having a breakdown. You're unfit to plead."

No I'm not.

"If that's not going to work, we go into court, you plead guilty and we go home. You are not going to abscond. I'll make sure of it."

How? Chain me up like Zed's father did?

"I've spoken to several friends who have knowledge of these things. There's a slim chance of you getting sent to a YOI, a Young Offender Institution. More likely, you'll be back at home with a smack on the wrist, you'll return to school and life will go on. This…blip on your record won't have any effect on the sort of job you'd get."

Caspian stared out of the window. *Fuck you, fuck you, fuck you.*

"You can't seriously want this to go to trial, to have our name dragged through the mud. The jury will hardly need to leave the courtroom to come to a decision."

But his father and brother would have to come to court and listen, to understand what Lachlan had done, to see what they were doing to Caspian and remember that for the rest of their lives.

They met the lawyer outside the Magistrates' Court. Caspian's head ached. He was exhausted. He just wanted this over with and the easy way was to plead guilty, but he wouldn't. He knew a jury would find him guilty, he accepted that. But he wasn't going to admit to what he'd not done. Ever.

103

"Have you been able to talk any sense into him?" Appleby asked.

"I've talked. He hasn't. Let him have what he wants. See how long he lasts without all the comforts he's used to." His father was stiff-jawed with fury.

It was over quite quickly. Caspian spoke in front of a panel of magistrates to confirm his name—the whole bloody stupid thing—and to enter his plea of not guilty.

His lawyer made him look a flight risk which saved Caspian having to try and run from the court. He wouldn't have got far but he'd have made his point. Caspian got what he wanted. A stay on remand in Woodbury Young Offender Institution in North London. His bloody father stood and said he thought it would be good for his son to come to terms with the seriousness of what he'd done. Caspian knew his father would never pay for what *he'd* done. Chosen one son over another. Chosen the guilty son over the innocent one.

Caspian was driven to his future home in a security van along with three others. He sat on an uncomfortable moulded plastic seat in one of the van's six cubicles. There were no seat belts. If he hadn't been wearing a seatbelt the day of the accident, he might have died. Would his brother have still moved him? Probably. Those in the van with him were discussing why there were no seatbelts and concluded it was in case any of them tried to hang themselves or kill each other. *Really? Could you do that?*

Refusing to talk in the van had made him realise staying silent was going to piss off people he really didn't want to piss off. Maybe he should only stay silent when questioned about what happened the day his life had shot in the wrong direction. There was no point making things more difficult than they needed to be.

He was led from the van to a windowless reception room and asked his full name and date of birth. *Oh fuck.* He had to give the whole damn thing again. The guy smirked. From there he was taken to another room where two prison officers were waiting.

"Stand there," one said. "We're going to take your picture for your ID card."

Caspian had always thought mugshots he'd seen on the TV were grim things. They made people look bad but maybe their expression came from the sudden realisation that they were swimming in a sea of deep shit. Caspian thought about smiling but didn't. Couldn't.

"Sit on the chair," the other guy said.

On the weird grey unit that looked like a cross between a badly designed set of steps and an uncomfortable wheelchair?

"What is it?" Caspian asked.

"A BOSS chair. Body Orifice Security Scanner. It'll tell us if you've stuffed a phone up your arse, or a memory stick, SIM card, shank, razor blade, handcuff keys, parts for a gun, metal cylinder with drugs, and a whole lot of other things."

Caspian cringed. The only thing he wanted up—right, not going there. He sat on the chair. He didn't expect there to be a beep but was still relieved when there wasn't.

"You can get up."

Caspian stood.

"Now take off all your clothes." The taller man stared at him.

"Why do I have to do that when the chair didn't find anything?"

"Do as you're told."

Caspian wasn't shy about getting undressed for games at school but these were men, it was different. It felt wrong. They pulled on rubber gloves and a light went off in his head. *Dare I? Why the fuck not?*

He took off his shoes and socks and set them aside. As he began to undress, he swayed as if he was moving to music. He fixed his gaze on the better looking of the two, shrugged off his blazer then slowly unfastened his tie. He twirled it around his head before letting it fly. The guard it was heading toward flicked it aside. Caspian pushed open the buttons of his shirt, pulled it off, struggled to get it over his cast, then held it out before flicking his fingers and letting it fall. Caspian gave a long sigh and swept both hands down his chest, skipping over his scar, to his trousers.

Maybe they were interested to see if he kept going because they didn't stop him. Caspian had been trying to annoy them off and it hadn't worked. He removed his last item of clothing, his boxers, turned around and bent over. He'd made it a little less humiliating, but it was still embarrassing. Fortunately, the inspection of his arse and balls was over quickly and he was told to get dressed. His blazer and tie were placed in a plastic container. A sheet of stickers showing his picture and prison number had been printed off and one was stuck to the container.

"Sign here," he was told.

He signed.

"Are you going to get other clothes brought in?" the guy asked. "Prisoners on remand are allowed to wear their own gear."

Caspian shook his head. He had no idea, but he suspected not. His father would expect him to grovel for help and that wasn't going to happen. He was handed a see-through plastic bag that apparently held blankets, sheets, pillowcase, T-shirt, jeans, jumpers, pants, socks, white trainers, basic toiletries. He missed some of what was said but they gave him a list. Another signature required. It all had to be returned at the end of his stay. Did they think he'd want to take it with him? His hospital medication, painkillers and antibiotics, were handed back to him. Well, not all the painkillers. He had to ask for those if he needed more.

Reality was beginning to sink in.

"You'll spend the first night in isolation. Your PO, personal officer, will interview you and make sure we know what you need and you know what we expect from you. Okay? You'll get a medical too. You're just out of hospital, aren't you?"

Caspian nodded.

"Nice strip," one of them said and they both laughed.

"You could have given me a tip," Caspian flung back.

"Not that nice," said the other.

He hardly had time to take in the clunk of the cell door locking and register how small and powerless he was, that this was a place he couldn't get out of, that he wasn't like the others in here, before the door opened again.

A stocky, heavily built man walked in. "I'm your personal officer, James Naughton."

Caspian automatically held out his hand. The red-haired guy had a complexion that was more freckles than clear skin. He looked to be in his forties, wore an earpiece and carried a clipboard. He stared at Caspian's outstretched hand and laughed. Caspian let his hand drop.

"I know what you did. None of your little pals in here do—yet, but they'll ask. Be careful what you say. Three girls dead because you were in a fucking hurry. I have an eleven-year-old daughter and a son just older than you. You're a piece of shit. Try not to get under my foot or you'll be smeared all over the floor. Sit down."

Caspian dropped onto the bed.

"Call me sir. You do not use my name, nor that of any officer in here. You address us all as *sir*. You come to me if you have any problems. Everything you do gets written up in here." He brandished a folder. "Don't make work for me." He took a pen from an inside pocket. "Have you ever had any feelings of self-harm or suicide?"

Yes. "No."

"Some might say that was a pity."

"Who do I report bullying to?" Caspian stared straight at him.

Naughton laughed. "Me. Who do you live with?"

"Mother, father, sisters, brother, housekeeper." *Oh shit.* There had been no reason to mention the last.

The guy tsked. "Oh dear. Not sure you're going to fit in here."

Caspian kept his face blank.

"Do you have any mental or physical health problems? I can see the broken arm."

I've had my spleen removed, I broke some ribs as well as my arm, I fractured my skull and I'm depressed as fuck. "I was discharged from hospital this morning. They gave me antibiotics and painkillers."

"Hand them over."

Caspian passed him the bag. The officer looked inside and handed it back.

"You take drugs?"

"Nothing illegal."

"Drink?"

"Just a small dry sherry before dinner."

Naughton laughed. "Any particular dietary requirement?"

"Apart from the sherry? I prefer fillet steak to any other cut."

His PO rolled his eyes. "Smoke?"

"No."

"Member of a gang?"

Apart from the Rock Paper Scissors Society at school? "No." He'd been thrown out of every other group he'd joined.

"Are you gay?"

Oh shit and fuck and bollocks. "Why?"

"Because if you're gay and receive abuse from other inmates, you can be transferred to the VP unit, for vulnerable prisoners. But once in there, you only get one morning session of basic education a day. The rest of the time you'd be in your cell. So are you gay?"

"No."

"Is there anything we need to know about you that might make your stay here more…comfortable?"

"I'd like 400 thread sheets and a fifty-inch TV."

Naughton chuckled. "Wouldn't we all. Well tonight, your highness, you get room service. Your meal will be brought to you together with a breakfast pack for tomorrow. Watch yourself. Smart-Aleck comments can get you into trouble. There are a lot of tough young men in here and it's clear you're not one of them. That sets you apart and anything that does that, can be dangerous."

"Right."

"You're not a hardened criminal. You're a kid who's made a mistake but a bad one. Behave yourself and you'll be fine. We operate on a system of rewards for good behaviour. Bronze, silver and gold. I want you at gold and I want you to stay there. Understand?"

"Yes."

"You do not wreck your pad. You do not get into fights. You do not put one fucking step wrong or you and I will be having words. Got it?"

"Yes."

Naughton left and a woman came in with a prison officer. "I work on the health wing. I need to assess your medical needs. You were discharged from hospital this morning?"

"Yes."

"It says you had your spleen removed. You had broken ribs as well as your arm and you fractured your skull." She looked at him. "Do you need any more painkillers?"

"No."

"Have you ever self-harmed?"

Not in the way you mean. "No."

"Considered suicide?"

"No." *Yes.* Suicide would really show his father. Caspian swallowed hard. But it would also make him look guilty.

And that was it. She left. His meal arrived. Curry and rice, an apple, water and a breakfast pack containing cereal, bread, jam and a carton of UHT milk. *Ugh.*

The curry was lukewarm and too spicy but he ate the rice, and followed that with the cereal, bread and jam. There was no way he could drink UHT milk. He put the tray by the door and curled up on the bed.

Please don't let this be a mistake. Had anger with his father and brother stopped him thinking straight? It probably had. His whole world had just fallen apart. Everything he'd taken for granted had gone. His own space. His ability to choose on every level. Zed was gone. Now all Caspian had was himself and his thoughts. And they weren't good ones.

A whole load of yelling and catcalling and abuse echoed up and down the corridor. He couldn't make out what was being said, but it sounded like a cacophony of devils, just as if he'd landed in hell. He told himself not to cry but looked like he had no choice about that either. Tears rolled down his cheeks. *Fuck.*

The following day he was led by Naughton to the second floor of Mako wing.

"All the wings are named," Naughton said. "Tiger, Bear, Cobra. Stupid idea in my view. Now you all compete over which is the fiercest. We're not supposed to have remand prisoners in with those already sentenced but we're short of room. You'll have to manage."

Caspian looked straight ahead, didn't make eye contact with any of those out of their cells who were watching him pass. He looked the other way at the netting strung across the gap between the parallel line of cells.

Naughton saw him staring. "To prevent you being thrown down rather than to stop jumpers."

Would it stop him if he wanted to jump? Caspian thought he could probably clear it. Find an edge to slide through. Dive to oblivion. Or to paralysis. *Maybe not.* Anyway, he'd decided against killing himself.

Naughton pushed open a cell door. "Here you are, your highness. TV is no bigger in here, I'm afraid."

Bunks. At the end of them, a steel toilet with no seat and no privacy. One window with bars as thick as his wrist, but the window was open and he could see blue sky.

"Stow your gear in the empty locker. Looks like you're on the bottom bunk."

Caspian put his bag on the floor. The pillow and mattress looked disgusting, covered with stains every shade of yellow and brown. When Naughton had gone, Caspian gave a heavy sigh. There was a pile of sweets on the bed—Polos, Refreshers, a finger of Fudge, a Twix, wine gums and some orange squash. A welcome pack and for some reason it made him want to giggle. But the sound that emerged was a strangled sob.

He took a deep breath and walked out onto the landing. This wasn't so different to boarding school. Newcomers needed to show they weren't afraid, start out as they meant to go on. Except Caspian *was* afraid. He felt like a baby as he made his way downstairs. These guys had serious muscles and looked older than him.

As he reached the ground floor trouble broke out. Someone who was cleaning the tables sprayed disinfectant over another guy, punches flew and all hell broke loose. Guys began fighting everywhere as though they'd been waiting for the excuse to thump the person nearest them. Caspian backed off, but his route to the stairs was blocked by two tough looking black guys and one white guy wearing matching silver tracksuits and white T-shirts.

"What's your name, fresh fish?"

"Caspian." *Huh, so much for not speaking.* Still, they hadn't asked him what he was in for.

"The ghost," the tallest boy said.

"That was—" Caspian was going to correct him, tell him he was thinking of Casper, then thought again.

"What you in for, Ghost?" the same boy asked.

"Causing death by dangerous driving."

Prison officers rushing in to break up the fight pushed Caspian aside. A pathway opened to the stairs, and he fled to his cell to find a black guy lying on the top bunk eating his sweets.

"Lesson one, man. You leave anything unattended, it's fair game. You should have gone for the smoking pack. You could have traded."

Caspian strode over and slammed his cast against the guy's stomach. *Ouch.* "Lesson two. Don't fuck over your cellmate." He grabbed what was left of the sweets, then threw the Refreshers back on the guy's chest. "Don't like those."

Caspian started to empty his plastic bag, stowing the clothes and cheap white trainers in his locker.

"It's shit stuff. Don't expect it to fit neither. Don't you got your own gear?"

"No."

Caspian made his bed. The guy dropped down, sat on the desk piled with books and car magazines and watched him. "I'm Jason."

"Caspian. Sorry about the thump."

"Don't fucking apologise. You did right. I was out of order. You have to stand up for yourself. Lesson number three. If you get involved in a fight, it don't matter whether you win or lose, you just have to show people you're not some bitch they can push around. And you have to be prepared to land some kicks and punches if required."

"Even if you're outnumbered?"

"'Specially if you're outnumbered."

"You didn't thump me back."

"Yeah well, next time. Hey?" He laughed. "We're sharing. Unless you do something to piss me off, we look after each other's backs."

Caspian nodded.

"They take our clothes and our names, give us numbers, feed us shit food, treat us like they can't wait to go home and wash us off their skin. All we have left is our dignity. Stand up for yourself or you'll go under."

Just like boarding school.

"What you in for, posh boy?" Jason asked.

"Causing death by dangerous driving."

"That's okay."

No, it fucking wasn't. "Compared to what?" Stabbing someone to death with a screwdriver? He didn't say that just in case that was what Jason was in for.

"Being a nonce."

"What's that?"

Jason laughed. "Christ, you really don't know nothing. It's a sex offender. Someone who fucks around with kids. Course you might be a nonce and just been told to say you're in for death by dangerous driving. Though you look like a kid yourself. How old are you?"

"Seventeen. I'm not a nonce."

"Fucking seventeen? Shit, they must short of space. Eighteen to twenty-two-year olds in Mako. You're a baby shark."

"But I'm still a shark."

Jason smiled and nodded. "Good thinking. I was done for drug dealing. Second time in. And last. I want to see my kid grow up."

Caspian gaped at him. "You have a child?"

"Yeah. Billy. He's five. I was a dad at fourteen."

Christ.

The room darkened and Caspian turned to see a huge guy blocking the doorway.

Jason jumped to his feet. "Hi, Lewis."

"Fuck off."

"Dignity and respect," Jason whispered as he passed Caspian.

"Cigarettes." The guy held out his hand to Caspian.

"I don't have any. I don't smoke."

"Then get them. You pay to be in this wing if you want to stay in one piece." The guy walked out again.

What the fuck? He knew it was only intimidation, but it was still scary. He shot to the door and called, "Fancy a tube of Polos instead?"

"Bend over and I'll shove them up your arse."

"They're already up my arse."

Caspian held his breath, but the guy laughed. Back in the cell, Caspian sat on his bed with the induction booklet. He tried to read it—and failed to read it. Anxiety made his dyslexia worse. Words were dancing off the page onto the walls. He ate the finger of fudge while he still had the chance, then drank the juice. One thing he definitely needed to hide was that he was gay. Though he wondered if it mattered, if TV shows were right, that bending over in the shower wasn't a good idea for anyone. He shuddered.

A short time later, he was taken to a classroom where he and three others were given a two-hour talk by a squeaky-voiced woman about what to do and what not to do. There was an exercise yard, but he had to move around it in a clockwise direction. Or was it anticlockwise? *Shit.*

The long list of prohibited items included wax, chewing gum, magnets, plasticine, toy guns, phones, Blu Tack, metal cutlery, explosives—*well duh*—wire, computer memory sticks and umbrellas. *Umbrellas?* If they didn't have pointy ends, or poisonous tips was that okay? Though Caspian guessed the wire spokes could be used for all sorts of things. Stuff that would be carefully monitored included tools, yeast, cling film, rope, vinegar, glue and tin foil.

Education was obligatory until he was eighteen. *Shit.* The one thing he thought he'd escaped. Not only was he in jail but he had to attend school as well? How crap was that? At least there was a huge choice of subjects to study ranging from Islam to parent craft to industrial cleaning. *Fucking wonderful.*

The woman went down the list too fast for him to follow on the handout. But he did catch that he'd be paid forty pence for each class he attended which could be spent on chocolate or credits for phone calls. Classes started at 8.30 but staff began searching boys earlier so they could be moved in small groups to the education block.

The more he listened, the more freaked out he became. Stress dried his mouth and made his heart pound. He'd forgotten almost everything the woman had said by the time she'd finished speaking. But it was all helpfully detailed in yet another booklet he'd struggle to read.

He had his compulsory talk with the chaplain. Well, the chaplain talked, he didn't. All he wanted to do was curl up on his bed and pretend he was somewhere else.

Chapter Eleven

When talk ceased downstairs, Zed slipped into bed. The front door slammed as he pulled the covers over his face. *Oh God.* He had to be careful. One wrong step, the wrong expression on his face and he'd give himself away. Do anything that might reveal a word of what he'd listened to and he was dead. There was no misinterpreting what he'd heard. Not another story from a master storyteller, but an actual plot. *Jihad.* They were going to detonate bombs at the Olympics.

Well, not Fahid. He was the one behind it, but he was giving the honour of destruction to others. Parwez would be somewhere in the crowd for the 100 metres final. Wasim and a guy called Saheed would be at exits to the athletics stadium ready to destroy those fleeing once Parwez had detonated his bomb. Another guy, Javid, would blow himself up in the Westfield Stratford City shopping centre thirty minutes after the first device had exploded, the place where fleeing people would have been told to go.

According to Fahid, the BBC and the internet had helpfully provided details of the security measures put in place. Bags and backpacks would be searched on the way into the Olympic Park, unarmed troops working alongside civilians. There would be dogs that could sniff out explosives but Fahid seemed to think they'd be no problem. They only had around thirty animals to cover the whole venue and they could work for just thirty or forty minutes before they became bored or distracted.

Timing was everything. If any of the three of them were approaching a place where a dog was working, or a guard looked straight at them, choose another line. If one of them was caught, he should detonate immediately. The other three would follow once they heard the first blast.

Zed was still shaking as he thought about it. He heard Fahid coming up the stairs and froze. To his intense relief, Fahid continued past his door. Zed would have pretended to be asleep if Fahid had looked in on him. He was too freaked out to attempt to look normal.

Fahid had spouted the crap about seventy-two virgins waiting for martyrs and Zed had heard them tease Parwez, telling him his first time would be even better than the wonder he'd hoped for. Zed's brother had once told him the notion of virgins as a reward for martyrdom was a wilful misinterpretation of phrases in the Quran, a twisting of sentences

114

in the Hadith. But people heard what they wanted to hear, believed what they wanted to believe.

Suicide bombers! Zed bit back his moan. Was Fahid going to ask him to be a bomber too? *Make* him be one? He gulped. Once they'd fastened an explosive belt around him, locked it in place, what could he do? Yell at people to keep clear? *Fuck.* Zed forced himself to take deep breaths as panic gripped him. How could he even face Fahid now he was aware of what they were planning?

Then he worried whether Tamaz knew anything about this. He was friends with Fahid. He had a key to his house! If Zed reported Fahid, he'd drag Tamaz into this whether he was innocent or guilty. Bile surged up Zed's throat. He forced it down but the bitter taste remained. *What can I do? What can I do?*

There was little sleep to be had that night. He went over and over every possible way he could get out of the house to tell the right person what he'd heard. He'd have to sneak out but leave his bag because he'd probably have to come back. If he didn't, when the others were arrested, Fahid would know who'd betrayed them. And who was the right person to tell? Who'd believe him? Zed fled to the bathroom and was violently sick.

He felt the hand on his back, Fahid gently patting him, soothing him, and fear made him throw up again. Zed clung to the toilet and kept his face averted for as long as he could, until there was nothing left inside him to throw up, no reason to stay on his knees other than abject fear.

"Feeling better now, little brother?" Fahid asked.

A glass of water was pushed into his hand. Zed swilled out his mouth and spat out the water. As he stood, Fahid flushed the toilet.

Zed washed his face and drank the rest of the water.

"Hope that wasn't something we ate," Fahid said.

Okay to look worried now. "Oh no. You don't feel ill, do you?"

"I'm fine." Fahid pressed a hand to Zed's forehead. "You're hot. Sweaty. Go back to bed. Stay in bed. When I go to the mosque for *Israq*, I'll tell the imam you're not well today."

Zed nodded and made his way back to his room. Had he just been handed an opportunity? *Israq* was the sunrise prayer so Fahid would be leaving around five. Not back until almost six because he inevitably found someone to chat to. Zed lay awake, watching the red lines on the digital clock mark the time down.

But as he thought it through, he worried this wasn't the moment to take. On virtually empty streets he would be seen.

He thought some more. He needed to call the police but use the new non-emergency number 1-0-1.

When Fahid came downstairs at five, Zed was waiting. "I feel okay now. I want to go to the mosque."

"I'm delighted to hear that. No shalwar Kameez?"

"It needs washing." It didn't, but he didn't want to wear it today.

Zed had his question ready as they left the house. "Do you think a tally is kept of the number of times we pray?"

"Our private prayers or those at the mosque?"

"Both. I can't shake off the thought of angels holding lists of names ready to tick off when you've prayed."

Fahid laughed. "You're thinking too literally. I'm sure all our good and bad actions are known to Allah—peace be upon Him. A good Muslim should pray five times a day plus Friday prayers, but beyond that there is no particular number of private prayers that each person is required to make. It would hardly be fair on those who died early through accident or disease."

"That's true."

As he'd hoped, his observation set Fahid off and he talked all the way to the mosque allowing Zed to hide his nervousness.

They completed *wudu* side by side, sitting on the special seats to wash. Once their *du'as* were said, they waited for entry into the place of worship.

"Are you able to work for the imam today?" Fahid asked.

"Yes. I'll speak to him after *Israq* and ask what he needs me to do."

"You'll have to wait. He'll be busy."

"I'll find somewhere to sit and be patient."

When *Israq* was over, Fahid went off to speak to someone and as soon as he was out of sight, Zed slipped out of the door in the midst of an exiting group and hurried to the Tube. He wanted to run but he made himself walk. The less attention he drew the better. There was a public phone near the ticket office.

He walked straight up to the phone. There was no point hesitating. The longer he waited, the more likely he'd lose his voice. His heart pounded as he listened to a recorded message telling him he was being connected to his local police service centre. Zed was torn between

116

keeping his face hidden and checking to see if there was anyone around who knew him. But if the latter was true, he'd had it anyway.

Finally, a man spoke. "Can I help you?"

"I want to talk to someone about a bomb attack at the Olympics. I overheard them plotting. I can't speak for long now in case I'm missed. I need to meet someone. Not anyone in a police uniform."

"O...kay. What's your name?"

"I don't want to tell you."

"Then tell me more about this plot."

"Four suicide bombers. Three at the 100 metre final on Sunday, August the fifth. The other at the shopping centre that's near the Olympic Park."

"Who are they? Where do they live?"

"Not now. I can't. There's no time. I'll meet someone in St James's Park. There's a bench that looks onto West Island. Today at eleven. If not, tomorrow at the same time. This isn't a joke. I'm telling the truth. Please send someone."

He put the phone down, looked around, saw no eyes on him and hurried back to the mosque. The relief that no one was around to see him slip back inside was tempered by the worry that he'd been missed. He went into the bathroom, flushed the toilet, washed his hands and emerged to find the imam talking to a man Zed didn't know. Zed stood to one side and waited.

When the guy walked off, the imam beckoned Zed. *"Al-salaamu alaykum."*

"Imam. *Wa 'alaikum assalam.* Fahid said that you might have work for me. I wasn't well last night and I thought I was okay this morning, but I don't feel well again. I'm sorry but I can't work for you today. I waited to ask what work you require me to do, the hours and where I should work." *Argh, too much blathering.*

"Ah, I did mention to Fahid I was looking for someone but I've already promised the work to another young man. I thought I'd told Fahid."

"Oh. I'm glad you've found someone. *Ma'aasalaama.*"

Zed backed away feeling relieved but worried. For Fahid to have sent him for a job that no longer existed seemed strange, though not dissimilar to what had gone before. Maybe Zed was looking for problems. If it was a test, what was Fahid testing? Zed found himself heading away from the house. He could claim he'd been disappointed

117

there had been no job and wanted to keep looking. Would that convince Fahid?

It had to.

He headed back to the Tube and when he reached St James's Park station, he bought water and a salad. *Fuck the fasting.* That made him think of Caspian and he smiled. That would have been exactly what Caspian would have said. Zed didn't want to fast, but he did need to fit in. The salad and water in the bag he carried felt like scarlet letters.

Zed didn't want to believe anyone could be following him, but it was hard to shake off the feeling he was being watched. He didn't go into the park but wandered down the Mall, back up Birdcage Walk, searching for faces he recognised, until he convinced himself of his stupidity. His pulse still raced as he headed into the park. People were sunbathing on the grass. Others were walking dogs. Children were playing games. Normal lives, and he carried a secret that would rock the world.

He made his way around the lake to the west end, then sat on the bench—an hour too early.

Would anyone come? Would he be believed? Would he be arrested?

He drank the water but he couldn't eat the salad. He worried he'd throw up. So he went down to the lake, and fed the ducks the lettuce, peas and cucumber, followed by grapes he'd bitten in half. He wasn't sure about nuts, so he didn't throw those.

When he turned to go back to the bench, a man was sitting there holding a newspaper as if he was reading it but watching him. He wore a T-shirt and jeans, had curly brown hair and glasses and looked to be in his mid-thirties. Was this who'd come to speak to him? Zed sat down at the other end of the bench.

"Glad to see you're not feeding them bread," the guy said. "It's not good for them."

"I know." *Oh crap, is that the best I can do?* Zed kicked at the dirt with his heels.

"Do you like to do good things?"

Zed shot him a quick glance. "I'm not going to suck your cock."

The guy laughed. "Thank goodness for that."

Zed had figured if this wasn't the guy he wanted it to be, he'd have got up and walked away after a comment like that.

"My name's Jackson. I don't wear a uniform."

Zed exhaled.

"You have something to tell me?" Jackson spoke quietly from behind his newspaper.

"Are you a policeman?" Zed whispered.

"MI5. You know what that is?"

"Yes. British Intelligence. Thank you for coming." He released a shaky exhalation. "I don't know where to start."

"The beginning is always a good place."

But maybe not if he could keep Tamaz out of this.

He took a deep breath. "I ran away from home a few weeks ago and was given a place to stay by a man called Fahid." He told the man the details of what was planned for the Olympics, every name he knew, every address, and how he'd sneaked away to make the call that morning and then come to the park today.

"You didn't write anything down." Zed glanced at him.

"I've recorded it."

"Oh." He felt stupid for not thinking of that.

"Do you think you'll be asked to take part in the *jihad*?"

"For a while I worried that might happen, but now I think Fahid has deliberately kept himself away from the others physically, and I live in Fahid's house. I think that keeps me safe. He must know he'd get asked questions after the attacks, but there would be nothing to link him to the others apart from them being acquaintances. But he knows a lot of people. The house is always full of different guys. All Muslim."

"So why not you? Why didn't he send you to live with the others?"

"Maybe he doesn't feel he knows me well enough to trust me. Maybe he thinks I argue too much. Maybe he has something else planned for me or perhaps I'm his alibi. He thinks I'm a good Muslim. I go to the mosque. I'm fasting for Ramadan, well—until today, but I'm not a good Muslim. I'm…" *Can I say it?* He swallowed hard. "I'm gay."

The guy didn't react at all. "Is Fahid gay?"

"No. I'm… No." He'd been going to say he was sure, but he wasn't.

"No one knows about you being gay?"

"No." *Only Caspian.*

"Tell me about your family."

"No."

119

"Mother, father, brothers, sisters?"

"I won't talk about my family."

"Where did you use to live?"

"I won't tell you."

"Your name?"

"You can call me Zed. You could trace my family through my real name."

"Right. You aren't prepared to trust us enough to give us your name. How do we know we can trust you? How do we know you're not deliberately sending us in one direction while havoc is wreaked in another? How do we know this isn't some prank? A dare that you've been forced to go through with or chosen to go through with to impress a friend? Do you know how many reports we've been given of possible terrorist activities while the Olympics is on? You think you can overwhelm us, spread the security services thin?"

The guy never raised his voice but his words made Zed tremble.

"I've told you the truth. I've told you everything I've seen and heard."

"Have you been to the house where Parwez and the others are living? Seen bomb making equipment? Belts? Explosives? Timers?"

"No."

"So they might be testing you, letting you overhear to see what you'll do."

Zed's shoulders slumped. "Maybe. But I wasn't followed here. I was careful. I went in circles for a while. No one was watching me."

"I was, as soon as you came anywhere near this end of the park. I have your picture in my phone now."

"Okay." What was he supposed to say? The moment he'd set up the meeting, he'd known everything in his life was going to change.

"We need more detail. We need to know if the explosives are at that house. If not, when will they arrive? How are the three of them getting to the Olympic Park? If Parwez has a ticket, where is he sitting?"

The list of what he wanted to know went on and on. Zed had understood in his heart that the authorities weren't going to go straight to the two houses and arrest everyone, but he'd nursed a little hope that was what would happen.

"Can you find out more? Safely?"

120

"I can try. When you arrest them, you have to arrest me too so they don't suspect me."

"We can keep you safe."

Zed wasn't sure that was true. "I need to go now. I'll have to explain where I've been most of the day."

"Visiting a friend?"

"I don't have any friends."

"You do now."

No, he didn't. Jackson wanted to use him. He wasn't his friend.

"Where can we meet that's safe for you?"

Zed thought for a while. "The piano in St Pancras Station."

"Okay. Wednesday. One o'clock. You can follow me to a café. Can you remember a phone number?"

"Yes."

Zed repeated it back to him, thought of a way to keep it in his head, then nodded. "I've got it."

"Good," Jackson said.

"All you have to do is stop them," Zed whispered and he walked away, dumping the empty water bottle and the rest of the salad in a bin.

Before he'd left the park, he'd thought up an excuse for having come into the city. He'd buy a gift for Fahid to thank him for his hospitality.

When Zed emerged from an Oxfam shop with a *rehal,* an X-shaped foldable wooden bookstand for Fahid to rest his Quran, he saw a dark-skinned man watching him. The guy looked away quickly but Zed had seen him when he'd left the park. He remembered his yellow shirt. Jackson's guy or Fahid's? If it was Fahid's then Zed would have to think of a reason why he'd spent the best part of an hour sitting in St James Park. His heart thumped.

He could do that. His mother's favourite park. They used to feed the ducks there together. It was true. If it was Jackson's guy, so what if he followed him? If he went all the way to Islington he'd know Zed wasn't lying. But it was a tense journey, wondering what he was going to be confronted with.

Fahid wasn't in. He owned a few travel agencies and went to each of them in turn. Zed wrapped the bookrest in some kitchen towel and put the Oxfam bag under the sink with the other carriers. He wasn't sure whether Fahid was eating at the house that night, but Zed prepared a meal anyway. There was always plenty in the fridge.

Bademjan. Aubergine and tomato stew. He began by cutting and frying the aubergine, followed by the onion. No garlic. Fahid wouldn't eat it. You weren't supposed to have either onion or garlic before you went to the mosque but how could you make a stew without onion? Concentrating on preparing the meal calmed Zed's mind. He wished he was brave enough to go into Fahid's room and look through his things. Caspian would have. Zed decided he'd take the risk if he couldn't get information in any other way.

Finally, the shimmering red-gold stew was done, a sheen on the surface indicating it had cooked long enough for the oils to rise to the top. The rice would be ready by the time the sun went down and they were permitted to eat. Another twenty minutes. Zed would eat alone if—The door slammed and Fahid walked into the kitchen.

His face was tight with fury but when he saw Zed, he smiled. "You tempt me to break my fast at this very moment with that delicious smell. What is it?" He lifted the lid on the saucepan and sniffed. "Ahhh."

"It's an Iranian dish my mother used to make. *Bademjan.*"

Fahid sat at the table. "My poor stomach. Sit down. What have you been doing today?"

"I asked the imam about the job, but he'd already given it to someone else. So I went back into London to see if I could find work. There was nothing. Then I went to St James's park and fed the ducks. My mother…" He let his head drop and took a deep breath. *Does he believe me?*

"Oh, I bought you a gift." Zed jumped to his feet and handed Fahid the badly wrapped present. "To thank you for letting me stay here."

Fahid unwrapped the bookrest and for a moment Zed thought he'd made a mistake, until Fahid beamed at him. "*JazakAllahu khair.*" May Allah reward you with goodness.

He reached across the table for Zed's hand and clutched it tightly. "You're a good boy."

No, I'm not. Not for you.

Prayers were over and Zed had just put the stew and rice on the table when there was a knock on the door.

122

"Shall I see who it is?" he asked.

Fahid nodded. He was already helping himself to the food.

When Zed opened the door, Wasim pushed past him and went into the kitchen. Someone else in a bad temper. Zed followed him and Wasim stopped talking when Zed came in.

"Get a plate for Wasim," Fahid said. "Sit down, Wasim. Eat with us. Zed has cooked. I think maybe this boy needs to work in a restaurant."

"*Bismillahi wa 'ala baraka-tillah,*" Wasim said. In the name of God and with God's blessing.

Fahid smiled. "*Bismillāh-ir-raḥmān-ir-raḥīm.*" In the name of God, the gracious, the merciful.

Zed muttered under his breath.

"You need to learn how to cook rice," Wasim muttered and poked at the solid lump on top of the rice.

"That's the *tahdig*. The best part," Zed said.

"It's burnt." Wasim scooped rice from below.

"*Tahdig* means the bottom of the pot," Zed said. "In Iran the rice is boiled then steamed and it leaves behind this buttery slab. I put it on top because it's the treat. If you don't want it, I'm happy to have all of it."

Fahid laughed, broke a piece off and put it in his mouth. "Don't eat it, Wasim. You won't like it. More for me and Zed."

Zed smiled.

Every mouthful of the stew and rice was eaten and Fahid put his fork on his plate. "That was magnificent."

"It was very good," Wasim said. "*Alhamdulillah il-lathi at'amana wasaqana waja'alana Muslimeen.*" Praise be to Allah Who has fed us and given us drink, and made us Muslims.

Fahid repeated it and Zed said, "*Alhamdulillah.*" Praise be to Allah. "I'm glad you enjoyed it." He got up to clear the table.

Wasim caught his arm. "Leave us."

Zed nodded and went into the lounge. He put on the TV and sat in the chair closest to the door.

"Javid is panicking," Wasim said. "We assembled the belts this afternoon and he freaked out. I don't know if we can trust him. If he looks like he does now, anxious and sweaty, he'll get stopped before he's in position."

"He could change roles with you or Parvez."

123

"But then he might betray three rather than just himself."

"You think he'll run?"

"He might. What about using him?"

Me? Zed froze.

"He's not ready," Fahid said. "I'll come and talk to Javid. What about everything else? Any problems?"

"No. Everything is ready. We're excited. This is our chance to show the world who we are and what we believe in."

"You're a good, brave man, Wasim. Your reward will be great. I'll come with you now to speak to Javid."

"Bring him. You might as well see what he's made of."

"No. His time is not yet here. This belongs to you and Allah. Peace be upon Him."

Fahid opened the door of the lounge and Zed sat up on the chair and turned to face him. *Look normal.*

"I'm going out. I'll be back in a couple of hours." Fahid glanced at the TV. "Everest?"

"A series about the world's greatest mountains. I wish I could climb it."

"There are higher things to aspire to," Wasim said at Fahid's back. "Like getting a job."

"I'm trying. But no one wants me."

"You're a young Muslim. What did you expect? We're the last choice when it comes to employment."

Fahid patted Wasim on the back. "Come, let's be off."

The door closed and Zed shuddered. How could Wasim and the others strap explosives to themselves and look into the faces of those they were about to murder? How could they see happy families and children and not care about what they were about to do?

The thought of what might happen gave him new resolve. There was still enough light in the house not to need to put on lights. He went upstairs and cracked open the door of Fahid's room. A bed, wardrobe, chest of drawers, a desk and open curtains. Zed went inside. The desk was hidden from the window which meant the laptop was too but it was switched off. Zed didn't know enough about computers to risk turning it on. Fahid was bound to have a password.

Zed didn't really know what he was looking for. There were lots of utility bills and piles of receipts but only from supermarkets or to do with the travel agencies. Nothing about bomb making equipment.

Though Zed had no idea how a bomb was built. Maybe some of the things *were* relevant. There were lots of business files but everything seemed relevant to the travel agencies. He was really careful to put things back how they were. For all he knew Fahid had the sort of memory that would instantly tell him someone had been messing around with his stuff.

Maybe it wasn't Fahid that Zed should be looking at, but Parwez.

Chapter Twelve

Caspian and Jason had nothing in common except for being locked up in the same cell. When Jason talked about his woman and how much he missed not just fucking her but spending time with her, touching her, her softness, her laughter, even her moodiness, Caspian thought about Zed. When Jason went into details about hand jobs he'd had, sensational blowjobs, condomless sex, Caspian imagined that with Zed and turned himself on. Ironically, his erection convinced Jason he was into girls—if he'd needed convincing.

"You need to watch yourself," Jason said. "You're too good-looking. Stick with me and you'll be okay but some of these guys don't care if you've got a cock. There was an incident a couple of weeks ago. A guy ended up in hospital, his arsehole ripped. He had to have two hundred stitches."

Caspian clenched his arse cheeks, his muscles opening and closing like the wings of a bee. Prison rules said sexual activity between prisoners wasn't allowed and yet the booklet also said there was a 'condom policy'. It was almost enough to make Caspian laugh. However long he was in here, sex was not going to happen. Not with anyone other than himself.

"Don't smile like that," Jason said. "If you do get cornered and that's what they want from you, either to fuck you or stick their cock in your mouth, don't fight. It'll hurt less."

How can I not fight?

"Yeah, I know what you're thinking because I thought that too, but there's only one thing that's important, getting out as soon as you can. You can't let this place get to you and it will fucking try. Choices are everything. Choices make your time here something you can deal with. Use this staircase, not that one. Choose this programme on the TV, not that. Find classes and go to as many as you can. Fill your time. Borrow as many books from the library as you're allowed."

Yeah, right, well one should last him a month.

"Enjoy the decisions you *can* make," Jason said. "'Cos the stuff you have no choice about, like being banged up every night, when to eat, when to go outside—that eats away at you."

He knew Jason was giving him good advice, advice that would make the time he spent in here something he could cope with. If

126

Caspian wanted to survive with his head intact, and maybe his body, he had to make the most of what he could control.

"And say no to drugs," Jason told him with a grin.

Caspian laughed. "I thought you were a drug dealer."

"Outside of this place yeah, you buy my dope, though I'm not going to do it no more. In here, leave it the fuck alone. There's more trouble over drugs than anything else. Who you buy it from, where he gets it, where you keep it, if you end up buying stolen gear… There's always an excuse to make trouble. Drugs is a slippery slope. I'm off it and I'm not going back on it."

Caspian wondered why Jason didn't ask him more about his life outside, but it seemed to be an unwritten rule that it was off-limits. Caspian wondered whether he ought to lie, assuming it ever came back as an accepted topic of conversation. Telling anyone about the life he'd had, the sort of home he'd lived in, the holidays he'd taken would set him apart from the rest. His voice already did, though he'd tried to tone down his accent. Blending in was key. Blending in until no one noticed you were there was the answer. Caspian hated conforming, but he wanted to survive with his arse and teeth intact.

Only day one on the wing and he'd already seen what happened to those who were perceived to be different. The way an effeminate man was bullied. The way a pale-faced guy labelled as a nonce was tripped, spat at, beaten up though the fight had started elsewhere over something entirely different. The names he was called: kiddie fiddler, animal, beast, along with fuckhead, dickhead, bastard, shithead and bacon bonce—that one Jason had to explain, bacon bonce rhymes with nonce, though Caspian still didn't get the bacon part. Prison had a language of its own. The guy was moved to the vulnerable prisoner unit with a broken jaw.

Caspian's first night was a sleepless one. The noise went on and on. Banging on the pipes, guys calling to each other, passing messages along.

"New fish in 47," someone shouted.

"That's you," Jason muttered.

"Sing us a song," the voice called.

"Don't," Jason said. "They're the Window Warriors and they won't let up."

"Twinkle, twinkle, little star. Sing it now or we'll fuck you over tomorrow."

127

Caspian's mouth was so dry he couldn't have sung even if he'd wanted to and he didn't want to.

"Sing it, sing it, sing it."

The demands went on and on. Lots of guys shouting now, threatening.

"If you sing it, they'll tell you to sing it again, and again," Jason said. "And when you finally stop and say you won't do it anymore, they'll do what they threatened to do if you didn't sing it in the first place."

Caspian stared at the wall and tears fell again.

The next day, Caspian kept his gaze down and was careful where he walked, showing respect to both inmates and screws was rule number one. But trouble walked into him in the form of Lewis Wilcox.

"You owe me," Lewis said. "You want to keep your pretty face, I want a packet of cigarettes before dinner."

Caspian fled back to Jason and told him what had happened. "What do I do?"

"It's Lewis. I'd give him what he wants. Buy them from Des in 22. He's reasonable."

"And when he wants another packet?"

"When you give him the first, you make it clear it's the last."

"What if that doesn't work?"

"Just hope there's new blood he can pick on."

Caspian bought the cigarettes. Used a chunk of his precious money, and quietly seethed.

Just before it was time for dinner, Lewis came to the cell. "Fuck off, Jason."

Jason fucked off. Caspian didn't blame him. He'd have done the same.

Lewis held out his hand. His huge hand. He was tall, only a few inches taller than Caspian but he was all muscle.

Caspian had intended to hand over the cigarettes, but he could see the future unfolding in front of him. If he gave in now, he'd have to give in forever. Even if Lewis ended up walking out with what he'd come for, the harder Caspian made it for him, maybe he wouldn't ask again. Or alternatively, Lewis would beat him to a pulp for being awkward.

"No," Caspian said and then wondered if that had really come out of his mouth.

Lewis swung a fist and Caspian ducked. He was good at avoiding, less good at landing punches, and in the end, no match for Lewis who'd probably boxed his way out of his mother's body. But Caspian didn't give up. He kept fighting, kept getting back to his feet after Lewis had knocked him down. They were both bleeding when Lewis stopped hitting him. Or maybe it was all Caspian's blood.

The doorway was blocked by spectators who dispersed once the action was over.

"Give me the fucking cigarettes." Lewis wiped his mouth with the edge of his hand.

Caspian stood there panting.

"Your teeth or the cigarettes." Lewis held out his hand.

He left with the cigarettes.

Everyone watched the Olympics, either in their rooms or in the communal area on the ground floor. There were a whole range of nationalities in there, everyone roaring support for athletes from their countries. But it seemed everyone, regardless of where they came from originally, was rooting for Usain Bolt, the fastest sprinter in the world, ever.

Caspian imagined himself being that good at something, the best in the world. How brilliant would that be? The men's 100 metre final was the following Sunday and guys were betting on the exact time Bolt would take to win. Caspian hadn't joined in. He saved every penny he got. No way was he asking his father for money.

Interest in going to the gym increased, as if they thought it gave them a chance to be like the athletes they were watching. Caspian had made good use of the one hour a day he was allowed, building his muscles, trying to make himself harder, tougher inside and out. Lewis hadn't bothered him again. Caspian had been asked about his injuries by his PO but he knew what to say—that he'd slipped, that it was an accident. His PO didn't even press him.

So far he'd refused to see any of his family. He had to refuse to see Betsy too because he worried his mother would be mean to her if he agreed to see her. Because Caspian was only on remand, visitors could come seven times a week for up to ninety minutes. As far as he knew, his family had only tried to see him on three occasions. The idea that he was causing them pain was of some comfort. Even his mother. Let them imagine what they wanted. His father thought he'd beg to come home and that wasn't going to happen.

They wrote to him. Somehow his brother found out he was allowed a games console. An Xbox, Wii or PlayStation. *Let me see you and I'll bring you whatever you want.* His mother had asked—did he want clothes, toiletries, his fucking teddy bear? *Seriously?* She had no idea. Probably thought Woodbury was like a hotel except you didn't get a key to your room. His sisters wrote letters where they talked about what they'd done that day. Everything he couldn't do. When he read that they'd been into the treehouse, he was filled with fury. But it faded. He could do nothing, so there was no point getting bent out of shape about it. He had to learn patience.

Because Jason was right. All he needed to do was get out as soon as he could. Behave. Survive.

Zed seized his opportunity when he saw Parwez at the mosque and grabbed the spot next to him when they knelt to pray. He'd never really liked Parwez who always seemed angry about everything. But Zed's head was filled with horror at the knowledge that Parwez was counting down the days left in his short life. Was he scared? Excited? Resigned?

At the end of prayers, Parwez turned to him and said, "*Assalamu alaikum wa rahmatullah.*" Peace be upon you and God's blessings. But he glared at Zed as if he was disgusted by him.

Zed spoke the same words in return, then Parwez got up and walked away. Once Zed had collected his shoes, he hurried to follow Parwez outside.

"Are you angry with me?" Zed asked. "What have I done to offend you?"

Parwez stared at him. "You ran from your home. You had a home and you ran from it. You had a father and you ran from him. You ran to Fahid."

Ah, you have no father and you think Fahid is yours. Zed struggled for the right thing to say. "I was afraid my father would kill me."

"What did you do to make him want to do that?"

"Failed to be the best in everything I did. I tried. I worked hard, but no one can be good at everything. Even the things I was good at, I still wasn't good enough. He made me feel worthless."

That wasn't true. His father had tried to make him feel worthless but the way he'd treated Zed had made him believe he deserved better, that he could make his life what he wanted it to be and not what his father wanted.

"I only ever tried to make him happy, make him proud but it was impossible," Zed said. "He stared at me and saw failure."

Parwez looked at him a little differently then, as if something had hit home.

Zed sighed. "I don't want to be a failure."

Fahid clamped his hands on his shoulder and that of Parwez. "My little brothers." He beamed at them. "I have something that needs collecting from an address in Tower Hamlets. Go together. Keep each other safe." He handed Parwez a piece of paper and asked, "You have money?"

He nodded.

"Come straight back."

Parwez looked at Fahid as if he were looking into the face of God. Such love, such awe, such desperation to please, and Zed understood part of why Parwez was intending to do such a terrible thing. Whatever Fahid asked, Parwez would do and Fahid would make it seem as if Parwez was a hero.

They set off toward the Tube, Parwez with his hands tucked into his pockets and his head down.

"How long have you known Fahid?" Zed asked.

"A year."

"How did you meet him?"

"I came to this country hiding in a lorry with six others. The police stopped the driver and I ran. I was the only one to get away but I had no money, nowhere to go. I'd been living rough and begging for two months when Fahid saw me. He brought me to his home, gave me food and a bed. Then he found me a job and a place to live. I was falling and he caught me. He made me see there could be joy in life, that *my* life could be important."

"How?"

Parwez glanced at him.

"Only I haven't got to that point yet," Zed said. "I'm still falling."

131

"You have a home."

"But no job. It's not fair. I'm fed up of being treated badly because of my religion and the colour of my skin. The way people look at us…"

"I know. Well, they'll learn."

Zed's heart thumped. "When? It'll never happen."

"Yeah it will."

They went down into the Tube station. Zed knew he had to be careful. Parwez might be misguided but he wasn't stupid. They stood together on the train surrounded by those travelling to jobs in the city. Most people were messing with their phones.

"I wish I had a phone," Zed said, though he had no one to call.

"You don't have one?" Parwez gaped at him.

"My father wouldn't let me."

"You're not at home anymore."

Zed forced a smile to his face. "That's true though I have no one to phone."

"You have a brother. Maybe Fahid will give you a phone."

Zed felt as though something was clamping around his chest, squeezing his ribs. He didn't want Parwez to talk about Tamaz. Was Tamaz in any way involved with this? *Oh fuck.*

"You know my brother?" Zed asked, aware that Parwez had been at Fahid's house at the same time as Tamaz.

"I've met him a few times. He seems like a decent guy, a good Muslim. He's at uni, isn't he?"

"Yeah."

They got off the train at Whitechapel and Parwez pulled up a map on his phone. Zed tried to think of what information he could get out of Parwez that might be useful to Jackson.

"What's Wasim like to live with?" he asked finally.

"He's cool. Though I liked it better with Fahid. There's always more to eat in his house."

"Did me coming push you out? I'm sorry. I didn't realise I'd taken your room."

Parwez shook his head. "I'd already moved out weeks before. I think…" He sighed. "I was jealous of you, that's all. But I'm not now."

"Good." *Shit.*

The address they went to was a flat above a barber's shop. Parwez rang the buzzer.

132

"Hello?"

"Fahid sent us," Parwez said.

A moment later the door opened to reveal a guy in a white thobe, an ankle length long-sleeved gown. He had the darkest, shiniest skin Zed had ever seen and the biggest, whitest smile. It was impossible not to smile back.

"Parwez?" He looked at Zed.

"I'm Parwez."

The guy handed him an envelope. "*Asalamu Alaikum Wa Rahmatullahi Wa Barakatuh.*" May the peace, mercy, and blessings of Allah be with you.

He closed the door again. They set off back to the Tube.

"What's in the envelope?" Zed asked.

"My destiny."

"What?"

"Not really." Parwez laughed but it sounded forced. "Tickets to the games."

"The Olympics?"

"Yep."

"You're joking," Zed said.

"No."

"Which event did you get tickets for?"

"The 100 metre finals."

Zed let out a cry of astonishment. "Really?" Then he huffed. "No way. I'm so easy to fool."

"Look." Parwez opened the envelope and showed him a purple and white ticket. Seat 352. Row 30. There were a couple of other tickets in there but Zed couldn't see the details.

"Wow," Zed sighed. "That's amazing."

Parwez put the envelope in his pocket.

"You lucky thing." *You poor thing.* "How did you manage to get that?"

"A reward for doing…good."

"For Fahid?"

"Yes. One day you might be as fortunate."

I hope not. "Guess I'll have to just watch Usain Bolt on the TV."

"Look for me in the crowd."

Zed made himself laugh. "Oh yeah, like I can spot you among the thousands watching."

"You might be surprised."

No, you will.

Zed changed the subject entirely to chat about what he was going to cook that night. He didn't want Parwez to end up telling Fahid what they'd talked about.

Zed had to work hard to hide his anxiety around Fahid. He worried Fahid would come up with something he needed him to do at the time Zed had arranged to meet Jackson. Zed behaved perfectly. He did exactly what he was told. He cooked, cleaned, went to the mosque. He also tried very hard to be as invisible as he could.

On Tuesday, Fahid took him to one of his travel agencies. While Fahid sat in the office with the door open, Zed tidied the literature, ran errands, cleaned the staffroom and toilet, and washed the windows. When there was nothing left to do, he curled up on a chair and read the brochures, wondering if he'd ever get to see any of the exotic places he was reading about.

"Have you ever participated in *Hajj*?" Omar, one of the two travel clerks asked him.

A pilgrimage to Mecca? Zed hadn't even been out of the country. "No, have you?"

Hawaii looked beautiful and interesting. He'd like to try surfing. "Not yet."

Maybe Caspian could teach him.

Zed stifled his groan. He needed to stop thinking about Caspian.

Fahid came out of the office. "Talking about *Hajj*?"

"Have you been to Mecca?" Zed asked.

"Yes. You must go. In *Hajj*, we are all equal. It's the most wonderful experience to kneel before the Kaaba with Muslims of every ethnic group, colour and status, and praise Allah together. Peace be upon Him."

"One day, *inshallah*," Zed said. God willing.

Fahid smiled which was Zed's intention. No way was Zed ever going to Mecca.

Fahid turned to Omar. "We're leaving now. Don't forget to speak to Richard about the tickets."

Omar nodded. Zed added another name to the list in his head. Jackson had said that any little detail might be important.

"Come on." Fahid beckoned Zed.

134

Fahid had driven them there that morning. The travel agency had a small parking area at the rear.

"Did you enjoy yourself today?" Fahid asked as he pulled onto the street.

Not enough to come back tomorrow. "It was okay."

Fahid's belly laugh was loud. "What's the expression? Damned with faint praise. You were bored."

"A bit."

"What am I going to do with you?"

Zed didn't answer. He just hoped Fahid wasn't thinking of explosives in his future.

"You want to go back to school in September?"

Zed was saved from answering because Fahid took a phone call on hands-free. "Wasim. Whassup?" He laughed. He said the same thing every time he spoke to Wasim on the phone.

"I need you at the house." Wasim sounded stressed.

"A problem?"

"Parwez is freaking out."

"On my way." He ended the call.

"Do you want me to make my own way back?" Zed asked.

Fahid sucked air between his teeth. "No, come with me."

Zed was torn. He didn't want to go with Fahid, but he knew this might be a chance to get more information.

"What does *jihad* mean to you?" Fahid asked.

"A fight against the enemies of Islam. A fight inside yourself to stand against anything that might not let you be a good Muslim." Zed had prepared that answer.

Fahid glanced at him. "You wage *jihad*?"

"Don't we all?" Zed's heart was trying to beat a way out of his chest. "If enemies of Islam produce the trainers I want to buy, should I refuse to buy them? If enemies of Islam made the food I eat, should I turn it down? How can I always do what's right? Everything in a Muslim's life is *jihad*." Zed didn't believe any of that but he'd overheard Wasim saying something similar.

Fahid slapped his hand on Zed's thigh and Zed jumped.

"You are right, little brother. We fight all the time. I heard an expression—*We are screams searching for mouths.* Exactly true. This world is a bad place. Teenagers stabbed for no reason. Prostitutes on the streets. Gay men and women marching half-dressed with rainbow

135

banners. Women wearing offensive clothing. Drug addicts everywhere. *Haram, haram, haram, haram, haram, haram.*"

Fahid fired out the word like a machine gun.

"A beautiful world made terrible by our enemies," Fahid said. "We have a duty to make it better."

Zed took a deep breath. *"Ah, my Beloved, fill the cup that clears today of past regrets and future fears. Tomorrow? Why, tomorrow I may be myself with yesterday's seven thousand years."*

Fahid glanced at him. "You quote poetry?"

"Omar Khayyam," Zed said. *Shit.* Had he gone too far?

"And what is he saying?" Fahid asked.

"That we should cherish each moment because we don't know what tomorrow will bring. Live each day as if it's your last. Find inner peace in order to cope with past mistakes and fear of future wrongs. Life is good. We can make it good."

"We can."

But not by blowing up innocent people.

"Do you know the whole poem?" Fahid asked.

"No. My mother used to read it to me."

"How you must miss her. Can there be anything more tragic for a child than to lose his mother? She converted to the faith before she married, Tamaz told me."

"She did."

"Tell me about her."

"She was a good person. Kind and gentle. She told wonderful stories. She was a brilliant teacher. Children loved her. They bought her presents. Made them for her. She kept them all, even the ones that weren't very good. She said they'd been made with love and so they were special." His father had thrown them away after she died.

"Was it hard to share her?"

How could Fahid guess he'd sometimes felt jealous? "She always made time for me and Tamaz."

"My mother had ten children."

"Wow, that's a lot."

Fahid laughed. "We fought but we loved each other. We drove her mad."

Now Fahid was talking about himself, Zed let himself relax a little.

136

"But one day I will be with her in Paradise, God willing. And you will be with yours."

Zed swallowed hard. *But not yet, thank you.*

Wasim let them into the house. Zed had only ever been to the door before.

"Why did you bring him?" Wasim snapped.

"Because I like him." Fahid's eyes narrowed. "He's a calming influence."

"What does he know?"

"Let us see." Fahid glanced at Zed and his stomach churned.

They went into a lounge with cheap furniture and bright green wallpaper that was peeling away at the top of the walls. Parwez lay curled up on a brown couch. Fahid sat next to him and patted his ankle.

"Do we have to change our plans?" Fahid asked quietly. "Do you no longer believe in *jihad?*"

"I believe," Parwez whispered. "But I'm scared."

"Of course you are scared. All great warriors are scared. The sacrifice is all the greater if you are afraid."

"I don't think I want to do this." Parwez bit his lip.

Zed leaned against the door, wishing he could take Parwez's side and tell him he didn't have to do anything. How much should he admit to understanding? Fahid knew he was bright. It was too dangerous to play dumb.

"*This* is the most important thing you will ever do." Fahid stared at Parwez intently. "This is your path, your *jihad,* for the love of Allah, peace be upon Him."

"I've never even done *hajj.* Shouldn't I do that first?"

Fahid waved his hand dismissively. "*Hajj* is a lower level of faith. Action is the highest. You will be doing Allah's will, peace be upon Him. There is no greater love, no greater sacrifice, no greater reward. There will be no pain. There will only be blissful happiness. Everyone will know of your sacrifice. You will be revered. Your name will be remembered."

Oh bloody hell. No way could that be misinterpreted. *Can I get details?*

Zed watched and listened as Fahid pulled Parwez back from the edge and felt guilty for being glad because the alternative might have been him taking Parwez's place.

137

Then Fahid turned to look at him and Zed tightened the muscles controlling his bladder.

"Do you see?" he asked Zed.

What is he asking me? If I know what's happening? "What do you wish me to see?"

"A pure heart. A brave young man. A warrior." Fahid stared straight at Zed.

"I see a scared guy." Zed's heart was racing. "What is he going to do?"

"You know." Fahid reminded him of a cobra. Zed couldn't move.

"*Jihad,*" Zed said. "A suicide attack."

"Not suicide," Wasim shouted.

"I'm sorry." Zed gulped.

"Parwez's action will strike terror into the hearts of unbelievers," Fahid said. "He will make his family proud. His mother will smile on him forever. His father will have a son who stands above other sons. This…moment of concern will pass. It was the final test to see if Parwez is worthy and he is. I know this." He banged his fist against his heart.

Parwez clutched Fahid's hand.

"You see how brave he is?" Fahid asked.

Zed nodded. "Braver than me."

"Hear that, little brother?" Fahid pulled Parwez into his arms.

"What are you going to do?" Zed asked. "How—?"

"Not now." Fahid glared at him and Zed shut up.

Parwez gave a shuddering sigh. "I am ready."

So was Zed.

Chapter Thirteen

Caspian came around with an awareness that he was not emerging from sleep but from a state of unconsciousness much like he had in the hospital. With that awareness came a blast of pain and a certainty that he was in trouble. He wasn't lying on his bed but on the floor of his cell. Though still in his boxers and T-shirt. Everything hurt, particularly his head. He could see trainers on feet that he didn't want to belong to Jason, though he suspected they did. But he couldn't lift his head any higher and whether it was Jason or not would make little difference to the fact that Caspian couldn't move.

A foot slammed into his hip and Caspian curled up groaning. *Oh Zed. Is this how much it hurt? How could you bear it?*

"I don't got any choice," Jason said with a moan, then leaned down and punched Caspian in the throat.

Pain and shock ricocheted through Caspian. No air reached his lungs and he doubled up, gulping for breath that didn't come. *Fuck. I'm going to die.*

"It's you or me." Jason paced across the cell. "Oh for fuck's sake. I don't want to do this but I have to."

Caspian began to crawl toward the emergency call button. To his intense relief, he found he could breathe again. But what the fuck was going on? Jason caught hold of his feet and pulled him away.

"Don't," Caspian groaned.

"I told you to just give them to him. Now it's my fault for not teaching you right."

This was about Lewis and the fucking cigarettes? A foot slammed into his back. Caspian jack-knifed and howled.

"I have to teach you a lesson. Fucking scream unless you want your face destroyed," Jason hissed the words into his ear, then dragged something across his stomach.

Caspian rolled over and screamed. Not because he was told to.

It seemed a lifetime before guards bustled in. There was a brief scuffle, then Jason was handcuffed and taken away. Caspian was lying on something wet. Had the fucker pissed on the floor? But when he was turned by a prison officer, Caspian realised he was bleeding and the concern on the man's face freaked him out.

Next time Caspian opened his eyes, he wanted to be in a hospital. His eyelids fluttered closed.

He woke on a moving trolley. There was a towel draped over him.

"We're taking you to Healthcare," a guy said.

So I'm not dying. It was almost disappointing.

The bars on the entrance door were painted in red, blue and yellow. Caspian guessed that was to make it look friendly and welcoming to inmates who'd been attacked for no fucking reason. *I gave Lewis the cigarettes. I didn't snitch.*

As he was lifted onto an examination couch, he grunted in pain.

"I'm Doctor Mike Jones. You know where you are?"

"The Dorchester? Please tell me it's not the Ritz."

The doctor smiled. "I'm going to check you out."

He lifted the towel and touched Caspian's stomach in several places while Caspian winced and clenched his teeth.

"You've got a wound dehiscence."

"And in English?"

"A complication in which a wound ruptures along a surgical incision. Your splenectomy scar has been opened up by a thump or a kick or maybe a knife."

"A knife," the guard said.

Caspian's head swam with pain.

"Right. I'll stitch you up and do an ultrasound check to exclude any internal injuries."

The injection of anaesthetic hurt but Caspian guessed that sewing him up would hurt more without it. It didn't take the doctor long.

Hardly worth the bother," the prison officer said.

"Sorry my guts aren't hanging out," Caspian muttered.

The doctor shot the officer a glance of annoyance, then turned back to Caspian. "It won't leave a further scar."

"Good. Didn't want to discount a career in stripping when I get out."

He lay still while the doctor examined him, feeling around Caspian's head, checking his arms, legs, ribs and his eyes.

"I can see you got a kicking. He touch you anywhere else?" the doctor asked.

"You mean did he stick his cock in me? No."

"Is the pain bad anywhere in particular?"

"My head hurts the most."

140

"So what happened?" the doctor asked as he cleaned him up.

"Nothing."

"Is nothing likely to happen again?"

Caspian bit his lip. "Maybe."

The doctor turned to a computer, tapped on the keys and tsked. "You're not long out of hospital. And you're on remand? Why the hell are you in Mako wing?" He glanced toward the prison officer standing by the door, then looked back at Caspian. "How old are you?"

"Seventeen."

"He shouldn't be in that wing," the doctor snapped.

The officer shrugged. "I'll speak to his PO. It's likely a matter of available accommodation."

"I'm not sending him back in there. He's underage and vulnerable. The Senior Officer needs to be informed. There's grounds for a complaint."

"I can complain?" Caspian widened his eyes. "The mattresses are really shitty. I wouldn't let my dog sleep on one, if I had a dog. I'm not keen on the cottage pie and I'd really like Sky TV."

The prison officer came up to him, "And I'd like to get through the night without you scumbags causing trouble."

Caspian pressed his lips together.

"What did you do?" the officer asked.

"Nothing."

"So Jason attacked you for no reason?"

"It was Jason?" Caspian asked. "I had no idea."

Don't snitch on your pad mate was another rule. *Don't carve up your pad mate* probably wasn't.

"Do you feel suicidal?" the doctor asked.

"No." Though only yesterday Jason had helpfully explained how to make a noose from a bedsheet and where to hang it.

"I'll keep you in Healthcare for a couple of days," the doctor said. "Do you need painkillers?"

Yes! "No thanks."

"Hmm. Take these two tablets anyway."

He helped Caspian sit up and handed him the pills and a glass of water.

"You'll be in a room on your own but monitored at all times. If you need anything, there's a button to press. I'll come and see you first thing in the morning."

The cell was clean and so was the bed. He was safe in there but the shouting and banging were just as bad. He could trust no one. *Don't forget that.*

Imagine a world where trust doesn't exist
Where you're told where to walk
How to talk
What to eat
Where to sleep
Imagine a world where everyone hates
Where time has stopped
No place is safe
Where you have no worth
Where you're all alone
Imagine a world that's not like this
Missing it hurts.

Fahid shook Zed's arm. "Wake up, little brother."

Zed blinked and rolled his shoulders doing his best impersonation of someone waking up. He'd been scared to ask more questions and instead had pretended to sleep and listened.

"We're going home."

Zed pushed to his feet, yawned and stretched. He hoped he wasn't overdoing it. He looked around. "Where is everyone?"

"Cooking. We can leave now."

Zed followed him to the car. "Is Parwez okay?"

"He's calm."

Calm enough to wear a suicide vest on Sunday? Zed had listened to Fahid repeatedly tell Parwez that it wasn't suicide he'd be committing—which guaranteed an eternity in hell, but martyrdom—which would send him straight to heaven and his multitude of virgins. Wasim had even gone into detail about how to fuck them. How lovely for the virgins.

"Would you like me to ask Tamaz to come for the weekend?" Fahid asked.

Oh shit. Zed turned to him and smiled. "That would be great. Thank you."

"I'll call him now."

Was this a test? Maybe for both him and Tamaz?

Tamaz's phone went to voicemail.

"I'll call him tomorrow. Or you can. Is there food in the fridge?"

"Enough for me to make us something." *Which I'm not going to be able to eat.*

But he did his best. Fahid was happy with a cheese omelette, new potatoes and salad which was about as much as Zed could stomach even though he hadn't eaten since that morning. The man whose table he sat at, the man whose hospitality he had accepted, was evil. Not just misguided but pure evil. If he believed in what he preached, in the destruction of all those who weren't Muslim, why didn't he blow himself up in his cause instead of persuading others to do it?

Fahid's world was narrow, hateful and bigoted. There was no belief in the old traditions of tolerance and inclusion. The new way was the only way and as a result Islam was being destroyed from the inside out and the idiots couldn't see that. Zed might not believe, but he was sad about the way Islam was burning, because he understood how many needed the support of their faith and that for most it was a good thing. The actions of a few were hurting so many.

Zed found it hard to sit next to Fahid and pretend friendship, but the knowledge that a boy would bring down this man kept him focused, kept him calm. Dawud and Jalut. David and Goliath. *I can stop this happening. I just have to keep calm.*

Even so, Zed was relieved when Fahid told him he was going out.

"I think I'll go to the mosque to pray for Parwez," Zed said. "Is that okay?"

Fahid squeezed his shoulder. "A fine thing to do. I'll walk there with you."

Shit.

The good news was that Fahid left him outside the mosque. The bad news was that Zed couldn't tell whether Fahid trusted him or not. No way was he not going inside. He completed the ritual washing and slid into the prayer room. How long should he stay? Would Fahid be outside watching? Or had he asked someone else to watch him?

He stayed fifteen minutes before he risked emerging. The imam had seen him just after he'd arrived, but no one was around when he left. Zed hurried to the Tube station and called Jackson.

"Hello?"

"It's me. Zed. Tomorrow. Three at the piano."

"I'll be there."

Zed went a roundabout way back to the mosque and prayed again. He had too much information to keep until Wednesday. When Fahid joined him, he nearly jumped out of his skin. Zed went through another *rakat*—prayer cycle and then rose to his feet. Fahid followed him.

Does he know? If he did, he wouldn't do anything now or on the street. He'd wait until they got back. Maybe not even then. He'd drive him somewhere, then kill him. Zed's heart pounded so hard, he could hear it in his head. But Fahid emerged smiling and they walked back together.

"How many *rakats* did you do?" Fahid asked.

"I didn't count. I just wanted to pray."

"You're worried for Parwez."

"I worry that whatever he's going to do, is the right thing to do for Allah, peace be upon Him."

"If it isn't meant to be, then it's not the right thing and won't happen. *Inshalla.*"

You won't let it not happen. You're not Allah.

The following morning, when Fahid asked him if he wanted to go to work with him again, Zed didn't hold back his groan. Luckily, Fahid laughed.

"So what are your plans?"

"I need new trainers. These have a hole." He lifted his foot to show him. Though the hole had been helped into life by a kitchen knife.

"Will you cook another Iranian meal tonight?"

"Okay."

Fahid handed him twenty pounds. "Keep what's left over."

"Grass salad and bread then."

Fahid laughed all the way out of the house.

Zed went back to the mosque that morning just to check if anyone was watching him. He was ultra-suspicious of everyone, familiar faces and new. He called in at the supermarket, bought the ingredients to make *khoresh fesenjan*, chicken stew with walnuts and pomegranate sauce and prepared it before he ventured out.

When he thought he saw a face he recognised from the mosque, he pretended he hadn't noticed the guy. Just because they were both using the Tube didn't mean he was being followed. Even when he pursued Zed onto the Victoria line, he wasn't too perturbed. Only when the dark-haired guy got off at St Pancras and stayed on his heels did Zed worry. He changed his plans and boarded a train to Oxford Circus.

He got on and off three trains before he was convinced he'd lost him. He had to move without leaving a shadow. He bought a pair of trainers from the first shop he found, dumped the others and headed back to St Pancras. He was early and there was no one playing the piano so he sat down and launched into Mozart's *Rondo alla Turca*. He'd almost finished before he realised Jackson was watching. Zed completed the piece, pushed to his feet and followed Jackson across the busy concourse.

They sat inside a café but although Zed would have loved something to eat and drink, he refused the offer.

"I thought you weren't a Muslim." Jackson stirred his coffee.

"I'm not but if I'm seen with you, I can lie about you who are. If I'm seen eating or drinking, I can't excuse that."

"And you can the piano?"

Zed sighed. "No, but it's an indiscretion more likely to be forgiven than breaking the fasting rules of Ramadan."

"Why have you brought the meeting forward?"

Zed told him everything that had happened. All about the tickets, about Parwez and everything else he'd heard.

"You've done well. You have a good memory, Hvarechaeshman."

Zed groaned. "I shouldn't be surprised. You're just doing your job. Can I borrow your phone to call my brother? Is there a way to stop your number coming up on his phone?"

"There is but why do you want to call him?"

"Fahid wants to invite him for the weekend. I don't want him to come. By then I won't even be at Fahid's house, will I?"

"You can't call him."

"Why not?"

"Because you stopping him coming will make him suspicious. He might say something to Fahid and Fahid might change his plans."

"But Tamaz has nothing to do with this."

"Are you sure? If your brother is involved, you can't save him."

Zed shuddered. "He's not. He wouldn't."

"How can you know for certain?"

"Because he wouldn't put me in danger." Zed put his head in his hands. Was that true? He looked up. "I can't run the risk of meeting

145

you again. There's no way for me to get more information. You have enough to act. You know where the bomb making equipment is. You know who's involved."

"You seem more scared than you were before."

Zed let out a shaky breath. "Yeah, I'm more scared. If Parwez has fallen to pieces once, who says it won't happen again. Javid too. He panicked. Who will they use instead? What if they hold Tamaz and threaten to hurt him if I don't do what they say? *That's* why I'm scared. I'm afraid of what I might get asked to do. Save my brother or kill dozens of innocent people. Maybe a lot more than that."

"Calm down."

"Easy for you to say."

"I know."

"I wouldn't ever be a suicide bomber. I don't understand how anyone could do it. But they do."

Jackson patted his arm. "Yeah, they do but maybe not as many as you might think. The person doing the detonation isn't always present."

Zed straightened. "You mean there's someone ready to detonate the bomb if the person carrying it gets cold feet?"

"Yes."

"Oh fuck."

"If you think you're in any danger of being involved, you make an excuse to get out of the house and you run and call me. Otherwise, sit tight. Do exactly what you've been doing. There will be a raid. I won't tell you when and your reaction will be genuine. You'll be arrested. No one taking part in the raid will know you've talked to me. It keeps you safer. Don't resist. Do exactly as they tell you. I'll come to the police station afterwards. Okay? Go back now."

Zed pushed to his feet.

"Oh, and the piano playing? You're very good."

"Thank you."

"You're also good at spotting when you're being followed and slipping the net. Well done."

The praise put more of a spring in his step than his new trainers.

Fahid was in when Zed got back. He put the change from the food shopping on the table. "I didn't need it, thanks."

Fahid looked down at Zed's grey and red trainers. "Will they make you run faster?"

146

"The guy in the shop said they would."

Fahid chuckled. "They look nice."

"They're really comfortable and now I don't have to worry about outrunning velociraptors."

Maybe Zed was wrong, but it seemed to him that being able to joke made Fahid more relaxed with him. Four days until the bombings were due to take place. How long before the police raided? The thought smothered him. Heaviness filled his gut and his heart.

He and Fahid went to the mosque, ate together and Zed went to bed leaving Fahid in front of the TV watching the Olympics. Zed didn't believe in God but he muttered a silent prayer that night for everything to go smoothly, for no one to get hurt.

Zed sat bolt upright in bed. *What the hell was that?* Another crash downstairs and he gulped. Four twenty in the morning. Was this the raid? His heart pounded as he listened to guys downstairs shouting, "Clear... Clear... Clear..." Then his door flew open and two men slammed into the room and moved apart. They were dressed in dark clothing, had helmets on their head and guns in their hands. Red laser sights flickered over him and Zed shook.

"Hands in the air. Get out of bed. On the floor!" a man screamed.

Zed put up his hands and slithered onto the floor, his throat dry with fear.

"Hands behind your head."

Even as he complied, he heard others yelling "Clear... Clear..." and fear galloped in his chest. Zed told himself everything was going to be okay, but he was terrified. He'd set all this in motion and had no idea where it would stop.

He lay still while he was handcuffed, and it gradually began to dawn on him that he hadn't heard Fahid's voice.

"Who else lives here?" a guy yelled at Zed.

"Just Fahid."

"Where is he?"

Oh shit. "I don't know."

Had he managed to get away while they were breaking in? Or before? Maybe he'd left after Zed had gone to bed. It was possible he'd never intended to stay around until Sunday. *But did I fuck up?*

147

Zed was allowed to get dressed once his clothing had been checked. He was escorted from the house and shoved into a police van. Three anti-terrorism officers piled in after him, still wearing their helmets, the bottom half of their faces covered. Two of them pulled him onto a seat, fastened him in and sat either side of him. Zed kept his mouth shut and his head down. They hadn't been rough, not really, but he could feel their anger, their disgust, almost taste the adrenaline. No one spoke. All he had to do was keep quiet and wait for Jackson.

Except—where was he supposed to go after that? The few possessions he had were still in Fahid's house. And his money. How could he get it back? When would Tamaz find out what had happened? Would he tell their father? Even if Zed's name was kept out of it, Tamaz knew he was in Fahid's house. It would be on the news. *Shit.* But maybe Tamaz's place had been raided too. Zed trembled.

Even though he currently sat in a police van and the guys with him thought he was a part of terrorist cell, Zed wished Caspian was with him. Maybe he could ask Jackson to find out about him, check he was okay, discover why he hadn't come to the station. *Wherever he is, Caspian can't be worse off than me.* The thought made Zed feel better.

He was bustled from the van into a police station, taken to a room with a table and two chairs, told to sit down and left on his own. There was a camera in the top right-hand corner and Zed guessed he was being watched. He put his arms on the table, rested his head on them and closed his eyes. He was exhausted and yet his mind still raced. Did they have Fahid or not? What about the others? *Please not Tamaz. Where am I going to go? What am I going to do? How will this end?*

It seemed hours before the door opened but when it did, it was Jackson who came in carrying a bottle of water and a sandwich.

"Here you go."

"Thank you." Zed opened the water and took a long drink.

"Are you okay? Were you treated properly?"

Zed nodded. "I'm okay. I was scared. I forgot I hadn't done anything. What happened with the raids? Did you get everyone?"

"We have Wasim, Parvez, Javid and Saheed in custody. There are other people being questioned as well, including the man who gave Parvez the tickets. The houses are being searched as are the travel agencies. We've found the explosives."

"My brother?"

"Has been taken to a police station in Canterbury."

148

Zed groaned. "He had nothing to do with this. What about Fahid?"

"He's the only hiccup. He wasn't in the house. Nor was he at the mosque. We're still looking for his passport and he's taken out a large quantity of cash over the last couple of weeks. There was no sign of that either. Did he give you any hint he might be worried that the plan had been compromised?"

"No. Last night he was normal. We went to the mosque, ate and I left him watching TV when I went to bed."

"Not having him in custody gives us a problem." Jackson circled his index finger on the desk as he looked at him.

Zed sighed. "You can't let me go."

Jackson gave a brief laugh. "You are amazingly quick for a sixteen-year-old. Two years too young for MI5 or I'd make sure you were offered a job. Yes, you're right. If we let you go, and Fahid or anyone who knows you sees that we've released you, you'll be seen as the traitor because we'll have everyone else in custody."

"What had you intended to happen to me? I should have asked you before. I have no place to live. Little money. I won't go home. It isn't that I want any sort of reward for what I've done. I really don't, but now you've even taken my brother away from me."

Zed's throat hurt.

"You're old enough to live on your own. We could help you with that, but we think it would be better if we found you a family to live with. You could go to school, university if you wanted. We weren't just going to desert you."

Zed unclenched his fingers.

"But to keep you safe in the short-term, you need to be seen to have been treated like the others. Charged and remanded in custody, just until we find Fahid. You *won't* be charged, we just need to make it look as if you were. Because you're only sixteen, there'll be no name, no photo in the paper but the press release will make it clear a sixteen-year-old was taken from a house in Islington and has been remanded in custody in relation to terrorism offences."

"So where do I go?"

"A Young Offender Institution. Only for a short while. I won't forget you're in there." Jackson smiled.

Zed thought about asking him to find out about Caspian but maybe it was better that he didn't think of him anymore.

Chapter Fourteen

Caspian spent two days in Healthcare, during which his cast was removed. The relative quiet, the lack of a roommate, particularly one who might have killed him, and the chance to take a shit and shower in private made Caspian even more resentful of what his brother and father had done.

Though it was partly his own fault he was in here and he wasn't resentful enough to want to beg to go home. *So no whining!* He wasn't sure he'd be allowed home anyway. Though maybe if he promised to be a good boy and not run away, and his father promised to keep him in line, it would be enough to get him released until the trial. Except while he was at home, his father and brother would be playing on his guilt complex to persuade him to change his plea. *Fuck that.*

Naughton, his PO, had been to see him wanting to know what was behind Jason's attack. *What did you do?* Naughton had asked. *I just fucking lay there and got hit.* His PO's attitude made Caspian quietly seethe. Jason had kept his mouth shut and so did Caspian.

He passed the time watching the TV. There'd been a plot to set off bombs at the Olympics and a load of people had been arrested. Hopefully all of them. Various countries were threatening to pull out which seemed stupid to Caspian. The plot had been discovered so everyone was safe now, weren't they?

He didn't go back to Mako wing. He was put where he should have been placed at the start, Dolphin wing for those on remand aged between sixteen and eighteen. What idiot thought that sounded a good name? And a dolphin wasn't a fucking fish! The atmosphere wasn't much different. A load of slightly younger testosterone-filled boys who were either trying to big themselves up into men or disappear into the woodwork like worms.

Caspian was given a cell to himself, which—on thinking about it—had been worth getting beaten up for. But there was another bed in there, so he might not be alone for long. There was also a shower in the corner and a TV too, though probably not for long either because Caspian hadn't yet reached the silver behaviour status to warrant his own TV. Fucking unfair that getting attacked kept him off the privilege ladder. He'd thought everyone had a TV, but Jason was a gold inmate—back to lead status now, Caspian assumed, or whatever came below bronze.

Served him the fuck right.

After he'd sorted his stuff that had been brought over from Mako, he wandered into the communal area with its screwed down chairs and tables. He needed to get a feel for how things worked in the wing, who to avoid, who thought they were in charge, where he should and shouldn't sit or stand. Then he looked up and saw Zed.

Not that he believed it. His eyes playing tricks, his brain turning whoever was coming out of that cell into— Well, not Zed, just someone who looked a lot like him.

But then the guy turned and Caspian saw those eyes and the room began to spin faster and faster. He couldn't even think about taking a step because a gaping chasm loomed in front of him. He opened his mouth to say something before the mirage slipped away, but nothing came out, no words, no cry, no name, no moan, nothing.

Not real. I'm a fool. How can this be Zed? Why would he be in here?

Caspian's throat filled with sand and it hurt to swallow. The spell broke and he went back to his cell before he burst into tears and ruined his street cred as the hard guy with a bruised face and throat, and a cut stomach who'd survived a Mako attack. As he slumped on his bed, a figure appeared at the door.

"It *is* you," Zed gasped.

Caspian straightened. The voice was the same. The smile the same. It was impossible, but Zed was here. Everything in Caspian's world had changed, but Zed was the same. Caspian pushed to his feet. Zed hadn't moved from the door. He looked as shocked as Caspian felt. Caspian was desperate to touch him, prove to his sceptical brain that Zed was real. Only feet away and it felt like miles. But unless Caspian touched him, he couldn't know for sure.

Zed took one step.

"The door," Caspian choked out. This moment had to be theirs. Only theirs.

Zed reached back and closed the door.

It was Zed who walked towards him, Zed who touched him, reached out for Caspian's hand and brought it to his mouth. He kissed the tip of each finger, then his palm, before he pressed his mouth to the pulse on Caspian's wrist. Then he took Caspian's other hand and did the same. And he brought Caspian back, kiss by kiss. Zed looked at him as if he were the only boy in the world, the only thing that mattered to him and Caspian's battered heart began to heal.

He wrapped his arms around Zed and Zed pressed his lips against the bruise on his cheek, kissed the line of his chin, the dip in his throat before he came back to his mouth. Everywhere he touched with his lips was like an electric jolt bringing Caspian back to life, keeping him alive. His cock throbbed, tenting his sweat pants. His heart banged so hard against his ribs, his chest hurt.

When their lips finally met and stayed together, Caspian was almost overwhelmed with emotion. Zed was so gentle. It was as if they were the only two people who existed. The only two people who had ever kissed, who had ever felt this pull, this desperate yearning. Caspian wanted more, wanted to strip them both of their clothes so they could lie skin to skin and melt into each other, become each other, join forever.

But the kiss ended, because all kisses do, and the questions poured out.

"What the hell are you doing here?" Caspian asked at the same time as Zed.

"You didn't know I was in here?" Caspian had been sure Zed must have known, done something stupid to get sent here and…

"I had no idea. I thought you were still in Lower Barton."

Caspian pulled him down to sit next to him on the bed. "Tell me everything. Why are you in here?"

"Why are you?"

"You go first."

Zed shifted in discomfort. "You have to promise never to breathe a word of this. Ever. I shouldn't tell you. I'm not supposed to tell anyone. Plus, I'm not sure you'll believe me."

"Tell me." Caspian pressed against him, trapping their entwined fingers between their thighs.

Zed chewed his lip. "I waited until the last train that day and you didn't come."

Caspian groaned. "I was in an accident. I ended up in hospital."

"Oh fuck. Fuck, fuck, fuck. I called you. Your father answered but he didn't tell me that. He said I wasn't your friend anymore, not to call again. I wasn't just going to accept that but when I tried your number later, it was out of service."

"He cancelled my phone. He didn't tell me you called." *The complete and utter bastard.* "So you got on the train?"

Zed's face was bleak. "I couldn't go home. I told you I'd stolen my father's money and his phone. He'd have killed me. It was late when I reached St Pancras. I called Tamaz. He sent a friend of his to get me. I hadn't asked him to. Now I'm sort of torn on whether I should be glad or not that Fahid came." He took a deep breath.

"I ended up in Islington in Fahid's house and I discovered he'd organised a group of extremists to blow themselves up at the Olympics. It was supposed to happen tomorrow at the 100 metre finals."

Caspian gasped. "Fucking hell."

"I told the authorities and two days ago they arrested everyone except for Fahid who managed to escape. Because Fahid might guess it was me who betrayed them if I'm not in custody, they put me in here. It won't be for long."

That should have made Caspian happy, but it broke his heart all over again.

"Now you," Zed said. "What are you doing in here? And what happened to your face and your neck?"

"You know you said I never had to tell anyone what you said, well the same applies to what I'm going to tell you. But there's a difference. If I spoke out about what you did, I'd put you in danger and I'd never do that. If you revealed my secret, it would destroy my family, but it would probably help me."

Zed stared at him and Caspian took a deep breath. "The thing is, you'll want to tell someone. You're going to think it's not fair, that it shouldn't have happened to me and you're right, but it's done now. You have to promise you won't breathe a word to anyone. Promise no matter what happens in the future, this stays a secret between us."

"I promise. I swear."

Caspian told Zed what had happened and watched Zed's face pale in shock.

"I don't know who to be angrier with," Zed said. "Lachlan or your father. What fucking shits!"

"Yeah," Caspian muttered. "The family name would be ruined if Lachlan fucked up but not if I did. So little was expected of me that having a conviction for causing death by dangerous driving wouldn't wreck my life because I was never going to amount to anything."

153

Zed opened his mouth, then closed it again, but he reached for Caspian's other hand where it lay clenched on his thigh and held it tight.

"I could have gone home to wait for the trial. It could take a year to come to court, but I didn't want to go home. I can't bear to look at any of them. I'd rather get beaten up in here." He gave a short laugh.

Tears rolled down Zed's face and he gulped back sobs. "Oh fuck, Caspian. How can they do this to you?"

"It's done. What proof do I have that I wasn't driving? My father gave Lachlan an alibi. My sorry excuse for a brother apparently put my hands on the wheel and the door handle before he went home so if the police checked, they'd find my fingerprints. To use prison lingo—they stitched me up."

"Oh shit. The fucking bastards."

"The one thing they want me to do is plead guilty. I'd get a lesser sentence and the girls' parents wouldn't have to go to court and hear distressing evidence. I get all that, but I won't plead guilty. I'm not going to speak at all at the trial." He gave a heavy sigh. "I know I'll get found guilty. That's a foregone conclusion. But I'm not going to say I was driving when I wasn't."

"I didn't know you could drive."

"I passed my test when I was at school. I thought when the GCSE results came out, and my father sat there rolling his eyes, I could tell him I passed my driving test at the first attempt and at least that would be something to impress him. Lachlan took his test three times. But I even shot myself in the foot with that because if I hadn't passed my test, I might get a lesser sentence, which doesn't seem right to me."

"How long are you talking about?" Zed's eyes were wide.

"The lawyer seems to think I might just get a slap on the wrist. A ban and a fine. Community service. But it could easily be a prison sentence. Maybe this time on remand will help. But three girls died. Their families deserve more than me getting told not to do it again and having to tidy some old person's garden for a few months."

"They do deserve more but not from you. Your brother was responsible. He should accept the blame."

"It was partly my fault. If I hadn't run from the house, Lachlan wouldn't have come after me."

"It was not your fault," Zed spoke through gritted teeth. "Are you listening to me? Not even partly your fault. It's entirely your brother's.

154

If he wasn't fit to drive, he shouldn't have driven. He should stand up and take the blame. What the fuck is he thinking? How can your father let this happen? I thought my father was a bastard, but this…? This is fucking awful."

"Nothing's going to change. Once I discovered my father had given Lachlan an alibi, that ended any hope the truth would come out." Caspian released a shaky breath. "I'm so happy you're here. Telling you the truth has made me feel as though some of the weight has lifted from my shoulders. I thought I'd lost you forever. I knew you wouldn't come back to the village. I've thought about you all the time. Wondered where you were. If you were okay. If you'd…found someone else."

Zed pulled him down gently so they were lying on the bed. Zed spooned behind him and pressed his mouth to Caspian's ear. "There will never be anyone else for me. Whatever happens, I'll always wait for you."

It was hard for Zed not to cling onto Caspian too tightly. He'd not been able to believe his eyes when he'd seen him. Even battered, he was still beautiful. Zed was furious with Caspian's father and brother. And maybe with his mother too. Did she know what they'd done? Zed wanted to do something to make things right even though he'd promised Caspian, but there was nothing he could do. Appealing to Caspian's father and brother would get him nowhere and even if Zed broke his promise and told the police, maybe told Jackson, it could be hard to prove Caspian wasn't driving.

Lachlan hadn't been injured so didn't that imply the driver's side of the car had been less damaged? How severe had Caspian's injuries been? But if Caspian had been found in the driver's seat, then why look for anyone else? If Zed talked, he'd destroy what little love remained between Caspian and his family. Not only that, he'd be betraying Caspian's trust.

It wasn't Zed's choice to make. *That* was the truth, whether Zed liked it or not, and he didn't like it.

"Think they'll let me move in here with you?" Zed asked.

"We can ask."

"And not take no for an answer."

Caspian chuckled. "Good luck with that. Who's your PO?"

"Naughton."

"Mine too. He's a prick."

Zed wanted to go and ask right then but he equally didn't want to move away from Caspian.

"Does Naughton know you're not in here for long?" Caspian whispered.

"No. They told me only the governor knows."

"Who's *they*?"

"MI5."

Caspian rolled over, stared at him, then smiled. "Zed Bond."

"Bond was MI6."

"Were you scared?"

"Terrified. But you're the brave one, not me." Zed stroked Caspian's face and ran his finger over his lips. "I was the boy who never swore, always said please and thank you. I wanted to be the type who skipped school to go to the seaside, the boy didn't always do his homework, took risks, drew crop circles. A boy who recognised what he really was, someone who could admit to being gay. You showed me I had that boy inside me. The best thing that ever happened to me in my whole life was finding you up that tree. The. Best. Thing."

Zed closed the gap between them and brushed his lips against Caspian's, breathing in Caspian's expelled air. "You made me feel as though I'd never truly been alive. You made me believe I could escape. I won't let you go. Ever." He winced. "I don't mean that in a freaky way."

Caspian closed his eyes. "I'm imagining this. I have to be."

Zed slipped his hand between them, fondled Caspian's cock through his clothing and Caspian juddered against him. He kissed his way down Caspian's neck into the hollow of his shoulder, ran his teeth along his collarbone and smiled as Caspian's breathing turned ragged.

"Oh God," Caspian gasped.

"No, just me," said a voice.

They sprang apart and turned to see their PO standing at the door. Caspian pushed to his feet. "You're supposed to knock."

Zed stood at his side.

"Sexual activity between prisoners is not allowed."

Caspian glared. "Why is there a condom policy then?"

"In case you're at risk of catching an STI. Wouldn't want you to be passing on any nasty diseases." Naughton looked from Caspian to

156

Zed. "You were both asked if you were homosexual. You both said no."

Caspian edged closer to Zed so their hips bumped. He clutched Zed's fingers out of sight of their PO.

"It's difficult, if not impossible, for prison staff to be sure whether a relationship between inmates is consensual or not."

Zed squeezed his fingers. Maybe warning him to keep quiet.

"An inmate observed as being openly affectionate towards another inmate can be given a warning under the IEP scheme. Incentives and Earned Privileges, in case it's slipped your mind."

"We're in my pad. We weren't being openly affectionate," Caspian said.

"I'll be the judge of that," Naughton snapped.

Shit.

"You work fast," Naughton said to Caspian. "You only moved in here this morning." He narrowed his eyes. "Do you two know one another? Because prisoners in a relationship can't share a cell."

"No," Caspian said quickly.

"No." Zed shook his head. "We're not in a relationship. So we'd like to share a cell. Can I move in here, please?"

Naughton smiled. Caspian was sure he was going to say *no*, but Naughton nodded. "Contrary to what you lot might think, I'm not anti-gay. What you get up to at night when the door is locked is up to you but for your own safety, you don't take this outside the cell. Understand?"

"Yes." Caspian nodded.

"And if you need to talk to someone in Healthcare about the condom policy, you ask me."

"Can—?" Caspian said.

"Yes. I'll put a slip in. Move your stuff over here."

That afternoon, after Zed had moved his things, a prison officer came to tell him he had a visitor. Jackson. Zed was given a yellow top with *Woodbury Young Offender Institution* on the back and led to the visiting room. Jackson sat at a table near a vending machine and pushed to his feet when Zed came in.

"How are you doing?" Jackson asked.

"Okay."

157

"You want something from the machine? A drink, crisps, chocolate?"

"Please. Anything. Thanks."

Jackson came back to the table with a whole load of stuff. Zed wanted to share it with Caspian so he only opened the water.

"Have you caught Fahid yet?" Yesterday, he'd have wanted the answer to be yes, now he sort of didn't.

"No. We suspect he's left the country, but we need to be sure."

Zed nodded. "Better to be sure."

"Parwez has done a lot of talking, unlike the others. He confirmed everything you told us and that you weren't involved."

"You thought I was part of it?" Zed clenched his fists.

"No, I didn't think you were part of it, but others weren't so sure."

Zed sagged.

"You're a good kid, Zed. You spoke out when many would have kept quiet. You risked your own safety and you saved lives. You did a brave thing."

"Right."

"Parwez's confession has saved you needing to give evidence."

"Give evidence? You mean I'd have had to go to court? Stand there in front of them?" His heart banged against his ribs.

"Your identity will always be protected. If necessary, we'd relocate you, get you a new name."

"Okay." It wasn't okay but Zed had known once he'd made the call that he was in danger.

"How are you coping with being in here? You're not desperate to get out?"

"It's all right."

There was something about the way Jackson was looking at him that made Zed think a little harder. Could he have fixed this? He knew Zed's full name. Not difficult to find out where he'd lived in Kent. Zed had told him the date he'd run away and arrived in London. Zed hadn't mentioned Caspian's name but how hard would it have been to find out the rest? Zed running on the same day that three girls had been killed in a nearby village? How much did Jackson know?

There were lots of places Zed could have been sent. A safe house with a family. A secure children's home. A different Young Offender Institution. But he'd ended up here.

158

For a long moment he was torn. He wanted to tell Jackson that Caspian had been set up but he'd promised not to tell anyone. If he did tell the truth, Caspian's family would implode and maybe Zed would never be forgiven. He wouldn't tell.

"You arranged it, didn't you?" Zed looked straight at him.

"Arranged what?"

But the smile told Zed he was right.

"Thank you."

Jackson nodded. "You're very quick." He smiled. "You have another visitor waiting. I was told he was coming to see you and I needed to speak to you first."

Zed froze. "I won't see my father."

"No, not your father. Your brother."

"You haven't arrested him?"

"No."

There was something in the way Jackson said *no* that put Zed on edge. Not the definite *no* he'd have liked to hear.

"I want you to speak to him, see what he knows," Jackson said quietly.

"And then tell you."

"I'd like to record the conversation."

Zed's exhalation was shaky.

"You think he's done nothing wrong, so what do you have to worry about?" Jackson asked.

Goose bumps shot down Zed's arms.

"We can't use anything later in court that he might say to you now. It's just to…tie up loose ends."

"Has he already been questioned?"

"Yes."

"What did he say?"

"That he had no idea what Fahid was planning, that he had no idea if you knew."

Really? "Record it then."

Jackson took a small grey machine out of his pocket and slid it across the table under his hand. "Make sure you're not seen. Tape it under the table by your thigh."

Zed checked they were unobserved before he did what Jackson had asked.

159

"I'll come back after he's left. I'll return these snacks then too. Not a good idea to let him wonder if you've had another visitor."

Zed couldn't believe Tamaz would have known about the plot and not done anything. But for his brother to say he had no idea if Zed knew… Something about that pissed him off.

The door opened and Tamaz came in with a prison officer. Zed pushed to his feet and his brother rushed over. The officer stayed by the door.

"Zed!" Tamaz threw his arms around him, then pushed him back and held him by the shoulders to look at him. "Are you okay?"

"Yeah." Zed wriggled free and dropped back into his seat.

Tamaz sat opposite. "What happened?"

Don't you know? "I was in bed when I heard a loud crash. Two guys burst in with guns and yelled at me to get on the floor. I had no idea what was happening. I was so scared. They were shouting about Fahid. *Where is he? Where's he hiding?* I thought he was asleep in his room but turned out he wasn't in the house. I got taken to a police station and asked a lot of questions and…" He let out a little moan that wasn't entirely put on. He had been scared. He still was.

"Did you ask for a lawyer?"

That was all his brother was bothered about? "No. I didn't ask. I didn't think I needed one, but they appointed a guy." They had, sort of, though he worked for MI5. "I haven't done anything."

"They must think you have or why remand you in custody?"

"An accessory, I think they said."

"Did you tell them anything? What did they ask you?"

"Tamaz! I was scared. I was dragged out of bed in the early hours of the morning and you don't even sound concerned."

"Of course I am. You're not the only one it happened to."

Zed made himself gasp. "You as well? Why?"

"Because I'm a friend of Fahid's."

"Why?"

"What do you mean why?"

Zed was trying to give Tamaz every chance to say he had no idea what Fahid was up to. He didn't want to be the first one of them to mention suicide bombers.

"How did you meet him? Why is he your friend?"

"I knew him from when we lived in Lewisham. He lived there then."

160

"Seven years? That long?"

"He's a good, kind man. Clever. A true Muslim. He went to get you from St Pancras because I was worried. He gave you somewhere to live. He fed you."

And he would have used me as a bomber if he'd thought he could. "So why are the police looking for him? Do you know where he is?"

"I've no idea where he is. The police... They think he's involved in a plot to plant bombs at the Olympics."

Zed put his head in his hands. He'd thought about how he'd react if Tamaz said it first. There was no right or wrong way. Maybe the only way was the truth. But modified. He looked straight at his brother.

"I think he was," Zed whispered.

Tamaz widened his eyes and yet... Zed didn't want to see anything other than disgust.

"He took me with him when he went to see Parwez," Zed said. "You remember Parwez?"

"The moody one."

"Yeah. Well, Parwez was upset about something and... Things that were said made me wonder what they were planning. *Jihad* came up. I was with Parwez when he collected tickets for the Olympics. I suppose I'd started to put two and two together. I didn't say anything to Fahid, but I was going to move out the next day."

"What have you said to the police?"

You're not shocked enough, brother. What are you mixed up in? Zed still didn't want to believe it.

"I don't know anything. I haven't told them anything. But I was living in Fahid's house. They want to talk to him. Sure you don't know where he is? Maybe this is all a mistake? Fahid doesn't have to be involved. Though why would he run if he isn't?"

"Because the police have already decided he's guilty. Just as they have you. But you haven't done anything. They'll have to let you go sooner or later. I'm sorry I asked Fahid to go and get you from the station."

That felt like the truth but Zed suspected Tamaz was hiding something.

"Don't tell Dad where I am," Zed said. "He doesn't know, does he?"

161

"No." Tamaz pushed to his feet. "This'll all get sorted out. Don't worry. When they let you out, come and live with me. We can squeeze you into the house."

"Thank you." *But no.*

Tamaz hugged him and left.

Moments later, Jackson came back in with the vending machine snacks and surreptitiously retrieved the recording.

"Were you listening as well?" Zed asked.

"No. What do you think?"

Zed took a deep breath. "I think you need to watch my brother."

Chapter Fifteen

Zed walked into the cell carrying the snacks Jackson had bought him and put them on the desk. "I was bought treats. We can share."

Caspian got up from the bed. "I got treats too." He took Zed's hand, pulled him over to the locker and opened it. "Three condoms and lube."

"I was hoping for food."

"We...don't have to use them," Caspian said.

"Well...I don't want to catch anything."

Caspian gaped at him, then laughed. "You little..."

"How long until we're locked in?"

"Long enough for us to decide whether we want to use one, two, three or none."

Zed put his hand in his pocket and pulled out three condoms and some lube. "I made a detour on the way back from the visiting room."

Caspian chuckled. "We need to go back to Healthcare right now for more. Think how shocked and impressed Doctor Jones will be."

"Except he told me that if you ask for too many you get sanctioned."

"What does that mean?"

"I guess they might take away the TV."

"Shit. We have to choose between sex and the TV?"

Zed laughed. How good it felt to be able to do that. "He told me that some prisons only give them out one at a time and you have to take a used one back before you get another."

"Ewww. Why?"

"I guess because you can do other things with them."

Caspian frowned. "I suppose. Smuggle drugs. Or maybe fill them with sand or dirt and use them as a weapon. Water balloon fight. Waterproof anything small enough to fit inside your arse. Cut them up and use them as elastic bands."

"Have you been thinking about it?"

Caspian grinned. "Ever since I heard that a guy in South Africa made a bungee cord out of 18,500 condoms and jumped off a 100 foot tower."

"Wow. Did he die?"

"No."

163

"Would you do a bungee jump?"

"Not with a rope made out of condoms, but yeah."

Zed grabbed one of the chocolate bars, sat on the bed and opened it. "I don't know if I could. I'd be thinking of everything that might go wrong. Rope too long, they might forget to tie me on, my eyes might get injured because of the increase in pressure, or I could hurt my neck or my back. What if the cord wrapped round my throat when I jumped? I'd hang myself." He chewed a mouthful of chocolate and moaned. "Oh that's nice. I've missed chocolate."

"When did you last eat it?"

"A couple of days ago."

Caspian rolled his eyes. He picked up a bar and dropped onto the bed next to him.

"I'm a wuss," Zed said. "Sorry. I never got the chance to do anything exciting after my mother died. And not much before, to be honest. *Don't go near the edge, Hari. No roller skates for you. No skateboard.* I've never been on a roller coaster, never climbed a mountain, never surfed, never skied, never even been abroad. I bet you've done all those."

"I'm not as brave as you think. I might have been abroad a lot but we always went to the same place, ate at the same restaurants, skied on the same slopes, swam and surfed off the same beach. You're the brave one. You put up with an abusive father. You risked your life talking to MI5. You saved hundreds of people. Are you still in danger? Was it the MI5 guy who came to see you?"

Zed screwed up the wrapper and lobbed it into the bin. It missed and he got up to put it in before settling back next to Caspian. "Yes, it was Jackson. They've not found Fahid yet. My brother came to see me too. Jackson wanted to record him talking to me."

Caspian sat up from his slouched position. "Oh fucking hell."

"I said yes. I was almost positive Tamaz would have had nothing to do with it and he didn't say anything to contradict that."

"I heard the word *almost* and I sense a *but*."

Zed leaned against the wall and pulled his feet up onto the bed. "Yeah, there's a *but*. The truth is, I'm just not sure about him and it kills something inside me to admit that. He wasn't shocked enough or angry enough on my behalf. He didn't ask to speak to my lawyer or rail against the injustice of me being in here. He's definitely become more devout over the last few years. We used to joke about how strict our father was, and Tamaz stopped doing that. I don't know anything for sure. He asked me if I wanted to go and stay with him when I get out. But I don't. I didn't tell him that."

Caspian took his hand. "When I get out, we can live together."

Zed smiled and then his smile faded. "I'm going to be out sooner than you."

"When I get out, we can live together," Caspian repeated.

"Yes. That would be great."

"Okay. That's sorted. Now let's make a list of everything we want to do."

"I bet you already have a list," Zed said.

Caspian grinned. "Maybe. Do you?"

"Yep. Have my own piano. Buy a cello. Play the guitar. Learn to surf. See the northern lights. Stay in an ice hotel. Hike to the top of Kilimanjaro and look at the stars. Fly into space. Bike down a volcano in Hawaii."

"I want to do a parachute jump, visit a nudist beach and go skinny dipping, get a tattoo and a piercing, go scuba diving with sharks, invent something brilliant, invent something else brilliant. Wear eyeliner. See you in eyeliner. Get a blowjob. Give a blowjob. Get rimmed. Go rimming. Lose my virginity. And do all of those with my best friend."

Zed pouted. "Not with me?"

"Ha ha."

A lump grew in Zed's throat. "Er...no sharks."

"Okay. Forget the sharks."

"Not sure about the parachute jump."

Caspian sighed. "Okay, forget that as well. The rest?"

"Where are you thinking of getting pierced? Ear?"

"No."

"Nose? Please don't."

"Not my nose."

Zed frowned. "Lip?"

"No."

"Tongue?"

Caspian shook his head.

"Eyebrow?"

"No."

"I'm running out of body parts. Oh nipple?""

"My cock."

165

"Oh fuck." Zed grimaced. "Really?"

"Maybe." Caspian put his mouth to Zed's ear. "I can't wait to be locked up tonight. Words I never thought I'd say."

They talked and talked, shared dreams, made plans. They tried to keep their hands off each other in case a prison officer looked into the cell, and it turned into a game.

"You touched me," Zed said in mock-horror.

"No, you touched me."

"You touched me like this." Zed brushed his fingers over Caspian's hand.

"More like this." Caspian did it back.

They laughed and teased and joked and Zed's heart lightened to the point he felt he'd float. They were still in a mess, their immediate futures uncertain, but there was hope and they both clung to that. They emerged from the cell to eat dinner and collect their breakfast, then watched the Olympics for a while with the others in their wing, but they were both fidgeting, high on anticipation, fizzing with energy, both tugging down T-shirts to hide hard-ons. That Caspian was as nervous as him reassured Zed because he didn't want to be the timid one. Having time to think about what they were going to do was good and bad.

If Zed was being honest with himself, he wasn't sure he wanted to lose his virginity in a prison cell. He didn't want to be worried about making a noise, about being disturbed. There were plenty of other things they could do they hadn't tried. And yet, he wanted Caspian with all his heart.

"Changed your mind?" Caspian whispered as the lock-up bell sounded and they returned to the cell.

"No."

Caspian brushed his hand against Zed's.

The clank of doors closing made Zed jump. Locks engaged. Almost immediately the banging and calling started. It had freaked Zed out the first night he'd been in there. It still felt threatening. His chest tightened and he leaned against the wall by the door. "Why do they do that?"

Caspian stood on the other side of the cell next to the window. "For attention. To ask for help—except help doesn't always come in time. To aggravate the prison officers. And I guess they do it just because they can. Too many guys in here are bullies and like taunting those weaker than them. It's all about power. Some of them think if they make themselves sound big, they won't get picked on. But if you keep your head down and make yourself as small as you can, you might still get picked on. In the end you can't win, whatever you do."

"You never told me how your face and neck got bruised."

"My former cellmate was ordered to teach me a lesson after I got mouthy about getting cigarettes for an older guy. He did this too."

Caspian lifted his T-shirt to reveal stitches at one end of a scar.

"What the hell?"

"I had to have my spleen taken out after the accident. My cellmate managed to cut me in the same place. I've forgotten what the doctor called it but I'll heal. I'm sort of grateful it happened because as a result, I was put in here rather than going back to Mako wing."

"He could have killed you."

Caspian didn't react to that. "You know you can watch TV until two in the morning? I wasn't allowed to do that home." Caspian tsked. "No porn channel though. There's only crap or repeats on at that time of night."

You're nervous. Maybe more nervous than me. "What's going through your head apart from what's on TV?" Zed asked.

"You don't want to know."

"Yeah I do."

"If I can make it all the way over to you, nine difficult steps, without stumbling? If I can touch you when you're naked without coming? If my heart could beat any faster without exploding? What if I faint? Will you give me the kiss of life? Is it possible to feel any hotter without melting? Will my hands do what I tell them? Do you feel all of this too? Any of this? Will my fucking mouth stop babbling anytime soon?"

Zed smiled. He walked across to Caspian and Caspian gave a little grin before spinning Zed round to face the wall. When Caspian pressed up against his back, Zed's cock sprang the rest of the way to full attention.

"Your nine steps saved me completing the cell marathon, and hey, guess what? I managed not to come in my clothes." Caspian let out a shaky breath. "Oh fuck, I want this to be perfect. I don't want to disappoint you. I don't know if I'm…"

167

"If you're ready?" Zed whispered and squirmed around to face him. "I don't know either. We're going to play, that's all. Whatever we do, we both want or we don't do it. Okay? I hadn't figured my first time would be in a cell, so…"

"It'd be something to tell the kids."

Zed laughed out loud. Then Caspian leaned in, and pressed his mouth into Zed's smile, his hard cock rubbing against Zed's hip as they rocked their bodies together. *Oh fuck, coming in his jeans seemed more and more likely.*

This wasn't a sweet kiss. This was a desperate invasion. This was licking, nipping, sucking, pulling at lips, teasing, eating at each other while Caspian's hands roamed everywhere. Fingers wandered up and down Zed's spine and across his shoulder blades, exploring the sharpness of his bones under his T-shirt, then back and forth over his stomach and chest, running along his ribs, sliding up his pecs, brushing his nipples, twisting, pinching—*ouch, oh God, GOD*—and down the back of his jeans onto the cheeks of his arse and squeezing hard before diving into the crease, which made Zed lurch violently against him.

Zed's breathing was all over the place, as if the inbuilt mechanism in his body had developed a temporary—hopefully—fault.

"Can't breathe," Caspian gasped.

They rested their foreheads together, inhaling and exhaling into each other's faces.

"We contract and relax our respiratory muscles about thirty thousand times a day," Zed said panting.

"Unless you're sexed up, then it's a lot more."

Zed smiled. "A billion times for a lifespan of ninety years."

"Two billion if I'm doing this with you."

The way Zed felt about Caspian scared him because it was beyond understanding, reason or comprehension. Fantasy had become reality. But he was scared of hurting him. He had stitches. This wasn't the right time. And yet they kissed their way out of their T-shirts, barely breaking apart. If lips weren't together, then hands were. Caspian licked his way from Zed's mouth to his nipple and a bolt of sensation shot to Zed's cock. He slammed his hand over his crotch and shocked his balls into painful submission.

Trainers were toed off. Socks somehow discarded, and they kissed their way to another world where there were no bars at the window, no doors and no locks. The backing track of prison, the shouts, insults and sobs, the singing of nursery rhymes over and over, the slamming of doors, the authoritative voices of prison officers with their jangling keys telling them to pipe down—it all faded away.

Caspian unfastened the button of Zed's jeans, eased down the zip and Zed groaned with relief. He tugged down Caspian's tracksuit bottoms until they pooled at his feet. Their cocks tented their underwear and they reached out at the same time to wrap their hand around each other's length.

"Hey," Caspian whispered. "I'm thinking we should come at least three times before we try to do anything more than touch each other."

Zed laughed. Above Caspian's black Y-fronts dark hair swept up to his navel, like a swirl of the magnetised iron filings they played with in physics. The scar under his left rib cage made Zed swallow hard.

"I won't break," Caspian said.

God, you're already broken.

Zed brushed his fingers over Caspian's belly, squeezed his erection and was rewarded by a long groan.

"Naked. Now," Caspian gasped.

As Caspian yanked off his underwear, Zed kicked off his jeans and pushed his boxers down his legs. Caspian took his hand, pulled him to the bed and sat down, tugging Zed to sit on his lap so his knees were either side of Caspian's thighs. Zed arched toward him, then their chests were together, and so were their cocks and mouths and—*oh fuck.*

Zed was sprinting toward release but he wanted Caspian to come at the same time. As he slid a hand between their bodies, Caspian did the same and with fingers slick with precum wrapped around their dicks, they squeezed them together until their kissing and rutting turned frenzied. Within seconds they were coming, gulping into each other's mouths as cum spurted between them.

They swallowed each other's shuddering moans as they fell back from the high, and Caspian slid down to lie on his back, dragging Zed with him. When Zed worried Caspian couldn't breathe under the weight of him, he rolled onto his back at Caspian's side, his chest heaving.

Their fingers threaded together, bellies sticky and hearts happy, they fell into an exhausted sleep.

Caspian woke first and nudged Zed awake. "Shower." He breathed the word into Zed's ear.

"Are we allowed?" Zed asked.

"I don't give a fuck." He pulled Zed to his feet and into the small cubicle near the door where there was barely enough room for one let alone two.

They'd hardly washed each other clean before a guard banged on the door. "No showers at this time of night," he shouted through the slot.

"How are—"

Zed slapped his hand over Caspian's mouth mid-yell and switched off the shower. The footsteps moved on past their pad and Zed took his hand away.

"What were you going to say?" Zed asked.

"How are we supposed to clean off our spunk?"

Zed stifled a laugh. "Lick it off?"

Caspian whined. "You could have told me that before."

When Zed started to step out of the shower, Caspian pulled him back.

"What?" Zed asked.

"I want to do something."

"What?"

"I think you'll like it."

"What? Oh fuck. I'm stuck on repeat. What, what, whaaaat."

Caspian had dropped to his knees and when he looked up at him, Zed gulped. One lick from Caspian's hot, wet tongue along the length of Zed's cock, which had been frisky from the moment he'd woken, and Zed turned to iron.

"Where did you learn to do that?" Zed whispered.

"What?" Caspian asked and sniggered.

"Send me hard with one lick."

Zed had managed to lick his own cock a couple of times when he'd been smaller and more flexible but—*Oh hell, this feels so good.*

One shove from Caspian and his back hit the wall. Caspian's fingers encircled the base of Zed's dick and Zed spread his hands flat on the tiles.

"Tell me if I do something wrong," Caspian whispered.

"How would I know? How could any of this be wrong? Unless you bite. Don't bite."

When Caspian tentatively wrapped his lips around the crest of his cock, Zed clenched his fists, unclenched them, then clenched them

170

again before he grabbed Caspian's hair. Zed couldn't help bucking, wanting Caspian to take more and when Caspian widened his mouth and let him drive into him, Zed's knees shook. He could feel Caspian's tongue darting around the head of his cock, sliding around the ridge, pushing into the slit—*Jesus,* then he sucked hard before pulling away to let his cheek rest against Zed's thigh as he got his breath back.

"You okay?" Caspian panted.

"What? Are you kidding? Your mouth, my cock, no biting—how could it not be okay?"

Then Caspian's mouth was back around him, sucking hard, sucking slow, sucking fast and every time Caspian glanced up at him, Zed's heart physically hurt. Those dark eyes, that cheeky, crooked smile plus the sight of his cock disappearing into Caspian's mouth made Zed shake like a jelly. *Thank fuck for the wall because my knees... My cock.*

Think of something unsexy. Fast.

Terminal velocity.

Zed almost laughed. He was *at* terminal velocity. Falling faster and faster. Except no, that wasn't right. He was falling at a constant rate which was... *Oh, my balls.* Caspian was licking them and his fingers were behind them stroking that strip of skin in front of his arsehole.

"You know rimming was on my list... Can I?"

"Oh fuck." Zed twisted around in the small space to face the wall and the next moment, Caspian's face was up against his backside, kissing him, licking, nipping and Zed let out a strangled sound that definitely wasn't human. *Don't come. Don't come. Please!* When Caspian slid his tongue between the cheeks of his arse, Zed barely managed to get a hand to his balls in time, to push down, delay the inevitable. Try to delay it. Not so difficult when he was in charge of making himself come but impossible when he wasn't.

Caspian's tongue. Every stop it made travelling down the seam of his backside had Zed quivering and whimpering. Each push against his hole forced him to grit his teeth to stop himself moaning. Caspian was elbowing his way between his legs to do what? And—*oh fuck, inside me. His tongue is inside me!* It felt like the best thing ever. Hot and wet. Long sweeps. Short jabs.

Zed wanted this to last a lifetime.

171

Yet couldn't cope with another second of it. Five seconds of it. *Oh Christ*. He came all over his fingers. Short, hard spurts that made his gut clench and his heart ache with joy that it had happened and annoyance it hadn't lasted longer. *He* hadn't lasted longer.

He turned the shower back on, tugged Caspian to his feet and kissed him. Caspian turned the shower off.

"You want them to split us up?" he whispered.

No, but it was going to happen anyway.

They fell asleep tangled in each other's arms.

They woke tangled in each other's arms.

Inside the cell they were inseparable, one part of them always remaining in contact with the other. Caspian kept trying to push back the knowledge that Zed was going to leave soon and he wasn't. They talked about the future, but maybe Zed sensed Caspian's heart wasn't in it because Zed always let him change the subject. Yet that hurt.

He's going to leave me.

Maybe they were both in their own ways getting ready to be parted. Not that it showed in what they did to each other. Caspian went hard thinking about it. They did everything except fuck. It was as if there was an unspoken agreement they wouldn't go that far, that this wasn't the right place. The condoms stayed in the locker.

It's not fair for me to take that first time from you.

How long do we have?

Caspian was waiting for the day that Jackson came again because he knew that marked the end. Perhaps of everything. Because once Zed had started a new life, he wouldn't need him anymore. Not a guy who'd been in prison. Caspian wasn't even sure he could leave the country once he had a criminal record. He'd google it except he wasn't allowed to go online.

Their kisses became more desperate. They came in each other's hands and mouths as often as they could. It was as if they were trying to fit a lifetime into a few weeks.

I am going to lose him.

At night, long after Zed had fallen asleep in his arms, Caspian lay awake committing every inch of his body to memory. He did it time after time. Zed had told him he felt as if he was being examined like a stone, as if Caspian was finding the direction of the grain, looking for flaws. *There are no flaws.*

172

Caspian made up poems, traced them and his name onto Zed's skin with his tongue. Wrote over his back. Over the faint scars left by his father's beatings. Over his heart. Wanting him to remember, knowing he had to let him go.

Then one day, even before the call came for Zed to go to the visitor's room, Caspian began to push him away. *Not let him go,* make *him go.*

"It's been fun."

"This has been great."

"You're too good for me."

"You can be anything you want to be."

"I'll hold you back."

"You have a future. I don't."

"You have to go and be happy."

"Forget me."

Those were the two words that choked him. The two words that gave him away because his voice broke when he said them.

Zed pulled him into his arms. "Shut up. I know what you're doing. Don't. Don't tell yourself or me that it's for my own good. Without you my future is nothing. I will never desert you. Don't think that I will. This is our story. We can make it whatever we want it to be."

And I can make it what it needs to be.

Zed went to see his visitor and when he walked back into the cell Caspian knew their time was up.

"When?" he choked out.

"Tomorrow."

Caspian nodded and bit his lip to hold back his sob.

"Jackson has found a couple with no kids to take me."

"That's great."

"The moment you get out," Zed said, "we'll make a life together."

How can I let you walk away from your future? He forced a smile to his face.

"I'll come and see you in here," Zed told him.

"Until you're eighteen you have to be accompanied on visits."

"Oh. But I could get someone to bring me."

173

"I don't want you to come. I think we should stop this now. There's no point waiting for me. I suspect I'll be spending years inside. I don't want you to wait. Promise me you won't."

He hated the look of disappointment on Zed's face, but he wasn't going to change his mind. Though Zed didn't promise and that kept Caspian's spark of hope still burning.

Almost as if their bodies knew what was coming, they slept unentangled for the first time in two weeks. Caspian slipped into the other bed and lay watching Zed sleep knowing this was the end.

Their last kiss was so chaste and sad that Caspian's anger over what his brother and father had done bubbled into hatred. Zed walked out and Caspian slumped onto the bed.

Fifteen minutes later Naughton came in and handed him an envelope. "GCSE results."

Caspian sat up and opened it.

Cs in physics and Design and Technology. Ds and Es for the rest. He screwed up the paper and threw it at the bin. Missed. He was useless.

Chapter Sixteen

Zed hated leaving Caspian in prison, hated the way they'd parted. He'd expected to wake next to him that last morning but when he'd opened his eyes and Caspian lay on the other bed, he'd known what was going to happen. Zed wasn't going to give up on him.

Jackson collected him in person from Woodbury, told him Fahid had left the country. Zed would have preferred hearing they had him in custody. He walked with Jackson to his car, a black Honda. The relief in being free was spoiled because he'd had to leave Caspian behind.

"So how was it?" Jackson asked as he set off. "Glad to be out?"

"Yes." *And no. What about Tamaz?* "So Fahid is definitely out of the country?" Zed felt bad that he needed Jackson to say it twice, but he did. He also wanted Jackson to volunteer information about Tamaz.

"He took a flight to Pakistan. We have him on CCTV using a different passport at Heathrow."

"Okay." Zed took a deep breath. "What about my brother? He wasn't involved, right?

"No."

Zed didn't like the way Jackson had said no because it sounded a little too much like *he might be.*

"How's your friend?"

Zed wasn't going to answer that. He didn't want to talk about Caspian with Jackson. There was too much risk of him blurting out the truth. "Where am I going now?"

"Greenwich."

"That's where I'm going to live?"

"Yes. I'll let Jonas explain everything. Jonas Mallinson. It's his house."

"You know my brother asked me to go and live with him."

"Do you want to?"

"No. But he's going to want to know why I don't."

"We'll come up with a plausible story. Tell you what, why don't you try to think of one?"

"Is this a test?"

Jackson laughed. "I have a feeling you'd ace any test we gave to an eighteen-year-old. See what you can come up with."

Zed thought about it. "I don't want to be a burden to my brother who's in the middle of his degree course. He can't afford to look after me and it might make his relationship with our father difficult. I can't go home and Tamaz will understand why not. The local authority would take me into care for the next couple of years enabling me to stay on at school and do A levels, but I was lucky there was a family who offered me a place to live close to a good school."

He glanced at Jackson.

"Not bad. There is a slight issue however."

"The school's not good?"

"I think you'll love the school."

Zed's shoulders slumped. "My father."

"Yes."

"What has he said?"

"He wants you home. He claims he's always acted in your best interests and that things have been difficult between you since your mother died, but he feels you can rebuild your relationship."

Zed wrapped his arms around himself. "No, that won't happen."

"He could decide to go to court to try and get you back."

"He…" Zed took a deep breath. "I think he's bluffing. He doesn't want me. He just wants to look as though he does. I won't go back. I'm sixteen. He can't make me do anything. Court's not an option."

"What did he do?" Jackson asked in a quiet voice. "You wouldn't tell me before. Will you now? Should we be thinking of involving the police?"

"He beat me. He kept a crop on top of the door and sometimes he used that. Other times it was his belt, his fists and feet."

"Because you're gay?"

"He doesn't know that. He beat me for a lot of stuff but not because I'm gay."

"For what then?"

"Not eating the food in front of me even though it would make me throw up and then I'd get beaten anyway. He hit me for being disrespectful. Islam commands that a child shows kindness, respect and humility to parents on a daily basis. No matter how hard I tried, I was never going to be the son he wanted. He hit me for not getting better marks. Not cleaning well enough. Forgetting to polish his shoes."

"Didn't your teachers notice your bruises?"

"Not often. He was careful to hit me where it couldn't be seen. Usually my back or backside. When he got really angry, he forgot and hit my face. Sometimes I was asked what happened, and I always lied.

176

He broke my arm a couple of years ago and didn't even take me to hospital. Caspian told someone and then the police came and I had to lie and say some boys attacked me. I don't know why my father would want me back. I don't know why he hates me so much."

It was as if a dam had burst. Zed couldn't stop talking. "He won't let me play an instrument or study music because it's *haram*. I could only do it at school without him knowing. I couldn't choose the A levels I wanted. He chose them for me. He never gave me pocket money. I had to take a few coins from wherever I found them around the house. I rarely had new clothes, just Tamaz's cast-offs. I wasn't allowed to read fiction. He found me reading one of Caspian's books and he ripped it to pieces. Things were better once he had a girlfriend because he paid me less attention, but life was still shit." He sucked in a breath. "Sorry."

"I'm the one who's sorry. Okay. We'll tackle a court case if it comes to it, but you're right. He can't make you go back and he won't want you telling a judge why. Is there anything from your home that you want?"

"The only things I wanted were in the bag at Fahid's place."

"They're now in Greenwich."

"Thank you. Tamaz said he'd send for my National Insurance Number. I don't know if he did or if he just told me he was going to."

"I'll check."

Jackson turned right off Trafalgar Road and drove up the side of Greenwich Park. Just before they reached a small traffic island, he swung left through open black gates, the iron staves topped by golden *fleur-de-lis*.

Zed gasped when he saw the house. "Here? It's huge."

"They don't live in all of it. It's divided up into four three-story blocks. They have the largest area though."

Zed's heart started to pound. What if he didn't like them? What if they didn't like him? How many were there of *them?* What did they do? Why did they want to give him a place to live? Questions bubbled and made him queasy.

He was slower getting out of the car than Jackson and by the time he'd joined him, a tall, slim, brown-haired guy in glasses had reached them. He looked to be in his mid-thirties and was wearing chinos and a pale yellow shirt.

177

"Jonas!" Jackson shook his hand and turned to Zed. "Zed this is Jonas Mallinson. Jonas meet Zed."

Zed held out his hand. "Pleased to meet you, Mr Mallinson."

"Call me Jonas. I'm pleased to meet you too. Are you coming in, Jackson?"

"If Zed wants me to."

What difference would it make? He had to stay here for the time being at least. "I'll be fine. Thank you."

Jackson smiled and headed back to his car.

"When was this built?" Zed asked as they walked along the gravel path towards a door.

"Early eighteenth century."

"Wow." Zed followed Jonas inside. "So what was this building originally?" He was trying to make conversation. He wanted Jonas to like him.

"A family home until the early twentieth century. Then it became a school operated by the Royal Air Force Benevolent Fund for the sons of RAF personnel killed in service. That ended in the mid-seventies and afterwards it was restored by the Blackheath Preservation Trust and finally sold for residential use." He turned to Zed, "Would you like a drink?"

"Some water would be great, thank you."

"I'll get you a drink and show you round."

The kitchen was lovely, with dark blue cupboard doors lower down and white above. French doors led to outside and in front of them was a battered looking table holding an open newspaper, a pen and a half-drunk coffee. It looked as though Jonas was doing a Sudoku puzzle.

"I'm addicted to those," Jonas said. "Do you do them?"

"I've done a few at school."

Jonas drew the water from the dispenser on the American-style fridge-freezer and handed it to him.

"Thank you." Zed carried his glass as he followed Jonas.

"Just off the kitchen is the music room."

Zed gasped when he saw the grand piano. "Wow!"

"Thought you might like that."

There were violin cases propped in the corner, a music stand and sheet music piled on the floor.

"Who plays?" Zed asked.

178

"Me."

"Will I be able to play too?"

"Go ahead."

"Now?"

Jonas nodded. "Try it out." He took the glass from Zed's hand.

Zed moved the seat forward slightly and ran his fingers over the keys before playing a short piece by Bach. He winced when he made a mistake and stopped. "I'm rusty."

"You're very good. You're welcome to play anytime I'm not using it."

"I'm at my best at three in the morning."

Jonas laughed. "Ah, maybe we'd better set times. Come on, I'll show you the rest of the house."

Zed took back his glass and followed Jonas through a large reception room with modern furniture, books everywhere, a brick fireplace and a big TV.

"We spent most of our time in here. Though we both work unsocial hours on occasion."

"Who else lives here?"

"Just me and Henry. And you now, assuming you want to."

Henry with a y or an i? Zed supposed it might be short for Henrietta but when he thought about it, he hadn't seen any women's shoes or coats or makeup, any of the sorts of things his mother had left around.

"This is the gym. Small but it works. Henry uses it more than me. If you don't know how to use the equipment, ask him."

They went up the stairs. "Three bedrooms up here. All with their own bathrooms. This one is ours."

It was so large there was a living area at one end with two couches and a fireplace. And even more books.

"You can choose one of the other two bedrooms or maybe you'd like to sleep in the basement."

"Compete with chains and a rack?" Zed pressed his lips together, regretting the quip but Jonas chuckled.

"Wait and see." They came out of the bedroom and Jonas started up another set of stairs. "These lead to the roof."

At the top was a small glass conservatory which opened onto a large decked terrace set out with dining table and chairs, modular seating and a hot tub.

179

"You can see the grounds from here. Two and half acres of sloping communal gardens. Not to be used for ball games I'm afraid, but the park is across the road."

Greenwich Park and the Observatory lay in one direction, the Thames and London in the other. *Oh no, this can't be right. This place is too good for me.*

"We're very close to Maze Hill station but it's not far to the town centre. A quick walk."

"I think…" Zed swallowed hard. "Has there been a mistake? You really want me to live here?"

"Yes, but only if you want to. Come on, let me show you downstairs."

"Have you had a lot of… boys staying?" Zed asked.

"You'd be the first."

Zed sucked in a breath when he saw the basement room. A brightly lit white tunnel with modern furnishings and a small kitchenette. There was a bedroom at the end and beyond that a bathroom. One side of the room was a wall of glass doors and outside there was a small private deck with chairs and a mosaic topped table.

"The benefit of being on a slope," Jonas said. "Two patio areas." He led him from there to a room the other side of the stairs. Racks of wine lined one wall. "Do you drink?"

"No." *I'm too young.* Was that a trick question?

"We don't allow smoking but you could go outside to light up until we convince you to stop."

"I don't smoke."

"Good. Drugs are a definite no." They headed back up the stairs.

"I've never taken anything."

Jonas turned and smiled at him. "I knew we'd get on fine. Well, I think that's the tour done. Your bag is here." He took it from a hall cupboard and set it at the bottom of the stairs. You can take it up or down later. Where would you like to sleep?"

"Upstairs." There was too much space downstairs. He didn't feel old enough or worthy enough to have his own virtual bedsit.

"Let's go back to the kitchen and I'll make us something to eat. There's a letter for you too."

"A letter?"

"Exam results I believe."

He'd forgotten. Now his heart thumped.

180

Zed put down the glass on the kitchen table and Jonas handed him the envelope. "Nervous?"

"A little." He took out the paper. Read it once, then read it again before he smiled.

"Did you do okay?"

"I got eleven A*s."

"That's brilliant! Well done."

"You knew."

Jonas laughed. "Damn. I've lost my touch. Yep, I knew. When Henry gets home we'll talk about your options for A levels. What you'd like to do and where we think you might like to go. But for now, what do you want to eat? A sandwich? Cheese and pickle? Ham? Smoked salmon?"

"Just cheese, thank you. Can I help?"

"Find some plates and cutlery. Just open cupboards and drawers. It'll take you a while to discover where everything is kept. Assuming you want to stay." He stared at Zed.

"Is the alternative a bedsit in Deptford?"

"I think they could do better than that."

"Do you work with Jackson?" Zed began opening cupboard doors.

"No, I'm a musician."

Zed only just held in his whine of pleasure. "I'm really grateful for... Thank you. I'd like to stay if that's okay. If Henry wants me too."

"He's looking forward to it."

"Really?" Was Henry Jonas's son? But only one bedroom was in use. *Oh.* Zed smiled and snapped it off his face as Jonas turned.

"Yes, really."

"Should I tell you my bad habits now?"

"No." Jonas chuckled.

"I hope it'll be okay if I have that bedroom upstairs with the white wooden bed and the desk and the bookshelves. I like the view."

"Absolutely. When we've had lunch, we'll go out and buy you a few things. Okay?"

Okay? Zed felt he'd just won the lottery.

By the time they returned late that afternoon, Zed was tired. They'd wandered around Greenwich buying all sorts of stuff that he both needed and didn't need, then Jonas had driven him to the supermarket for him to choose the food he liked. Zed had taken his own money but Jonas insisted on paying for everything. He told Zed they'd be given money to look after him, and he'd also have pocket money.

Zed felt as if he'd been transported to a different planet. No one had ever been this kind to him.

"Can we stop and have a drink?" Zed asked.

"'Course we can."

Jonas drove to a café and parked just past it.

"I want to buy us something. What would you like?" Zed asked.

"Black coffee and carrot cake. Thank you."

Zed chose water and a cream-filled meringue. Jonas gave a quiet groan of delight when he took a mouthful of the cake. "My favourite."

When Zed's fork shattered the meringue over the plate and table he wished he'd picked something else, though it tasted lovely.

"What do you do as a musician?" Zed asked.

"I'm a violinist with the LSO, the London Symphony Orchestra."

"Oh wow. That's fantastic. You played at the Olympics."

Jonas smiled. "Yep, we did. I go all over the world with the LSO. We're going to New York in October."

"I read that the LSO can play anything you put in front of them, instantly and how the conductor wants it. That you're the world's greatest collective sight-readers."

"I *knew* I was going to love you."

Zed sighed. *Please don't let anything spoil this.*

It took them three trips to unload everything from the car. Jonas helped him carry everything upstairs.

"What happened to him?" Jonas picked up Zed's bear.

"My father. He pulled him apart. I sewed him back together but not very well."

"Shall I have a go?"

"If you think you can fix him."

"I'll try. Why don't you put all your things away and then we can make dinner together."

"Okay."

Jonas left the room with Teddy Robinson and Zed dropped onto the bed. His head was buzzing. *My bedroom.* Not what he'd thought he'd have when he set off from Kent a couple of months ago. No Caspian for a start but there really was nothing he could do about that no matter how much he wished otherwise.

He choked up yet again as he lined up toiletries in the bathroom and hung his new and old clothes in the wardrobe. He seemed to have spent the entire day trying not to cry. He put the three adventure books Jonas had recommended onto the shelf. Zed imagined that one day, it would hold lots of books and his throat thickened once more.

He showered, changed into shorts, T-shirt and flip-flops, and made his way down the stairs. He slowed when he heard Jonas talking to a guy.

"I really like him," Jonas said.

"You've only known him a few hours."

"Plenty of time. You'll see. He's polite, funny, smart, interesting, cute and—"

"You can't call him cute."

"I love you, Henry. But he is cute. He has the most beautiful eyes. One glance and you'd remember him."

"Not necessarily a good thing. He's had a terrible home life. Jackson told me his father beat him."

Zed winced.

"His life is going to be different with us. He's a good kid. He played the piano so beautifully."

Zed decided to go into the kitchen before he heard something he didn't like. Jonas was talking to a tall man in a charcoal suit. Henry had short grey hair and looked about the same age as Jonas. Jonas had his back to Zed and was unfastening the guy's tie.

Henry tapped Jonas's shoulder, gestured with his eyes and Jonas turned.

"And here he is," Jonas said. "Zed meet Henry Steele."

Zed walked towards him and held out his hand. "Hello."

Henry smiled at him, shook his hand then turned to Jonas. "Yep, he's cute."

Zed blushed, Jonas groaned and Henry laughed.

"You heard us," Henry said.

"How did you know?"

Henry smiled. "Step up from the bottom creaks very slightly."

"I'll remember that." Zed smiled.

"Henry has ears like a bat." Jonas took a bottle from the fridge.

"Champagne?" Henry raised his eyebrows.

"Tell him about your GCSE results." Jonas handed the bottle to Henry to open and took three tall, thin glasses from the cupboard.

183

"Eleven A*s."

"That's better than I managed. Well done." The cork popped out.

"Give Zed half a glass too," Jonas said. "Special occasion."

"Good lord, you're corrupting him already?"

The guys chinked their glasses against Zed's.

"Congratulations on your exam results, Zed," Henry said. "Here's to the start of your new life."

"Thank you." Zed sipped the champagne, the bubbles popping against his tongue.

"Like it?" Jonas asked.

Zed nodded.

Henry put his glass down. "I'll go up and get changed. What's for dinner?"

"Zed's offered to make an Iranian salad. I'm doing salmon to have with it."

"Sounds good."

They went up to the roof terrace to eat. Jonas and Henry finished off the champagne while Zed had water. He kept wanting to pinch himself because this all seemed too good to be true.

"This couscous salad is delicious." Jonas helped himself to more.

"What's in it?" Henry asked.

"Pine nuts, pumpkin seeds, pomegranate, mint, parsley and feta cheese," Zed said. "And couscous."

"Do you like cooking?" Henry asked.

"Yes. Well, only the things I like to eat."

"What don't you like to eat?" Henry asked.

"Tongue."

The two guys looked at each other and laughed.

Zed knew he was blushing but hoped they didn't notice.

"What else?" Henry asked.

"I don't like meat on the bone or bony fish."

"Will you eat pork?" Henry put his cutlery straight on the empty plate and pushed it away.

"I might have been brought up as Muslim but I'm…" *Gay* "…not a follower. I don't mind eating pork." He took a deep breath. "Do you both know what I did, where I come from, all about me?"

"We don't know *all* about you," Jonas said. "We know you got caught up in a bad situation and did a brave thing. The rest—well, you can tell us as much or as little as you like."

Henry put his glass down. "We do need to have a talk about rules."

Maybe this was the bad news. Zed put his hands on his lap.

Henry pinned him with his gaze. "Don't tell anyone what you did. I think that goes without saying but you really mustn't."

Does he know I told Caspian?

"We've had to change your name to protect you. You can keep the Zed but it's now short for Zayne. Zayne Mallinson. Jonas's nephew. His eldest brother's only child. Your father died recently in a plane crash, your mother some years ago of cancer. Your mother was a teacher. Your father worked for a bank. You used to live in Lewisham. Keep to the truth where possible. If you're not sure what to say, then don't say anything."

"Okay."

"Be careful what you invent because it's easy to get caught out in a lie."

Zed nodded.

"There's a school very close to here but we'd like you to go to a private school to do your A levels," Henry said. "Colfe's School is co-ed, very good, only a few miles away and I know the head. It was decided you were safer not going to the closer school. You can walk to the top of the hill and catch a bus to Lee Station or if one of us is available, we'll take you in. We need to know what A levels you want to do so we can tell the school, then we'll buy your uniform and you're all set for September."

He took a key from his pocket and put it on the table. "This is for the house. We'll show you how to use the alarm in case no one's here when you get back."

"Who's paying for me to go to school?"

"The government."

Zed swallowed hard. "I don't deserve—"

"Yes, you do." Henry patted him on the shoulder. "No more about that. Right, the rest of the rules. No inviting anyone here unless you check with us first. If you're asked, I work in the Department of Health and Jonas is a musician. If you want to go out at the weekend, that's fine but we need you back here by eleven at the latest. We also need to

185

know where you're going or else you can't go. Knock before you enter someone's bedroom. Do your fair share of chores such as washing dishes, emptying the dishwasher, setting the table, taking out the rubbish, doing laundry, vacuuming and dusting. You're not our slave. Just do your share. Keep your own room clean, make your bed every morning, put clothes for laundry in the basket and not on the floor." He turned to Jonas. "Have I forgotten anything?"

Jonas gaped at him. "Clothes for the laundry in the basket and not on the floor? You know that and yet you still think your socks make the journey on their own?"

Zed laughed.

"My socks are well trained." Henry smiled. "Just a little slow."

Jonas huffed.

"We'll give you an allowance of ten pounds a week," Henry said, "but we'll pay for clothes, books, travel costs, trips out, anything required by the school. The ten pounds are for you to do what you like with. Spend or save. If you need something big, ask us. Oh, and I'm getting you a phone and a laptop."

Zed seriously worried he was going to cry.

"Any idea about A levels?" Jonas asked.

"Music, geography and maths."

"And further maths too?"

Zed nodded. Could he manage that?

"I'll get onto the school tomorrow." Henry pushed to his feet. "There's no TV in your room. Do you want one?"

"No thanks."

Jonas held out his hand and Henry put a five-pound note in his palm.

"Jonas said you'd say no."

"I'd like it in the bathroom, please," Zed said.

Both men laughed.

They cleared the table, took everything back to the kitchen and loaded the dishwasher.

"Like to play us something?" Jonas asked.

"Okay."

When Zed walked into the music room, he stopped so quickly, he stumbled.

"A gift for you," Henry said.

A cello. Then Zed did cry. It was Jonas who wrapped his arms around him and Zed clung to him.

"Happy tears?" Jonas whispered.

Zed nodded but they were guilty tears too because he was thinking of Caspian and how Caspian's world had shrunk while his had grown.

The following evening, Jonas gave Teddy Robinson back to Zed.

"Wow. He looks fantastic. Thank you." He wanted to hug the bear, but he was too old to do it in front of anyone.

"These are for you too," Henry said and handed over a laptop and phone.

"Thank you. Those two words don't seem enough. But thank you. I should phone Tamaz."

"Yes, you should," Henry said. "What are you going to tell him?"

"That I don't want to be a burden to him, that I've been found a place to live in Greenwich and I'm going to go to school to do my A levels. I think I need to give him that much or he'll be suspicious, but I can say I don't want to tell him the address because if our father asks, I don't want Tamaz to lie. I should offer to meet him."

Henry nodded. "I suggest the park. But tell me when and where."

"You're going to watch me?"

"We don't want your father swooping in. Or anyone else."

Zed shuddered. "Let me call him while you're listening. Then if it looks as if I'm saying something I shouldn't, you can stop me."

"Fine. This is how to put the phone on speaker."

Zed tapped in the number. Henry sat next to him while Jonas sat on the couch and watched.

Tamaz answered quickly. "Hello?"

"It's me."

"*Alhamdulillah!*"

Of course the first words would be to praise Allah.

"Are you okay? No one would tell me anything. Are you still in Woodbury?"

"Yes, I'm fine. Not in prison. My lawyer told me Parwez confessed to planning to detonate a suicide bomb at the Olympics but said I wasn't involved."

"They believed him?"

187

Zed glanced at Henry. "Well, I wasn't involved but he implicated Wasim and…" Henry shook his head. "…some others so I guess they thought if I was involved, he'd have blamed me too."

"Where are you? I'll come and get you."

"There's no need. Social services have found a family for me to live with. They're really nice. They don't make me eat *zaban*."

Tamaz laughed. "I wouldn't make you eat it either."

"I know, but I'm okay here. More than okay. You have enough to do without having to look after me and I don't want to make things difficult for you with Dad. It's better that I stay here. I have my own room and they bought me a… laptop." He'd nearly said cello. "And this phone."

"Where are you living?"

"Greenwich. You want to come and see me? Not at the house. Maybe in the park?"

"Why not at the house?"

Henry shook his head.

"I'm not supposed to have people here while they're at work." Zed winced. That was weak. "I mean, they don't know me yet. I might run off with their TV. Though it's humongous."

Tamaz chuckled. "All right. Where then? What time?"

"The Pavilion Café in Greenwich park? Whatever time works for you. Still the school holidays for me for a few more weeks."

"Eleven thirty tomorrow. I'll buy you lunch. I hear they do *zaban*."

Zed mock-gagged and they ended the call.

"Well done," Henry said. "Now we need to practise what you say."

Tamaz was waiting at the café when Zed arrived. He flung his arms around Zed and hugged him. Henry had told him someone would be watching, just in case, but it wouldn't be him or Jackson.

"Inside or out?" Tamaz asked.

"Out. It's too nice to sit indoors."

They ordered from the waitress. Tamaz insisted on buying Zed lunch.

"I'm so glad you're out of Woodbury," Tamaz said.

"I was really scared."

188

"Dad is still going on about you coming home."

"I won't. Now I'm sixteen he can't make me. I want to do the subjects I like at A level and not the ones he picked for me."

"He only wants the best for you."

"He thinks he can beat that into me?"

Tamaz sighed. "So how did you do in your GCSEs?"

"Eleven A*s."

Tamaz gaped at him. "That's amazing." Then he frowned. "I thought you were doing ten?"

Shit. "I did a GCSE in Farsi in my own time."

That earned him a broad smile.

"Have you heard from Fahid?" Zed asked.

The smile vanished. "He's gone back to Pakistan. Don't talk of him again."

"He left me in the house and ran. I might have been trawled up in what they were planning. I *was* trawled up. I went with Parwez to get the tickets for the event he was going—"

Tamaz grabbed his wrist and squeezed hard enough to make Zed yelp. "No more about Fahid."

"You think he was wrong though, don't you? I was worried you had something to do with it."

"I said no more. Forget it ever happened."

Oh shit.

Zed went back to the house and told Henry everything. He could almost remember it word for word. Henry made no comment apart from praising him for his quick thinking on the GCSE, but Zed worried he'd just hammered a nail into Tamaz's coffin.

School was better than Zed could ever have imagined. He wasn't bullied. He'd made friends. The work was hard but studying subjects he liked made all the difference. He joined the orchestra and started to learn the guitar as his third instrument. He'd even been asked to be in a band. Not that he'd be telling his piano or cello teachers, but Zed thought he liked the guitar best. If it hadn't been for Caspian, Zed would have thought life was more or less perfect.

But he would not forget Caspian.

189

He saved up his allowance and bought propelling pencils, notebooks and an MP3 player and posted them to Woodbury. He wrote to him every week but Caspian never wrote back. Zed knew he didn't like writing, but he still thought he might have managed a short note.

In the end, worry drove him to ask Henry to find out if Caspian was still in Woodbury. He was. Zed didn't give up. He was careful about what he said to Caspian because going on about how great his life now was when Caspian was locked up in prison was just going to hurt him.

But his life *was* great because it was full of music. He played the cello while Jonas played his violin. He accompanied Jonas on the piano. He went with him to LSO rehearsals and sat at the back listening.

One day Jonas told him he could play the piano after they'd finished rehearsing. Zed crept onto the stage and played the powerful opening chords of Tchaikovsky's Piano Concerto No. 1. It sounded so much better in a proper auditorium. While he was playing, Jonas came back with his violin and played alongside him. Then another person joined him and another until about half the orchestra had returned. It was the best feeling ever.

SUMMER FOUR

Chapter Seventeen

2013

Caspian's case came to court the following May. He'd been on remand in Woodbury longer than almost anyone in there. He'd have been in court sooner but the mother of one of the girls had killed herself a few days before Christmas. His PO had told him on Christmas Eve the reason why his court appearance in February had been postponed. Caspian was pretty sure the timing was deliberate.

He hardly moved off his bed the next day. He didn't have anything to eat, even though it was supposed to be the best meal of the year. His pad mate, who worked in the kitchen, had gone on and on about it and Caspian had pulled the pillow over his head, part wishing he could suffocate himself.

He'd wondered if Lachlan had spared the woman a thought or whether his brother had by now convinced himself he hadn't even been fucking driving that day.

Christmas had probably proceeded as usual at home. Only artistic decorations allowed. Strategically placed holly, red berries compulsory. Colour-coordinated baubles on trees in the dining room, drawing room and hall. Elaborate parties pre and post-Christmas Day.

They exchanged gifts after breakfast. Tasteful, expensive presents to be opened carefully, admired by everyone, followed by a huge amount to eat. Games played. A bit of TV watched. Everyone having fun. A ski trip to follow. Caspian bet they'd still gone skiing. He tried not to torture himself wondering what Zed was doing, but it was hard. He'd find out soon enough. Zed was still writing to him every week even though Caspian didn't write back. He lived for Zed's letters but he couldn't let him think they had a future.

Every time his lawyer came to see him, he asked Caspian if he wanted to change his mind about pleading guilty, pointing out that silence would allow people to assume the worst. Caspian didn't care. Appleby didn't ask if Caspian had been driving. He just assumed that was the case. Efforts to try and get him to explain exactly what had happened on the basis the charge might be reduced to careless driving failed. When the lawyer said they could use Caspian's dyslexia in his favour, that a psychologist would produce a report, Caspian had told him to fuck off and not come back, but he had. He had no power to stop him.

Caspian had been *persuaded* to attend a course about forgiveness because he refused to engage about what he was supposed to have done. He did the course but wouldn't speak. He also wouldn't speak to the prison psychologist who knew all about him, his background, his education, his dyslexia, everything except the truth. *What are you afraid of?* the guy had asked. The answer, though Caspian maintained his silence, was that if he started to talk, he wouldn't be able to stop.

He also had to see a probation officer who was responsible for writing a pre-sentence report that would be given to the judge and prosecution and defence lawyers. The report was supposed to consider Caspian's age and maturity, the seriousness of the offence, his family circumstances, any previous offending history and whether he admitted what he'd done. Caspian gave some personal details, but he refused to discuss what happened that day, refused to show remorse and refused to admit the offence.

When the report was done, Caspian was given it to read. It took him a while. He didn't come out of it looking good. *Unable to come to terms with his situation. Unwilling to cooperate or engage with those trying to help him.*

His lawyer was furious with him. *How am I going to get you out of here if you sabotage yourself?*

The first thing Zed sent Caspian were propelling pencils, an eraser and sketch books. An MP3 player that Naughton had delivered with the comment—*someone's getting preferential treatment*—was hardly ever out of Caspian's pocket. Along with the music he and Zed had listened to, Zed had recorded himself on the piano, cello and guitar. There was a song called *For You* that Caspian found hard to listen to without choking up. Zed's voice was… *perfect.*

Always for you
Only for you
I long for you
I breathe for you
Please breathe for me
Please long for me
I'm waiting for you

Zed's letters were all about school and the two guys he lived with. Tamaz was rarely mentioned. Caspian worried when a letter didn't

192

arrive from Zed, yet he also wished Zed wasn't writing to him. Zed was making it all so much harder. Though Caspian devoured the words because they gave him life, kept him breathing. He'd wanted to let Zed go but he couldn't, not until Zed let go of him.

Caspian decided to write back and he'd managed to write short letters and poems only to rip them up again. He was supposed to be pushing Zed away, though what was there to say? His world was tiny and repetitive, unsafe, always teetering on the brink, subject to unpredictable eruptions and there was nowhere to run. Caspian knew everyone in the wing but had no friends. No one did, though they might think otherwise.

It wasn't easy to hear about the outside world without feeling jealous. He knew Zed was being careful about what he told him, playing down fun stuff. He had a life and Caspian didn't begrudge him that. How could he? But it hurt because it was a life without him.

Zed couldn't visit on his own until he was eighteen. He'd tried to come on several occasions but Caspian had refused to see him. He didn't want to hurt him, but Zed was hurting himself by clinging to the hope that they could have a life together. From the moment Lachlan had hit the girls with his car, Caspian's future had been set in stone. In the brief time he'd had in here with Zed, he should have been building a wall, pushing him away and instead he'd clung to him until the last moment. Zed had the chance to fly without him and Caspian had lost the chance to make him see that. Now all he could do was not write to him, not see him.

Caspian wouldn't accept visits from his family either, he ripped up every letter they sent, refused every gift, destroyed his birthday cards, tore up photographs and wouldn't use the money they put in his account. He kept every one of Zed's letters. He could read them without faltering because he knew them off by heart.

He was polite and respectful, but only spoke when he had to. He attended lessons and tried to learn but still struggled. The teachers were kinder and more patient than he was used to but Caspian felt doomed to his level of literacy. Almost half of those in Woodbury had some form of learning difficulty; dyslexia or attention deficit something or other. Eighty percent had a type of mental disorder. Caspian thought he probably fell into that category too. Being locked up made the sanest person crazy.

Most of them didn't pay attention in class, particularly in maths. They knew they needed it to get a job but the majority were worse than Caspian.

"What's five times one?" the teacher had asked one guy.

The idiot had fucking got it wrong.

"What's 560 pence in pounds?"

A different guy had said, "560 pounds. No...er...56 pounds."

Caspian had looked out of the window in despair. He saw now how disruptive boys who didn't want to learn or couldn't learn could be. There was a one-way mirror on the side of the classroom, allowing security staff to monitor what was happening inside. But they were looking for violence not chatter.

Sometimes the teacher picked up on it. "Let's not talk about beating someone up, boys. It's not a nice conversation."

Yeah, right.

Pens were removed from them at the end of the lesson and they were searched before they could leave. Yet Caspian was allowed pencils in his cell. Sometimes rules made no sense.

Taking classes filled time and that was all Caspian was interested in, apart from the money he earned and used in the vending machine to buy essentials like toothpaste. Hard to express any enthusiasm for studying creative writing, healthy living, catering, motor vehicle maintenance, horticulture or industrial cleaning.

Nor did he want to work in the kitchen, laundry or library, but he needed money for basics so he chose to work in the gym, tidying equipment, wiping it down, cleaning the floor. He took guitar classes in the evenings and finally found something he enjoyed and was good at. But guitars weren't allowed in your pad. Strings could be lethal. The guy in with him now seemed okay but how could Caspian know what he was thinking—planning?

While his conventional education stuttered along, he learnt plenty of stuff he wasn't supposed to know. Put in prison to be taught a lesson, they learnt the wrong lesson instead. He overheard others discuss the best way and right time to break into houses, the make of cars still easy to steal, how to rob convenience stores, how to weigh up drugs and sell them at the best profit, how to get visitors to bring you drugs, which prison officers could be bribed. His cellmate was yet another drug dealer and because Caspian didn't touch them he was apparently the perfect person to share a pad with. But sometimes, when he saw the blissed-out state that could be attained, he wondered about the point of denying himself a way out, even if it was a temporary one. Unhappiness and anxiety were hard to cope with day after day.

Few people bothered him. He tried to stay out of trouble, but trouble happened, so he learned how to fight. Being quick was the most important thing. Any altercation would only last seconds, maybe minutes before a guard stepped in, not always fast enough to stop an inmate getting hurt. Caspian never started any fight, tempting as it had sometimes been because there were some dickheads in there, but he'd been attacked and been glad he'd known how to defend himself, how to hurt the other person as quickly and efficiently as he could, where to kick, bite or punch. When to back away. Never to snitch.

He drew the line at making shanks or shivs but he admired the inventiveness. Toothbrushes were turned into weapons by heating handles with a lighter or by short-circuiting a battery. Caspian had heard that one guy had even made a shank by melting sweets and moulding them inside tin foil. There was no way Caspian was risking making a weapon.

Today was the first time he'd leave the prison in almost a year. He didn't want to return to serve a sentence at Woodbury or anywhere else, but he knew that's what would happen. He was resigned to it. He just hoped it wasn't for long. Maybe another year. He could do that. Yet how could a couple of years satisfy the parents of the girls who died, the father who'd lost his wife as well? Not pleading guilty made him look uncaring, but… He just couldn't.

Caspian's school trousers and shirt were too small. Time spent in the gym had broadened his chest and he'd grown taller. A dark blue suit, white shirt, grey tie and black shoes had been delivered to his cell, presumably purchased by his father. Caspian put them on. They were all too big and somehow diminished him. Maybe that was deliberate. Making him look like an eighteen-year-old boy not an eighteen-year-old man.

He had to take his belongings with him to court. His lawyer said they didn't know how long the trial would take and until it was over, he'd have to spend the nights in a police station because it was too far to keep taking him back and forth to the YOI. At the end, he might get sent to a different place anyway. Maybe a nice cottage by the sea, Caspian thought and managed a half-smile. He was put in handcuffs to be transferred to the vehicle and his plastic bag of clothes and toiletries, notebooks and letters were stored in a locker under the van used to transport him.

There were men and women already in the vehicle, collected from other prisons. Caspian couldn't see them because they were behind screens, but he could hear them calling him and each other. He stayed quiet. He was put in a small cubicle with a plastic seat and a yellowing Perspex window that was hard to see through. Graffiti had been scratched onto the panels: names, swear words and images like the one he and Zed had made in the wheat field. Once his cuffs were removed, he was locked in.

He had a moment's panic thinking if there was a crash he'd be trapped, before he pushed the worry back. There were worse things ahead of him. The lack of seat belt meant every time the van accelerated around a tight corner Caspian was thrown sideways and banged his knees or head. The driver's erratic driving drew a chorus of protests from the other occupants though he doubted the driver could hear or would care.

Caspian pressed his face to the window and watched a yellow-tinged world flashing past. Once he knew how long he'd be inside, he'd start planning his future. He needed a job so he'd have to pick from the training courses offered even if he didn't fancy any of them. He wouldn't be asking his father for help when he came out. Though was he just cutting his nose off to spite his face? Yeah, he would be. He'd already done that in spending the year at Woodbury.

When the van turned and came to a stop, instead of the abusive calling coming from inside the van, it came from outside and Caspian flinched away from the window. People were banging on the sides, photographers pressing their cameras against the Perspex and Caspian covered his face. *Not for me.* He didn't warrant that sort of attention.

Or did he? His heart rate soared.

He was handcuffed before he was led off the vehicle and he was horrified when he realised they were in an area overlooked by the clamouring public who were jeering and shouting. Someone spat at him but missed. His guard rushed him inside at such speed that Caspian almost fell. He was taken to a booking-in desk, given his rights to read—*forget that*—and then led to a court cell where his handcuffs were taken off. After a pat-down search, he was locked in.

He waited. And waited. He could feel his anxiety level climbing. Whatever happened today wouldn't be good. Lachlan wasn't going to stand up and confess. The accident would be rerun in minute detail and everyone was going to look at Caspian and hate him, even his own family.

When the door opened, Caspian glanced up from the bench he sat on. Appleby came in with Caspian's father and a tall, black guy in a wig and gown.

"Right, this ends here," his father said. "You've made your point. Plead guilty. Say you're sorry and you can be home with us tonight."

"Er…Sir Gerald," Appleby said. "There's no certainty of that."

"Even so." His father continued to stare at Caspian. "It's not too late to do the right thing."

No, it isn't. But Caspian *was* doing the right thing. It was others who weren't.

"Spare these girls' families further distress," his father snapped.

Because my distress doesn't matter. How dare he snap at me? No word of concern for him from his father. No rush to hug him after not seeing him for so long. No choked emotion. Not even a whispered *sorry.*

"The jury are going to find you guilty." His father glared down at him. "Even at this late stage, a guilty plea is better than letting the trial proceed."

Caspian stayed silent and finally, realising he wasn't going to speak, his father stormed out. The black guy held out his hand. "I'm Jonathan Cross, your barrister. Did Robert explain how today is going to go?"

Caspian nodded, then stood and shook his hand.

"Still determined not to speak?" Cross asked.

"I won't speak in my defence. I don't want you to challenge what the prosecution say. I don't want you to suggest anyone else might have been driving."

"It's the only defence I can put forward. Your reluctance to give up a friend. Or if you'd explain exactly what happened there might be a case for careless rather than dangerous driving."

"No," Caspian said. "There was no friend. Let them say what they want to say, then offer no defence."

The barrister sighed. "The judge is going to ask why you didn't just plead guilty."

"Maybe I wanted my day in court."

197

"You'll regret it," Cross said. "Particularly when you have to sit and listen to the victim impact statements."

"Then they'll get their day in court."

"Is this your way of punishing yourself for what happened?"

It's not me I'm punishing.

Cross stared at him. "Don't you think being remanded for a year was punishment enough? Do you *want* to serve more time in jail?"

"No," Caspian whispered. "But I accept that's what will happen."

The barrister sighed.

Caspian's heart moved from a canter to a gallop as he was led in handcuffs from the cell. The court room was like an over-sized headmaster's office, the walls clad in wooden panels. It was overpowering, intimidating. There were rows of desks and a raised platform and bigger desk where the judge would sit. Caspian was put behind a three-sided wooden barrier and his cuffs removed by the custody officer who sat close by. Behind him was the public gallery. He hadn't looked that way when he'd been brought in, but he could hear people muttering. Not only would his parents be there but so would those of the dead girls. He swallowed hard.

Everything seemed to happen so fast. Everyone stood for the judge who was an old man with glasses.

"Please state your full name and address," a woman said to Caspian.

Oh fuck. "Caspian Ulysses Octavian Nathaniel Tarleton. Woodbury Young Offender Institution."

"Your home address?"

To which he'd never return. "Barton Hall, Lower Barton, Kent."

"Are you maintaining your not guilty plea?"

"Yes."

That brought a ripple of shuffling noises and whispers from behind him.

A jury were sworn in but Caspian didn't look at them. He kept his gaze fixed on his lap. The prosecuting barrister stood and introduced himself and Caspian's barrister to the jury. The guy on the opposite side was a hyena, someone who'd rip Caspian to shreds to get what he wanted. The way he outlined the case against Caspian had some members of the jury gasping even before he called a number of witnesses.

198

No one had seen the accident, just the aftermath. A policeman, a paramedic and a scene of crime officer spoke. After listening to what they had to say, Caspian would have found himself guilty. The skid marks on the road an indication of excessive speed at several points along the road. Photographs were shown to the jury. Caspian had been found behind the wheel. His fingerprints were on the wheel. Why would they look for anyone else?

When the prosecuting barrister sat down, Cross stood up. "My Lord, I should now present the case for the defence, but I find myself in a difficult and rather unique position. My client maintains his not guilty plea. He declines to give evidence, as is his right, and has instructed me to make no defence on his behalf."

"He's eighteen years old. He doesn't know what he's doing," Caspian's father shouted from the gallery.

"He was old enough to drive and kill my child," someone called.

"Order," the judge banged his gavel. "One more word and I'll have you removed from the court." He turned to look at Caspian and Caspian met his gaze. "Is what your barrister said correct?"

"Yes."

"You maintain that you're innocent, but you won't offer evidence to prove it?"

"Yes."

A few moments later, after the judge had summed up and made it clear Caspian's silence was not to be taken as a sign of innocence or guilt and they were only to consider the evidence, the jury were ordered out. Caspian returned to the cell. Fifteen minutes later, he was back in court. The verdict was guilty. Caspian was surprised it had taken them that long.

Listening to the victim impact statements read out by the prosecuting barrister had Caspian pressing his nails into his palms. The policeman's daughter had wanted to be a ballerina. Another loved animals and hoped to be a vet. The last had been a gifted mathematician. She was the one whose mother had killed herself. Slit her wrists in the bath to be found by her husband.

Caspian had been told the statements weren't supposed to materially affect the tariff imposed by the judge but how could anyone fail to be moved by the tears of the girls' parents for their lost children, for futures that wouldn't happen.

When Cross rose to his feet, Caspian froze. "While my client declines to offer any defence, I do wish to say a few words about him on behalf of his family."

Caspian rose to his feet. "No."

The custody officer pushed him down.

"Don't speak on my behalf," Caspian said.

The judge sighed. "Your barrister wishes to make a statement of mitigation. You know what that is?"

"Yes, and I don't wish him to say anything."

"Very well." The judge looked over his glasses at Caspian. "Stand up."

Caspian pushed to his feet.

"You have been convicted on overwhelming evidence of causing the death of three young girls by driving dangerously on the morning of July 29th last year. You had only passed your test a month earlier. You took your father's car without permission and drove it recklessly at an excessive speed along a narrow country lane failing to have proper regard for vulnerable road users. No prison sentence can reflect that three young lives have been lost, that three families will grieve forever, that one father has not only lost his child but his wife because of your dangerous driving.

"You have some agenda of your own for appearing here today that you decline to share with us. You have wasted court time in not offering any defence. You have obligated these grieving families to relive their ordeal. You have shown no remorse for your actions. Indeed, you appear to be in denial about what happened."

Caspian's heart thumped hard and he clenched his teeth.

"But I'm taking into account your age when the incident occurred and although the lives of three young girls were lost, you did not set out that day to cause those deaths. It was a tragic accident but one that could so easily have been avoided. You will have to live with that as will the families and friends of those three girls. I sentence you to ten years in a Young Offender Institution, minus the time already served on remand, plus a two-year driving ban on release."

There was a buzz of noise, but all Caspian could hear was the word *ten. What the fuck?* He was led out of court in a daze and put back in the cell he'd been in before. *Ten years?* How long was he going to be locked up? He'd serve at least half of his sentence and more if he got into any trouble. Five years and he'd served one, so another four years. *Fuck.* He hadn't thought it would be that long.

The door opened and the custody officer stepped inside.

"Your parents want to speak to you."

"No...thank you."

The door closed again. What would they say? *It serves you right, you stupid boy?* He could hear his father arguing on the other side of the door, talking about an appeal, but eventually he went away. Caspian felt numb. He was having difficulty taking in that all this had actually happened. His life destroyed to save his brother's. He straightened his shoulders. Not destroyed or ruined or wrecked. Not unless he let it be. Why hadn't he just pleaded guilty? *I should have. Oh fuck.*

The door opened again. "Someone else to see you."

"Who?"

"Me." Zed moved into sight.

Caspian gasped. The last person he wanted to see. The only person he wanted to see. Zed walked into the room, flung himself into Caspian's arms and the door closed. Caspian told himself not to hug him. He'd refused to see him all this time, hadn't written to him because he needed Zed to be free, but his treacherous, pathetic, needy arms crept around Zed and he clung to him as if Zed was the only thing keeping him from being swept away in a raging flood.

But then he came to his senses and shoved Zed so hard, he almost fell. *At least four years in jail. I will not do that to him. And after I come out, who would want a guy with a prison record?*

"Caspian." Zed stood with his arms hanging limply at his sides, his bright eyes brimming with tears.

"I don't want to see you again." Caspian kept his voice as cold and calm as he could. "Didn't you get the message?"

"I know you don't like writing. I didn't mind not hearing from you."

"I threw your letters away without reading them." *Oh fuck.*

Zed dragged his arm across his eyes. "I sent you an MP3 player."

"That? I sold it to buy drugs."

It killed something inside Caspian that he was hurting Zed, but it was the right thing to do.

"You ought to know that I hooked up with my new pad mate. Fuck...the things he's taught me."

"Oh."

201

"And don't get it into your head that I'm lying about any of this, some sort of *cruel to be kind* crap. I've grown up and moved on. Which is what you need to do."

"Caspian." Zed took a step in his direction.

Please. I need this to work. "We had fun. But that's it. We're done. Just fuck off now like a good boy."

Zed turned his back and knocked on the door to be let out. Caspian's heart broke into so many pieces, he knew he'd never be able to put it back together.

Appleby came in and Caspian rubbed the tears from his face.

"We'll appeal," he said. "That sentence is too harsh."

Caspian didn't say anything.

"Though unless you admit your guilt, I'm not sure there's much point."

Caspian felt as if heavier and heavier weights were being piled on him.

"Are you okay? Your parents would like to see you."

"No."

"Let them talk to you."

"No."

"Is there anything you want to ask me?"

"Such as."

"I usually get asked—*what happens now?*"

Caspian shrugged.

"You don't want to know?"

"What does it matter?" Caspian turned his back.

Chapter Eighteen

The moment the door closed on Caspian, Zed crumpled into Jonas's arms. "He doesn't want me."

"Oh Zed." Jonas wrapped his arms around him and held him tight. "Come on. Let's get out of here."

Jonas bundled him down the corridor and a security guard opened the door for them to get back into the public area.

Henry had fixed it for Zed to see Caspian and yesterday, Zed had been so grateful and excited, and now he wished it undone. Jonas guided him out of the building past a TV crew doing an interview with the parents of the girls. Tears blurred Zed's vision.

"Ten years is nowhere near long enough," said a man who had his arm wrapped around his sobbing wife. "Our girls are gone forever. He should have been given the maximum sentence—fourteen years. And spend that time behind bars, not be released after he's been inside for five."

"Are you considering an appeal?" a reporter asked.

Zed groaned as Jonas hurried him along the pavement, his arm still wrapped around him. Zed was stumbling, barely holding it together. He wanted to fall to the ground and weep. He wanted to bang his head on the pavement until it bled, let that pain swamp the pain in his heart. Jonas helped him into the car, fastened his seatbelt when Zed's hands shook too much to do it, and squeezed his hand.

"We'll go home and talk."

Zed turned his face into the window, pressed his forehead against the glass and closed his eyes. When he'd seen Caspian walk into the courtroom, his heart had leapt. In spite of what was happening Zed was still thrilled to see him. But Caspian was wearing a suit that was too big for him and he looked pale and scared which made Zed want to rush over and hug him. The people sitting in front of Zed and Jonas were clearly the parents of the girls who'd died. Zed had felt their anger, seen it in their tight faces as he'd passed them, and now he'd heard it on the steps of the court. He didn't blame them. He blamed Caspian's father and brother.

Lachlan had sat on the far side of the gallery next to the wall. Whenever Zed had glanced at him, Lachlan had his lips so tightly pressed together they'd lost all colour. Caspian's father was grim-faced.

The woman in the pink dress and sunglasses had to be Caspian's mother. How could they just sit there and let this happen?

When the foreman of the jury said the word *guilty* Zed wasn't shocked yet it hurt just as much as if someone had suddenly thrust a knife into his chest. He'd wanted to stand up and yell out the truth, but he'd promised and though it killed something inside him, he kept his promise. Even if he *had* spoken out, then or earlier, would he have been believed? And if he was, and Caspian's mother knew the truth, she and her husband could get sent to jail. What would happen to Caspian's sisters then? Whichever way Zed looked at it, Caspian had been trapped from the moment Lachlan left him behind the wheel. Lachlan was…a despicable bastard. He'd left his brother injured in a car that could have caught fire. Zed wished him nothing but unhappiness for the rest of his life.

But when he heard the words *ten years,* he'd felt as if he was falling from the top of a tall building.

"What does ten years actually mean?" Zed whispered to Jonas.

"He'll only serve half of his sentence in prison, the rest he'll be out on licence. So that would be five years. But he's been on remand for a year so four more years inside."

That was longer than they'd known each other. By the time he was released Zed would be twenty-one and Caspian twenty-two.

The journey back to Greenwich seemed endless. Day one of a week off school and Zed needed to revise for his AS exams, some of which he'd already done, but there was no way he could concentrate on his school books today.

Caspian had tried to finish things a year ago when they'd been together for that short time in Woodbury, told him they were over, and Zed had chosen not to believe him.

Did he now?

Not one letter from Caspian in an entire year. No phone call even though Zed had given him his number. But for a brief moment in that courtroom cell, Caspian had returned the hug Zed had given him, even if he'd pushed him away a moment later.

That small embrace proved nothing. Caspian didn't want him anymore.

Zed couldn't think straight. His head ached. His body ached. He felt as if he had the flu. His face was wet with tears.

When Jonas pulled up on the drive, Zed jerked back to reality. Jonas patted his knee.

"I want to play my cello," Zed blurted. *Not talk. I can't talk.*

"Okay. Can I sit with you?"

Zed nodded.

Back in the house, Zed went straight to the music room. He put his jacket aside and opened the cello case. Once he'd tuned up, he started with Shostakovich's cello sonata, just mournful enough for his mood. Hunched over his instrument, he did little more than play the right notes at the right tempo before his head began to clear. His eyes fluttered closed and he and his cello melded into one. Emotion poured from the strings and from Zed's heart, swirling around the room until his throat thickened and breathing became hard.

Caspian didn't care. Nothing mattered anymore. Zed didn't want to think. He could lose himself in music. It would happen. He'd keep going until it did.

An hour of Shostakovich, Dvorak, Brahms, even the music from *The Game of Thrones* with thoughts of Caspian woven throughout before Zed finally gave up. The music had helped but not cured. Nothing could do that. He'd been asking for too much. He loosened his bow and put it away, unscrewed the end pin and returned the cello to its case.

"Hungry?" Jonas asked.

Zed shrugged but followed him out of the room. Jonas rarely pushed him, unlike Henry. Henry was the practical one, the stricter, stronger one who said *no* and meant it, when Jonas was more likely to say *yes.* Henry asked *why* and *for what purpose,* when Jonas encouraged without question. Zed liked them both more than he'd ever hoped he could. He needed Henry to rein him in, he needed Jonas to let him fly. The pair were balanced, one with his head in the clouds, the other with his feet on the ground. Zed was in the middle.

Their harmony brought him comfort. He liked that they were okay about being gay and were openly affectionate in front of him, though cautious outside the house. Their friends and family all knew they were gay and were fine about it. Zed had met many of them and he liked them all, especially Henry's parents. Jonas's father was dead but his mother was lovely. Zed couldn't have asked for a better place to live or better people to live with but every time he tried to say that, he choked up.

Jonas put bowls of home-made gazpacho soup on the table along with a wooden board holding a walnut loaf from Tesco that they both loved, and a dish of butter. He brought over two glasses of water then sat next to Zed.

"Did the cello do its work?" Jonas asked.

"It tried."

"I wondered. You seemed distracted but not in the right way."

Jonas understood when Henry couldn't, how music could soothe Zed's soul, but this time it hadn't worked.

"Music can comfort but sometimes you need the human touch." Jonas reached for Zed's hand and held it.

Zed leaned against him, let his face fall against Jonas's shoulder. "It hurts."

"Then it hurts me too." Jonas pressed his face against Zed's hair.

Zed sighed. "I don't want you to be hurt."

"You think you can live here for a year and us not be affected by things that upset you? We care about you."

"I know you do. You and Henry are so good to me. Every time I think of how lucky I am, I can't breathe. Then I think of how unlucky Caspian is and it breaks my heart."

"Unlucky?"

Zed tensed.

"You can tell me whatever you like. It will go no further. Not even as far as Henry if that's what you want."

"I wouldn't do that. It's not fair. Whatever I tell you, you can tell Henry."

Jonas squeezed his fingers and let him go.

Zed sat up. *Don't say too much.* "I met Caspian three years ago. He's... He was the first real friend I've ever had. Someone I could have fun with. Someone to talk to. He was the first person I'd ever told about my father beating me. I liked him so much. He was the boy who could, I was the boy who couldn't. But he changed me. He was fun and brave and adventurous, and he made me laugh."

"You don't think you're fun and brave and adventurous?" Jonas raised his eyebrows. "Take another look at yourself."

"I told you he changed me. Before Caspian, if I'd seen a sign saying—Don't walk on the grass—I wouldn't have. Caspian would have leapt over the sign and danced on the grass. I followed every rule. Caspian ignored them. He persuaded me to dye my hair, take risks,

206

enjoy myself. He's clever, brilliant at inventing things. He has sketch books full of his ideas, but he's dyslexic and he struggled at school. He got expelled and sent to a really strict place in Scotland."

Zed sagged. "The day of the accident, we were planning to run away together. I didn't want to leave until I was sixteen and couldn't be made to go back. Caspian's brother caught us together in the treehouse and went to tell his father. I waited all day and when he didn't turn up by the time the last train pulled in, I had no choice but to go to London on my own. I thought Caspian must have changed his mind or been made to change it. I ended up with Fahid and you know that story.

"I didn't find out about what had happened that day for a long time. Jackson arranged that when I was remanded for safety reasons, I went to the same place as Caspian. I guess when Jackson investigated me, he found out about Caspian. Everything was perfect between Caspian and me in Woodbury until the day I was due to leave. Caspian said we were over, that it was better to finish it then. He told me to forget him, but I didn't. I've been writing to him all year. I sent him pencils and drawing pads and an MP3 player. I saved up my allowance."

Zed glanced at Jonas. "But he never wrote back. Not even to thank me. I told myself it was because he hates writing, and he does, but today he said he'd thrown my letters away without reading them, that he'd sold the MP3 player for... that he was in a relationship with his cellmate and..." Zed gulped.

"Pushing you away again."

"I miss...him," Zed hiccupped.

"Why didn't he let his barrister speak on his behalf?"

Zed shrugged.

"I can't understand why he didn't plead guilty. He'd have gotten a lesser sentence."

"Yep."

"He wasn't driving, was he? Someone else was."

Zed froze.

"Was it you?"

"No," Zed gasped. "I was at the station all day. The guy in the ticket office saw me coming and going. I don't know how to drive. I wasn't in the car. How could you think I'd let Caspian go to jail if I was responsible?"

207

Jonas took his hand and wouldn't let Zed pull away. "I'm sorry. I didn't think you were, but I had to ask. Who was driving?"

"I promised not to tell. I won't tell."

"He really wasn't driving?" Jonas gaped at him.

"I promised. Please. Even if he doesn't want me, I won't break my promise."

Jonas sighed. "How far did things go with him?"

"We did…things but not… We never… I love him… I loved him…. I love him." He groaned. "Shit. Sorry."

"Don't be sorry. You've been hurt. You're allowed to be confused and sad. Was he the first boy you were ever interested in?"

Zed nodded.

"What you had was special. A first is special to everyone. Eoin was my first. I met him on a school orchestra trip to Ireland. He played the violin like me, yet nothing like me. He made it up as he went along. The conductor used to roll his eyes when Eoin carried on playing when we were supposed to pause. I used to wonder if he was a faerie. His fingers moved so fast. Those fingers… Magic fingers."

Jonas smiled briefly. "When I was with him, it was as if I came alive. I knew I was gay but suddenly I *was* gay. Everything was brighter, clearer, shinier. My brain had never experienced anything like it before. He'd awakened something in me, triggered a rush of teenage hormones that overwhelmed everything. Being near him was a kind of agony, a kind of ecstasy. I caught fire in his vicinity. My cock was constantly hard. So was his. We were blind, deaf and dumb to anything but each other. Sound familiar?"

"Yes."

"We wrote for a while but the distance between us meant it was a relationship destined to fail. The letters petered out and I was heartbroken. We'd spent every moment we could exploring each other's body and I thought I'd never love anyone in the way I loved Eoin. But several years later, I met Henry and realised I was wrong."

"Several years?"

"Five to be exact. And I had plenty of flings in between. Henry and I met at university. One look and that was it. You *will* find someone else. But I know it hurts now."

"What if Caspian doesn't mean it? What if he's pushing me away so I don't feel trapped in a relationship with him?"

208

"That might well be what he's doing but he's going to be behind bars for at least four years. I think you have to respect his wishes and let him go."

More tears fell from Zed's eyes and Jonas gathered him into his arms. The feeling of being held by someone who truly cared was almost too much. Zed felt safe and secure, and for the first time in a long while he felt loved. Maybe Jonas was right. By the time Caspian was out, Zed would be graduating from university. All those letters and not one letter back. He'd be stupid to waste any more time thinking about him.

Yeah, well he was stupid. He couldn't just forget him. In a way, he was fortunate he had to spend the week revising. He hadn't thought he'd be able to concentrate on his schoolwork, but the desire to do well combined with worry about letting Henry and Jonas down made him push thoughts of Caspian as deep into his mind as he could. He would never forget him, but Zed had a life too.

Even so, he wrote another letter and sent it to Woodbury, figuring they'd pass it on if Caspian had been sent somewhere else.

A reply came on the day of a maths exam. He wanted to open it before he went to school but Jonas convinced him to wait. He was glad he did because on the single sheet of paper inside, Caspian had written in ugly block capitals—STOP WRITING TO ME.

The trial of Wasim, Parwez and the others was held behind closed doors. Jackson had come to talk to Zed and told him that the prosecution had successfully argued that if the media were allowed to publish details of the trial, national security would be threatened. He promised Zed his name wouldn't be used.

The papers and the TV were full of it. *Olympic Bombers. 100 Metre Blast. Security Services Superb. Threat Level Still Severe.* It made Zed feel ill thinking about what might have happened if he hadn't overheard that discussion, if he'd not risked contacting the authorities.

Reporters from all over the world had come to London to cover the trial even though what they could say was limited. Zed didn't want to read about it or watch the news but it was impossible to ignore what was happening. He'd spoken with these guys. Eaten with them. Been to the mosque with them. Zed was guilty of nothing, but he felt ashamed just for knowing them.

They were all found guilty and sentenced to life imprisonment. But Fahid was still out there.

Zed had met up with Tamaz a couple of times and his brother had taken him out for a meal in Greenwich last week, but things weren't right between them. Zed was constantly on alert for a question he didn't want to answer or some comment that he didn't want to hear. Tamaz seemed too careful in what he talked about. Maybe their relationship would always be broken.

When the exams were over and school was finished until September, Jonas and Henry took Zed out for a meal at the top of the Shard. The view was spectacular, London was lit up in all directions. Zed was given a glass of wine but when he pulled a face after he'd sipped it, Henry laughed.

"Have we wasted that on you?"

"Tip it into my glass," Jonas said. "What would you like instead?"

"I'll keep trying with the wine."

"I do need it more than you after today," Jonas said.

"I thought you were rehearsing?" Henry asked.

"Yes, but an open rehearsal so there was an audience. Zed was there."

Zed knew the story Jonas was going to tell Henry and he laughed.

"We didn't get off to a good start," Jonas said. "The conductor turned to the audience and said, "If you feel like it, you can clap between the movements." Well that was what he meant to say. What he actually said was "If you feel like it, you can crap between the movements." We cracked up. It was a wonder we managed to play anything."

Henry laughed. Jonas and Henry both made Zed laugh but Jonas was the one with the funny stories. Henry never spoke about work. Zed had no idea what he actually did, but he knew the answer to everything. Henry liked to spout obscure trivia and Zed thought it was cool and played along by doing the same.

"How's the lobster?" Henry asked him.

"I like it. Did you know that lobsters communicate by peeing at each other?"

Henry laughed. "Yep, they have bladders on either side of their head."

"Their brains are the size of the tip of a ball-point pen," Zed countered.

"The biggest lobster—"

"Shut up the pair of you," Jonas said.

Henry looked at Zed and grinned. "Word fact, please?"

"The fear of long words is called hippopotomonstrosesquippedaliophobia."

"Well done," Henry said. "Give me a word in English language with the letters in alphabetical order."

"Beefily."

"Excellent."

"You two are such show-offs." Jonas said. He pulled a box from his pocket and offered it to Henry. "While I can get a word in edgeways, happy anniversary."

Zed was mortified. "Your anniversary! Why did you ask me to come? You should be eating on your own. I'll go home." He started to push to his feet.

Henry tugged him down. "Sit still. You're here because we wanted you here."

Zed sucked in a breath. Henry took an envelope from his jacket pocket and handed it to Jonas. "Happy anniversary."

"What anniversary is it?" Zed asked. "The day you met?"

"No," Henry said.

"The day one of you asked the other out?" Zed tried.

"No." Jonas grinned.

"When Henry was at a Japanese rope bondage workshop and needed someone to tie up and you volunteered?"

Henry barked out a laugh. "Try again."

"When you were bitten by a snake and Jonas sucked out the venom from somewhere interesting?"

Both guys gaped at him.

"How much wine have you drunk?" Jonas asked.

"'Course you're not supposed to suck venom out," Zed said. "Did you know that in America only ten percent of snakes are venomous while in Australia, about sixty-six percent are? I'd worry if I was going on holiday there."

"Hmm. Open your present," Jonas said to Henry.

Henry flipped open the box and his eyes widened. "Are you crazy? You bought this?"

211

"No, I borrowed it to show you. Of course I bought it. It's the one you want, isn't it?"

"Yes. The exact one. Thank you. I'll…thank you properly later."

Henry took off the watch he was wearing, put the new one on his wrist and showed Zed. "It's a Tag Heuer."

"It's lovely. Can it tell you how many feet you are above sea level?"

"Why yes it can. And if aliens are invading." Henry held out the other watch. "Would you like this one? It does feet below sea level and what's on TV. No warning of alien invasion though."

Jonas laughed.

"You mean you'll give it to me?" Zed asked.

"Most people use their phones to tell the time but I like wearing a watch." Henry pulled up his cuff and admired his new one.

"I'd love it, thank you." Zed put it on, but the metal bracelet was too big.

"I'll take you into town and get it altered. Put it in your pocket." Jonas smiled at him and turned to Henry. "Shall I open the envelope now?"

Henry nodded.

Jonas pulled out a card. Whatever he read must have shocked him because he gaped at Henry and didn't say anything.

"We g-go on Monday?" he finally stuttered.

"Unless you've something better to do. You've booked the time off, haven't you?"

"Yeah, but I thought…" Jonas smiled and turned to Zed. "A two-week holiday in the States."

"A touring holiday. Mount St Helens in Washington State, then to Portland, a bit of white water rafting before we go down to Crater Lake, drive south-west to look at the redwoods, back up the coast, dune buggy riding and whale watching before we get back to Portland. All the hotels are booked. Nothing to stress about except what to pack and the weather. Oh, and driving on the correct side of the road." Henry held out another envelope to Zed.

"You don't need to send me to a summer camp. I'll be fine in the house on my own. No wild parties. I promise."

"Open the envelope," Henry said.

Zed opened it. There was a passport inside.

"You're coming too," Henry said.

212

"But…you need time together. You don't need me."

Jonas grabbed his hand. "But we do need you."

Oh God. My heart.

"And now I'm aware you know there's such a thing as a *wild party*, you're definitely coming," Henry said. "Pour Zed some more wine, Jonas. He looks like he's going to pass out."

Zed drank too much. He'd never been drunk in his life but he had a feeling that was part of why he felt so happy. Or maybe not. Maybe it was just life with Henry and Jonas.

His happiness lasted all the way to London Bridge station. Henry and Jonas were holding hands. He didn't think he'd ever seen them do that before in public. Then he heard someone call his name and looked around to see Tamaz hurrying toward him.

"My brother," he whispered to Henry before he walked into Tamaz's arms.

Tamaz hugged him tight. "What are you up to?"

"Nothing." Maybe Tamaz wouldn't realise he was with Jonas and Henry. "What are *you* up to? Been following me?"

Zed was joking but he saw from Tamaz's expression that he'd got it right. Jackson had known of every meeting Zed had had with his brother. Was he aware of what Tamaz had done?

"I worry about you," Tamaz said. "You need to be with a good Muslim family or at least a family that encouraged you to keep to your faith. But you're with *them*."

Zed couldn't talk past the glass in his throat.

Henry stepped forward and held out his hand. "You must be Zed's brother. Zed lives with us."

Tamaz didn't take his hand. He looked at Zed. "You live with two men?"

"They're kinder to me than our father ever was."

Zed flinched as Tamaz wrapped his fingers around his arm and Zed pulled away from his grip.

"This is the *family* you didn't want me to meet? They're filthy homosexuals," Tamaz spat out the words and Zed's happiness crumbled a little more.

"So am I," Zed said.

Tamaz's eyes widened, then he turned and walked away.

Chapter Nineteen

On the day of the trial, Caspian had left the court late in the afternoon after all the cases had been heard. He wasn't taken back to Woodbury but a different YOI in Surrey. Shawton was a much older place. It looked more like a prison inside and out. He went through exactly the same entry process as he had a year ago when he'd been remanded to Woodbury, except this time he had more possessions with him. His own clothes, including his suit, were put in a bag to be kept until release, and others handed over. He had to wear the same as everyone else now; blue T-shirt, grey sweatpants and grey trainers.

He was disappointed but not surprised to learn that he was back at the bottom of the incentive scheme. He had no idea whether that was down to the rules, or the whim of his new personal officer, Steve Webster—*call me sir, do not make work for me,* which sounded familiar—but he knew there was no point questioning his lowest of the low status.

Induction was as confusing as it had been a year ago. Too much information given at one go for him to take in, too much information handed to him to read. Why didn't they use pictures? From what he'd seen at Woodbury, hardly anyone in there was a good reader. Guys in the library picked up the book with the most pictures because they didn't want people to know they couldn't read or write. Caspian had a half-formed thought about creating a different induction leaflet with more images than words.

Falcon wing—birds this time—was to be his new home. He had a room of his own but no TV until he'd proved he could be a good boy. Once he had all his stuff stored away, including the pile of induction literature he wouldn't be reading today, or tomorrow probably, he made his bed, lay down on it and curled up.

The smell in Shawton was stronger than in Woodbury. Piss, shit, body odour and jizz mixed with whatever was being prepared in the kitchen. Boiled something or other. The pad he was in had a window too high for him to see through unless he stood on his chair on tiptoe. The walls needed repainting, but the mattress looked new which made him wonder what had happened to the old one and who had previously occupied this room.

He told himself not to think about Zed, but he'd never been good at taking his own advice. Caspian knew he'd hurt him when he'd pushed him away. He'd hurt himself, but there was no choice. *Shit.* Well yeah, there was a choice but not one he was prepared to make. Without Caspian on his back, Zed could cross rivers, climb mountains, fly high, see the world. Zed was better off without him. Two objects falling from the same point and Caspian would hit the ground first.

He closed his eyes and hoped for oblivion except he already knew that wasn't what he'd get. He was tired, weary of everything, but he couldn't switch off. He reran the trial in his head, recalled the glance he'd snatched of his parents, their stricken faces, Lachlan's paleness. Any sense of satisfaction he'd hoped for in them seeing what their lies had done vanished under the length of the sentence. But the hardest thing to bear was remembering the way Zed had felt in his arms for that brief moment before Caspian had pushed him away and knowing that feeling was lost to him forever.

Caspian rolled over to face the wall. He was more scared than he had been before. He hadn't particularly wanted to go back to Woodbury but now he wished he was where he knew how everything stood. Here he was a baby again. The eighteen-year-old who'd had a privileged life living with hardened criminals: murderers, drug-dealers, burglars and rapists. The voices echoing around the cells sounded harsher, more threatening.

When asked, Caspian told his PO he wasn't gay, though he wondered if he'd made the right decision. Not through any sense of guilt about climbing back into the closet but because he might not be able to cope in general population in this new place. *Oh fuck it, I just have to.* While he was still eighteen he could take lots of classes to make the time pass more quickly and if he was classified as a VP, vulnerable prisoner, classes and chances for exercise would be limited.

This time he'd accepted the smoker's welcome pack. At least he had something to offer if he was threatened.

When he was threatened.

It didn't take long. He'd been persuaded to hand the cigarettes over the next day yet didn't know whether he'd given them to someone of power, someone who mattered or just a con artist. He didn't want them anyway. Smoking held no appeal.

He was about to come out of his pad for lunch, hunger was one thing that never went away though his ability to eat ebbed and flowed, when three guys blocked his path. Two were white, one black. All three

215

were bigger than him. Caspian was shoved to the rear of his cell and he backed up as close to the emergency button as he could get.

"Don't like the way you walk," one of the white guys said. "Strutting as if you own the place. Don't like the way you talk either. Think you're better than the rest of us?"

Caspian had only emerged from his pad once, and made a point of neither strutting nor speaking, but had shambled along with his head down, avoiding eye contact. But he knew any excuse would serve for what they were about to do. *Try* to do.

"We need you to take a nicking," said the black guy. "Screws found tablets in Steve's washbag. You say you put them there, that they're yours."

"No."

"What?" The biggest of the white guys gaped at him.

"I don't take drugs. They won't believe me. In the block I was in before they always used my piss for the tests. I'll do that but I won't take a nicking."

"You'll do whatever we fucking want you too," the black guy said.

No, no, no.

"Saw on the TV you killed three little girls," one of the white guys said, and Caspian's heart lodged in his throat.

"Fuck 'em first did you?" snarled another.

What? Caspian's moment of frozen shock allowed them to wrestle him onto the floor. He was held down, a hand pressed over his mouth while they fumbled with his sweatpants. Strengthened by fury and fear, Caspian kicked, lashed out and managed to wriggle just far enough to smack his hand on the emergency button. By the time the prison officers arrived, his attackers had gone, his sweatpants were back over his arse and his nosebleed had almost stopped.

No, Caspian had no idea who they were.

No, he didn't need medical treatment.

He looked at the blood on his T-shirt and thought of what the guys had threatened then said as they'd left—*you're bird food*. Yes, he wanted protection.

The governor agreed, and Caspian was moved to the VP wing. Overwhelming his sense of relief was shame he'd not lasted longer in general population. There were never any positive feelings in here. It was all negative. Guilt, humiliation, anger, frustration, fear, misery, loneliness, depression.

He didn't expect the protective wing to be easy but almost immediately, he was on edge. This was a home for the eighteen to twenty-one-year-old wild things: a jungle holding beasts, snitches, chesters, bent pigs, crooked kangas, radio rentals, pilchards, cucumbers, all manner of fraggles along with guys who were loudly gay and those who were quietly gay. *That would be me.*

Prison language was elaborate and inventive. Caspian still didn't know what it all meant, why there were several words for the same thing. The child molesters were beasts and chesters. Crooked screws were kangaroos—kangas. The mentally ill were pilchards and radio rentals—mentals, but why pilchards? The rest, he had no idea about.

He was surrounded by those who were too fragile—*fraggles*—to cope with life inside in any wing including this one. They were outcasts from the prison community yet seemed to have made no effort to form a community of their own. They stayed in their cells like nocturnal zoo animals, emerging only to feed.

Except that first quick assessment proved to be wrong. There was a hierarchy even among the misfits. The cliques of the ordinary wings existed here too. People from different parts of the country stuck together. Gang members united against other gangs.

In the other wings, the sex offenders lurked at the bottom of the heap, the child molesters were on a journey to the centre of the earth. Armed robbers were at the top, admired as some type of Robin Hood figure because when you had no money, stealing from those who did and redistributing wealth was viewed as a noble thing. *What fucking crap.* Caspian kept his views on that to himself.

In the VP wing, sex offenders ruled the roost, not those who'd gone after kids, they were just as despised, but guys who'd raped women, often multiple times, swaggered around bullying the rest. The most normal guys were the crooked cops and bent prison officers but they kept themselves to themselves, forming protective circles when they were out of their cells on recreation, a bit like gazelles watching for prowling lions. Caspian felt like a deer that had mislaid his herd. It was a matter of time before he was prey of the day.

All I have to do is survive.

Zed helped him. Caspian wasn't supposed to be thinking about him. He'd physically pushed him away, tried to get him out of his head,

217

but he'd done that before and Zed had known, understood and had still written. Those letters were in his locker, in his head, written in his heart. *He'll write to me. I love him. He loves me.* Too soon to say the words. Maybe too soon to even think them, but memories of Zed brought him joy. The only source of joy he had.

He knew he was fixating, obsessing, fantasising—whatever the word was—over the way he felt about Zed, but he was incapable of letting go. Something about being locked up made him think differently.

Caspian wanted it to be love, so he made it love. At eighteen years old he thought he'd found the meaning of life, the reason for living. But he had to hide it, lock it away in a box in his head with Zed's letters because he didn't want something beautiful tainted by his current home. When he was low—though he was always low—he'd open that box and happiness would flood out, providing enough joy to let him carry on. Love gave life meaning. That was what he clung to. Caspian could exist without it. He could survive without it but with it—he was invincible. He would survive.

But when no letters came, love—if it ever was—slowly and steadily dissolved, became corrupted, then turned to hate. He might have told Zed to forget him, told him he'd hooked up with his cellmate but why had Zed believed him? Couldn't the idiot see what he was trying to do? Caspian had offered him the chance to fly without him but hadn't really meant it. In moments of lucidity, Caspian understood the flaws in his logic, his stupidity, but with too much time on his hands, his mind wandered back and forth over the same things, telling himself he was right, telling himself he was wrong.

When a letter came, clearly forwarded from Woodbury and judging by the length of time it had taken to get to him, rerouted via the North and South Poles, he was on an up cycle, he was coping, life was okay, and had the strength to not read it. He scrawled a note telling Zed to stop writing and posted it before he slid down a snake which would make him change his mind.

The snake bit him the next day.

There were no more letters.

Caspian kept his head down and his mouth shut. Opportunities for education, the gym and outdoor exercise were as limited as he'd expected. But faced with a choice between boredom in isolation or stimulation in danger, there was no choice. He tried to exercise in his cell but that didn't last long, his motivation wilting like his dick. Wanking failed to make him feel good for even those fleeting moments when he came. It took him longer and longer to get to the point of coming, and he stopped bothering.

Depressed and lonely, he began to fade. He didn't touch his sketch books. His idea for an image-driven induction leaflet dried up. He ate very little. He lost weight. The times for meals were off-kilter. Lunch at eleven, dinner at four with a breakfast pack for the next morning handed over at the same time, which almost all of them ate there and then. An eighteen-hour gap without food unless you had the money to buy snacks. He didn't. Not without touching the money his father was sending. But Caspian didn't want them anyway.

But when his good behaviour meant he was allowed a guitar to play in his cell—while it was unlocked—time finally passed more quickly. He couldn't stop playing. He played until his fingers bled, played until someone came and threatened to break his fingers if he didn't *shut the fuck up*.

There were drugs to buy that made you not care anymore. Spice was cheaper than tobacco. Sent into the prison in impregnated letters or magazines, it was easy to get. Spice offered a brief escape from reality but it turned the person who'd taken it into a zombie. No way was Caspian taking drugs but sometimes guys were tricked into it just to give the others something to laugh at in the yard. Entertainment was everything. The prison officers seemed helpless to stop it.

When dogs were brought in to sniff for drugs, Caspian liked watching them work. Their tails wagged so hard. Even though there were no drugs in his pad, he still worried when the dogs went in, in case someone had hidden their stash so Caspian got the blame. But they never found anything in his cell.

There seemed less of an issue with drugs in the VP wing and he was grateful for that. In a block already populated with snitches, people were quick to tell on others and drugs weren't so easy to get. When they *were* finally offered to Caspian, because he couldn't sleep, they were prescribed by a doctor and carefully handed to him one at a time. Caspian wasn't sure they made any difference, but he took them. Then he started to pretend to take them and stored them instead. Knowing he was building a way out gave him some comfort.

As did figuring out ways to hang himself in his pad. Jason had told him everyone thought about suicide and Caspian had promised himself he wouldn't. But…

Time was his enemy.

Zed was no longer his hope. Caspian knew he'd never forget him, but his life, if he ever got it back, would be one without Zed. He didn't hate him anymore. He saw him as one bright beam of light in the darkness.

When Caspian's stash of pills was discovered, he dropped to the bottom of a snake from halfway up a ladder. No guitar in his cell. No TV. The idiots failed to see that both those things kept him sane, kept him normal. He was sinking into a hole entirely of his own making. Well, he hadn't made the hole, Lachlan had, but the rest was Caspian's fault.

All he'd needed to do was tell the truth or plead guilty. Say he was sorry for something he hadn't done. He reran the trial in his head, playing a different hand, getting a different outcome. Saying he was sorry might have helped the families of the girls, might have helped him get a lesser sentence. He *was* sorry but if he'd said it, they'd have seen it as an admission of guilt. *I could have just fucking said it anyway.* Everyone except his father, brother and maybe his mother, and Zed, thought he was guilty. That wasn't going to change when he came out.

A short sentence might have made him less desperate to push Zed away. With a shorter sentence, they could have had something.

A phrase kept running through his head. They'd studied Coriolanus for English lit GCSE. A banished hero of Rome allies with a sworn enemy to take his revenge on the city. Caspian had thought it sounded good until he came to read it. The play was about a guy who struggles to change his nature. That was about all Caspian understood. He'd tried to read it and given up after a few pages. He did manage to read a summary and watch a film version, and he learnt some phrases off by heart to pepper any answer in his exam regardless of relevance. He'd written the essay he'd practised that would have to serve for any question. No wonder he got a D.

The phrase he was thinking of now was *Never shame to hear what you have nobly done.* Was taking the blame for what Lachlan had done stupid or noble? Caspian was ashamed he'd not refused. He'd lost his family anyway, though that was his choice.

He was safer in the VP wing, but still careful. One thing he could do nothing about was being disliked for what he was. His nickname was Posh Prick which he supposed was better than Cunt. There was a group in there that didn't like him and one day, he found out just how much they didn't. Three of them pushed him into his pad and barricaded the door. One sat on the bed with his arm around Caspian's throat, a shank in his hand. Two stood watching and one negotiated.

They wanted to be moved to a prison in the north of England where they came from. Even Caspian knew the governor wouldn't agree to that. If he did, this situation would happen every day. Caspian didn't resist. He sat quietly and hoped. They held him for three hours before they let officers into the cell. Then he seethed because he was treated no differently to the three who'd held him, as if he'd been in on the fucking thing.

One prison officer really didn't like him though he had no idea why that was. Maybe he had an eleven-year-old daughter. The guy enjoyed winding inmates up, particularly Caspian. It felt as if he was trying to get Caspian to lose his temper and lash out and get into more trouble. He wanted to make a complaint but one of the kangas told him if his complaint wasn't accepted, he'd be at risk of being put on a charge for making a malicious accusation. So Caspian kept quiet and tried to keep out of the guy's way.

But one day, towards Christmas, when he'd wanted to clear the rubbish out of his pad, he went to the door with his bin only for Officer KD347 to tell him to stay put.

"The bin's right there," Caspian had pointed out. The main bin where they all emptied their crap, pushed around by an inmate, was outside Caspian's door.

"Do as you're told and don't argue."

When the guy pushing the big bin started to move on to the next cell, Caspian stepped out of his pad and emptied his crap into it. The officer grabbed his arm, hauled him into his cell and laid into him. He gave Caspian a black eye without Caspian lifting a finger. In a review of the incident, two officers who'd been nowhere in sight reported that Caspian had lunged at the man.

Back down the snake.

Chapter Twenty

Zed flopped onto the couch facing Henry and Jonas. A few weeks back at school and the fantastic holiday in Oregon was a distant dream.

"Right," Henry said. "We need to talk."

"Jonas has already done the birds and bees," Zed said. "I know more about BDSM, fisting, felching, watersports and pony play than I ever wanted to."

Henry's jaw dropped and Jonas creased up laughing at his side.

"What the hell?" Henry stared at Jonas.

Jonas rolled his eyes. "He's a teenager with a laptop. He probably knows more than we do."

Henry cleared his throat. "That wasn't the sort of talk I had in mind."

Zed straightened. Was this going to be another gentle lecture about going out and meeting people? "I'm not a hermit. I go out."

"To orchestra rehearsals, to practise with your band, to watch Jonas, to the British Library," Henry said. "Not to parties, the cinema, bowling with friends. We know you're not shy. You get on well with all our friends. You can perform in front of hundreds of people without freaking out. But that's not what I want to talk about either."

Zed's heart did a couple of loop the loops. Did Henry know already? Zed had been given time to tell him, but he'd put it off.

"We have to talk about the future," Henry said. "Which university you want to go to? What subject you'd like to study? Whether you want to take a gap year?"

Jonas leaned back with his arms crossed behind his head. "Or don't go to university."

Henry frowned. "I just said he can take a gap year."

"I mean he doesn't have to go at all."

Henry huffed. "He's too clever not to go." He stared at Zed. "The school must consider you an Oxbridge candidate."

Zed squirmed. He was predicted to get 5 As in his A levels. The school wanted him to apply for Oxford or Cambridge, but he wasn't going to.

"Royal Holloway is very good for music," Jonas said.

Henry tsked. "Music is not a good choice."

"I did music," Jonas said indignantly.

"Precisely." Henry laughed as Jonas swatted him.

"Zed loves music. You're not going to just wipe it out as a choice," Jonas said. "The big advantage in doing music is it gives you time to focus on practising. If you're doing any other subject it's difficult to maintain the level of intensity you'll need to succeed as a musician. Plus, you'll make contacts for the future. Success is as much down to who you know, as how you play."

"No matter how good Zed is, and I know he's good, the chances of him becoming a successful musician are low. No matter how talented someone is, how hard they work, they need a certain amount of luck. Am I right?"

Jonas gave a heavy sigh. "Yeah, you're right."

"You were always practising," Henry said. "You worked harder than I did."

"And you earn five times as much as I do."

Zed knew that even in a prestigious orchestra like the LSO, the pay wasn't brilliant.

"But you don't do it for the money." Henry squeezed his fingers.

"Don't tell the director that."

Henry smiled.

"If you want a gap year, we can help sort something out," Jonas said. "Saving turtles in Costa Rica, working with elephants in Namibia, teaching in South Africa, ski instructor in Canada, there's a music project I know of in Senegal. I think a gap year would do you good. What do you think?"

"I don't want to take a gap year. I love music, you know I do. But I don't want to study it at university. I like listening to it, playing and composing, but not studying music theory and history and yes, I know that all feeds into playing and composing, but that's not what I want. I'd like to study computer science and maths at Imperial College." Zed took a deep breath. "And I want to keep living here with you."

His gaze flicked between the two of them. He wasn't ready to leave them. Plus there was something he hadn't yet told them. They weren't going to be happy.

But their silence made him nervous. "I can move out if you want."

"Going to university is as much about growing up as it is about what you study," Henry said. "You rarely go out. You never mention friends. We told you that you can bring people back here, but you never have. You don't go to parties. You don't want us to throw you a party even when we promised not to lurk."

223

"You don't spend hours in your room on the internet," Jonas said. "You're not constantly checking your phone. I know we shouldn't complain about any of that but it's…"

"Not normal." Henry took over when Jonas hesitated. "We're worried you rely on us too much."

"Yet we appreciate you're the perfect teenager in many respects. You've never caused us a moment of anxiety. You're polite, kind, considerate."

Zed curled his fingers into fists. "I'm too good? You want me to be bad?"

"Of course we don't," Henry said. "We're just worried about you. Is it the cost of living elsewhere? Don't worry about that. It'll be taken care of."

Jonas was watching him carefully.

"It's not the cost. Almost every student has to go into debt. I accept that. Why should I be different? I really want to stay here, not to save money on accommodation, but because…because this is my home and I love living here more than you could ever know. I…" *Say it!* He couldn't. He had two fathers in these guys who were a million times better than the father he'd been born to. "But if you've had enough of me, if you took me in thinking I'd only be in your hair for a couple of years before you got your lives and your privacy back, then I understand."

"We want you to leave because we think it would be good for you," Henry said. "That is the only reason we think you need to move out."

"I'd miss you," Jonas whispered.

Henry sighed. "You're supposed to be encouraging him to spread his wings."

"I know but I will miss him. I'll miss playing with him, talking to him, cooking with him."

"I've got a job lined up," Zed blurted while he could still speak.

Jonas frowned. "For next year?"

Henry pushed to his feet. "Hold on a moment. You're telling us you want to go to Imperial *and* do a job? What sort of—? Oh no." He shook his head. "No, you are not."

"What are you talking about?" Jonas asked.

"I'll kill Jackson," Henry said through gritted teeth. "I'm right, aren't I? He's persuaded you to work for MI5."

"Not persuaded. I want to."

"Right. There is no way you're living anywhere but here with us for the next three years," Henry snapped. "Maybe the next ten. Quite possibly the rest of your life." He pulled his phone from his pocket and walked out of the room making a call. "Jackson. You are in so much fucking trouble."

Jonas switched seats to drop next to Zed.

"Do you mind that I don't want to study music?" Zed asked.

"Of course I don't. It's your life. You can do whatever you like and I know music will always be important to you. We'll support you, whatever you do. I just wish…"

"What?"

"That you had someone in your life apart from us. Working for MI5 will make you even more isolated. You can't trust anyone. Can't confide in anyone. It's not easy. What does Jackson see you doing?"

"Keeping my eyes and ears open while I'm at university. Maybe joining a few societies I might not have joined. After I graduate, I think I'd like to be involved in intelligence gathering, not necessarily out in the field but desk-based."

"You really need to talk it all through with Henry. Don't commit yourself to anything. One more year at school. Three at university and you might decide you want to be a farmer. I think you're right not to want to do music and not because I don't think you could make it, but you're better than you think you are. I've seen your teachers pulling you in every direction. How do you choose between the piano and the cello? And the violin. You're good at that too now and you only took it up a short time ago. We both learnt the guitar at the same time and you are streets ahead of me. Do you even know which instrument you like the best?"

Zed winced. "It depends on what mood I'm in."

Jonas laughed. "See! My advice is to keep your options open."

"Well if I write some songs and get a record deal maybe I'll be a popstar."

"I think Henry would prefer that to you working for MI5."

Zed pushed to his feet. "Is there anything we need from the supermarket?"

"That is not going to fool Henry."

"I just want to give him the chance to cool down."

"You mean for me to cool him down. Go and buy some chocolate. That will help."

"You're right. I'll feel much better after I've had a Mars bar." Jonas laughed.

Zed crept out of the house and set off down Maze Hill toward Trafalgar Road. It was Jackson who'd approached him and asked if working for them was something he'd be interested in. There was no obligation to join one of MI5's graduate schemes when he'd finished at university, but Zed thought he probably would. If they'd have him, because Jackson had told him that Tamaz had left the country and not returned on the flight he was booked on. Zed hoped there was an innocent explanation.

He wondered how Caspian was getting on. Just being told not to write didn't stop Zed thinking about him. If he really had been...doing stuff with his cellmate, that had ended after the trial because he'd been sent to a different prison. Zed had found that out after Caspian had eventually written back telling him to stop writing. But Zed thought what he'd said about his cellmate was a lie, the most powerful shove in Zed's back that Caspian could manage.

So long as Caspian didn't do anything to have to serve all of his sentence, he'd be out in the summer of 2017, and Zed would be graduating from university, assuming he went. Their lives were entwined. Zed knew he was waiting for Caspian.

Chapter Twenty-One

SUMMER EIGHT

Four years later 2017

Caspian had tried not to count down the days until release in case something made it not happen. Fights kicked off all the time over stupid things like towels getting misplaced or someone's stuff being moved. For the last four months, he'd had a cellmate who was okay most of the time, but also prone to unexpected bursts of fury. When Mick and Caspian played board games in their pad, Caspian often deliberately lost to keep the peace.

Being locked in a cell for up to twenty-one hours a day was enough set anyone on edge. The closer Caspian was to being free, the more paranoid he became about staying out of trouble. He'd already gone two months beyond the date he could have been released because each case was dealt with in chronological order of eligibility, and Shawton was two months behind. Fucking unfair but what could he do?

He didn't sleep the night before he was due to be let out. By the time the cell door's double bolts were unlatched, he was ready and waiting. He picked up his bag of belongings and Steve Webster, his PO, took him to the reception area. For some reason Caspian couldn't fathom, he was strip-searched, and his belongings checked. What the fuck did they think he wanted to take out of there other than the few things he had in his plastic bag? The only things he cared about were Zed's letters, the MP3 player and his sketch books, full of dreams and badly scribbled poetry.

He dressed in his own clothes, the creased suit he'd worn in court that was the right length now but too broad in the shoulders. Still, it made him feel less like an ex-con. He handed the prison gear back in return for a pile of paperwork.

"Sign here, here and here," Webster said.

Caspian signed.

"I'll sum up the conditions of your licence or we'll be here all day while you read them." Webster smirked.

If Caspian hadn't gone through *ready, steady* and been waiting for *go* for the last few hours, weeks, months, he'd have taken issue with that, or made Webster wait while he *did* read it. But *go* was too close to mess things up now.

"The point of being released on licence is to allow you to reintegrate into the community, rebuild family ties and help prevent re-offending," Webster read.

The first two were already disasters waiting to happen. The last—he wasn't going to put a foot wrong.

"You're being released on licence because you're not considered a significant risk to the public. The conditions of release are that you maintain good behaviour, keep in touch with your SO, supervising officer, in the way he's specified and reside permanently at the address he's approved. If you want to stay one or more nights elsewhere, you have to have his permission. No work unless he's signed off on it. No leaving the country unless he's said you can. No driving for two years. Break any of those, commit an offence and you're back inside. Got it?"

Caspian nodded.

"Sign here, here and here."

Caspian scribbled his signature.

"Copies of this will be kept by the prison as well as being sent to your SO. Copies will also be sent to the local police force in the area where you're going to be living and to the National Identification Service at the Metropolitan Police."

Why not add fucking Interpol and the FBI?

Webster stared at him. "Almost forty percent of young offenders end up back inside within twelve months. I don't want to see you in that number. When I look at a lad, I have a good idea of whether I'll be seeing him again. I don't see you coming back here. You made a bad mistake, three girls died, and you'll live with that for the rest of your life, but you're not beyond redemption. When you eventually get behind the wheel of a car, remember what you did and don't let it happen again. You're only twenty-two. You have the rest of your life ahead of you. You're lucky you weren't sent to an adult prison after your birthday."

Caspian wanted to say *I wasn't driving that day* but he wouldn't be believed and if he was, all this time inside was for nothing. He kept quiet.

When he reached the final exit point and stepped outside, the door closed behind him and he took a deep breath, exhaling shakily. As well as feeling apprehensive, he was excited. The air tasted different. The

228

world looked…amazing. Enormous. Caspian tipped his head back. The sky was huge. Not a cloud in sight. A warm day in June and he was finally free. Though with the small amount of money he'd been given, he wasn't going to get far. He wouldn't even take his father's money to pay for a ride home.

He heard his name called and turned to see Lachlan hurrying toward him. *Shit.*

"Caspian."

Lachlan looked as if he didn't know whether to hug him or not. Fortunately, he decided on not, otherwise Caspian might have been tempted to commit an offence right at the prison door. He didn't want to be touched. It freaked him out.

"You've grown. You're almost as tall as me. The car's this way. I drove up this morning. Set off at five. Didn't want to be late."

His brother was nervous. Not the brother he remembered. Caspian followed him to the car park. Lachlan had stopped talking and Caspian thought how quiet the outside world was. Prison was loud almost all the time. Even in a cell on your own, there was constant yelling among inmates, doors slamming, keys turning, officers yelling instructions, the intercom doing the same. With a cellmate he had to put up with snores, farts, chatter and the sounds of wanking. Now there was nothing. Not even a bird.

"This is my car," Lachlan said.

A silver Honda. Not a smart, new snazzy one which was a surprise. Caspian's heart thumped at the thought of his brother driving him anywhere. He swallowed hard. Not much choice about whether he got in or not. Caspian threw his bag in the boot, along with his suit jacket, then climbed in and fastened his seatbelt. Why had anyone thought it a good idea for his brother to drive him home? Couldn't his father have come? *Did I want him to?* He had, sort of. *Home. Huh.*

Caspian hadn't wanted to go back to Barton Hall but his SO, Glenn Woodrow, made it clear Caspian needed a stable base in order to be released and that home was by far the best option, one that many ex-offenders didn't have. And did Caspian really want to go into a hostel that wasn't much different to being inside? *No.*

He'd almost stopped cutting off his nose to spite his face. It was time his father and brother paid him back for what he'd gone through. He needed time to…reset himself, and then he wanted a job. He had plans for what he'd like to do and he required help.

Lachlan's speed had Caspian gripping the sides of the seat but when he checked how fast they were going, it wasn't over the limit. His world had been slow for the last four years. Now it was going to speed up. He stared out of the window and watched real life flash by.

"Want to stop and get something to eat?" Lachlan asked.

"No thank you."

"Would you—"

"Could you stop talking to me please." He'd dreamt of this moment for a long time. He didn't want his fucking brother to spoil it. He took in everything they passed—houses, shops, garages, traffic, people, dogs. Streets of houses gave way to villages in the countryside and Caspian thought how much he'd missed this openness, fields that went on and on. The colours. The brightness. The sky clouded over but it didn't dampen his mood which was improving the further he was from Shawton.

Not long after they'd joined a motorway, Lachlan pulled off into a service station.

"I need to pee, sorry."

Caspian did too. He walked with his brother along the lines of parked cars toward the entrance, thinking that everyone who looked at him must know he'd just got out of prison. Mick, his pad mate, had warned him about that. Caspian loosened the tie around his neck but didn't take it off. He liked the strangeness. Even walking this far without meeting a barrier was something to be cherished.

The bathroom made his heart beat faster. No one watching. He could take his time. No threats. He stared into the mirror as he washed his hands. *I look tired.* His face was whiter than he'd ever seen it. Prison White. A new shade on a paint chart. He started to think about a palette that kids might like. Bogie Green, Vampire Red. Bat Black. He smiled and for a moment, glimpsed the old him.

"Sure you don't want anything to eat?" Lachlan asked as Caspian joined him outside the bathroom. "Something you've missed eating?"

Until Lachlan had added the second question, Caspian had been considering asking for a burger. Now he shook his head and pressed back his irritation. He had the feeling he was going to be irritated rather a lot over the next few days, weeks…*oh fuck it*…months.

"Can I talk to you yet?" Lachlan asked.

"No."

Caspian waited until Lachlan had pulled up in front of the house before he spoke again. "Does Mum know exactly what happened?" He wasn't sure what he wanted the answer to be.

"Yes. I told her. Early on."

Caspian bit down on the inside of his cheeks. "What did she say?"

"Not what she should have said. She was upset, but she never told me I should have spoken up. I—"

"Betsy?"

"No."

Caspian climbed out of the car. He had a sudden, violent desire to run to the treehouse before he told himself he was an idiot because Zed wouldn't be there and it would only be delaying the inevitable. Lachlan took his stuff from the boot and Caspian went with him into the house.

The hall was full of flowers. It looked like a funeral parlour waiting for the corpse—ah, which would be him. His mother rushed towards him in tears and wrapped her arms around him. Panic surged and Caspian pulled away. *Don't touch me. Don't hold me.* He backed right off and she stifled a sob.

"Caspian. Let me hold you. Please. All this time and you've not let me see you. Please."

He shook his head. His heart was hammering, his breathing laboured. No one had held him without violence in mind since Zed. "No," he whispered.

He watched the way his mother pulled herself together. All emotion gone. Turned off like a tap. "We're so thrilled to have you home."

It sounded like the way she greeted her guests. *We're so thrilled you could come.* But for a moment, a brief moment, Caspian felt sorry for her. She had no voice. She played her role as his father's wife.

"Araminta and Cressida are out," she said. "I didn't want you to be overwhelmed. They'll be here for dinner."

"Where's father?"

"At work. He'll come back early."

Is that all I warrant? That he'll come back early? But Caspian was the one who'd cut off contact. This was just his father setting the ground rules again.

"Your room's the same," she said. "We didn't change it. Of course, you can do whatever you like with it. It's a boy's room, not a…"

A man's. Caspian nodded.

"We'll buy you new clothes and get you… Well, we'll talk about it later. I *am* glad to have you home again."

Caspian picked up his plastic bag and went up the stairs. He heard his mother whispering to Lachlan. "What's wrong with him? Did he talk to you?"

"No. Give him time. Let him settle in."

Caspian opened the door of his bedroom, stood on the threshold and gave a quiet laugh. Everything looked the same, just tidier and dust-free. His sketches were still in place. Charlie Bear sat on his bed. The marble Zed had given him was still on his bedside table. But the laptop was new. Next to it was an iPhone and a bank card. Caspian switched on the bedroom light, then switched it off again. He did it twice more before he stopped. He'd not been able to turn a light on or off in prison.

He closed the door and dropped his bag on the floor. *Carpet.* He toed off his shoes and pulled off his socks. A couple of steps over the soft surface and Caspian sighed. *That feels so good.* He shed the rest of his clothes on the way to the bathroom. He could shower for as long as he wanted. Have the temperature hotter than was allowed inside. The shampoo and conditioner were ones he'd never used before. Probably the most expensive his mother could find. He suspected that was the way she was going to handle *the problem of Caspian.*

When he finally switched off the shower and reached for a towel, it was so soft, he caught his breath. His heart started to pound, and he swallowed hard. *Christ, am I going to freak out every time I remember what I missed?*

His old clothes no longer fit him. His jeans were too short and too tight. None of the seven dress shirts hanging in his closet were big enough. A couple of T-shirts were passable. He tried on everything, including his shoes, underwear and swimming trunks. By the time he was done, the bed was piled with stuff that didn't fit. He was sitting on the floor in black boxers when there was a knock on the door.

"Who is it?"

"Me," Lachlan said.

"Come in." Caspian almost laughed at being able to tell someone to come into his room until he remembered how Lachlan had never knocked before but just barged in.

Caspian pushed to his feet.

Lachlan looked from him to the bed and kept his gaze there. "Nothing fits?"

"Not much. None of the things on the bed."

"Would you like some of my clothes until you go shopping?"

"Do you still live here?"

"No, but I keep a few items in the wardrobe. We live in Tunbridge Wells."

"We?"

"My wife and I."

Caspian tried not to look shocked. *He* was the one who'd chosen to keep his family at bay and it wasn't as if he'd ever thought Lachlan would ask him to be his best man.

"If you'd been out, I'd have asked you to be my best man."

Fuck. Had his brother developed mind-reading abilities?

"I shouldn't have done what I did," Lachlan said. "I'm sorry."

Caspian didn't answer.

"It was the worst thing I've ever done, that I will ever do, and I know it's unforgivable. I want—"

"Is your wife coming tonight?"

"Not tonight. But Elise is looking forward to meeting you once you've settled in."

Caspian doubted it. Both her looking forward to meeting him and his settling in. "Is she the one who was doing medicine?"

"No, she dumped me. Elise was on my legal practice course. I'll go and get you some jeans. Anything else?"

"A pair of trainers if you have any. Would you bring some black bin liners as well, please. This can all go to a charity shop."

"I can do that." Lachlan looked pathetically grateful to be given something to do.

Caspian knew Lachlan wanted to talk to him but he wasn't sure he could cope with that today. Being sorry wasn't enough.

Lachlan returned with bin liners, a couple of pairs of jeans and some T-shirts. "If there's anything else you need, I'll be downstairs."

The smallest jeans were the best fit but he had to thread a belt through the loops to keep them up. The trainers were fine. Black Nikes with a purple stripe. Lachlan had bought a new pack of socks too. Caspian filled three black bags with his old clothes and dragged them down the stairs to the hall. His mother emerged from the drawing room as he carted down the last heavy bag.

"Lachlan says he'll take them to a charity shop," she said. "To get them out of the way."

Along with sweeping under the carpet anything she didn't like to think about.

"Tomorrow we'll go and buy you whatever you need." She smiled at him.

Caspian didn't smile back.

He was fighting the pull of the treehouse. He needed to see it. Just to be sure.

"Betsy's in the kitchen," his mother said.

He took the hint. He doubted he could let Betsy hug him and he knew she'd try. As he approached the kitchen he could smell baking. The moment he walked into the room, Betsy dropped a spoon and rushed towards him.

"Master Caspian. Oh, you've grown so much."

Caspian managed to not pull away before Betsy let him go, but only because she didn't hold him for long and he didn't have time to panic. She wiped her eyes with a tissue.

"Are you all right?" she whispered.

Caspian nodded. *No, I'm not.*

"Was it awful?"

He shrugged because it was but he'd never be able to tell anyone how awful because they wouldn't understand.

"I keep thinking back to that day, the way you crept out of the kitchen and how Lachlan went after you. If I'd seen you come back and get the keys to the Jaguar, I'd have stopped you. I wanted to come and visit you but your parents told me not to, that you didn't want to see or hear from anyone, otherwise I would have come and I'd have written. Don't think I didn't care or that I didn't worry about you."

"It's okay, Betsy. It's all over now." He swallowed hard. "Can I smell chocolate cake?"

"Your favourite. The one with the fudge icing. I've made white chocolate chip cookies too and I'm doing peppered steak and salad for dinner. You still like peppered steak?"

He nodded. Not that he'd tasted steak the whole of the time he'd been inside. Well, not anything that would pass for steak in a restaurant.

"Would you like anything to eat now?"

"No thank you."

"You look too thin."

"Not for long if you're going to bake all the things I like to eat."

She pushed a huge cookie into his hand and he slipped out of the house. The same door that he'd left through that day. It seemed a lifetime ago. One bite and sweetness flooded his mouth. Another bite and he'd eaten the entire thing. *Shit.* He knew he was too thin, but he'd have to be careful.

Caspian ran to the treehouse, though he didn't manage to get far before he was out of breath and slowed to a walk. He needed to get fit. He needed to do a lot of things. As he made his way through the wood, he tried to calm his heart rate. He wasn't stupid, so why did part of him think Zed might be there?

The place that had featured in so many of his dreams was now a ramshackle structure with missing planks and holes in the roof, the whole thing overwhelmed by ivy. He climbed up the ladder, that at least was sturdy, and pushed open the hatch. The floor seemed solid though he was careful where he put his feet. Everything had been taken out, the mattress, books, lights. The shelf hung at an angle. If there had been a message from Zed, that had gone too. Not even one origami flamingo had survived. He thought for a moment about rebuilding, but there was no point. He couldn't put the past right. All he could do was move forward.

By the time he got back to the house, the bags of clothes had gone and the Terrible Twins were home. He evaded their hugs and saw the hurt in their eyes. Too bad. Once they'd asked the obligatory questions, including whether he'd been raped in the shower—his mother had let out a muffled sob at that—they were full of what they'd done. They were off to Bristol University in October, assuming they got the grades. Cressida to study history, Araminta law.

Caspian felt relieved the pair were leaving in a couple of days to spend the summer in France. They were staying in the family's holiday home with friends from school. He felt a pang of jealousy at the idea of lying by the pool in the sun.

"You should come," Araminta said. "You're really pale. Mum and Dad aren't coming out until August, but you should come now, shouldn't he, Mum?"

"You'd like our friends," Cressida said.

He doubted it. "I'm not allowed to leave the country."

Cressida gaped at him. "Why not?"

"Because I'm still serving the sentence I was given. When you're on licence there's stuff you can't do."

"That sucks," Araminta said.

"Is that your considered legal opinion?" Caspian asked.

Everyone laughed at that. Maybe too loudly.

"What else can't you do?" Cressida asked.

"Stay overnight anywhere but here. Commit another offence."

"What constitutes an offence?" Araminta asked.

Caspian shrugged. "Anything that breaks the law."

"Even littering?" Araminta gaped at him.

"I suppose."

"Wow, so if you were stopped by the police for something really minor, you could go back to prison?" Cressida asked.

He nodded.

Caspian managed to escape on the basis of being tired and went up to his room. The phone was charged up, ready for use. Next to it was a sheet of paper with the number, and also those of his father, mother, brother and sisters. Caspian wrote his number on a piece of paper to give his SO tomorrow. Glenn Woodrow had told him he'd be at the house at nine. Caspian took Glenn's number from the information sheet he'd been given and entered it into his phone. He didn't put the other numbers in. Why would he want to call any of them?

He spent an hour messing around with the phone and laptop. Technology had changed so much. Once he'd worked out how to get online, he used Siri—fucked that up, then googled Zed and found page after page about Zed, Master of Shadows, League of Legends champion. Not his Zed. Caspian had no idea how to spell Zed's proper name but checking Iranian boys' names gave him the correct spelling only for him to find no results for Hvarechaeshman Zadeh. Nor for Tamaz. He did find Zed's father, Majid, in a couple of entries connected with a pharmacy in Maidstone.

This is fucking pointless. Not because he hadn't found anything but looking in the first place. What did he want to see? Zed's life had nothing to do with him. *Leave him alone.*

Caspian took all his sketches down from the walls, leaving greasy marks behind. He struggled to remove Blu Tack from the back without ripping the paper. Some of his early inventions still had promise, some were so crap they were funny. There were drawings of a time travel machine, an easy way to eat peas that looked suspiciously like a spoon, a diagram of a dinosaur go-kart, a machine that made toast, buttered it and spread it with marmalade, and a way to turn a house into a haunted mansion for Halloween.

He put them all in his desk. In the notepads he'd brought back from Shawton, there were four ideas that he wanted to pitch to his father because he doubted the prospect of turning Barton Hall into a place people would visit to be scared would be a winner.

The knock on the door made him jump.

"Yes?" he called.

Lachlan poked his head inside. "Father's back. Dinner in ten minutes."

"Okay."

"Is there anything you need?"

"No thank you."

Caspian was being careful to be as polite as he could manage because it kept his rage at bay. Before he left his room, he slipped the marble Zed had given him into his pocket. Maybe it would give him courage.

As he reached the bottom of the stairs, his father emerged from his study.

"Caspian! At last."

There was no attempt at a hug. Instead his father held out his hand. Caspian wrapped his fingers tighter around the marble. He didn't want to shake his father's hand. He ought to but...

His father dropped his hand. "You've grown."

You look older.

"How are you? Anything you need?" his father asked.

"I'd like to talk to you about—"

"Later. Come along. Let's eat."

When Caspian walked into the dining room, he drew in a breath. The table was laid with all the best china, glasses and silverware. Two ice buckets held bottles of champagne and there were flower arrangements the length of the table. Christmas without a tree. His mother beckoned him to the seat next to her. The twins and Lachlan were opposite. When everyone had a glass of champagne, his father stood.

237

"Tonight, the family is once again complete. Welcome home, Caspian." His father held up his glass then sipped the champagne.

Caspian wasn't sure if he wanted him to say anything else or not, but when his father sat down, he found himself feeling disappointed. The food was great but much as he'd looked forward to eating something other than the repetitive prison diet, he found himself struggling to swallow. Feeling his mother watching every mouthful he took, didn't help. He left half of his smoked salmon starter. He made himself eat all the steak because he knew he needed to eat something, but he couldn't face the potatoes or any of the vegetables.

Conversation had flowed, probably because he wasn't talking. His mother was still doing lots of charity work and currently arranging a summer ball for a cancer charity that would be held in a marquee in the grounds. It was the biggest event she'd ever arranged and apparently a couple of royals were coming.

Then Lachlan surprised him. Caspian had assumed his brother would be a hotshot corporate lawyer working long hours and earning a lot of money. That might still be true, but Lachlan was also part of a scheme called *Lawyers in Schools* that partnered lawyers with students in economically and socially disadvantaged communities. Judging by the scowl on their father's face, he didn't approve.

Betsy had made Eton mess for dessert. Caspian's favourite. He managed half of what had been put in the dish.

I don't belong here anymore. This had been his life, but it wasn't now. He felt as though he was in a kind of limbo. He didn't want to be here, but he had nowhere else to go.

When the meal was done, he followed his father to his study. Caspian had removed the four plans from his notebooks that he wanted to show him. He took them from his pocket and unfolded them. His father sat behind his desk and pointed to the chair in front of it.

"I've sorted things out," his father said.

Caspian tensed.

"Obviously you need a job. A suitable job. I've had a word with a friend of mine. You remember Malcolm Dennison? He owns FunKit. He has stores all over the place including one on Oxford Street. I think even you could manage to sell clothing and accessories. You never know, you might possibly work your way up to become a store manager."

238

Fuck you. He slipped his hand into his pocket and wrapped his fingers around the marble.

"His daughter Poppy works in the Oxford Street branch. She was a bit of a wayward child too."

A goth who never said a word whenever Caspian had met her. She hid behind her long straight black hair.

"Her father and I think you and she would make a good match."

Caspian almost missed that. "What?"

"She's a... nice girl."

So she wasn't nice. Caspian opened his mouth to remind his father he was gay, then shut it again. *Timing.* He got up and laid the four sheets of paper on the desk.

"This is what I want to do. A business of my own. I've come up with a number of ideas and I selected these four. I'd like you to back me on one of them."

His father picked up the first sheet.

"That's a use for 3D printing," Caspian said. "I saw a programme about it on the TV and I was thinking of ways to use the technology and came up with something to help children with cerebral palsy who have to walk with sticks or crutches. They could have tailor made supports constructed for a reasonable sum so..."

His father tossed the drawing aside and picked up another.

"Tattoo ink that's not permanent," Caspian said. "Something that would last maybe a year and then fade. By then the person would know if—"

"You know nothing about biology and chemistry."

"But I have the ideas, that's—"

"Caspian. You're not bright enough to follow these through. What's this one?" He picked up another sheet of paper. "A hot tub?"

"No, it's a water treadmill. You exercise in it. Everyday exercise or physical therapy. It takes up a lot less room than a pool. Though you could use it as a hot tub after. It generates electricity too."

His father rolled his eyes and Caspian felt as if he was sinking in quicksand.

"The last one is a gadget you put on your tap that saves water. It turns the flow into a spiral. It's attractive and practical."

"How do you know it saves water?"

"Because the shape of the spiral means less water is flowing than if you just had the tap turned on." Caspian took a deep breath. "This is what I want to do, not work in a clothes shop. I want you to provide the funding for me to get a prototype made of one of my ideas. Please." The last word stuck in his throat, but... "I have other sketches too if you—"

"No. I'm not throwing money away on ridiculous ideas. I'll give you a couple of weeks for you to get used to life and then I'll buy you a rail card. You can come on the train with me to London. Work in Malcolm's shop. Prove you can hold down a job and then we'll talk again. I've invited the Dennisons over for lunch next weekend."

Caspian's despair was a physical pain in his chest, a gnawing agony that blocked his throat and shrivelled his lungs. Breathing became impossible let alone speaking. He grabbed his drawings and rushed out.

Chapter Twenty-Two

Only after all the graduates of a particular department had crossed the stage were the audience expected to applaud, but as Zed shook hands with the dean, he heard Jonas's loud whoops and bit back his smile. Zed hadn't even wanted to come to the ceremony, but Jonas and Henry had insisted and when Henry told him his plans for the rest of the day and asked for his help, Zed had given in.

Once Zed had returned his hired gown, he made his way out of the Royal Albert Hall, and headed for where he'd arranged to meet the pair. They weren't looking his way and Zed stopped for a moment and took in the two of them, dressed in dark suits, heads together as they chattered and felt a jolt of love so powerful it made him well up.

Jonas was the first to spot him and rushed over to wrap his arms around him. "Congratulations!"

"Thank you for embarrassing me."

Jonas laughed. "Henry elbowed me so hard I'm pretty sure he broke a rib."

"I can't take my whooper swan anywhere. Congratulations, Zed. A first in Computer Science and Maths. Fantastic. We couldn't be prouder."

"Thanks for not whooping."

Henry chuckled. "I only whoop in private."

"So where are we going for my birthday lunch?" Jonas asked.

"Wait and see." Henry moved to the kerb, put up his hand and waved, and within moments a cab had pulled up.

"Good grief. That never works for me," Jonas said.

"I have the magic touch."

Jonas sniggered and Zed put his hands over his ears which made Jonas laugh out loud.

They piled into the black cab which transported them a few miles to Trafalgar Square.

When they were out of the cab, Henry checked his watch. "We're a little early for the reservation. We're eating at the Portrait Restaurant inside the National Gallery. Zed, would you go and see if they'll take us now?"

"Can't you just call them?" Jonas asked.

"They're more likely to respond favourably to someone in person." Henry smoothly turned Jonas to face the other way and Zed went to get his cello.

The instrument was already set up and tuned. Zed sat on the edge of the fountain, raised his bow and began playing Beethoven's Ode to Joy. Jonas instantly turned and gave him a bemused smile.

Zed played his heart out. People stopped to listen. Another cellist joined him, then another and the double basses. One by one most of the members of the London Symphony Orchestra joined in and Jonas's jaw dropped. Everyone that could come, was here to celebrate Jonas's fortieth birthday with a flash mob. Violinists and wind players played as they wove through the crowds to congregate in front of Jonas and Henry. The timpani were there and the brass section stood on the raised area next to the steps leading to the National Gallery. Zed hadn't had much trouble persuading them. He'd been to so many rehearsals with Jonas that Zed knew almost all of the orchestra members.

Beethoven's powerful music rolled around the square and soared into the air. Tourists were gaping and smiling, holding up phones, taking pictures and videos, and then the choir joined in, people jumping as those around them burst into song. The sound was electrifying. Jonas stood wide-eyed in shock as Henry moved from his side over to a small group of singers and sang in German with them.

The music was an invitation to sing for joy and that's what everyone did, voice and instruments combined. The line *Diesen Kuß der ganzen Welt*—this kiss is for all the world was the perfect way to describe what was happening, but for two men, it was going to be more than that.

When the last note faded, everyone clapped and as instruments were put away and players dispersed, Zed was given his guitar and the other members of his band joined him in front of Jonas and Henry.

Zed sang a verse of a new song he'd written.
"Thank you for loving me
I may not say the words as often as I should
But you're the one that I love
Thank you for loving me
I never dared to dream that someone like you
Would ever want someone like me
Thank you for loving me
You lift me up when I fall down

There's nothing I wouldn't do
To spend the rest of my life with you
Thank you for loving me
When others turn away
You've never let me fail
You raise me up and fly with me
Thank you for loving me"

Henry dropped on one knee in front of Jonas and held out a ring. "Will you please marry me?"

Zed had never seen Jonas so shocked. *Never.* He looked as stonelike as the Trafalgar lions, his puppyish charm for a moment stilled.

"I need an answer," Henry said. "My knee is killing me."

Jonas hauled him to his feet. "Yes."

Henry put the ring on his finger and they kissed. The orchestra members who'd sneaked back clapped and whistled. Zed thought the moment was just perfect. Life was made up of moments. Some good, some bad, some like this one that swept everyone up in a burst of sunshine. This was a moment you wanted to swallow whole so you could absorb every second of it.

Finally, the pair broke apart. Jonas beckoned Zed over and flung his arms around him and Henry.

"I get the birthday lunch as well, right?" Jonas asked.

Zed laughed and left them to it. He had things to do.

Jonas and Henry arrived home around six. There was no sign of anything different, but when Jonas opened the door, everyone cheered and Jonas fell back into Henry's arms. Henry and Zed had arranged a surprise party. Caterers had been employed along with wait staff, and the house was full of people. Zed had invited the members of his band and they were going to play.

"There's nothing else going to happen, is there?" Jonas asked. "No naked guys jumping out of cakes? No pole dancers? Only my heart can't take much more. Er... Actually, it could take the pole dancers."

"I've cancelled the strippers." Henry took hold of his hand. "Let's get changed into something more comfortable."

"Don't take too long," someone shouted. "We know what you two are like."

Zed helped himself to a glass of champagne from a waiter's tray and joined his band. Electric Ice. There were four of them. Jonesie on drums, Akash on bass, Zed and Fin on guitar. Fin was the one in charge. He and Zed wrote the songs and did most of the singing. Only Zed had been at Imperial. Jonesie was a plumber. Akash had just graduated from the London School of Economics and Fin had studied music at Royal Holloway and graduated three years ago. A chance meeting with Fin at a concert had led to Zed being asked to audition after their other guitarist walked out.

Plans for working fulltime for MI5 were sort of on-hold. The band had been playing small gigs all over London and putting their music on YouTube had attracted the attention of a guy who wanted to work as their manager. Pete Corrigan found them a booking agent and everything suddenly seemed to be moving lightning fast. Jonas and Henry had told him to follow his heart. Except Zed didn't know where his heart was taking him.

"I like the suit," Fin said in his ear. "Very sexy. Maybe we should all wear them."

"It's been done before. The Jam, The Clash, The Beatles."

"Even so. It would give us an identity."

Zed felt Fin's arm slide under his jacket onto his back and he pulled away. "I'm going to get changed."

"Can I help?"

"No."

Zed made his way upstairs to his room. Fin wouldn't take the hint that he wasn't interested. Zed wasn't sure if it was going to cause problems with the band if he kept saying no, but that was always going to be his answer.

The party was great. After the band had finished, Jonas persuaded Zed to play the piano and Zed played and sang whatever people asked for—choices that ranged between *You're Welcome* from *Moana* to Adele's *Make You Feel My love,* Hosier's *Take Me To Church* and *The Boogie Woogie Stomp.* The furniture had been moved back so that people could dance and they'd have had Zed playing all night if Henry hadn't insisted someone else took over.

Zed was on his way to get another drink when Jonas threw his arm over his shoulder. "You are so good. Really good. You have no idea how good you are. You're as good as…"

You're drunk. "You?"

244

Jonas laughed. "You're a lot better than me. You come alive when people are listening and you do something so special that… I wish… No, I don't wish, I know. You're our son in every way that matters, you know that, right? The best we could have ever hoped for. I wish we'd had you sooner. I wish you hadn't ever been hurt. You've got to be our best man at the wedding. Oh shit, I wasn't supposed to ask you yet. Pretend I haven't. Fuck, he'll guess. You know I can't hide a thing. Still try though."

Zed hugged him. "Okay."

Jonas was whisked away by someone Zed didn't know. A hand landed on Zed's shoulder and he turned to see Jackson. Zed had spotted him earlier but they'd not had the chance to speak.

"Congratulations," Jackson said. "A first from Imperial is quite an achievement."

"Thanks."

"Can we go outside and have a chat?"

Zed nodded. He hoped Jackson didn't want a decision about the job. Zed had passed on a few pieces of information during his time at university. They ranged from observations on students who seemed slightly off-kilter, about others who were brilliant in their field and might be useful to MI5, plus comments about mosques he'd visited, imams he'd met. He found nothing suspect about Imperial's Islamic Society. But they hadn't known he was gay. Zed had stayed firmly in the closet.

Jackson ushered Zed deeper into the garden. "I wasn't sure whether to tell you tonight but there's no good time to give this sort of news."

Oh fuck. "Tamaz?" Zed whispered.

"He's left Pakistan but we don't know where he went. It's not him I need to talk to you about." He looked Zed in the face. "Your father died this morning."

Zed swallowed. He waited for it to sink in but when he felt nothing wondered if it had. *I don't care. I should but I don't. He hated me. What am I supposed to feel?* He struggled to find memories of a time when he'd been loved, when his father had held him and smiled, when he'd praised him, laughed with him and not at him. Zed found nothing. *That* made him sad.

"How did he die?"

245

"He was undergoing surgery for bowel cancer in Maidstone hospital and there were complications. His heart stopped and they couldn't get it started again."

Oh, so he had a heart?

"We've been keeping an eye on him, in case Tamaz got in touch. We don't think he has."

Zed felt himself crumbling, the weight of responsibility suddenly heavy on his shoulders. "I'll have to arrange everything. The funeral. The house. Tell his family in Iran but I don't know how. I don't know what to do."

"We can ask people to sort out the funeral."

"I can pay for it. I have money."

"He can pay for it. He must have money."

"I don't want to go to the funeral. Shit, do you think I should?"

"It's entirely up to you."

"Yeah, I should go. Okay. I'll go."

"You might see if anyone at the mosque he attended knows how to contact Tamaz."

Zed nodded. *Oh no, don't ask me to do that to my brother.*

Jackson sighed. "If he's joined Isis…"

Fuck. He won't have. But if he has… "I'll ask, okay?"

"Right."

"Don't tell Jonas or Henry about this. Not today. I don't want them to be upset. I'm not upset. I'm just…nothing."

"All right. I feel I should say I'm sorry, but I'd be lying. Was he ever a good father?"

"Not to me."

"Will he have made a will?"

"Very likely. One thing I remember from the summer school from hell is that it's the duty of a Muslim who has anything to bequeath not to let two nights pass without writing a will about it."

"And will you get anything?"

Zed shrugged. "Islamic law states it's absolutely prohibited to deny an heir his share. Once a person dies, they have no rights over their assets. Their wealth passes to Allah and it's distributed according to His will as stated in the Quran. So even if my father didn't want me to have a penny because I was a disobedient, disrespectful, bad son, he can't stop it happening. But, as I no longer practise the Muslim faith, I'm pretty sure that means I don't inherit."

246

"You've spent the last three years appearing for all intents and purposes to be Muslim. That should continue. Take your share of whatever your father has left. Do some good with it."

"I could donate it to an organisation my father would have hated." Zed smiled. "A LGBTQ charity. 'Course, he might have spent it all or re-mortgaged the house. If there is anything it might be swallowed by debts. And I've just thought of something. I have no proof I'm his son. You gave me a different name."

"Yes, you're right. Which is why I've brought you this." Jackson handed him an envelope. "Your National Insurance Number as Hvarechaeshman Zadeh and a copy of your birth certificate."

"Am I going to be pleased?"

"Depends what you want to see. I'll make arrangements for the funeral and whatever else needs doing and call you."

"Thank you."

"Made a decision about working full-time for us?"

"Not yet."

"Have a break this summer. You've worked hard. You deserve it."

Zed went back into the house and went up to his room before he took the certificate out of the envelope. Majid Zadeh was named as his father. He went back downstairs and got drunk.

By the time Zed emerged from his room the next day, it was close to lunchtime and the house had been returned to its pre-party state. He'd already had a conversation with Jackson that morning. His father's funeral would be the following day. Ten o'clock at the Everlasting Gardens, a Muslim burial ground near Maidstone. *Janazah salah*, prayers for the deceased, would be performed on site by an *alim*, a religious scholar.

Theoretically, he should have been buried sooner but Zed had apparently been sick which also meant he'd not had to wash his father's body at least three times. Jackson had arranged for someone else to do that as well as wrapping the body according to Islamic practice.

What sort of sick? Zed had asked.

Stomach bug. Easiest get out clause Jackson told him.

Zed poured himself and Jonas a coffee, then headed for the music room where Jonas was practising. He put Jonas's mug on the coffee table, then sat and listened to some moody modern piece he'd never

247

heard Jonas play before. The throaty sound he was pulling from his violin was brilliant. Sounded like a pissed off tiger. Zed put down his coffee, closed his eyes and leaned back.

If he worked for MI5 how much time would he have for music? Would he still be able to be in the band? If the band took off, he couldn't do a daytime job as well. But even if the band was successful, that success might not last. The chances of making it were small no matter how talented you were. His heart pulled him to music, his head toward the job.

"Have I sent you to sleep?" Jonas asked.

"Not with those discordant sounds." Zed opened his eyes. "Can I borrow your car for a few days?"

"Yep, why?"

"My father's died."

Jonas put down his violin and dropped on the couch next to him. "Damn. Is that what Jackson told you last night? I was on the roof. I saw the two of you in the garden."

"Yes."

"He could have bloody waited."

"Muslims have to be buried quickly and he knows what my relationship with my father was like."

"How did he die?"

"In hospital. He'd been admitted two weeks earlier with bowel cancer. His heart stopped in the middle of an operation and they couldn't get it started again." Zed turned to look at him. "And you know what I thought? *So the bastard actually had a heart?*" He gave a short laugh.

"Oh damn, Zed."

They sat in silence for a moment or two.

"How did he treat you before your mother died? Is there some memory you can pull up of him being kind?"

"He was never kind. Before she died, the best I could say of him was that he was tolerant. I knew he liked Tamaz the best. He didn't try to hide it. Mum did all she could to make up for it. Which made Tamaz jealous of me."

"Families can be messy things."

"Not ours." Zed took Jonas's hand.

"No, not ours." Jonas hugged him. "So what about the funeral. Do you need help to arrange it?"

"Jackson has arranged everything. Well, got someone to arrange it. Tomorrow at ten. I just have to turn up. I don't even *have* to do that but I feel I should."

"You want me to come with you?"

"No, I'll be okay. Thanks for offering. I'll probably go and stay at the house for a couple of days afterwards. The things my father went into hospital with will be given to me at the funeral. That includes his keys. I need to sort stuff out, find out how to contact his parents, assuming they're still alive, see if there are bills to pay. Put the house on the market, I guess."

"Let me help."

"No. I can do it. It'll give me time to think about what I'm going to do with my life."

Jonas gave a little smile. "You're all grown up. When did that happen?"

The last funeral Zed had attended had been his mother's. He'd knelt beside his father and brother and now he was alone in front of his father's body for *Salat al-Janazah*, funeral prayers. He'd dressed in his graduation suit and Jonas's black tie. The other mourners were in a mixture of suits and shalwar kameez.

Zed had thought he might have felt something by now, but he didn't. Not even when he helped put his father in the ground, positioned to lie on his right side facing the Kaaba, the sacred building at Mecca. Ropes were removed from the head and feet and a layer of wood laid to cover the body, so soil didn't directly touch it.

More prayers, three handfuls of dirt thrown by Zed, then by the other mourners before the grave could be filled in. Jackson had arranged for a meal to be served and Zed did what Jackson had asked him to do and talked to those who'd come, noted in particular the names of any who asked about Tamaz.

People lined up to shake his hand and tell him how much they'd liked his father, what a good man he'd been, a good friend, a good employer, a good Muslim, a caring pharmacist. They were talking about a different man, one Zed had never known.

He recognised a few faces from when he'd attended the mosques in Lewisham and Maidstone, and one man from the pharmacy. He got no hint that anyone had known he'd run away from home and

249

wondered just what lies his father had told. When one guy in his thirties, who said he was from Maidstone mosque, had asked him about Imperial and said how thrilled his father had been by how well he'd done, Zed's throat clenched. He had no idea that his father had known. His name was different. *How had he known?* Maybe he hadn't.

Zed would give this guy's name to Jackson. Basem Nadir. He tried to find more about him but no one else there seemed to know him which was strange. When Zed spotted Nadir leaving, he slipped to the window and took a picture with his phone of him and his car. *Something or nothing?*

Jackson had taught him that even thinking that meant there was most likely something.

Zed reached the house in Upper Barton at two that afternoon. At the funeral, he'd been handed a bag with his father's clothes, copies of his death certificate, his phone, wallet and keys. His father had been taken to the hospital by ambulance so his car still sat on the drive. A new BMW. Zed pulled up behind it.

He was about to get out of the car when he instead sank back in the seat. He'd sworn never to come back here and here he was. The house had been his home but it hadn't felt the same after his mother had died. He exhaled. He hadn't thought he could come here without thinking about Caspian and he'd been right. He should be out of prison so maybe he was at home. So near and yet a world away. He wondered about trying to get in touch with him and could almost hear Jonas's voice in his head. *Leave him alone.*

Zed opened the car door and climbed out with the house keys and his phone. He left everything else in the car and locked it as he walked to the door. The garden was an overgrown mess. He'd never seen it looking as bad. The lawn barely recognisable as a lawn under a riot of weeds. Nothing had been touched for far longer than a couple of weeks. He'd assumed his father had taken ill quite recently but maybe he was wrong. The windows were dirty and piles of leaves had blown up against the walls and accumulated in every corner. The outdoor furniture was filthy. *Fuck.*

There was no longer anything to hurt him in this place but Zed hesitated before he turned the key. It was a warm day but as he pushed open the door, which scraped and stuttered across the floor in reluctance, it was as if he'd opened the door on winter. The chill hit him like a physical blow and he caught his breath. Inside it was dark, damp and dusty, the air still and heavy. Zed kicked aside the mail and walked through to the kitchen. It was warmer in there, brighter, the sun shining through the grimy windows. *Unloved* was the thought that went through his head. The house had been loved once, but love had died with his mother.

He wished Jonas and Henry were with him. He called Jonas.

"Hi, how did it go? Are you okay? Where are you?" Jonas asked.

"It went okay. I'm fine. I'm at the house."

"Is it fit to stay in? Are you sure you're okay?"

"Honestly, I'm fine. I'm going to sort out something to eat and I'll give you a call tomorrow. Sure you don't need your car? My father's is here so I can probably use that."

"No, I don't need it. Be careful, okay?"

"I will. Bye."

Then he phoned Henry, who'd also asked him to call.

"I'm at the house," Zed told him. "And I'm fine."

"You didn't fall to pieces at the funeral?"

Zed chuckled. "It's not allowed. No wailing or gnashing of teeth. You can cry but I didn't bother."

"I hope you'd shed a tear for me."

Zed sucked in a breath. "Don't you dare die. Don't. Don't." He heard the break in his voice and was helpless to hold back his sob.

"Zed, Zed," Henry whispered. "It's okay. We're not going anywhere. Sure you don't want one or both of us to come down?"

Zed pulled himself together. "No. I'll be a few days sorting things out then I'll come home."

"Be careful," Henry told him.

"I always am. Bye."

His final call was to Jackson. One that lasted twice as long as the other two. Zed went over everything that had happened, who'd he'd spoken to, his thoughts about them, particularly about Basem Nadir, and he sent Jackson the pictures.

He put his phone in his pocket, opened the fridge and slammed it shut again as the smell of rotten food rushed out. *Fuck.* He couldn't face that for a while. The freezer was only half full, but he spotted a four cheese pizza he could eat later.

Zed went back out to the car and brought in the bag of his father's things, and his own bag. He took the latter upstairs. He needed to get

251

changed. He didn't want to wreck his suit. When he pushed open the door of his old room, he let out a startled gasp. It was totally bare. A carpet but no curtains, no furniture. *Please let there be a bed in Tamaz's old room.* Or he'd be sleeping on the sofa because there was no way he was lying in his father's bed.

Tamaz's room looked just the same as Zed remembered. Almost as if his brother had just stepped out for a while. Zed changed out of his suit and hung it in the empty closet. He stripped the bed, went looking for sheets in the airing cupboard and was relieved when he found them. Once the bed was made, he felt better.

Then he slowly pushed open the door of his father's room and for a moment, he thought he saw him standing by the window. "Dad?" But the sensation had gone in an instant. Just as fucking well, really. It would be a cruel twist to find this had all been some massive lie.

The room smelt awful. Zed raised his arm to his nose and blocked it, breathing through his mouth as he walked over to the windows. Once they were unlocked, he opened them wide, then retreated from the room and returned downstairs. He picked up the mail in the hall and put it on the kitchen worktop. Nothing looked important.

He left his father's study until last. His computer sat on the desk. Zed went to get his father's phone from the living room and then returned to the study. He opened the top drawer of the desk, found the phone charger and plugged it in. A quick look through the desk drawers revealed plenty of labelled folders but no address book. Zed picked up the phone and looked through his father's contacts. Tamaz wasn't there.

Chapter Twenty-Three

Caspian was kicking gravel on the drive when Glenn Woodrow, his supervising officer, pulled up in front of the house, thirty minutes late. Glenn got out of his car holding an orange folder and headed towards him.

"Morning." Glenn blinked a lot. *Stress, a nervous disorder or maybe he was a vampire?* "Let's get out of the sun."

Definitely a vampire. Caspian walked into the house and led Glenn into the dining room. His father had said they could use his study but Caspian didn't want to.

"Would you like a coffee?" Caspian asked.

There was a machine on the side table that Betsy had shown him how to use and she'd baked lavender shortbread biscuits. Caspian doubted they'd soften Glenn up.

"Yes, thanks. Black, no sugar."

Glenn laid out his paperwork while Caspian made the drinks. He carried them over to the table along with the biscuits.

"How was your first day?" Glenn asked.

Bloody awful with moments of fucking brilliance. "It was okay."

"It takes time to adjust. Don't expect too much of yourself or anyone else. They're unsure how to talk to you or behave around you. And I'm sure you're the same with them."

Sadly, that didn't apply to his father who sounded exactly as he always had. Domineering, bombastic and intolerant. Nor to his mother who was the ultimate ice queen. Nor to his self-absorbed sisters. But Lachlan… Something was different about Lachlan.

Glenn yet again went through the conditions for Caspian being released on licence. There ought to be a pictorial guide for this too, Caspian thought, then dismissed the idea. He wanted to forget about the last five years.

"You must *not* miss an appointment to see me. And be on time."

But it's okay if you're not? "Are you always going to come here?"

"No. You'll mostly need to go to Ashford. No driving, remember. This is a list of the times, dates and places of meetings for the next year. Don't turn up drunk or on drugs. Sometimes I might call you instead of us meeting up. The probation service is overworked and very busy. Respond promptly to my texts or emails. If there's any sort of emergency where the police are involved, call me."

"Do I have to live here?"

"For the time being, yes. I need to approve any place you want to live."

"If I found a bedsit…"

"I'm not in favour of your parents supporting you living elsewhere. You have to learn how to look after yourself."

"I can get a job."

"Doing what? You don't realise how lucky you are, living rent-free in a house like this. Meals provided. No doubt your laundry done for you, your room cleaned. Why on earth would you want to leave? You're the first person I've ever had on licence with a home this size. The conditions aren't onerous for someone in your position. I don't see us having any issues." He looked at Caspian over his glasses. "Do you?"

"No," Caspian muttered.

"Now, training. Here are details of some courses you might like to sign up for. IT, office skills, that sort of thing. I can't force you to go to any of them, but if you're still unemployed after three months, you might be compelled to attend one or more. You have to report to the Job Centre and abide by the rules. Have you made an appointment yet?"

Caspian shook his head.

"You might be able to support yourself with savings but they'll run out eventually. The first job you get might well not be what you want—preparing food, labouring, warehouse work but it's a chance to prove you're dependable and self-reliant, and therefore a stepping stone to the next level."

Caspian dutifully nodded. *Fuck you.*

"Don't forget, if you get a job you have to tell me. I need to approve it."

No acting in porn movies then? Caspian thought but didn't say.

"You're very fortunate," Glenn said. "You have a supportive, wealthy family. You're not violent. You're not an ex-gang member, a sex offender, a habitual thief or a drug addict. I don't believe you're bad. You made a mistake and now you need to be the best person you can to make up for what you did."

He stared at Caspian and Caspian stared back.

"You've never talked about the day of the accident," Glenn said. "Maybe you should. Maybe it will help you."

Fucking go away.

Glenn stared at him but Caspian didn't speak but a slow rage filled him.

"Just saying the words—*I did it*—would be a step in the right direction. If I can put on my report that you've admitted what you did, understood the damage you'd done and were truly remorseful..."

Then you'd look good and probably get a clap on the back.

Caspian kept quiet and Glenn sighed.

More forms to sign, then less than fifteen minutes after arriving, Glenn was driving away. Never again would Caspian compromise himself or make himself unhappy just to satisfy the demands of another person. He'd been seventeen years old when he'd suffered the worst betrayal of his life. He'd never let that happen again. He'd rebuild his life and be who he wanted to be.

But he knew it would take time.

Caspian had money in the bank. His grandfather had set up a savings account for him and paid into it monthly until he'd died. Caspian had added money given to him for birthdays and Christmas. He had over twenty thousand pounds. The money put into his prison account was in the process of being transferred to him. He hadn't touched it while he was in there but now his father had set fire to his dreams, Caspian had less qualms about using it.

Though Glenn was right about one thing. The money would run out. Caspian had to find a job.

He carried the dirty coffee cups and the plate of biscuits back to the kitchen. No one was around to ask him how he'd got on. Lachlan and his father were at work. Lachlan would be returning at the weekend with his wife. *That should be fun.* The Terrible Twins had gone shopping in London. His mother was meeting friends in Tunbridge Wells and it was Betsy's day off. His mother must have forgotten she'd offered to take him to buy clothes.

Caspian pocketed his marble, phone and wallet, locked the house and walked towards the village. He set off feeling reasonably happy. His PO and Glenn had warned him that freedom might be harder to deal with than prison, but Caspian couldn't believe that was true. How could being out in the fresh air with views in every direction be harder to deal with than having to look at the same four walls for hours on end?

Everything around him made his heart sing. The crops growing in the fields, the new leaves on the trees, birds, the colour of the sky, being able to walk without stopping, without needing to check behind him. That was maybe the best thing of all. Yesterday and today and maybe for many more days, he'd be rediscovering the world—how fast traffic moved, how food *should* taste, how insubstantial doors felt compared to those in prison, how much pleasure small things could bring him—switching the light on and off, clean cotton sheets, soft pillows, fluffy towels, an endless shower in safety. The awareness of what it was like to be alive would return.

There was no point being angry about what had happened, he knew that. He'd been let down by his family and he'd let himself down too. He'd chosen to stay silent and thought he'd be treated like a…hero or something on his return. Instead his father was busy planning the rest of Caspian's life. That wasn't going to happen.

Caspian didn't think he'd ever be able to extinguish the rage that was on a slow simmer inside him, though he fucking hoped it eventually evaporated. Those moments when fury flared into his throat to choke him hadn't diminished over his time inside, but he didn't want to wreck the rest of his life seething with bitterness.

The sooner he was living somewhere else, the better he'd feel. Wouldn't he? Except along with that simmering anger at the unfairness of what had been done to him, at his weakness for letting it happen, lurked something that was almost more alarming—fear. It was like an octopus, its tentacles reaching out to strangle any pleasure. Even now, walking along a country lane with a blue sky overhead and no one waiting to stab him in the back, anxiety lurked like a raptor readying to pounce. A rustling bush and he'd freak out.

Before all this he'd never been nervous or hesitant. He'd seen life as one big adventure. He'd thought he could do anything, go everywhere, see the world, that he'd invent something brilliant and his father would be…would be proud of him. Now things were a challenge when they shouldn't be. The slightest thing made him jump or shake. The sudden flutter of a bird taking flight. The bang of a door. Sitting in a car. Choosing what to eat for breakfast. Trying to sleep in a comfortable bed. Trying to sleep when there was no one calling out or crying for their mother.

This isn't me.

If he was to break free of what held him back, which included his family, he needed a job, but the last thing he wanted to do was work in a fucking clothes shop because that was a trap set by his father. He clenched his fists thinking of what his father had said about Poppy. He was sure Poppy wouldn't want to marry him either. Their fathers were both dickheads.

Caspian was full of thoughts about what he *didn't* want to do. Not work in catering or carry materials around a building site or stack shelves in a supermarket. All considered suitable placements for an ex-offender like him who had mostly failed his GCSEs, read like a robot and whose handwriting looked like the trail of an epileptic snail. *I'm fucking useless.* His reading might have improved slightly, there was so little to do inside that when he couldn't play the guitar, he'd *had* to read, but he was still bad at it. His poetry wasn't bad, he didn't think, but no one had read it other than him and it wasn't as if there were loads of jobs for poets.

His list of possible occupations was distressingly small and largely unrealistic. He'd pinned his hopes on having his father's support to develop one of his ideas. Hope that had been destroyed. All those promises by his father and Lachlan about what they'd do for him had turned out to be lies. Caspian's irritation started to climb. Even a threat to reveal the truth would have no effect. After all this time he definitely wouldn't be believed.

By the time he'd reached the village general store, depression had smothered his anger though not his anxiety. Another new thing to conquer. All he had to do was walk inside, pick up a bottle of water or a bar of chocolate, pay, say thank you and leave. Simple enough yet the thought of it freaked him out.

Christ, do it! You're not a fucking coward. He pushed open the door and walked up and down the three aisles of the shop distracted for a few moments by the things he'd missed eating. Scones, crumpets, crisps, chocolate cake, unusual fresh fruit, croissant, peanut butter…

He picked up a Crunchie and a bottle of water and took them to the counter. He recognised the guy and saw in an instant that he'd been recognised too. A scowl replaced Don Dawson's smile.

Dawson picked up the chocolate bar and water and put them on a shelf behind him. "Get out. Don't come back. I don't want your custom."

257

Caspian returned his wallet to his pocket and walked out with his heart hammering. He passed a group of ramblers on their way in and kept his head down. Why hadn't he thought to wear sunglasses? *Why did I even fucking come out?*

While his heart was urging him to go home, instead he forced himself to push open the door of the post office. Of course it was the same woman behind the till in there as well and when she refused to serve him, his chest felt so tight he thought he might be having a heart attack. *I am not going home without fucking buying something.* But it seemed to him now that every person he saw knew exactly who he was and despised him. Logic told him that wasn't possible, people would have moved out of and into Lower Barton, but anxiety overpowered his common sense, turned reality on its head.

Christ. What if the families of those girls saw him wandering around? Why had he come back here? The pain deepened, a bit like indigestion except it didn't stay in his chest but spread down his arms and legs, up his neck, into his skull, into his face. It filled his head with fluttering wings, blocked his throat with a crawling sensation that he was convinced was insects, until he couldn't breathe. A complete system failure apart from his heart that pounded so fast and hard he could hear it, a frantic tribal drumbeat. He tried to move faster, get away, but everything wavered and wobbled. Things that should be still, like lampposts, were moving. Or was it just him? Caspian staggered as the ground rolled under his feet.

Need to get somewhere safe. My bed. My pad. He forced his feet into a clumsy run and stumbled. *The woods. Get to the woods. Hide. Oh fuck. I'm going to die. Oh God, I'm dying.*

He lurched a few more yards before he fell. Just about got his hands out to save himself, but still hit his head on the ground. Dazed by pain and shock, he tried and failed to get up. No one came to help him. He was pretty sure his eyes were open but he didn't know where he was. He could have been on another fucking planet for all he knew.

It's a panic attack. That's all. He'd seen guys have them inside. *Calm down.*

Oh fuck. As if he could *calm down.* Everything was out of control. He was scared he was going to die. All he could think was that this was too much, too overwhelming, too fucking intense. Caspian pressed his arm to his mouth and bit down—hard.

Pain jerked him back. He tasted blood in his mouth and realised he'd broken his skin. Luckily it didn't look like teeth marks. His heart no longer hammered. His lungs weren't struggling. His sense of doom was receding.

Caspian had no idea how long it took him to get back to his feet, how he even managed it, but he found himself walking down the road out of Lower Barton in the direction of Upper Barton. He'd take the long way home and cut across the fields on the other side of the next village rather than reverse his path. So much for the marble giving him courage. Zed had told him he was giving him the world but it was slipping through Caspian's fingers.

He had to stop a couple of times to pull himself together. He was safe. He wasn't going to die. He repeated the words over and over in his head.

By the time he reached the general store in Upper Barton, he was desperately thirsty. He went in to buy a bottle of water and thought he'd succeeded until a woman came out from the room at the back and stopped the girl serving him, pushing his money back across the counter. Caspian so very nearly left it lying there and walked out with the water but he didn't.

There was no panic attack this time just a deep-rooted hopelessness. But he made himself go into the pub and sighed with relief when he had a half pint of shandy in his hand. He scuttled outside to the seats in front and took several gulps of the cold liquid. But when he put the glass down on the table, a guy came up and spat in it.

"Fuck off. You're not wanted," the man snarled.

The temptation to throw the drink in his face was strong but even that might be enough to get him put back inside, so Caspian got up and walked away. He heard the splatter of liquid hitting the pavement behind him as he carried on down Middleham Road. One last shop to try. He might as well find out if he was barred from everywhere. It was a matter of pride now to face these demons at least.

When he walked in, there was a customer standing at the counter. A tall, slim dark-haired guy. Caspian went to the chiller section on the far side of the shop. He'd try and buy a drink and a sandwich.

"Six pounds fifty-two," he heard a woman say.

"Thanks. I'd like to put this help-wanted card in the window."

Caspian clung to the side of the refrigeration unit, his knuckles as white as bones. It couldn't be Zed, but it sounded just like him.

"Fifty pence a week."

"One week is fine. Shall I put it up on my way out?"

Why would Zed be back in this village?

"Please. There's a space at the bottom. Just slip it into the holder."

Caspian had to know, had to move, but for a moment, it was as if he'd forgotten the mechanics of walking. But he reached the end of the aisle, caught a glimpse of the side of the guy's face and gasped. *Too loud.* He pulled back out of sight. *Zed! Oh fuck. It is him.* Caspian peered over the top shelf and watched Zed slot a small white card into the plastic holder before he left the shop. Caspian took the card with him as he followed.

He stood out of sight in the shop doorway and watched as Zed opened the door of a silver car and drove off in the direction of where he used to live. Caspian walked after him. *Oh God, Jesus, fuck. What is he doing here?* He looked at the card clasped in his hand.

Help wanted

To clear overgrown garden

Larch Cottage

Middleham Road

£100 a day

Est. three days' work

There was a telephone number at the bottom. But now he had it, he didn't know what to do with it. Do nothing was probably the correct answer. But… *Oh fuck. I'll call him. No, I'll just turn up at the house.* He changed his mind. Then he changed it back again. Caspian stomped down the road furious with himself. This was a chance to put something right. To say he was sorry for being a prick.

Quite an irony that self-disgust had shoved panic aside. Still… It took him ten minutes to reach the point of tapping the number into his phone.

"Hello?"

Caspian couldn't speak.

"Hello?" Zed repeated.

"Hi there." Caspian changed his voice, put on an accent. "Saw your ad. I need the work." *Oh fuck, I'm Australian?* "Please."

"That was quick. You want to come and see what needs doing? The garden's a bit of a mess."

"I'm local. I know your garden. I'm good at sorting out messes."

And making them. He knew next to nothing about gardening. He hadn't even intended to go down that route with the call, but it had just happened.

"When can you start?"

"Whenever you like."

"I've got to go out now but you could make a start while I've gone. I'll open the shed. Everything's in there. Start with the lawn."

"No worries." *Did that sound Australian or South African?*

"See you later this afternoon."

No worries? Was he mad? Ten minutes later, from where he stood behind a tree, Caspian saw Zed pull out of the drive and head up the road away from him. *What the fuck am I doing?* For one childish moment he wished he could work a miracle on the garden and when Zed returned, he'd be so amazed, he'd smile and… *Yeah, right.*

When he reached the house and saw another car in the driveway, he hesitated. That had definitely been Zed in that car, so who did this belong to? A boyfriend? *No, his father, you idiot.* Which brought back the question of what Zed was doing here. Maybe his dad was ill or had died.

The state of the lawn and the garden made Caspian wince. It looked like an overgrown meadow. He'd jam up an ordinary mower. He'd have to cut the grass and weeds down first. Even as he pulled open the shed door he knew he didn't need to do this work, but he'd removed the advert and it didn't seem fair not to try. He wasn't going to bother telling Glenn. No way was Caspian taking money for helping Zed out.

There was an old pair of gardening gloves on a shelf in the shed and after shaking them in case anything had taken up residence inside, Caspian pulled them on. He left the lawnmower where it was but pushed out the wheelbarrow carrying a spade, rake, fork and a long-handled scythe. Keeping busy would stop him thinking what he was going to say when he was face to face with Zed.

It took a few swings of the scythe before he got the hang of it, though it was hard work. Swinging the scythe in an arc in front of him, he cut a path right up the middle of the lawn. Then he curved around at the top and came down again. An erect cock. So he hadn't lost his sense of humour, just mislaid it.

261

Zed pulled into the first layby he came to, switched off the engine and let out a shaky laugh. Caspian was crap at Australian accents. Zed had spotted him as he left the shop. It felt as if a hundred questions now raced through his mind. Why hadn't Caspian approached him? *Why did I get in the car and drive off?* Because he'd needed space to think and maybe that was what Caspian had needed too. Hence, the accent.

Now what am I going to do? Zed hadn't planned to go anywhere. He'd spent most of the morning sorting out the fridge. Things that he had no idea *could* dissolve, *had* dissolved or alternatively turned into rock. The glass shelves were still soaking in the sink. He'd been side-tracked by a smell from the dishwasher, then by out-of-date foodstuffs in the cupboards, flour milling with insects and hadn't had chance to look through his father's papers.

Fuck it. Stop waffling. Fridges didn't matter. His father's papers didn't matter. After all these years… Caspian… *And I've run. Stupid.* But Caspian didn't want him to know it was him. Had he phoned him then panicked?

Zed drove to Ashford. He went to the supermarket, and bought bread, butter, a couple of different cheeses and tomatoes for lunch. A jar of peanut butter. A punnet of strawberries. The ingredients for a chicken salad for dinner. Enough for two. A bottle of wine. Beer. Soft drinks. Then he drove back wondering if he'd be capable of eating anything. Would Caspian even be there?

Coward that he was, he parked away from the house and walked a 100 yards with the shopping, managing to get inside without being seen. He put the bags down in the hall and went upstairs. His brother's room, where he'd slept last night, had the best view of the garden. Zed snuck to the window and looked out from the edge of the curtains.

Most of the lawn had been scythed down and raked. There was a pile of grass cuttings at the bottom corner of the garden. Caspian was working with a strimmer, trimming the edge of the lawn. He looked the same and yet different. His jeans were low on his hips. They looked too big for him. His blue T-shirt was too tight. Zed still didn't know what to say. He was hoping the right words would emerge when they stood in front of each other.

Caspian switched off the strimmer and put it down. He pulled off his gloves and tossed them next to it before walking back toward the house. *Does he know I'm here?* He couldn't. Zed watched as Caspian reached for the hose that lay coiled on the patio like an enormous yellow snake. He dragged it onto the lawn and pressed the trigger on the gun, squirting water into his hand. Most of it sprayed elsewhere but Caspian lifted his hand to his mouth, then spat the water out. *I need to give him a drink. Go now.*

But then Caspian pulled off his T-shirt and nothing could have made Zed move. When Caspian's jeans came off as well, Zed gulped. He was long and thin and pale…and still the most beautiful thing Zed had ever seen.

Water went everywhere as Caspian removed the gun from the end of the hose. He held it directly over his head, let the flow cascade over him and Zed held his breath. Caspian's wet hair glistened in the dappled sunlight and every part of Zed was still, apart from his cock, which was struggling for room in his jeans and pressing hard against his zip.

Zed was mesmerised by the way Caspian's muscles moved under his sleek skin. He was like an otter. Caspian tipped his face to the sky and arched his back. Zed groaned as the water fell over that pale, slender body, following the curves, dripping from his hair, soaking his tight cotton boxer shorts and outlining his—*oh for Christ's sake.*

"Shit, shit," Caspian yelped and flung the hose away.

Zed smiled. He guessed all the water warmed by the sun had gone and been replaced by cold. Caspian shook his hair like a wet dog and water arced through the air. Zed moved away from the window and unfastened his jeans. A moment later, he had his cock in his hand. A moment after that, he was coming harder than he had for a long time. *Fuck, that was quick.*

He cleaned himself up, crept out of the house and went to retrieve his car. By the time he'd gathered up the shopping from the hall and made lunch, Caspian had gone. *Well, fuck.* Zed grabbed his phone to call him and saw he had a text.

Sorry. Something came up. Be back early tomorrow.

Zed was disappointed, though it did give him more time to think what to say when he next saw him. He cleaned one of the patio chairs and sat outside to eat a sandwich. If Caspian didn't come back tomorrow, Zed would drive to Barton Hall. They needed to talk. He wasn't leaving until they had.

Chapter Twenty-Four

When Zed could no longer put off looking through his father's paperwork, he took his plate and empty beer bottle back inside. The house wasn't quite as oppressive as it had been, but he took a deep breath before he opened the study door. One foot inside the room, his phone rang. *Jackson.* Was the guy psychic?

"Hi," Zed said.

"How's it going?"

"I checked his phone. There was no number for Tamaz, though he could have put him in under a different name."

"Bring the phone back with you. What about his computer?"

Zed switched it on.

"Password protected?" Jackson asked.

"Probably." The screen lit up. "Yes."

"Want to have a go at cracking it?"

"You're not worried I'm going to get a sign saying—*Warning. This machine will self-destruct in ten seconds?*"

"You can be out of the house in ten seconds, can't you?"

Zed smiled.

"If you can't get into it, bring it back with you. Bring it back anyway. The forensic guys can have a look."

"Okay." Zed knew that because Tamaz had disappeared overseas having had connections to a terrorist cell, any communication their father had had with him could be important.

"Thought I'd better give you a heads-up that Caspian has been released on licence and is back home."

"Oh."

"It'd be a good idea if you stayed away from him."

"Right." Zed kept his voice neutral.

Jackson sighed. "Well, I tried."

Zed groaned as he put his phone on the desk. How could he give himself away with one word? Or maybe Jackson just knew him better than he thought.

Before he started to guess passwords, he went through the contents of every drawer. Most people had so many passwords, they tended to write them down on scraps of paper, but his father's drawers were neatly organised—pens, pencils, notepads, scissors, stapler…

264

Along with files holding household bills, receipts, credit card statements, tax records, bank statements, medical records, house and contents insurance, life insurance, all the information about the car... Zed supposed his father's meticulous records were something to be grateful for.

Everything to do with the pharmacy was in a separate filing cabinet. He had a quick look through and was shocked to discover that a year ago, his father had sold the business to a national chain for four hundred thousand pounds. He'd carried on working there for six months until he'd left for health reasons. Zed hadn't seen any trace of that money in the bank statements. So where was it?

He checked the entire room for anything that might be hidden: behind the radiator, under the rug, inside the cushion on the chair, the bottom of the curtain—but found nothing. There were no hidden drawers, no buttons to press to reveal secrets or treasure, no oubliettes in a modern house. The only places he'd not thoroughly searched were his father's bedroom and the attic. The garage too, come to think of it.

Zed made his way upstairs. The bedroom window was still open and the odour much less intense. He could still see the indent of his father's head on the pillow, a few grey hairs remaining. The sheets were thrown back as if he'd just got up. Zed felt cheated he couldn't grieve. He should care that his father had died and he didn't. That wasn't right. Guilt surged in.

The bedside table was a cityscape of medicines. He'd need to return everything to a pharmacy for disposal. There could well be some dangerous drugs. He pulled open the drawer below and found an envelope labelled—*Will of Majid Zadeh*. He wasn't surprised his father had made a will though if he hadn't, Zed would have had a claim on his estate under English law. He was fairly sure he wouldn't be mentioned in the will he was holding.

He opened it up—*In the name of God, the Beneficent, the Merciful, this is the Last Will and Testament of me, Majid Zadeh.*

Zed wondered what it was like, knowing death was coming, creeping towards you like a lion or racing like a cheetah. Death was a possibility every day of your life, but faced with destruction by cancer, what had his father thought? Clearly, he'd had no desire to make things right with the son he'd mistreated. Had he sent that money from the sale of the pharmacy to Tamaz? Given it to charity?

He scanned down the page. Shaw's were the law firm that had produced the will. It had been witnessed by the elderly couple who'd lived next door to them in Lewisham. Zed looked at the date. The will was ten years old. Tamaz was the sole executor, tasked with paying debts, funeral expenses and handling any bequests. But there was no *wasiyya,* no mention of a bequest to anyone who didn't automatically inherit under Islamic law. There didn't appear to be any relatives Zed hadn't known about. Everything went to Tamaz along with his father's ring and personal Quran which had been among the possessions he'd had in hospital. Zed wasn't mentioned. So even then, his father had hated him.

As a gay, non-Muslim he was entitled to nothing under Sharia law. Though to everyone who'd known him at Imperial, he'd appeared to be a follower of Islam, albeit breaking the rules with his music. As for his sexuality, Zed hadn't had a relationship since Caspian. He hadn't kissed, hadn't touched, hadn't wanted anyone. He'd admired from afar. He wasn't immune to beautiful faces, bodies, arses, but he'd turned down all approaches.

Zed had told Tamaz he was gay, but Tamaz wasn't in the country. So if Zed wanted to challenge the will, he was pretty sure he could and that he'd win. It wasn't a path he wanted to take but Jackson might not be happy about Tamaz getting hold of his father's money. Once the house had been sold and the insurance policies cashed in, Zed thought there might be as much as a million pounds. Maybe Jackson would see that as a way to lure Tamaz back to the UK.

Where are you, brother? What are you doing?

The other things in the envelope were certificates. His father, brother and mother's birth certificates and one for her death, and the marriage certificate. Why wasn't his birth certificate there? Zed still suspected he wasn't his father's son despite the copy of the birth certificate Jackson had given him. He continued to search his father's room but found nothing but clothes and shoes. Not even a picture of his mother in a drawer. Islam might not support photographs being on display but it wasn't forbidden to have ones of your family. Did his father have a girlfriend when he died? Same one as he'd had when Zed had been at home? He didn't know and he didn't care.

Zed went back to the study and sat down. *So, a password...*

He started with his father's birthday, then his brother's, then his mother's. When he'd run out of significant dates, he brought his laptop in and linked the two machines. A rapid download of a programme he'd used before, and he was into his father's computer. Maybe he should have just done this to start with but he'd wanted to discover his father wasn't smart enough to use a complex password.

Getting into the emails was a little trickier, but Zed had a friend at Imperial who was an expert hacker. Maybe friend was too strong a word. Zed would have liked to be his friend but Nick was unsociable, maybe autistic, though absolutely brilliant with computers. Zed had sucked up the information about illegal ways to get at what you wanted. He'd recommended him to Jackson as a possible employee, or potential threat. There was far more money to be made in illegal work, though Nick didn't seem driven by money, more by the challenge of hacking into something no one else had managed.

Zed worked alphabetically through his father's emails, checked each contact, read a couple of the emails that had passed between them, starred any that might be worth rechecking before moving onto the next. It took him an hour to find Tamaz under the name radiotherapy@comcal.com. There weren't many emails to that address and it was clear both his father and Tamaz had been careful in what they said.

Honoured son. You do Allah's bidding, Peace be upon Him. If you provide details, I can transfer money to you to help with your humanitarian work. Blessed are the children you help.

Beloved father. You are the kindest of fathers. The most worthy. Allah's blessings upon you.

Blah blah fucking blah.

Zed picked up his father's phone and re-checked all the numbers that appeared to be hospital related. He found one for radiotherapy. The code was the same as the one for the hospital in Maidstone but the number looked wrong. Too many digits.

He called Jackson.

"Yep?"

"I found my father's will. Unsurprisingly made under Sharia law. Tamaz is the sole executor and beneficiary. It was signed by the couple who used to live next door to us in Lewisham."

"Who are now dead."

Of course Jackson would know that.

267

"I have an email address for Tamaz. Last email from him was a month ago. It's radiotherapy@comcal.com. I crosschecked the phone and have a number for radiotherapy at Maidstone that looks off. I think the country code has been changed so it appears to be a UK number. There's an extra digit. I want to call Tamaz on my father's phone, tell him our father is dead. It'll look odd if I don't."

"He thinks you have no idea where he is. How are you going to explain that?"

"I'll just say his number's on our father's phone."

"If they've been so careful to hide their correspondence, will he fall for that?"

Jackson was right.

"I'll say I found it on a piece of paper with his will."

"That works better."

"The other thing is that my father sold the pharmacy to a national chain for four hundred thousand pounds just over a year ago. That money never went into his bank account. As yet, I can't find any trace of it, but my father mentioned transferring money to Tamaz for humanitarian work."

Jackson sighed. "Send me the details of your father's email. I'll get someone to look at them as well. Call me on Skype on your laptop before you speak to your brother and I'll listen in. I'll guide you with a thumb's up or down if I think you're veering into dangerous territory."

"What country code should I try?"

"We know Tamaz left Pakistan. Try Afghanistan, then Syria."

By the time the Skype connection was established, Zed had made a note of the country codes. Tamaz answered from Syria. *Oh fuck. What are you doing there?*

"Father?"

Zed's heart jumped into his throat. "No, it's me. I'm sorry, Tamaz, but father's died."

Tamaz let out a long sigh. "*Inna lillahi wa inna ilaihi raji'un.*" We belong to God and to Him we shall return.

Zed had the strange feeling that Tamaz had already known.

"How did you get my number?"

"It was with his will. I've just come to the house and found it in his bedside drawer. I've had to have him buried. I didn't know how to get hold of you until now. Is there anyone I should call? Are our grandparents still alive? And where are you? What country code is this?

Can you come home? Please? He's left you everything. I don't know what to do." His anxiety wasn't faked.

"I can't come back yet. Our grandparents died a couple of years ago. There's no one in Iran to contact."

"Oh." Zed sighed. "What about the house? Shall I sell it? The business? I need help."

"Father sold the pharmacy a year ago. He sent me the money to open an orphanage in Afghanistan."

"Oh, that is such a wonderful thing to do." *What a crock of shit.* "Do you think he was trying to make up for the way he…?"

"Treated you? I think he was."

Fucking liar. "What do you want me to do about the house and everything else? His clothes, the furniture, the car."

"Settle all debts. He has life insurance. Cash it in."

"They're not going to let me have it. I'm not named on the will."

Tamaz muttered something Zed didn't catch. "Sort out as much as you can. I'll provide you with the authority to handle things on my behalf. What's your email address?"

Jackson put his thumb down.

"Banks aren't going to accept an email saying I'm acting on your behalf. I could have written it myself."

"Then…pretend there is no will. You'll be able to act as executor then. Say you have no idea where I am. Later, you can find the will and I'll let you know what to do with the money."

"Why the fuck should I bother?" Zed snapped. "He's left me nothing, not that I wanted a penny, but why should I do all the work? And lie for you?"

"Because Allah will reward your selflessness, Peace be upon Him."

Jackson was making a chopping motion with his hand. Presumably telling Zed to leave it.

"*Allahu alam,*" Zed said. Allah knows best.

"You're a believer, brother?"

"*Astaghfirullah.*" I ask the forgiveness of Allah. "I've grown up. I see things more clearly now. I'm still angry about the way Dad treated me but…"

"*Al hamdu lilah wa shukru lillah.*" Praise belongs to Allah and all thanks to Allah.

Zed doubted Tamaz believed in his return to the right path. "And the house? Do I sell it and the contents?"

"Do what you like with the house. Sell all that you can. When everything is done, call me." Tamaz broke the connection.

Zed checked the call had definitely ended, then turned to his laptop. "I think he already knew."

"Very likely," Jackson said. "Well done. We might be able to lure him back."

"You're convinced he's involved in something bad?" Misery churned Zed's stomach.

"We don't know, but him being in Syria is not good. And why would he be so reluctant to come home after your father's died? The last time you saw Tamaz, you didn't part on good terms. He asked you nothing about what you're doing, if you went to university, how things had gone. Whether you're still gay." Jackson gave a quiet chuckle.

"He can't think it's a miraculous cure."

"Maybe he does. I think pretending you've not found a will is a good idea, though. You have the legal right to act on your father's behalf."

"If anyone wants more than my birth certificate?"

"I'm getting you a driving licence in your birth name. By the way, the guy at the funeral who mentioned Tamaz to you? Basem Nadir? He doesn't work at the pharmacy. He's known to us by a different name. That could be how Tamaz knew about your father. Be careful."

Zed nodded and terminated Skype. He neither wanted nor had he expected any money from his father but it annoyed him that he was having to sort everything out. He found a site that explained what to do when someone died intestate and read it carefully.

Kent had a *Tell us Once* service that let him report the death to a number of organisations in one go, including HM Revenue and Customs, Department for Work and Pensions, Driver and Vehicle Licensing Agency, Passport Office and the local council. He paid for the mail to be redirected for three months to a post office box in London, then he started to make the rest of the calls to inform people his father was dead.

It was hard not to be distracted by thoughts about Caspian. All the feelings Zed had locked up tight for the last four years had burst back to life. He'd been waiting for this moment. It was why he'd not been out with another guy. He'd thought that when Caspian was out of

270

prison, they could try to rekindle what they'd once had. Zed smiled. When he'd watched Caspian hold the hose over his head, Zed had caught fire.

But Caspian was nervous and Zed understood that. He was nervous too. Then again, Caspian wouldn't have come anywhere near Larch Cottage if he didn't want to see him. Would he? Or had he just been checking Zed was okay?

We have to talk. If Caspian didn't turn up first thing tomorrow, he'd drive to Barton Hall.

Caspian made his way home across the fields wondering if he'd have stayed and spoken to Zed if his mother hadn't called him to remind him about shopping. He'd leapt at a reason to leave. *Fucking coward.* He'd be even more of a coward if he didn't go back tomorrow.

His mother was in the hall when he opened the door. She took one look at him and gasped. "What on earth have you been doing? You're filthy."

"I need to shower," he mumbled and ran up the stairs.

"Be quick."

After he'd towelled himself dry, he put on the dress trousers from the suit he'd worn at his trial. He had nothing else to wear. Betsy had already laundered the shirt, so he wore that too, though not the tie.

His mother smiled her approval as he came back down. "Lovely. I thought we'd go to the Designer Outlet in Ashford."

"Okay."

This would be the first time he'd been alone with his mother since before the accident. He wondered if she really knew exactly what had happened, or whether she'd been given a slightly different version, but it pretty soon became clear she wanted to talk about anything *but* the day of the accident. Caspian was hurt, then annoyed as she prattled on about the preparations for the charity ball.

"It's going to be a massive event. I just pray it doesn't rain." She smiled at him.

"Am I invited?" he asked.

That threw her. For too long a moment she didn't speak. "Darling, do you think it's a good idea? It would be a lot for you to cope with. All the attention. I'd hate for you to be distressed."

271

Like you'd hate to have to introduce me to your royal guests?
"Did you hate that I was distressed in prison?"

"Not prison. You were in a Young Offender Institution."

He sighed. "Still prison."

"Yes, of course I hated it."

"Do you think I deserved to be there?" Caspian held his breath.

"Absolutely not."

"When did you find out what Lachlan had done?"

"When you wouldn't come home and wanted to stay in… prison on remand, I couldn't understand why. Lachlan told me the truth. He was so upset. I knew in not coming home, you were punishing us." Her shoulders fell. "I was very angry with Lachlan but what was done was done."

"Angry with Lachlan and not our father?" Caspian gaped at her.

"What choice did your father have?"

Why had he hoped she'd feel differently to that? "Want to ask me what it was like inside?"

She glanced at him. "I tried to come and see you. You were the one who didn't want to see any of us."

"I didn't want to distress you," Caspian said.

"Oh, sweetheart."

Oh, Mother. Can't you hear my sarcasm? There was no point telling her what had happened to him today, how he'd been treated in the villages, how he'd been so crippled by panic he'd felt trapped in another reality with the only outcome death. She'd reach for the phone and call for a psychiatrist. Probably try and get him committed. Make him disappear so he wasn't a problem anymore.

He should tell her he was gay. What would her reaction be to that? He wanted to tell her. Maybe not when she was driving. He was nervous enough in a car as it was.

They started at Polo Ralph Lauren and Caspian was a good little boy and tried on everything his mother picked out, even emerging from the changing rooms for her *yes* or *no*. To be fair, he mostly agreed with what she selected, and she did allow him to choose a few things. He verged on enjoying himself but there was still that niggle of anxiety eating at his gut, worry about what life held for him. When she pulled out her American Express card, he let her pay. As he did in every store. He was astounded you could spend over two hundred pounds and still

272

get asked for five pence for each plastic bag. Something else that had happened while he'd been locked up.

As they made their way around the leaf-shaped shopping centre, the pathway sheltered from the elements by a sweeping tented roof, Caspian tried to pluck up the courage to tell her he was gay. He'd thought he could just say it, but it hadn't proved that easy. At least he had no sensation of an imminent panic attack while he dithered. They'd made it almost all the way around the shops before Caspian finally said, "By the way. I'm gay."

His mother turned. "So you're not marrying Poppy Dennison?"

He smiled, and for once it was genuine. "No, I won't be marrying Poppy Dennison."

"Thank goodness for that. She has no dress sense."

Caspian ate on his own that night. Everyone was out. A pizza from the freezer, topped with a whole packet of Parma ham. It was delicious. As was the glass of wine he'd helped himself to from a bottle next to the fridge. He played his guitar for a while, struggling with the transition back to electric. He showered—just because he could—then lay in bed trying to figure out how to handle whatever might happen tomorrow.

Zed might tell him to fuck off, in which case that's what he'd do. Maybe that was the best-case scenario. If Zed tried to hug him, Caspian might hit him. He wouldn't mean to, but he might. After all this time spent not letting anyone touch him, maybe he couldn't flip the switch back to *on.*

But should he knock on the door and let Zed see him? Or call him and tell him? Text him? Let Zed discover who he was for himself?

At four thirty in the morning, after a bad night, he headed across the fields dressed in his dirty jeans and a too-tight white T-shirt to work on Zed's garden. He was halfway there before he realised Zed might have locked the shed, but he arrived to find the padlock hanging loose. *You should have escaped while you had the chance, wheelbarrow.* At least Zed's car was there.

The sun came up as he worked on the borders, pulling and digging up weeds. Maybe this was something he could do, gardening work. Except he was already bored, he knew next to nothing about flowers and his back ached. For all he knew, he'd been pulling up things that had been planted rather than plants that had invaded.

By nine, when there was still no sign of Zed, Caspian's nerves wouldn't let him wait any longer. He'd run their conversation over and over in his head in so many variations that he felt sick. He pulled the mower out of the shed, breathed a sigh of relief when it started on the first pull, and he began to cut the lawn. The grass was still long and he kept having to empty the collection bag but each time he turned to start another row, he thought how good it was beginning to look. Pale but neat. No longer wild but tamed.

He was on the last stretch when he realised the bifold doors were open and Zed stood there watching him. Caspian's heart bounced on his stomach. He pushed the mower to the end of the lawn and switched it off. When he turned, Zed was right behind him.

"You missed a bit," Zed said.

"I left that for you to do."

Zed smiled.

Shit, my heart. Caspian took a shaky breath. "I spent most of the night and all of this morning trying to think what to say when we stood in front of one another."

"What did you come up with?"

"Nice weather we're having."

Zed laughed. "Always a safe topic of conversation."

"Along with… How've you been? What are you doing here? Read any good books lately? Got a holiday planned? Where did you get that T-shirt—those jeans—those shoes? How was uni? Are you working? Do you like it? Do you have a boyfriend? Are you married? Do you have kids? Do you want your marble back?" He held it out. "Do you believe in vampires?"

Zed raised his eyebrows. "Do you want a drink?"

"Oh, I never thought of that one."

"Drinking from the hose isn't a good idea."

"You saw me?" Caspian whispered.

"I was watching from the upstairs window."

"Why didn't you come down if you knew it was me?"

"I knew it was you in the shop."

Caspian huffed. "And the *no worries* gave me away, didn't it? *And* it's such a fucking lie. All I have are worries."

You're here, in front of me and it's as if we were never apart except we were apart and everything has changed. But you haven't. You're still the guy I—oh fuck. Caspian swallowed hard.

274

"Orange juice?" Zed asked.

Caspian nodded.

"The marble is yours for always," Zed said.

He watched as Zed went back into the house. Featuring strongly in his —*what might happen tomorrow/today*— musings, had been the thought that Zed might just throw himself into his arms. Maybe that was asking for too much. No maybes about it. It was. He'd told Zed to fuck off, that he'd hooked up with his cellmate, that he'd thrown away the letters, sold the MP3 player. Caspian pulled the MP3 player out of his pocket, put it on the patio table and waited to see what Zed would say.

Does he forgive me? Does he want me?

Chapter Twenty-Five

Zed's hands shook as he took two glasses from the cupboard and poured out the orange juice. He'd been woken by the sound of the mower, checked it was Caspian—though who else would it be—then lay back in bed trying to figure out what he was going to say. Apparently, Caspian had the same problem. *Oh fuck.* He looked too thin, too pale, too anxious. Still gorgeous but his confidence had gone. His spark wasn't there. There'd been a hint of it in that vampire comment but maybe it was too much to expect things to be like they were without them having to even talk. Zed wanted to put everything right, but he didn't know if he could.

He took the drinks outside and swallowed hard when he saw the MP3 player on the table. Caspian had left him the clean chair and was sitting on a dirty one.

"You didn't sell it." Zed put the glasses on the table and sat down.

"It's a miracle it still works. I got through hundreds of AAA batteries. I would never have sold it. When I was down, I listened to your voice. That was my favourite song. *Rudolph the Red-Nosed Reindeer.*"

Zed laughed. *I should have known. Had I not guessed?* He dragged his finger up and down the condensation on his glass.

"You understand why I had to say all that." Caspian's voice cracked as he spoke. "I couldn't ask you to wait. Not for four years. And it might have been more. Days were added to sentences all the time. I was careful but it was easy to get blamed for stuff you weren't involved with. That had already happened to me. A fight. Something contraband found near me. Someone lying about what I'd done. It was like walking on a tightrope all the time. It wasn't that I didn't want you to wait. But it wouldn't have been fair."

"You're right. It wouldn't have been fair to ask me, but you still should have. You could have said—*don't wait, see other guys but when I come out if you're not with someone, come and find me.* And I'd have said, *I've already found the one I want.*"

Caspian groaned.

Zed wanted to hold him but wrapped his hand around the glass instead. "I was hurt even though I'd figured out you were doing the same as you'd done before. Setting me free when you couldn't be free.

276

That first time, I kept on writing to you anyway, but the second time, after you'd been sentenced, it was pointed out to me that if I continued to write, telling you about all the things you couldn't do for the next four years, reminding you of what you were missing, then I'd be the one hurting you."

"I was scared that one day you wouldn't want to write anymore, that you'd find someone else. I wasn't sure I could bear *knowing* that. I felt guilty too. It was hard not to obsess about the fact that I'd brought this on myself, that if I'd pleaded guilty, expressed remorse, there would have been a chance I'd not even have been put inside. Or at least, not for long. All I've emerged with is a warped sense of pride that I never did admit to something I didn't do, but the price I've paid wasn't worth it. I'm not defiant, I'm broken."

"Then we'll get you mended."

Caspian gave him a sad smile. "Can't mend those girls though. However bad I felt, I thought of them and their families. If I hadn't run away, if—"

"If we'd never met. I know. But we can't bring them back. We can't change the past. Both of us will always remember what happened. I'll always be angry with Lachlan and your father, but this is your life. Your time. What's done is done. A price has been paid by the wrong person, but it's been paid. It's over."

"Only as long as I behave myself for the next five years. Free but not free. I'm not even allowed to spend the night away from Barton Hall unless I get permission. Not allowed to work without permission. Not allowed to go abroad without permission and I'll never be allowed in some countries because I have a criminal record. I'll never be allowed to adopt. Never be allowed to do a lot of things. And by the way, I never intended you to pay me for tidying the garden. If you're ever asked, I'm just doing you a favour… So has your father died?"

"Yes. I've come to sort out his affairs, clean up the house and put it on the market."

"Where's your brother?"

"Abroad."

"Not coming home?"

"Not yet." Before, Zed would have told Caspian about the will, but he kept quiet.

"How do you feel about your father dying?"

277

"Indifferent. I hadn't seen him since the night before I left. The last thing he did was beat me. Why should I be sorry he's gone?"

"I'm glad he's dead. You wouldn't be here otherwise. I wouldn't have seen you in the shop, wouldn't have picked up your card, wouldn't be talking to you."

Zed put his glass down. "I would have come to find you once I'd known you were out. You wouldn't have been able to find me."

"I googled you."

"And you couldn't find me."

"No."

"I have a new name. Zayne Mallinson."

"To keep you safe. Are you safe? I couldn't let myself think that you might not be."

"The past four years have been…"

"Tell me."

"Brilliant."

"I'm glad. I really am." Caspian exhaled. "Tell me about them."

"I still live with those two guys I told you about, Jonas and Henry. Henry just asked Jonas to marry him. We arranged a flash mob in Trafalgar Square with the London Symphony Orchestra that Jonas plays in. I really like the pair of them. Not like. Love. I love them. I think being with them saved me. Their kindness helped me when I grieved over you. I carried on living with them while I was at university."

"What did you study? Music?"

"No. Computer science and maths."

"I bet you got a first."

Zed smiled. "Yep, I did."

"Do you have a job lined up?"

"Maybe but I'm not sure what I'm going to do. I'm in a band. We might be getting somewhere. Our music's online. We have a manager now and a booking agent."

"That's great." Caspian drained the glass, set it down on the table and pushed to his feet.

Zed knew he was losing him. "Don't go." He stood up. "I've not read any good books lately. I've been too busy revising. No holiday planned. I got my T-shirt, jeans and shoes from Next. Uni was great. Hard work but interesting. I'm not married. I don't have kids and I don't believe in vampires. Did I answer them all?" He knew he hadn't.

"I'm…glad you're okay."

"Did I say I was okay?"

Caspian's eyes widened. "Aren't you?" He winced. "Sorry. Your father's just died. Your brother's not here. You're having to deal with all this crap on your own. 'Course you're not okay."

"My father's left everything to Tamaz." *Shit. That slipped out.* "But no one has to know that. It's a secret, okay? I don't give a crap about him leaving me nothing, but it annoys me he still has the power to hurt me even after the bastard died. But that's not why I'm not okay."

"My father…" Caspian sucked in a breath. "He's acting as if I've been away at summer camp. He promised he'd make it up to me when I got out and he's already told me he won't back one of my inventions. He wants me to marry Poppy Dennison, the daughter of a friend of his. He's fucking delusional. Poppy and me are completely incompatible. She doesn't have a cock. Well, I don't think she does."

Zed laughed.

"Yesterday I told my mother I was gay. She was… all right about it. But I have to tell my father myself. I think it might be easier to dress in pink and wear eyeliner and I know that's clichéd and unfair. But he might get the message without me having to say anything. Then again…"

They were talking about everything but the one thing that mattered.

"There was one more question to answer," Zed said.

"Was there? Did I remember to ask what you thought about global warming?"

"Caspian." Zed took one step toward him and when Caspian moved backwards, Zed froze.

"Sorry," Caspian whispered. "Instinct."

"I've only ever wanted one guy," Zed said. "He's the only one I've had a relationship with."

Caspian closed his eyes and shuddered before he opened them again. "Does he make you happy?"

"Yeah, and he makes me sad."

"Dump him. You need someone who makes you happy all the time."

"He's tried to dump me twice but I'm stubborn."

Zed watched Caspian's face as realisation finally sank in.

"You haven't been with anyone?" Caspian whispered. "Are they fucking crazy? You're gorgeous."

"I've turned everyone down."

Caspian let out a howl of pain and despair, some primal sound that tugged at Zed's heart. "Fuuuuck, Zed."

"Now are you going to tell me that you hooked up with someone inside, that you're waiting for him to get out so you can set up home and suffer the torture of Ikea together? Or that you were...you were forced to do stuff that—"

"No, I'm not. No, I wasn't. Fuck." Caspian clenched his fists. "I want to do this again. Meet you again. I'm going to walk around the corner and come back and we're going to pretend we're meeting for the first time in four years and we're going to do it properly this time and if I freak out, and I might, because no one has touched me, even put a hand on my shoulder without me getting pissed off or upset or worse, I want you to keep holding me. If you can.

"I might even panic, I panicked yesterday and I thought I was going to die. Literally die. I felt as if I'd been pulled into the heart of a thunderstorm. That might happen again, I'm not sure, but don't let me go. Please." He gasped for breath after delivering all that at breakneck speed, then disappeared around the corner.

For too long a moment, Zed wondered if he was going to come back. But then Caspian reappeared and as he walked towards him, Zed set off to meet him. Even in his desperation to pull Caspian into his arms, Zed remembered what he'd just told him and let Caspian take the lead.

Caspian put out his hand. "Delighted to meet you again."

Zed laughed. *He's coming back to me.* "The pleasure's all mine."

"No, it's not. It's really not."

Then they were in each other's arms and Zed couldn't have said who grabbed who first. Zed kissed him with all the passion and love he'd had locked up inside since he'd last seen him. Their tongues tangled as they ate at each other. Caspian clutched Zed's back, then his hips and they rocked together, holding each other tight, kissing until neither of them could breathe. They pulled back with choked laughs.

Zed barely had time to draw air into his lungs before Caspian was kissing him again, nipping his lips, pushing his tongue in and out of his mouth as if he were fucking him. Zed threaded his fingers in Caspian's silky hair and kept him close. The hard ridges of their cocks rubbed together and they moaned into each other's mouth. The kiss was brutal, hard and perfect. Zed didn't fight it, felt every moment of it, allowed it to swallow him as he surrendered to Caspian.

This was all he'd ever wanted.

Somehow they ended up lying on the grass, side by side, though Zed couldn't have said how they got there. Boneless legs, probably. He lifted his fingers to Caspian's face, cupped his chin and stroked his lips. Caspian kissed Zed's fingers.

"Not panicking?" Zed whispered.

"No. My head's buzzing but only with thoughts of what I want to do to you. I want us lying with no clothes on. I want to kiss you all over, lick every inch of you, suck every inch of you, taste your skin, taste your cum, swallow your cum, listen to you groaning in my ear, make you groan louder. I want you to do the same to me. I want your fingers everywhere. I want to tease you and stop you coming until you can't stand it and then make you come so fucking hard you won't be able to breathe. I want to fuck you and I want you to fuck me. I want to catch fire. I want to fucking fly."

"Have you been thinking about this for long?"

Caspian laughed, his face lit up and he looked like the old Caspian.

"I don't have any condoms." Zed hesitated. "Or lube. Plus we're outside. The postman might see us."

Caspian tried and failed to smother his chuckle. "Passion killer."

"Am I?" Zed mock-glared.

"No." Caspian slid his hand down and unfastened the button on Zed's jeans, then slowly eased down the zip.

Zed's breathing turned choppy. It stopped altogether when Caspian moved down and took Zed's cock into his warm, wet mouth.

"Oh wow, wow, wow," Zed stuttered. "We're not going to do the making me wait thing, are we? Because… Oh fuuuuck."

Caspian sucked his balls and Zed bucked. It felt as if Caspian was doing everything he could think of with his teeth, his tongue and his hand. When he managed to open his eyes to look at him, he found Caspian looking up at him. The jolt of lust almost made him lose control. Caspian's mouth was wet with saliva and precum and when he licked his lips and smiled, Zed moaned, his lungs locked, his hips bucked and he exploded. The pleasure was so acute, he cried out. *Oh God, oh God, oh God.*

He stroked Caspian's hair, as Caspian licked him clean. Aftershocks still rumbled through his body. He hadn't remembered how good this felt. Caspian squirmed up to kiss him again. Soft, slow kisses that shifted to deep and hard, then back again time after time.

"Let me suck..." Zed managed to gasp.

Caspian laughed into his mouth. "Too late."

They spent the rest of the day working on the garden together in their boxers. Zed had found suntan lotion in his father's bathroom and though it was out of date, they figured it was better than nothing. But applying it to each other made them hard. They messed around until they were soft again.

They had fun. Caspian squirted Zed with the hose, raced around the lawn after the water had turned cold and laughed as Zed yelped. Zed pinned Caspian down and found every place that was ticklish. They were the kids they'd once been and wanted to be for all the years they'd been apart. They lay on their backs on the lawn looking up into the sky.

"I feel as if I've been lying under a concrete slab and you've just rescued me," Caspian said. "I can breathe, smile, laugh. I'm sure I'll never have another panic attack."

Zed threaded his fingers with Caspian's. "Do they go away just like that?"

He felt bad when he saw the worry on Caspian's face, but Zed was worried too. If Caspian thought he wasn't going to have another and then he did...

"I was broken but the glue is right here." Caspian turned to look at him.

I want to be the glue but you have to help yourself too.

In between periods of mucking about or lying in the sun trailing their fingers over each other, they'd attacked the weeds and the hedge and by late afternoon, had transformed the garden.

"I can't believe how different it looks. Part of me wishes it was still wild."

"After all that work? I'll let you replant all the weeds."

Caspian grabbed his jeans and pulled them on. Zed took the hint about getting dressed and put on his jeans too.

"Do you need to do much to the house?"

"Empty it. I have to order a skip. Some stuff needs dumping. Maybe there's a charity that would like the furniture and his clothes. I've got more calls to make, appointments to sort out. Stuff like that."

"And Tamaz won't come back to help?"

"No."

Caspian tossed Zed his T-shirt and pulled his own over his head. "Can I help?"

"That would be great." Zed tugged Caspian into his arms and threaded his fingers in his hair. "I wish you could stay the night."

"So do I but I daren't risk it. One nosey person could wreck everything. I think most people in these two villages would like me to end up back inside."

"Most people?"

"Those who know who I am. They refused to serve me in most of the places I went into." He pulled out of Zed's hold.

"Want me to run you back?"

"No, it's fine. I like walking." Caspian tied his laces.

They both turned when they heard a vehicle pull up on the drive. Zed headed around the corner to see who it was. Jackson climbed out of a black Audi.

"What are you doing here?" Zed asked.

"I've brought you a present."

Zed turned to look for Caspian and he'd gone. *Shit.*

Jackson handed Zed an envelope. Inside was a driving licence and credit card in his birth name.

"The credit card is linked to a bank account we've set up for you. Use it for anything connected to your father. There's ten thousand in there. To be repaid at some point. The address on your licence is what you need to use when anyone asks. Okay?"

"Great. Thanks."

"I'll take the phone and the computer with me."

"Want a drink?"

"Please."

He led Jackson back around the corner to go into the kitchen through the bifold doors.

"Been working on the garden?"

"Yep."

"Seen Caspian?" Jackson asked as he entered the kitchen.

"Yes."

283

"Was that a good idea? You're not going to be staying here for long."

"Water or orange juice?"

"Water's fine."

Zed put a full glass on the work surface.

"How are things going with Electric Ice?"

"Pretty good. Since Pete Corrigan became our manager we're getting more gigs."

"You'll be playing all over the country."

"I guess so."

"Caspian won't be able to go with you."

Zed stared at him.

Jackson shrugged. "The terms of his release make that impossible."

"A compelling reason to work for you."

"You could look at it like that."

"Could you fix it that Caspian isn't bound by the terms of his release?"

"Why would we interfere with the justice system?"

"Because—" Zed so nearly blurted out the truth.

Jackson looked at him carefully as if he was trying to see what Zed had almost told him.

"I'll get you the computer and phone."

"I'll take some of the paperwork too. Let me look at what there is."

Zed sighed and led him to the study.

Caspian made his way home across the fields. Today had been more than he could have hoped for until that guy had turned up. Caspian had slid to one side when Zed went to see who it was, and when he'd heard *I've bought you a present*, Caspian had carried on sliding into a flat-out run around the other side of the house to the road. Not that he thought this was Zed's boyfriend. He believed him about that, but more because the impossibility of all...*this*...had slammed back on his shoulders.

How long would Zed even be in Kent? The only reason he'd come was to sort out his father's affairs, not because Caspian was out of jail. Zed had said he would have looked for him but why hadn't he known he'd been released? Hadn't he counted down the days? Caspian stamped angrily down the side of the field. It was as if everything positive was being strangled by negative thoughts. And it was his own fucking fault. Why should Zed have been anxiously waiting for his release. Caspian had broken things off. The mere fact that he'd hoped Zed wouldn't listen was just a pathetic attempt to... *Oh shit.* When his heart rate climbed he took deep breaths and made himself walk more slowly. *I am not going to panic. I won't let myself.*

There was a poem he'd had to learn for school when he was twelve called *Invictus.* Latin for undefeated. The whole class had to pick a poem, any poem, and learn it. He'd struggled and struggled until he could recite *Invictus* without faltering. He'd found himself waking in in the dormitory, saying the words out loud with the other boys laughing at him. When it was his turn to stand up in class, he'd been word perfect and for once, been praised by a teacher.

When things were dark in the YOI, he'd repeated the poem to himself. The guy who wrote it—Henley—had been sick with tuberculosis of the bone and the poem was about his fight to keep going despite everything. It ended *I am the master of my fate. I am the captain of my soul.* Whether Caspian survived or not, was up to him. Whether he made a life with Zed or not, was up to him, as long as Zed wanted him. Caspian hadn't had a serious disease like Henley but for the last few years it had been a struggle to hang onto hope in the darkness, to believe that his world would be light again one day. But now his life was his. Almost.

Today had been brilliant. He had to stop looking for problems. He was his own worst enemy.

I am the master of my fate.

He went straight to his father's study and knocked on the door.

"Come in," his father called.

Caspian closed the door behind him. His father sat at his desk.

"Yes, Caspian."

"I'm not going to work in a clothes shop. I want you to back one of my inventions. You promised to help in return for me taking the blame for what Lachlan did. Lachlan was young and stupid. The real crime was when you didn't call the police and tell them what had happened. Because of you, I was locked up for five years. I deserve something for that. And I'm not going to marry Poppy. I'm gay."

His father dropped his pen and stared at him. "Gay?"

285

"Yes. It means—"

"I know what it fucking means."

Caspian curled his toes in his shoes. His father rarely swore.

"Look. What you got up to on the day of the accident with that boy, it was an aberration. That means—"

"I know what aberration means, and it wasn't. For me that's normal behaviour, not a deviation."

"Spending time locked up with a lot of other young men, I understand you'd form attachments, and in a search for affection you became confused. Though the prison service has something to answer for in letting that happen. But that's all behind you. This is a fresh start. I'll look again at your ideas and speak to some people. Maybe we can set up a little business for you to run. If you don't want to marry Poppy, that's fine. Apparently, she wasn't too keen on the idea either, but gay? No, you are not gay."

Caspian let out a strangled laugh. "Why don't you ever listen to me? I know what I am."

His father pushed to his feet and came around to the other side of the desk, his face full of unarticulated fury. Caspian guessed the lack of articulation wouldn't last.

"No son of mine is going to be gay." He spat out the words and dotted Caspian's face with spittle. "Bad enough that Lachlan is doing work for that LG… whatever that ridiculous acronym stands for. Do you hear me? If you want money for your scheme, forget about being gay. I don't want to hear another word on the subject."

Caspian was the one filled with fury then. "You can't tell me not to be gay. It isn't a fucking choice. It's not an illness. It's not something to be ashamed of. I am what I am."

"Not if you want my money."

"Then I don't want your fucking money." Caspian turned to go, then spun round. "I blame you more than Lachlan, you know that? When he came back here and told you what he'd done, you could have called the police, told them he'd panicked. Did you even come rushing to the scene to see if I was still breathing? No, you did not. You couldn't even call an ambulance, could you? You sat here concocting my brother's alibi, while I might have been dying or burning to death. Easier for you if I had died. Lachlan's everything you wanted—a successful lawyer, everything you deserve—a lying bastard just like you."

286

The blow across the face took Caspian by surprise. He backed up to the door, opened it and fled. By the time he was in the woods, he'd shifted into full-blown panic. It wasn't just him that was rushing, but everything around him—bushes, trees, birds. He was so scared of what was happening that it fed his panic and panic fed his fear.

He stumbled up the ladder into the treehouse and threw himself in a corner, curled up with his arms around his head as if he were trying to escape from some wild animal. Just like before he couldn't breathe. He was able to understand that unfolding himself would help his lungs expand, but he couldn't. He couldn't bear it. His heart couldn't beat so fast without breaking. If he didn't manage to draw more air into his lungs, he'd die.

I'm coming apart.

I'm lying on a narrow ledge halfway down a cliff. If I move, I'll fall and I won't stop falling. So don't move. Don't move. Don't move.

Eventually, after minutes or hours, he pulled himself back, reassembled himself, regained control. He'd seen guys inside have panic attacks. He'd never thought it would happen to him. Death had seemed imminent, not just possible but probable, but it hadn't claimed him.

Now he could breathe, he knew it was all in his head. Maybe his father hitting him had caused it, maybe it hadn't been that at all. Maybe just the act of running had triggered it. But this wasn't something he could ignore because the likelihood was it would happen again. The thought depressed him. He wasn't cured. Having Zed in his life hadn't stopped this happening.

He forced himself to unfold and hauled himself up. He leaned against the window, dragging air into his lungs. One breath before the boards broke and he fell out of the tree.

Chapter Twenty-Six

When Jackson had gone, Zed went online to find the number of a local skip company and ordered the largest they had. It was too late to deal with the rest of those who needed to be contacted about his father's death and since it was Saturday tomorrow, it would have to wait until Monday. A weekend with Caspian.

As Zed stood in the shower, he wondered why he'd run off? *Does he think I'm ashamed of him?* Caspian might not be able to spend the night here, but *he* could spend the night with Caspian. Or if he didn't want him at Barton Hall, Caspian could stay at Larch Cottage until late and Zed would drive him back. He felt increasingly uneasy about the way they'd parted.

When Caspian didn't answer his phone, Zed felt more than uneasy. He wasn't sure whether to drive to Barton House or take the cross-fields route that Caspian would have taken, just in case anything had happened to him on the way back. He decided on the latter.

By the time he reached Barton Hall, he was hot and sweaty. *I should have brought water.* He rang the bell.

Betsy answered. She smiled when she saw him.

"Zed. How lovely to see you again." She pulled the door almost closed behind her. "Caspian's not here," she said in a whisper.

Zed frowned. "Didn't he come back about an hour ago?"

"I don't know. They're eating dinner and his father is angry he's not at the table."

"Okay. I think I might know where he is."

"He's…"

Zed turned back to face her.

"He's very sad," she whispered. "All his life, he's believed he could do anything and now that belief has gone, he's adrift. Find him. Make him believe in himself again."

Zed nodded and ran to the treehouse.

When he saw Caspian lying on his back at the foot of the tree surrounded by broken pieces of wood, his stomach dropped. He fell to his knees at his side. Caspian opened his eyes and Zed groaned with relief.

"It broke," Caspian muttered.

"Did it break *you*?" Zed ran his hands down Caspian's legs and arms alert for any sign of pain.

Caspian didn't make a sound, but there was blood on his face, a dark graze on his cheek.

"Can you move?" The words blocked Zed's throat but when Caspian wriggled his fingers and moved his legs, Zed could breathe again.

"My treehouse is broken," Caspian whispered. "Our place. Everything's broken."

"We'll rebuild it together." *Rebuild you together.* "Think you can sit up?" He helped Caspian to a sitting position, then checked the back of his head. A bump that made Caspian wince when Zed touched it, but no blood. Zed lifted his T-shirt. Caspian's back was scraped and bruised. "Where does it hurt?"

"I'm okay."

Caspian tried to get up and Zed stopped him. "Just sit a moment. What are you doing out here? Your family are eating dinner."

"You've been to the house?"

"Betsy answered the door. I guessed where you might be."

"I told my father I was gay and he hit me."

Zed bristled. "What?"

"All that time you were beaten and I thought at least my father doesn't do that. Only one blow but he shouldn't have done it."

"No, he fucking shouldn't have."

"Apparently, if I'm gay, I can forget getting any support for one of my inventions. Be a straight guy and he'll help me. My mother was okay about me being gay. I'd hoped my father… Shit. I don't want to be here anymore."

Zed pulled Caspian's head to his chest and kissed his forehead. "I'm going to help you. I'll figure out a way for you to leave here and live with me."

"Who was the guy who came to see you?"

"Jackson. The one who got us into the same YOI. He brought me a driver's licence. I told you I had to change my name but I can't sort out anything to do with my father without ID in my birth name. Jackson got me a copy of my original birth certificate, but I needed a driver's licence too. I'd have introduced you if you'd stayed. Why did you disappear?"

"Panicked. You still have something to do with MI5?"

He nodded. "I think I always will." He looked straight at Caspian. "I want to tell Jackson that Lachlan was driving. I think he can help you."

Caspian sagged. "How? Does he have a magic wand?"

"He might."

"Not one that would make everything right. Help me up."

Zed supported Caspian's weight as he struggled to his feet.

"Nothing broken." Caspian reached for Zed's hand and squeezed his fingers. "I know you want to help but don't say anything. I don't want all this to have been for nothing. I think Lachlan's changed. He's doing work with disadvantaged kids. Something with a LGBT group according to my father. My brother's married now. How can I knowingly destroy his wife's happiness?"

"But your happiness matters too."

"I *am* happy."

Zed thought about challenging him on that but let it go. "Did you lose consciousness?"

"Yep."

Zed groaned. "For long?"

"I don't know."

"You should go to hospital."

"No. I'll be okay. Help me back to the house." Caspian's voice was flat.

"Let me stay the night."

Caspian smiled. "I don't think my father will allow you inside."

"How old are you? Fifteen?"

"Still his house. His rules."

"Since when did you follow the rules? Well, apart from when you were locked up."

Caspian's smile widened, which was a relief.

"Sneak me in," Zed said. "You have your key?"

"Yes."

When they reached the house, Zed slipped his fingers into Caspian's pocket and pulled out the key.

Caspian groaned. "That was far too easy to find. You could have groped for a while."

"You're not in a fit state to be groped."

"I'll be fine by tomorrow."

"I look forward to plenty of groping."

Once they were in the entrance hall, Zed could hear the sounds of people laughing and something snapped. Instead of leading Caspian to the stairs, he tugged him towards the voices.

Caspian sighed. "This is not a good idea."

Zed pushed open the door of the dining room to find Caspian's parents and presumably his sisters sitting at the table.

He glared at Caspian's father. "Enjoying your dinner? Is this how much you care? I thought my father was a shit but you—you're actually worse."

Caspian pinched his backside and Zed got the message.

"What's happened?" Caspian's mother pushed to her feet.

"He fell from the treehouse and was knocked out. Would he have lain there all night without you even looking for him? Yeah, I think that's exactly what would have happened. You should be taking care of him."

Caspian's mother rushed to his side. "Shall we call the doctor?"

"I'll be okay," Caspian said quietly.

Caspian's father stood up. "Thank you for bringing him back. Now get out of my house."

Zed looked at Caspian. But Caspian nodded, so Zed left. Confronting Caspian's father had cost him the night in Caspian's bed, but he was glad he'd said what he had. He stomped back across the fields. He understood that this was a battle Caspian needed to fight on his own though he didn't regret firing the first bullet.

Well, not until he'd reached the house. Then he worried he'd gone too far.

Zed wasn't sure Caspian would come in the morning, but he turned up just as Zed finished breakfast, looking far more delicious than the toast he'd just consumed.

"That's a big skip," Caspian said.

It had been delivered an hour earlier. "There's a lot of crap to put in it. Sure you feel up to helping me?"

"I'm fine. I'm looking forward to the grope."

Zed laughed. The bruise on Caspian's cheek had turned an unhealthy shade of yellow but his eyes were bright, his smile wide.

"Where do you want to start?" Caspian asked.

"His clothes. I bought black plastic bags yesterday. The things that are in reasonable condition can go to a charity shop. The rest can go in the skip."

Caspian followed him up to his father's room and paused on the threshold. "Looks like he's just stepped out."

"That's what I thought too." He pulled open the wardrobe door. "Check all the pockets just in case he's stuffed them with twenty-pound notes."

It didn't take them long to clear the rail.

"Seventy-three pence and a button," Caspian said. "That's very disappointing."

Zed smiled. "I'll take the bags downstairs."

"Leave the one for the skip. We can put more in that."

When Zed got back to the room, Caspian had stripped the bed, bagged everything and was now dealing with his father's underwear and socks.

"I should do that," Zed said.

"It's okay. Who puts stuff away dirty?"

"But he was sick. He might have."

"Euuw. I'll wash my hands before I touch you."

Zed had brought up a smaller plastic bag and swept all the medicines into it. "This has to go back to a pharmacy. If there's anything similar in the bathroom cabinets, that can go too."

"Look what I've found in a drawer, under the lining paper."

Zed took the photo from his hand. A wedding day shot of his father in a dark suit and his mother in a long white dress. They were smiling at each other. She looked beautiful and happy.

"They loved each other." Zed swallowed hard. "At least they did then."

"You can always cut your father out."

"Yep." Zed put the picture by the door. The only thing he wanted to keep from this room, though he put the Quran aside for Tamaz, if he ever had chance to give it him.

Between them, they dismantled the bed and hauled it and the mattress down to the skip. The bedside cabinets and chest of drawers were still in good condition. Zed assumed whoever came to collect them would carry them downstairs.

"You want to get rid of the curtains?" Caspian asked.

"No, leave them."

"Now which room. Yours?"

"It's on the right. Take a look." He followed Caspian and heard his snort of laughter.

"I wonder if he disinfected the walls." Caspian walked into the room and turned in a circle. "When I got back, mine was exactly as I'd left it. Well, they'd probably changed the sheets. My drawings were still on the walls. Teddy on the bed." Caspian sat where Zed's bed had been, the carpet still bearing indents from the wheels. "This is where you slept." He lay down and wriggled his backside. "Oh yeah, yeah, yeaaahhh."

Zed dropped down next to him. "I used to like going to bed. I'd lie in my cave of sheets reading books, but after my mother died, I had one ear primed for my father coming up the stairs."

Caspian reached out and let his fingers drift across the wall. "This is where you planned your life. Where you dreamed. Where you wanked. Where you looked at yourself in the mirror and decided who you'd be."

"When I looked in the mirror I wondered when my spots would disappear. I used to turn and look over my shoulder at my backside, wondering if it was too small, too big, or just right."

Caspian laughed and threaded his fingers with Zed's. "Just right."

"I was desperate to know how long my cock would keep growing. If it was going to be as big as I hoped."

Caspian raised his eyebrows. "Theoretically, it could still be growing."

"I'm pretty sure I've gone through puberty."

"I'll let you into a secret. I have a guaranteed way of making it grow. Ready?" Caspian slid his hand over Zed's already hard cock. "Damn. You did it without me."

"Opening the door and seeing you was all I needed."

Caspian laughed as he let him go. Zed wanted his hand back.

"Your cock is just right too, by the way," Caspian said. "Not too short, not too long. Course I might rethink that when you fuck me."

Zed swallowed his groan.

"Did you know that Indian mystics, called sadhus— and doesn't that name say everything? —used to stretch their cocks right from when they were kids by hanging weights on them?"

Zed winced.

"And the Topinama tribesmen of Brazil encouraged poisonous snakes to bite their dicks to enlarge them."

"That is far too much information. Where did you read that? *Why* did you want to know that?"

"My brain works in a mysterious way. Ask me to decline the word *jugarum* in Latin and I'm lost. Ask me for some strange fact about cows and I'll tell you that there are some people in the world who think they're cows and live their lives like they're cows. It's called boanthropy."

Zed widened his eyes. "I'll save that one for Henry. He loves weird trivia. You'll really like him. And Jonas. Is *jugarum* a jug of rum?"

Caspian laughed and Zed's heart leapt. "Sadly no. It's a measurement of land." He rolled onto his stomach and humped the carpet. "I like to think of you lying here, wanking."

"While I was thinking about you," Zed whispered.

Caspian squeezed his fingers. "So you do have some good memories of this place."

"Yeah. Most of them are from just after we'd moved here, before my mother found out she was sick. She was so excited to be out of London, living in the countryside. I remember the food she used to cook, the cakes she made and let me decorate. I licked out the bowl. Raw cake mix was the best thing ever."

"Better than wanking while you thought about me?"

"No."

"Good."

"Mum was fun. She helped me learn how to do handstands and cartwheels. We made dens with sheets and blankets. She taught me how to swim when I was five. She'd read a book that said just duck your kids under and they'll pop up. I didn't pop up and she was mortified. She took me swimming three times a week until she knew I wouldn't drown."

Zed smiled when he thought about how determined she'd been. "She wrote down all the funny things Tamaz and I said. When I was four, I'd asked her—*What's a virgin?* She asked where had I heard that? I said—*You told me in the car we had to make a die virgin.* I don't know where that little book she wrote in went."

Caspian rolled onto his side. "Did she tell you she was dying?"

"Eventually. Only when she was sure that death was all that was left for her. She told us separately. I was last. I think I knew when I saw Tamaz crying in the garden. He was never a boy who cried. Not like me. She told me how proud she was of me, that I was a good, kind son and whatever life threw at me, I should stand tall and do the right thing. *Whatever you are, wherever you are, be happy* she said. *That's all that matters in the end.*"

"She was right."

"I asked her how she could love me so much when my father hated me. She said he didn't hate me." Zed let out a strangled sob. "But she was wrong."

Caspian pulled him over and kissed him. A sweet, gentle kiss. He tasted of orange juice and melon and Zed wanted more, wanted to go further, his cock was desperate to go further, but Caspian stood up.

"What next?"

You're next. Though Zed felt Caspian was mentally pulling away as well as physically. "The bathrooms, Tamaz's room and the attic. I need the mattress leaving in Tamaz's room for me to sleep on." *For us to fuck on.*

They found nothing hidden. Zed wondered if Caspian had noticed how thoroughly he searched, though he had no idea what he was looking for. But there was little trace of Tamaz ever having lived there. A few pieces of clothing but nothing in the pockets.

The skip was filling up.

Finally, upstairs at least, only the attic remained. Zed pulled down the ladder and climbed up, reaching for the light switch on the left. He crawled onto the boarded floor and Caspian followed.

"There's more up here than I'd thought. At least it's all boxed."

"You want to sort it out downstairs?" Caspian asked. "Why don't you go down the ladder and I'll slide the boxes to you."

"Okay." Zed went back to the landing.

It took them thirty minutes to clear the attic. He went up after Caspian had come down to make sure there was nothing left and there wasn't. Zed switched off the light and pushed the ladder back into place.

They carried everything downstairs into the living room. Zed got them both glasses of water, then they sat together on the floor.

"We'll go through these and then have lunch," Zed said.

The first one they opened held Christmas decorations.

295

"I thought your mother converted to Islam."

"She did but we still had Christmas until she died. She didn't want us to miss out. I'm not sure my father approved but he didn't argue with her on that. We always had a tree and stockings and a Christmas meal." Zed took a packet of gold baubles out of the box, then pushed them back.

"You should go through properly and see if there's anything you want to keep."

He did. There wasn't. The box joined the pile for the charity shop.

Another box held board games and jigsaws. "She loved jigsaws." He'd forgotten that.

"Someone will buy these."

There were boxes of Tamaz's computer games magazines. Old clothes. Buckets and spades for the beach. Baby clothes. Zed knew most of this had been kept by his mother, not his father.

Inside one plastic container they found two boxes, one marked Tamaz and the other Zed. Tamaz's was empty. Zed's held school reports issued prior to his mother's death, things he'd made for her, wonky clay bowls, Easter cards, Christmas cards, ones for Eid. There was a folder of paintings from primary school—ones of her with huge ears, long legs and a yellow triangle dress. And the book of the funny things he'd said. His throat closed up, his eyes filled with tears and Caspian's arm wrapped around his shoulders.

All his school diaries were there. A collection of coins for the year of his birth. A set of stamps for the same year. A plastic box with shells and stones he'd collected and given to her. An envelope of pictures Zed had taken with a disposable camera. Funny, often distorted images of her and Tamaz pulling faces at him or laughing.

He opened one of the diaries. "*Today my mummy took me to see her mummy.*" Zed had drawn a picture of his grandmother. "*She hugged me very hard.*"

"I like this one," Caspian said. "*Today I ran away from a dinosaur. It wanted to eat me.*"

"I remember that. I was shit scared."

Caspian laughed. "You have to keep all these."

Right at the bottom of the box was a brown envelope with his name on it. Inside was his birth certificate. It looked as though it had been screwed into a ball, then flattened out. Zed sighed and set it aside.

296

"You think your father did this and your mother rescued it?" Caspian asked.

"Probably."

"I think you were right about not being his son. Or he thought you weren't."

The moment Zed opened the last cardboard box, his heart rate doubled. "This is all Mum's."

"That box was right at the back in the corner behind the chimney breast. I almost missed it. Do you want to go through it on your own?"

"No. I want you to stay. There might be spiders."

"You haven't worried about spiders so far."

"Because you were here."

Zed took everything out very carefully. He clenched his teeth when he saw the photo albums. The first one he opened held pictures of him and Tamaz when they were babies, toddlers, growing up. There was one of Zed in his dad's arms in the hospital, a big smile on his face. What went wrong after that? More with his dad on the beach, at the park, playing football. Everyone looked happy. But photos never told the complete truth. You had to smile, that was the rule. Say cheese. But it *was* a happy time. Remembering that brought some comfort.

"You were a cute baby," Caspian said.

"'Course I was."

"I mean it. You were gorgeous. I was *not* gorgeous."

"You are now."

"Well of course."

His mother's school reports were there, her exam certificates, her university degree. Postcards, birthday cards, and letters were held together with a red ribbon. Zed undid it and flicked through everything. He opened a letter at random. It was from a girl called Sandra, apparently his mother's friend at school who'd emigrated to Australia.

One envelope was addressed to him. Zed opened it. "From my mother. And there's a will."

He read the letter quickly and groaned. "She wrote this before we moved here. She'd just been diagnosed with cancer. I didn't know she knew then. She says she chose this village because she knew a teacher in the secondary school Tamaz and I would go to and he'd look after me. He'd been her friend when she'd been in the sixth form. Mr Carter. My music teacher. He never said he knew her."

"He was nice to you. I remember you telling me that."

"He was." He sucked in a breath. "Mum wrote *Eric's gay.*" He gulped. "Did she know then that I was? At ten years old? I didn't know then. The house was hers. She bought it with money left to her by her parents. The will leaves it to me and Tamaz, not our father, though that makes no difference now. I don't know if Tamaz knows." Zed thought about that. "He said to me—*do what you like with the house.*"

"That doesn't mean he wasn't aware half of it was his."

"True. She says Dad's increasing religious fervour was a wedge between them. His requests, then demands for her to cover up in public wore her down. She couldn't leave him and take us, so she stayed." He looked at Caspian. "I remember when she gave in, covered herself up whenever she left the house. Her smile looked different after that."

Zed looked through the rest of the letters. When he saw one addressed to a Gulshan Pasdar, with no address, his skin prickled. He pulled it out and as he read it, his throat closed up. "Oh God."

"Oh God what?"

"I think I just found my birth father."

"Really? What does it say?"

"*My dearest one, you have a son. I've named him Hvarechaeshman. He has your eyes. Mine too. Blue and they'll stay blue. When he was put into my arms, I felt as if I was holding a small part of you and I knew that had to be all I could ever have. I won't send this letter. Better that you believe I went back to my husband because I loved him more than you. Better that he believes Hari is his son or I would lose Tamaz. Perhaps one day I'll be brave enough to look for you and tell you the truth. Or tell Hari and let him look for you. You were my world. You are still my world. You always will be. We met at the wrong time and yet the perfect time to make a perfect child.*

All my love, Sara"

"Oh fuck," Caspian whispered.

"My father must have found out somehow that I wasn't his, but never discovered this letter or he'd have destroyed it." Zed gave a little smile. "I feel weird now. I actually feel sorry for a guy who treated me like shit."

"Well don't. Just remember what he did to you. He doesn't deserve your sympathy. You have no idea why your mother cheated on him. I'm not saying he deserved it but you don't know the details. You can't judge."

"No."

298

"But now you can look for your birth father."

"Yes."

"Right now." Caspian pushed to his feet and pulled Zed to his.

Before they reached the study, there was a knock on the door. Zed grabbed Caspian's hand before he pulled it open. "No disappearing, Houdini."

When Zed opened the door, Jonas and Henry stood there.

Chapter Twenty-Seven

When Zed let go of his hand to throw his arms around each of the two men in turn, Caspian's heart pounded. Instead of backing off, he planted his feet more firmly on the floor. This had to be Jonas and Henry. The first man Zed hugged was tall and slim with floppy brown hair and wire-rimmed glasses. So he was Jonas, the musician. He had one of those faces that always looked happy. Henry was dark-haired and not smiling when he turned to look at Caspian. More…considering, deciding, judging. *Do not shrink from this guy.* Caspian straightened.

Zed turned to Caspian. "This is Jonas and Henry. Meet Caspian."

They put out their hands and Caspian shook them, relieved to manage that without freaking out. "Pleased to meet you." He wasn't, even though he knew they'd been kind to Zed. But he'd wanted Zed to himself. He'd wanted to look for Zed's father on the internet together.

"What are you doing here?" Zed ushered them into the living room.

"We were worried about you dealing with this on your own," Henry said.

He isn't on his own. I'm helping him! Then Henry glanced at him and Caspian realised who the '*this*' was. Not the house. *Me. You fucking shit.*

"Looks like you're doing just fine." Jonas smiled at Caspian who didn't smile back.

"Want a coffee or something cold?" Zed asked.

"Coffee," Henry said.

"I'll make it." Caspian reached for mugs from the cupboard.

"Thanks."

"We're here to help if you need us," Henry said.

Zed's face was so open and happy. *Fuck it.* Caspian knew he was jealous. He couldn't help it. These two men had been in Zed's life when *he* couldn't be. Been important to him. So important Zed hadn't even wanted to leave them to go to university. Caspian should feel grateful, pleased for Zed, but he didn't. His head ached. His skin felt as though ants were crawling on him.

He kept his back towards them and listened as Zed told them they'd been clearing the house, and what they'd found.

"Look at this letter. We were just on the way to the study when you arrived. I was right about why my dad hated me. I wasn't his. I think I found my birth father's name. He doesn't know about me though."

Caspian could hear the excitement in Zed's voice.

"His name's Gulshan Pasdar. I was about to google him."

"Ah." Jonas's eyes widened. "You don't need to. Well, yes you do because there could be hundreds of Gulshan Pasdars for all I know, but I *do* know of one. He's Iranian and conducts the Harley Symphony Orchestra in Boston."

"Boston in America?" Zed asked.

Of course Jonas knows Zed's birth father. Fucking great. The joy of the discovery had been ruined and Caspian knew he was behaving like a spoilt shit, but just as with the panic attacks, he couldn't help it. Zed would go to America and maybe he'd stay there with his newly found father to catch up on the life they'd missed out on and Caspian couldn't go, because with a criminal record, that was one of many countries he wouldn't be allowed to enter and... *Fuck. I can't breathe.*

My heart.

Caspian poured out the coffees, slopping the liquid onto the work surface. His lungs wouldn't work. But he wasn't going to fall to pieces in front of everyone. He slipped out of the room, out of the front door, managing no more than a few yards before the storm of energy brewing in his body exploded.

So this is what dying is like.

When Caspian came out of it, he gasped as if he'd just surfaced from a dive into deep water. He was no longer outside on the drive but inside on the sofa. He slammed his eyes shut again. Yesterday, he'd taken some of Zed's father's tablets and slid them into his pockets. They were hidden in his telescope bag in his room. A lot of use they were to him there. He couldn't keep on like this. He couldn't spend his life worrying he was going to fucking fall to pieces at the slightest thing.

He opened his eyes. Zed knelt on the floor at his feet. Jonas and Henry stood behind him.

"I'm okay." Caspian didn't try to keep the belligerence out of his voice.

He sat up and leaned back into the cushion. He wanted to leave but he wasn't sure his legs would carry him out of there.

"You're not okay. What's wrong?" Zed asked.

Caspian pressed his lips together. Jonas and Henry didn't like him. They thought he was wrong for Zed and Caspian couldn't argue with that. Nor could Zed if he was made to think more clearly. Caspian had been right to let Zed go. Now he had to do it again. Only in a way that didn't make Zed hate him.

"Post-traumatic stress disorder," Henry said quietly. "How often are you having these attacks?"

"What trauma?" Caspian snarled. "Going to jail? I didn't... I didn't have anything like this happen in there."

"The accident took place on a road somewhere around here," Henry said. "I know you've never admitted your guilt. I think that's a weight on your mind and now you've come home, the pressure of it is making you ill, sometimes making you panic until you feel as if you're going to die, as if your heart is racing out of control."

I want to die. Then it will all stop. The thought brought him more comfort than he'd imagined, than he liked. *But you're wrong about the reason why I panicked.* Then Zed took hold of his hand and Caspian held on so tight he had to be hurting him.

"Medicine might help. Something like diazepam." Henry stared down at him. "You could get counselling. I imagine there'd be a wait on the National Health Service, but your father could send you privately."

"My father won't send me for counselling." He almost laughed at the thought. The last thing his father would want was Caspian telling a stranger the truth, even if they were bound by some physicians' code to not reveal what he said.

"Why not?" Henry asked. "You need help. You need to talk to someone."

"My father won't let it happen."

"But why?" Henry stared at him.

"Because Caspian wasn't driving," Zed blurted.

Caspian sucked in a breath. "Shut up."

Zed opened his mouth, then closed it again. He'd already said too much.

"Don't push him, Henry," Jonas said. "Don't push either of them."

Caspian could almost *see* Henry thinking but the guy shrugged and stepped back.

302

"Let's go online and see if we can find a picture of your father," Jonas said. "Come on, Caspian. See if you can spot any resemblance. Are there any more clues about him?"

"He had to have been in this country nine months before I was born."

Jonas nodded. "A good point."

Caspian found himself being ushered into the study. He stood behind Zed and held onto the back of the chair as Zed went online.

"Gulshan Pasdar." Zed exhaled the name. "Well, there's only one. That makes it easier."

"Assuming it's him," Henry said.

"It is. I'm sure," Zed said.

Somewhere in Caspian's head he could hear Zed talking, going through where his father had been born, lived, worked. About his wife and four children and instead of feeling happy for him, he felt angry. *I am so fucked up.*

"Do I look like him?" Zed turned and caught Caspian's hand.

Pashdar was tall and dark with laughing eyes. Blue eyes. Caspian could see the likeness. "No," he said. *I'm a bastard.*

Zed frowned.

"We need lunch," Jonas said. "Local pub?"

"Just down the road." Zed was staring at Caspian and Caspian pulled free and stepped back to the door.

"You're coming too." Jonas got in the way of him leaving.

Caspian almost said that with him there, they stood no chance of being served, but decided to let them find out for themselves.

"We'll drive," Henry said.

Caspian got in the back of the car with Zed.

"Are you okay?" Zed whispered.

Caspian felt mean. *Snap the fuck out of it.* "Yep." He smiled. "You were right. All those times you wondered why he hated you. And it explains your insane gift for music. 'Course if you turn up as Gulshan's long-lost son, his family might not be happy." *Why did I even say that?*

Zed sagged. "Maybe I should just be happy I don't share my genes with the man who beat me."

"You should email him, ask to meet him," Caspian said. "Tell him you're the son of a friend of his. Give him your mother's name and see what he does."

"That's a good idea," Henry said.

"How will you find his email address?" Caspian asked.

"Find out where he's working now," Zed said. "See if he has an agent, look for him on social media, do a web search, check web directories, use the Dark Web, or guess—using his name."

Zed had made that sound easy.

"Are you a private detective in your spare time?" Caspian asked.

Henry laughed.

"Half-timbered houses and thatched roofs," Jonas said. "This is a pretty village."

"If you look past the seething mass of hatred and lies," Caspian mumbled. "Don't be seduced by the beauty of the English countryside—it can turn on you in an instant."

Jonas looked at him. "You're letting your problems spoil your view."

Of what, you fucking prick? "They won't serve me."

"What do you mean?" Jonas asked.

"Just what I said."

Henry pulled into the pub car park.

"I'll go and sit in the beer garden. If they don't think I'm with you, you might get served." He pulled a ten pound note out of his pocket and offered it to Jonas. "I'd like fish and chips and a shandy, please."

"Put your money away," Jonas said.

Caspian made his way to the rear of the pub and sat at the furthest table with his back toward the building. Zed sat on the bench next to him and when Caspian felt their thighs touch, he moved away.

"You're doing it again," Zed whispered. "Don't."

Caspian moved back. "Henry and Jonas are great," he lied.

"I sort of feel bad that I got so excited about finding my birth father. *Possible* birth father. Being with them has been like having the two best dads ever."

"They're pleased for you. I am too." *Liar.* Though he was trying. "I think you just have to set your expectations… Not low, but don't hope for too much. Then if he's excited to meet you, or didn't know anything about you, it'll be good for both of you."

Henry and Jonas came back with the drinks. Maybe it would be all right, as long as no one had seen him. They'd have lunch in the sun and everything would be fine.

"How long is it going to take you to sort things out?" Jonas asked.
"I have to go into the bank on Monday. I'll speak to an estate agent then too. Mum bought the house with money she'd been left and her will says it belongs to me and Tamaz. I spoke to Tamaz."

"Did you?" Jonas put his drink back on the table. "Is he coming back?"

"No. He told me to do everything. I'll get a charity organisation to collect the furniture and clothes on Monday. I'm not going to try and sell stuff. Caspian and I have sorted everywhere except for the ground floor, shed and garage. Once that's done, the house will be empty. Last thing into the skip, the mattress I've been sleeping on. I've changed the insurance on my father's car so I can drive it home."

Don't say anything. Don't react. Don't do anything.

"I want Caspian to come with me."

"I can't." Caspian spoke quickly before they could say no. He couldn't bear the idea of them disappointing Zed and they would.

"I know you have to stay living in the place agreed with your supervising officer, but I want him to agree to another place." Zed grabbed his hand. "If we can't stay with Jonas and Henry, we'll get somewhere of our own."

The food arrived and everyone fell silent. Caspian kept his face averted and hoped this wasn't the same guy who'd spat in his drink. *Oh fuck, how can I drink it now?*

He had little appetite but ate what he could.

"Do you like music?" Jonas asked him.

"Yes."

"Anything in particular?"

"No."

"Do you play anything?" Jonas pressed.

"Guitar."

"Could you play when you were inside?" Zed asked.

"An acoustic. There was one electric guitar, but everyone wanted to play that whether they were any good or not."

"You still have your electric at home?" Zed asked.

"Yes."

"The transition between acoustic and electric is tricky," Jonas said. "The electric guitar highlights every string, every note you play and when you're used to strumming rhythms on an acoustic, it can sound overwhelming when you change to an electric guitar."

305

"I'm no good anyway," Caspian muttered, though he didn't think he was bad.

"We're going down to Cornwall for a week," Jonas said. "Want to come?"

"Both of us?" Zed asked.

"Yes," Henry said.

Zed nudged him. "Ask your supervising officer if you can. I won't go if you can't."

Caspian sighed. "Zed, you can't put your life on hold for me. There's too much stuff I can't do. I'm just out. I need to…find my feet." *Fucking stupid expression.*

Caspian jerked forward and gasped as icy water hit his back. Henry pushed to his feet. "What the hell?"

"Sorry," the guy said. "I tripped."

Caspian stood and turned to find himself looking into the camera lens of a man standing next to a smug barman. There was a woman there as well.

"What's is like to be out?" she asked. "Have you been to see the parents of the girls you killed? What are you going to do if you bump into them in the village pub? Finally say you're sorry? Do you think the money your father paid them was enough?"

Caspian walked away, veering to one side when his path was blocked by the woman. The camera and the questions followed him.

"Leave him alone," Zed shouted.

Caspian suddenly found himself with Zed and Jonas either side of him. He let himself be bundled into the car.

"Oh God, Caspian, you can't stay here." Zed hugged him.

Caspian shrugged him off. "Last time they spat in my drink. I just need to stay away from local people. That's okay. I get they're upset."

"It is not okay," Jonas said. "It's unacceptable."

Henry climbed into the driver's seat and looked over his shoulder. "Seatbelts on, you two."

Caspian fastened his with shaky fingers. "Could you take me home, please."

"No," Zed said. "I've got a T-shirt you can wear. I don't want you to go home."

Caspian bit his lip. He'd walk. That was fine.

But when they reached the house and were out of the car, Jonas tugged him to one side. "Can I talk to you? Just the two of us."

306

Caspian hesitated, then nodded.

"You need a new T-shirt first?"

"No, it's okay. I'll dry in the sun."

"What are you going to say to him?" Zed asked. "Don't tell him that—"

Henry put his hand over Zed's mouth and pulled him into the house.

Caspian set off back down the drive towards home with Jonas on his heels.

"I'm sorry that happened," Jonas said. "I should have thought. We could have gone somewhere else quite easily."

"Doesn't matter."

"It's not okay for people to behave like that."

"And if your eleven-year-old daughter had been mown down by a reckless driver you'd be happy to see him drinking in the local pub? No, I get it. I'm not welcome anywhere around here and I accept that."

Caspian cut into the field and Jonas followed.

"Where are we going?" Jonas asked.

"*I'm* going home."

"My father once said to me that a man is only truly tested a few times in his life. Moments when he has to make a decision that will define or maybe destroy him. Does a happily married man with three small kids put himself in peril to save a child he doesn't know? Does a woman turn her back on a man she loves to stay with a man she doesn't for the sake of her children? Does a boy take the blame for something he didn't do and ruin his future to secure his brother's?"

Caspian quickened his pace.

"Does a young man who sees someone he loves struggling under the weight of lies, speak the truth not knowing whether that truth will ruin or save a life?" Jonas sighed. "Slow down. I'm not as fit as you."

Caspian stopped and turned to face him. "I'm bad for him."

"Says who?"

"Me."

"You see yourself as a failure. You're unhappy. Depressed. You are not a failure."

Caspian huffed.

"It doesn't matter what other people think of you. What matters is how you see yourself. You're sliding down and you need to put your hands out and stop yourself."

Caspian said nothing.

"My guess—and it *is* a guess because Zed has told us nothing, is that your brother was driving when those girls died. He moved you into the driver's seat and ran home. He was at Cambridge University, destined perhaps for greatness. You were a dyslexic younger brother who'd been expelled from a couple of schools and not expected to get even one GCSE. You went along with what your father and brother told you because in the end, what choice did you have? If you told the truth and the police believed you, you'd ruin your family. If they didn't believe you, your family would never have forgiven you anyway. By keeping quiet, you get their enduring gratitude."

Caspian was torn between being glad Jonas knew and anxiety that he did.

"Their enduring gratitude didn't last very long," Caspian muttered.

Jonas sighed. "If we can arrange it, will you come and live with us?"

That shocked Caspian before he snapped back to his snarl. "Another mistreated puppy you want to rehome?"

"Believe it or not, it's as much for Zed as it is for you. He's waited for you for five years. I think that's part of why he chose to live with us when he went to university. He wasn't a party boy. He hardly drinks. Until he joined the band, he rarely went anywhere. I don't think he'd even been in a club, gay or otherwise until he was in the band. There have been no boyfriends. He's been waiting for you. Please don't hurt him."

Caspian's heart clenched. *What about me? What about me being hurt?* He took a deep breath. "Maybe he doesn't yet realise it but he's better off without me." *The world is better off without me.* "I'm not completely free for another five years. Even then, freedom is an illusion because of my criminal record. But until the end of my sentence, I can't do what I like, or go where I like without permission. Zed will get over me."

"Love endures all things."

"People say that about friendship too, but they don't always last."

"They will if you want them to."

Caspian turned, ran up the field and only slowed when he knew Jonas wasn't following. He powered down his phone. He didn't want to speak to anyone.

He went home but didn't go to the house. Instead he went into one of the outbuildings to collect what he needed to mend the treehouse.

Working soothed him. Hammering nails into wood, finding the right piece of plank to block a gap. He climbed out of the window into the tree to check the roof, then clambered onto the sloped roof to examine the other side before he climbed back in.

If he was being honest with himself—and what was the point in lying? —the thought of suicide had on several occasions washed over him like a spring tide. Inside, the thought of being able to end everything had brought a sense of security. There was always an alternative to prison life. He suspected a lot of the boys in there thought the same at some point.

Suicide in a YOI wasn't uncommon. Four guys had hung themselves over the time Caspian had been locked up. He wasn't sure whether he'd ever really been capable of going through with it. Instead, when he was low, he daydreamed he'd created something wonderful that would make up for everything done and not done.

He was pretty sure he had enough of Zed's father's tablets to kill himself. He had a lot of reasons to take them but a lot of reasons not to. That was what it came down to in the end. Whether those reasons to do it overpowered the excuses not to. The balance of his mind wasn't disturbed, though that was undoubtedly what a coroner would say.

His mind was as clear as a fucking bell. Who, after maybe a short period of grief, wouldn't want him dead, out of the way, out of sight, out of mind? Seeing Zed again, being with him had let him hope. Bad idea. He was an albatross around Zed's neck, and his father's and his brother's and sisters' and his mother's. A lot of big ugly birds.

I could run. And go where, with what? He had no skills.

I could stay. Take the first job offered. Wait until he was really free and then hope there was someone out there looking for a broken, self-pitying piece of… *Oh fuck.*

I want Zed. I can't hide from that. It might be the only true thing in his pathetic life.

Caspian showered and dressed for dinner in dark chinos and a white linen shirt. Lachlan and his wife, Elise, had arrived. His mother and father had left the house to greet her. He heard laughter and thought what a difference to the way he'd been welcomed home. Caspian didn't want to be here. He could never forgive his family for

309

what they'd done. He slid his hand into his pocket, fingered the tissue-wrapped pills and the marble, and put a smile on his face before he left his room. *I can end this any time I like.* The thought gave him strength.

They were all in the hall when he walked downstairs.

"Caspian, come and meet Elise," Lachlan said.

Elise turned and Caspian saw as well as being a beautiful blue-eyed blonde, she was also heavily pregnant. She made as if she was going to hug him and Caspian thrust out his hand. "Pleased to meet you."

She shook his hand and smiled. "Lovely to meet you too."

He doubted it.

Caspian was perfectly behaved throughout the meal. Like a good little boy, he only spoke when spoken to. He said please and thank you, declined the wine, declined to join in with the pulling of Lachlan's leg regarding some outlandish behaviour with whipped cream at law school. Apparently, Elise was due to give birth in August. A boy.

"We're going to be aunts," Cressida said with a giggle.

Caspian was sure he wasn't wanted as an uncle.

Prison wasn't mentioned. It was as if Caspian had just stepped off the planet for a while and although he was now back, everyone had been warned not to talk about his experience.

Elise tried to include him, but he had nothing to contribute to most discussions.

"Lachlan tells me you like to invent things," she said.

"Yes."

When he didn't say anything else his mother glared at him.

"What's your most recent invention?" Elise asked.

"I had an idea for a band to wear on your wrist when you go swimming in the sea. If you get into trouble, you can press a button and it inflates a brightly coloured balloon that will both keep you afloat and let out a piercing noise. I thought that could be combined with something parents could activate if their kids strayed on the beach and became lost."

"Already been done," his father snapped.

Caspian deflated.

"Sounds like something I'd definitely want." Elise smiled at him but Caspian looked away.

"Me too," said Lachlan. "You remember that time Cressida wandered off in France and we couldn't find her? Some sort of alert system would have been brilliant. What else have you thought of, Caspian?"

Caspian ran through the things he'd shown their father and every time his father tried to shoot him down, Lachlan stopped him. It wasn't his imagination. There was some issue between Lachlan and their father. Lachlan was arguing for Caspian.

"Why don't you support him?" Lachlan snapped.

"I'm not putting money into something that has no value."

"You dare to sit there and suggest Caspian has no value? After everything he's done?"

"What has he done?" Araminta asked.

"Be quiet," snapped their father.

"No," Lachlan said. "They should know. They might not have been old enough then, but they are now."

Caspian held his breath.

Elise wrapped her hand over Lachlan's where he gripped a napkin.

"One irrational act. One moment of panic that changed everything. Caspian wasn't driving that day. I was. I killed those girls. I dragged Caspian into the driver's seat, ran home, ran someplace safe, and told Father what I'd done. I was panicking, petrified. I knew I'd done something terrible and not just to the girls, but Father told me to wash my clothes, hide my shoes, go to bed and we'd let Caspian take the blame."

"Oh shit," Cressida whispered.

"We thought he'd not even go to prison whereas I would, and it would put an end to me being a lawyer. I'm not trying to pass the blame to someone else." He raised his head to his father. "I was driving. It was all my fault. But you should have picked up the phone and called the police. You were the adult. I wasn't thinking straight but you thought logically about the consequences and sacrificed Caspian who you'd already decided was never going to amount to much."

Lachlan sighed. "I shouldn't have let it happen but I did." He looked across the table to Caspian. "Caspian kept quiet, just as we'd asked him too, but he wouldn't plead guilty because he wasn't guilty, so he ended up serving five years in prison."

"You girls keep your mouths shut," their father barked. "There's nothing to be gained from the truth coming out now."

"Did you know?" Araminta asked their mother.

311

"Yes."

"What?" the twins chorused.

"I have done Caspian harm in so many ways," Lachlan whispered. "We've all treated him badly. Pouring scorn on him. Teasing him for not doing well at school. Laughing at his sketches and inventions. Not trying to understand him. Not appreciating how difficult being dyslexic made his life. Believing him to be a failure when he's a better person than any of us."

Caspian swallowed.

"Outing him to Father the day of the accident started an avalanche of wrongs. I thought it was funny that you were gay. I was a prat. I've said I'm sorry and yet I can never say sorry enough. I've suffered too in my own way. I'm not asking for pity, of course I'm not, I don't deserve it, but guilt has eaten away at me for the entire time you were inside." He turned to their father. "You knew how I felt. You threatened that if I opened my mouth, I'd ruin more than my life. The whole family would suffer. So I kept quiet for my mother and my sisters, and for you with your political ambitions, and I hated myself."

Lachlan was shaking. He looked as if he was going to be sick.

"Is this why you hardly ever come here?" their mother asked.

"Hard to be courteous to an arrogant, domineering arsehole."

"The arsehole who paid your school fees?" their father snapped. "University fees? Accommodation? Paid for your car? The arsehole who's supported you for your entire life?" His face had reddened with fury.

"And what a role model you are," Lachlan snapped. "I was weak, but you are Caspian's father. I can't imagine doing what you did to a child of my own. I don't think you know what love is. Neither of you." He glanced at their mother who'd paled.

Had Lachlan really changed? Caspian had so rarely had support from his brother he found it hard to believe it was happening now.

"I promised Caspian I'd spend the rest of my life making up for what happened and that's what I'm doing. Helping disadvantaged kids has given me more pleasure than I could ever have dreamed. I like working for a firm that sees the value in letting their employees do pro bono work."

"You could have been earning twice as much with a magic circle firm. I got you in. All you had to do was say yes."

312

"I didn't want to. I left it too late, but I finally stood up to you. Working for free for an LGBTQ charity has opened my eyes to what life is like for those who are different, those who have to face prejudice and hatred because of their sexuality. I've had a privileged life. I'm not ungrateful for that but I wanted to give something back." He faced his father. "Your disapproval told me it was exactly what I should be doing."

"You're wasting your time and talents," his father shouted. "You won't make partner."

"I don't care. I want to be around for my son in a way you never were for us." Lachlan turned to Caspian. "I've wanted to go and speak to the police on so many occasions. I should have done. I didn't. But I want you to know that I am on your side. Elise and I are on your side." She squeezed Lachlan's fingers. "I don't have much money, but I'll help you with one of your schemes. Come and live with us. We don't have much space, but we'll make room."

"Get out of my house."

Caspian widened his eyes. Their father was on his feet waving his arms around. Lachlan and Elise stood up.

"Come with us," Lachlan said.

"I can't. I'm not allowed. I have to stay here."

But Caspian followed them outside.

"Five years too late," Lachlan said. "If you need to tell someone where you're living, do it and come to us."

Caspian shook his head. "I'd be a crap babysitter. You don't need me around."

"He's changed, Caspian," Elise said. "I promise he has. But if you want him to go to the police and tell the truth, we'll face the consequences."

Lachlan wrapped his arm around her.

"No. That's not what I want."

Lachlan exhaled. "You've got my number, right? If you need anything, call me."

Caspian nodded.

"I don't like leaving you when he's in this sort of mood."

"What more can he do? I'll be fine."

He watched until he couldn't see his brother's car anymore. Then he went back into the house.

"Study. Now," his father snapped and strode off.

313

Curiosity about what his father wanted to say pulled Caspian after him.

"Shut the door."

Caspian slammed it. His father glared.

"See what you've done?" his father yelled and Caspian's curiosity faded.

He stood while his father railed about his selfishness, his immaturity, his pig-headedness and he knew that the guy would never change. He blamed Caspian for Lachlan's outburst, for his brother's refusal to join the law firm his father had wanted, for Lachlan letting him down, letting the family down. When he finally paused, Caspian opened his mouth. "It was you who broke this family."

"Don't be ridiculous. If you hadn't run away that day, I wouldn't have had to send Lachlan after you. All this is your fault. You are not to take a penny from your brother. If you do, I'll make sure anything you do will fail."

Caspian's heart lurched. His father went on and on and even though Caspian told himself to walk away, he didn't. He just let the abuse and disapproval wash over him until it started to drown him. He wondered why he'd thought a hostel would be worse than this.

But then he wouldn't have seen Zed again. Probably.

Maybe that would have been for the better.

Finally, his father shut up and slumped in his chair.

"Want to add—*I wish you'd never been born*—into that?" Caspian asked.

He turned before his father could answer and saw his mother horror-struck in the doorway. Caspian edged past her. He wasn't part of this family anymore. He hadn't been since the day Lachlan had left him in the car. He grabbed a blanket from the cupboard next to the kitchen, a bottle of water from the pantry and made his way to the treehouse using a roundabout route.

Strange, when you were sinking, that you didn't always want to press the flotation device that would save you. Sometimes, you just wanted to keep going down. Caspian climbed up into the treehouse and dropped the hatch into place. Once the blanket was spread, he sat down, took the package of tablets out of his pocket and lined them up on a plank.

Twelve 60 gm tablets. He figured that was plenty. He stood the bottle of water next to them, then lay on his back.

314

In prison, he'd come up with a technique of deliberately un-focusing his eyes to make his surroundings blur. A way of making everything not real without resorting to drugs like Spice. He shouldn't want to blur the outside world. He should be drinking it in, but he hadn't countered on being so…disappointed.

He didn't know how long he'd been lying there when he heard someone on the ladder.

"Do I have to huff and puff and blow your house down?" Zed asked.

If Caspian let him in, let him see the line of tablets, that would be what he was doing to Zed's life—blowing it down.

"Go away, Wolfie," Caspian said.

"I'm not leaving until I've talked to you," Zed said. "Open the hatch."

Caspian reached over and flipped it up. As Zed climbed in, Caspian lay down again.

Zed sat beside him. "I take it they're not vitamins. Do they happen to be my father's tablets?"

Caspian nodded.

"Fuck you," Zed snapped. "How the fuck do you think that would make me feel, supplying the method for you to off yourself? Tell me you've not taken any."

"I've not taken any."

"Is that the truth?"

"Yes."

"Thank, Christ." Zed picked them all up and put them in a pile in the corner. "They need destroying. I don't want dead squirrels on my conscience either." He lay down next to Caspian so that their faces were inches apart.

You are so beautiful. Your eyes… If they were the last things I saw…

"Whatever you're on the edge of, fall on my side," Zed whispered.

"I'm not good enough for you."

Zed took Caspian's chin in his hand and stroked his mouth with his thumb. "That is not true. You have a choice now and it's a simple one. You continue to live the old miserable life, or you write yourself a new happy one. One with me. And I'll write it with you."

315

"I… I do want a life with you. I just don't know—"

Zed pressed Caspian's lips together. "Jonas and Henry have gone. Jonas brought me a present."

He put his hand in his pocket and produced a strip of condoms and several sachets of lube.

"Or I can just hold you," Zed said.

"Hold me." *Don't let me fall.*

Chapter Twenty-Eight

Zed wrapped his arms around Caspian and held him tight. He was struggling to stay afloat in a mountainous sea of emotions. He wondered if Caspian could feel how hard his heart was hammering. *I want to help you, but I don't know how.* Fuck, if he'd not come... If he'd arrived too late... He clutched Caspian even tighter.

He'd driven over, parked out of sight of the house and gone straight to the woods. Zed wasn't sure if he'd just *thought* things were going well between them before Henry and Jonas had arrived, or whether he'd been mistaken. Caspian had taken those tablets earlier in the day so had this darkness been waiting for the chance to smother the light? Zed wasn't going to let it. All that really mattered in Zed's world was Caspian and he wasn't going to allow anyone or anything to hurt him again. *Somehow.*

So Zed couldn't go to sleep. That silent sentinel of pills still sat in the corner and while part of him wished he *had* tossed them out of the tree house, they were also a reminder of how close they'd been to disaster.

"What made you come out here?" Zed whispered.

"Elise is pregnant."

"Wow, you work fast."

At least Caspian laughed. "Lachlan's wife."

"Are they going to ask you to be a godfather?"

"I doubt it."

"They fucking should. No one has done more for Lachlan than you."

"A godless godfather? It's not going to happen." Caspian sighed. "Lachlan stood up for me tonight. Told me he'd support one of my inventions, that I could live with him and his wife. He apologised for what he'd done. He's said sorry before but this time... This time I felt he really understood the consequences of what he'd done. He's doing pro bono work for underprivileged kids and working for an LGBTQ charity."

"That's good."

"Yeah. He offered to go to the police. I said no. The not insignificant fact that his wife is a lawyer and knows the truth means her career would be in jeopardy too. Lachlan didn't ask me to forgive him but I'm thinking I should."

317

"Really?"

"He wasn't much older than me when the accident happened. I think he's come to see that our father was wrong to let him get it away with it. He's not the good child anymore."

Zed huffed.

"He didn't take the job Father wanted him to. He's not quite the black sheep I am but he's definitely dirty grey. There's hope I think that one day I might not want to throttle him."

"Except I still do."

Zed dragged his fingers through Caspian's hair.

"I probably shouldn't spend the night up here," Caspian said.

"You're still technically at Barton House. It's only stretching your licence requirements." No way was Zed letting him go back to the house alone. What if he had more pills?

"Can you give me your supervising officer's number? Henry wants to call him." Zed held his breath and only exhaled when Caspian pulled his phone out of his pocket.

Zed let him go and took out his own phone. Once he'd texted Glenn Woodrow's number to Henry, he held Caspian again.

"Tell me about some of the things you invented while you were inside. What did you ask your father to back that he said no to?"

"They're not inventions, are they? Mostly it's just using things already invented for another purpose."

"That counts as inventing something. Tell me about them."

Zed listened as Caspian described a system to find missing children via a wrist band connected to the parent's phone. A flotation device inside the wristband that automatically inflated if you went below a certain depth or inflated if you pushed a button or for kids who couldn't swim that inflated if they hit water. Using satellites to follow pirates. 3D printed supports for damaged limbs. Tattoo ink that faded after a year. A water treadmill that doubled up as a hot tub and generated electricity. A water-saving gadget to put on a tap.

Caspian went on and on. The only problem was that Zed couldn't hear any enthusiasm in his voice. Not all of the ideas were good ones or original, but some maybe were.

"Now you talk to me," Caspian said. "Tell me about your band. Need someone to play the triangle?"

Zed's smile went all the way to his heart and calmed it.

"Can you play the triangle? It's not easy."

318

"Cymbals then. I like the idea of making a loud noise at an inappropriate time."

Zed kissed his forehead. "That sounds more like you. Well, the band is called Electric Ice. It's been through a number of names but that one stuck. There are four of us. Jonesie, he's a plumber, plays drums. Akash has just graduated, he's on bass. Fin did music at uni and graduated three years ago. It's his band. He and I play guitar and sing."

"You can sing?"

"Turns out I can."

"You still play the cello and piano?"

"Yes. I learnt the violin too. Sometimes I play a different instrument in the band instead of the guitar. Jonas and Henry bought me an electric cello for my birthday."

"Who does the band sound like?"

"Fin would say we have our own distinct sound and I suppose we do. I know every band wants to think that, but I guess we're a mix of The Killers, Wolf Alice, Radiohead, a bit of Coldplay. That type of thing. Melodic pop-rock with occasional sixties sounds. Strong hooks, strong beat. Great lyrics."

Caspian started to quietly sing and Zed froze in shock. *Thank you for loving me.* The song Zed had put on the MP3 player. Even flat on his back with his face pressed to Zed's shoulder, Caspian's voice gave him chills—of a good sort. His supple croons were superb, his voice so full of emotion that Zed temporarily forgot to breathe.

Then Zed joined in, singing in harmony and Caspian smiled.

"Shit," Zed said when they'd done.

"I should stick to the cymbals, yeah? I think a big clash at the end would work perfectly."

He snuggled deeper against Zed and a moment or two later seemed to have fallen asleep. Zed's mind was racing. Just as well because there was no way he was going to sleep. He had to keep Caspian safe, but it wasn't just that. Maybe Caspian could join the band, be lead singer. Fin would *not* like that, but Caspian had a better voice than either of them. *Who'd have thought...*

Zed jerked awake. *What the hell?* It was morning. Caspian wasn't there, but the pills were. *Thank fuck for that.* He sat up, winced at the pain in his back, and pulled out his phone. Eight thirty. A text from Jonas and one from Caspian. Caspian's read *Gone to get breakfast.*

Back in twenty. He'd sent it fifteen minutes earlier. Zed sighed in relief. Jonas's had been sent last night and was to let him know he and Henry were back in Greenwich and would be trying to find a way to help Caspian.

Today, he was not leaving Caspian's side. They'd walk back to the house and do the rest of the sorting out. Maybe by the end of the day, there'd be a call with good news, though it was a Sunday. Could anything be sorted out on a Sunday? But Zed wasn't driving back to London tomorrow without Caspian. There had to be a way to fix this.

"Are you decent?" Caspian called.

"Let me just finish wanking. Right. Done."

"Damn, that was bad timing." Caspian's head appeared in the hatchway. "Here, take this."

He handed Zed a bag, then climbed inside, dropping the hatch down behind him.

"Coffee in the flask. Croissants in the foil. Best I could do."

You look better. Happier.

Zed poured the coffee into two mugs.

"Almond or chocolate croissant?" Caspian asked.

"Half each?"

"Okay."

Zed had a mouthful of croissant when Caspian's phone rang.

"Glenn. My SO." Caspian let out a shaky breath.

"Put it on speaker."

"Okay. Hi, Glenn."

"Morning. Are you all right?"

"Why?"

If Caspian's father had called to tell this guy he hadn't spent the night in the house, Zed was going to find a way to destroy his father's reputation.

"I heard you had some trouble in Upper Barton."

Zed and Caspian exchanged glances.

"Did I not tell you to get in touch with me if there was any trouble? What happened?"

"I live in a small village. Everyone knows someone who knew those girls. They don't want me here. I understand that. I think they called the press. Someone took a picture."

"And you had water thrown at you."

320

"A guy spat in my drink the day before. No one will serve me in any of the shops."

Glenn tsked. "There's an offer to let you stay in a house in Greenwich. Someone with good connections. I'm okay with it, but I'll have to visit to approve the accommodation. Won't be for another few weeks. I googled the address. Nice house. Once I've signed off, I'll pass you over to someone in that area, but you can move address in the meantime. And you can take the holiday in Cornwall."

Caspian gasped. "Thank you."

Had Henry done that?

"I'll give you a call in a week or so and arrange a meeting."

"Okay."

"Bye."

Caspian gaped at Zed, opened his mouth, then covered his face with his hands. Zed pulled him into his arms.

One thing Caspian didn't let himself do if he could help it, was cry. When he'd begun to lose faith in human nature, the kindness of Jonas and Henry had restored it. He knew they were doing it for Zed but that didn't matter. All Caspian wanted was Zed's happiness anyway.

"We're going to go to your house and pack up all your things," Zed said. "I brought the car over last night so we'll go and get that first. We can't leave until I've been to the bank on Monday and got rid of the furniture, but I don't think your SO will mind about one night. No one's going to tell him. Finish your croissant."

Once Caspian had brought himself back under control, he felt different. Stronger. Lighter.

Zed slipped the tablets into his pocket. "I'll put them back with the others. We can take them into a pharmacy in Ashford tomorrow."

Caspian put the mugs and flask into the bag and followed Zed down the ladder. He paused at the bottom and whispered, "Thank you, little house."

"Are you going to speak to your parents before we start packing up your stuff?" Zed asked.

"I suppose I'd better."

He could hear them in the dining room when he and Zed went into the house. Zed squeezed his fingers, then let go.

"Go get 'em, Tiger."

321

"Except I'm a flamingo, remember?"

"Then do it in style. But don't stand on one leg, you might fall over."

Caspian walked into the room smiling. Zed was right behind him. Everyone but Betsy was in there.

"I've just come to tell you I'm leaving," Caspian said. "I have my supervising officer's permission to move out. Is it okay if I take a suitcase?" He didn't wait for a response. "Good."

He walked out and went to the kitchen. Betsy was sitting at the table drinking a cup of tea.

"I've come to say goodbye," Caspian told her. "I'm going to live with Zed in London."

She stood and threw her arms around him. Caspian found he didn't want to pull away.

"The press came here yesterday," she said. "Your father sent them packing but they're not going to leave you alone. You're right to leave."

Caspian nodded. "Do you have some plastic bags I can use to pack up my stuff?"

"'Course I do." She handed him several. "Good luck, Caspian."

It didn't take him and Zed long to remove everything he wanted. The clothes his mother had bought him, his telescope, guitar, his notebooks, his little collections of all sorts of bits and pieces. Charlie Bear. The marble.

As they came down to the hall with the final load, his parents and sisters were waiting.

"Will you let me know you're all right?" his mother asked.

When Caspian didn't say anything, Zed spoke. "Yes, he will."

Caspian left before any of them could hug him.

Back at Zed's father's place, they unloaded the car and put Caspian's things in a corner of the hall.

"Want to finish off the rooms and then it's all done?" Zed asked. "Sure."

It took them a few hours to go through the shed, the garage, the utility room, kitchen, study and lounge. They stuck Post-it notes on every item of furniture and bag that was to be taken away. The garden equipment was left for the new owners.

"Would you mind if I took a few of your father's tools?" Caspian asked.

"Course not."

Caspian slipped them into a cardboard box. Drill, hammer, screwdriver, bits and pieces.

When Zed opened the fridge to look for something to eat, he laughed. "Jonas doesn't want us to starve."

Caspian looked over his shoulder. "You should call and thank him."

"Yep. I'll go on Skype and you can thank him too."

Jonas answered immediately. "Hi."

"Thanks for the food," Zed said.

"Thanks for the lube and condoms," Caspian added.

"Shit. The neighbours are round for coffee and listening to this." Caspian winced.

"No, they're not," Zed said. "Jonas wouldn't say *shit* in front of the neighbours."

Jonas chuckled.

"Thank you for everything," Caspian said. "I should warn you I'm not housetrained."

"We'll leave that to Zed. He'll whip you into shape." There was a short intake of breath. "If you're into that. Perfectly fine if you are. Zed, did we have that conversation about boundaries and consent?"

"I already wash my own sheets."

Jonas groaned and Caspian felt his cheeks heat.

"We'll be home early evening on Monday, I guess," Zed said. "See you then."

"See you then."

Zed put his phone in his pocket and pulled food out of the fridge. "Picnic?"

"Sounds good. Oh look, there's strawberries, meringue and squirty cream." Caspian gave a long moan.

"The salad first. You want beer or white wine? It's Prosecco."

"Prosecco."

Caspian had a plan and a very interested cock. All the ingredients had been provided. Then the buzzer went at the front gate and he wondered if his afternoon was going to be wrecked. Zed went to open the front door with Caspian at his back.

"Your father," Zed said.

323

"Let him in."

Zed pressed the fob and the gates opened.

"Stay in the house and I'll talk to him." Caspian walked outside, his boner gone.

His father got out of the car and headed towards him.

"Did I forget something?" Caspian asked.

"No. I did. Your mother pointed out to me that I'd been rather unfair. I'd promised to help you when you came out of the Young Offender Institution and that's what I want to do. Stay here. I'll set up one of the outbuildings as a workshop and provide you with a hundred thousand pounds to develop one of your ideas."

Shit. That was a lot. "Which one?" Caspian wouldn't take his father's money, but he was interested to hear which idea he preferred.

"I don't care. Whatever you like."

And that said everything. "The instant ice-maker? The razor phone? Hair in a can?"

"Whatever you want to go with."

"Goodbye." Caspian turned and his father caught hold of his shoulder and spun him around.

"I'm offering you what you wanted. Don't be stupid enough to turn this chance down."

"I don't want your money." *I want something from you that I'm never going to get. An acknowledgment that what you did was wrong. That you're sorry.*

"A hundred thousand pounds and you don't want it?"

"No thank you."

His father laughed. "That just goes to prove what a dumb little shit you are. I only came over here because your mother pleaded with me. You're never going to amount to anything. I'm glad you're out of my hair. Your mother also asked me to give you these. Ten tickets for her ball." He held them out. "Don't come."

Caspian took them. "July the fifteenth. I think my cellmate should be out by then. We'd love to come. Thanks."

He walked back into the house smiling and heard his father spluttering behind him. Caspian closed the door.

"A razor phone? Hair in a can?" Zed laughed.

"And what's wrong with those?" Caspian looked as indignant as he could.

Zed rolled his eyes.

"Yeah, well, he didn't listen. The offer's come too late. Far too late." Caspian cracked open the door. "Close the gate. Pity he's got his car all the way through. I'd have loved to scratch his paintwork."

Zed pressed the buzzer.

They took the duvet off Tamaz's bed and spread it out on the lawn before bringing the food outside. Caspian took off his shoes and wriggled his toes on the grass. His shirt came off next and then his chinos so that all he wore were his black Calvin Klein knit boxers. Slightly more snug than usual.

"You're stopping now?" Zed's forkful of salad was in limbo on the way to his mouth.

"I'm very lazy. I might need help with these." He flicked the waistband against his stomach and yelped.

"Hmm." Zed put his laden fork in his mouth.

Caspian smiled, tugged off Zed's shoes and tossed them aside.

"I thought you were hungry?" Zed said.

"I am." He stared at Zed's groin.

"Oh God."

Caspian crawled to Zed's side, peeled his T-shirt up over his head and threw it onto his shoes. Zed's nipples were hard, tight copper disks. Caspian's mouth watered. When he reached for Zed's zip, he was shoved away. "Let me do it. I don't trust you."

When Zed only wore the same as him, grey boxers of a similar style, Caspian sat back and ate. Zed opened the Prosecco and handed him a glass.

Caspian touched his glass to Zed's. "To…happiness and a happy penis. Two happy ones. Four happy balls. Two happy mouths. Two happy arses. Maybe."

"Maybe? That was a quick backtrack."

"Nerves."

"Why?"

Caspian laughed. "Neither of us has done this before. I don't want to fuck it up in the wrong way." He frowned. "That came out wrong."

He finished the salad, filling his mouth to stop himself blurting out anything else, then assembled the meringues, strawberries and cream.

"I thought that cream was for something else," Zed said.

"You didn't tell me you were kinky. I did wonder about that conversation you had with Jonas about boundaries and consent."

"It was the funniest thing. He was so embarrassed. He told me afterwards that he and Henry had promised each other all sorts of things if the other one talked to me. I sat and listened, kept gasping and widening my eyes until Jonas finally got that I knew it all already."

"All?"

"Enough."

Caspian had googled since he'd been released and found out more than enough.

"This is lovely." Zed bit into the meringue and licked the cream from his lips.

"Yep." Caspian moaned and groaned his way through the dessert, slowly sucking his spoon, making a popping sound when he pulled it out of his mouth, and he never took his eyes off Zed.

"You definitely shut the gates?" Caspian whispered.

"Yes," Zed whispered back and smiled. "No neighbours close by."

Caspian moved everything off the duvet, putting the cream close to the Prosecco.

Zed lay on his back and stretched. "I feel lazy."

"But do you feel lucky?" Caspian crawled over him, knees either side of Zed's hips, forearms next to his shoulders.

"I feel very lucky."

"Not as lucky as me."

Caspian bent and nipped Zed's ear, then wrapped his mouth around it and Zed let out a choked moan. Caspian licked across Zed's cheek to his lips and gave him a soft kiss.

"You know how porn stars manage to keep going for hours and hours?" Caspian said.

"Yeah, they do, well not hours but how do you know?"

"My cellmate had a phone with porn on it. Het porn but I just watched the guy do his thing. He was into ears and toes. Anyway, the going for hours and hours thing. I'm assuming after we've done this a few thousand times I'm not going to want to come just by looking at you. But I feel as though I'm a rocket that's already had its touch paper lit."

Caspian planted his forearms more firmly on the duvet and rolled his hips against Zed's.

326

"Oh fuck," Zed muttered. "The gates are definitely closed, right?"

"Yeah. We only need to worry about planes and gliders." Caspian tipped his head back. "Oh and hot air balloons."

"What?" Zed checked the sky and scowled.

Another roll of his hips to brush his cock against Zed's and precum surged. *Oh fuck that feels good.* Zed's scowl vanished. Caspian had thought about making Zed wait but he was too impatient himself. He moved back onto his knees and slid his hands slowly up Zed's thighs inside his boxers onto his hips. He smiled at the wet circle where Zed's cock had reacted like his, then peeled his boxers down to his toes. Zed kicked them away. Zed's dark, thickly veined cock rose straight up over his belly, balls heavy beneath, shaved, and Caspian swallowed hard. He wrenched off his own boxers and leaned over Zed again.

"Close your eyes," Caspian whispered. "And keep them closed."

Caspian squirted cream all over Zed's cock and stomach, and gasped as he did it. "Oooh, oh fuck, fuck, FUCK."

Zed's chest shook as he laughed. Caspian squirted cream into Zed's mouth, then dropped down to wrap his lips around Zed's cock. One deep, hard suck and Zed grabbed his head.

"Turn around. Let's both do it."

Caspian handed Zed the cream and without him seeing, took a mouthful of Prosecco. The idea had sounded good but when Zed's lips were on his cock, Caspian almost choked and the Prosecco went everywhere.

Then they were laughing, twisting around, each trying to get on top, sucking each other off, licking, stroking, grasping, while the cream and Prosecco went all over them and the duvet. But when they were finally in position, their mouths full of each other, Caspian struggled to concentrate on what he was doing when Zed was making him feel so blissed out.

Focus!

He held on to Zed's cock with one hand and slid his mouth around the crest, lapping at the head, while the fingers of his other hand explored Zed's arse cheeks. When he burrowed into the seam, he felt Zed's reaction and pressed a finger hard against his hole. Zed gave a loud groan and came in his mouth. Caspian was so turned on, he came too.

When they could move, they swivelled around so they were lying side by side.

"I knew there was a bonus in us both being the same height," Zed said.

Caspian laughed as he kissed him and kept kissing him.

"Fuck," Zed gasped. "Let me breathe."

"Hurry then. Breathing is so overrated and you're interfering with my face-eating marathon to be followed by an arse-eating one."

Zed growled and pinned Caspian down by his shoulders. "I can think of something else I'd like to eat. But we need to shower."

Caspian glanced at the hose.

"And not with that," Zed said.

Caspian wriggled free, ran to the hose and sprayed Zed until he reached the safety of the house.

Chapter Twenty-Nine

Caspian emerged into the bedroom naked, having scrubbed every inch of his body. He felt ultra-clean and insanely nervous. Zed had showered in the other bathroom and when he came into the room and saw Caspian holding the condoms and lube, the rise and fall in Zed's throat showed he was equally anxious.

"No whip?" Caspian gaped at him. "No rope. No power tools? I'm so disappointed."

Zed dropped the towel he'd wrapped around his hips and if that hadn't been enough to shut him up, the kiss that followed was. He worked his tongue into Caspian's mouth and every cell in Caspian's body felt electrified. *Mine. He's mine.* He had to keep telling himself because he struggled to believe it was true, that Zed had kept wanting him as much as he'd kept wanting Zed. Yet, if Zed's father hadn't died, would they even be together? *Fucking stop it, you idiot.*

Their tongues slid together, along with their bodies. Skin to skin from mouth to toe, their thickening cocks wedged between them as they grasped each other's backside. When they finally tore their mouths apart, they were panting as if they'd been running.

"Do you have to suck all the air out of my mouth?" Zed gasped.

"Hey, I give it back."

"We'll pass out through lack of oxygen."

Caspian lifted a hand to Zed's face and dragged his fingers over his lips. "Once, I wasn't frightened of anything."

"Apart from murderous flamingos, as I remember."

"That goes without saying. Vicious bastards."

"What are you frightened of?"

Caspian took a deep breath, sucked on Zed's finger and then sighed. "You. Disappointing you. Getting it wrong. Wanting you too much. Messing this up. Hurting you." *Loving you.*

"It's the same for me so we cancel each other out." Zed rocked against him. "Do you want to go first?"

That shocked Caspian. He'd thought… "Do you?"

"I did, but I've changed my mind."

"Okay." *Don't ask him why.* "Why?"

"Because it doesn't matter to me whether I'm on top or not. This is still a first for both of us. I've not been fucked before and you haven't fucked anyone."

"So we get another first when we swap." Caspian bit his lip.
"Okay. That time is going to be somewhere of my choosing."

"Not with an audience."

"Fuck." Caspian smiled.

"Not even flamingos."

"Double fuck."

"Use a lot of lube." Zed knelt on all fours on the mattress and looked at him over his shoulder.

Oh God. Caspian dropped behind him before he fell down. "You are so cute."

"Are you talking to my backside?"

"Bearing in mind what I'm about to do I thought we should get acquainted first. It appears I have a *thing* for your arse." He kissed it, nipped it, then licked over his teeth marks. His reward was the hitch in Zed's breath. More than once.

Zed's arse was rounder than his. Smooth. Firm. Muscular. Beautiful. Caspian pulled away to admire it and reached back for Zed's feet. He drew his hands over the heels, his fingers trailing up his calves, teasing the back of his knees before dancing along the length of his thighs. Was Zed shaking or him? *Ah, both of us.*

He leaned over, sliding his cock into the gap between Zed's thighs as he kissed his neck.

Caspian whispered "thank you" in his ear, and Zed whined. "I might forget to say it later."

He ran his tongue into the shell of Zed's ear, breathed into it and Zed moaned and quivered beneath him. Caspian rocked his dick between Zed's legs as he licked his ear and Zed collapsed onto the mattress, Caspian on top.

"Broken already? Do you need new batteries?" Caspian breathed the words into Zed's neck, then licked down the length of his spine while Zed squirmed and humped the mattress which wasn't easy with Caspian's weight on him. When Caspian reached Zed's arse, he trailed his tongue down the crease, then pulled Zed back onto his knees and dropped down to mouth his balls.

"Oh God, fuck, just, fuck, yeah, ohh." Zed's babbling was even more of a turn on.

"Tell me if you like it," Caspian lifted his face to say. "Be clear. And use a language I understand."

330

Zed snorted. Caspian spread his arse cheeks wider and dipped his head to suck a mark in the line where Zed's thigh met his backside.

"Caspian," Zed wailed.

"Have I driven you mad yet?"

"Every time any part of you touches me—it drives me crazy."

Caspian pressed his face against the seam of Zed's backside and licked around the tight hole. Over it, circling it, spitting against it until he slipped a little way inside, then deeper inside as Zed bucked back against him. Caspian held Zed's hips up and continued to rim and ream him.

"Need more. Need you," Zed gasped.

"Turn over. I want to see your face."

Zed squirmed onto his back, looked into his face, then down at Caspian's cock and gulped. "How come you suddenly look twice as big?"

"I *am* twice as big. That's my superpower." Caspian reached for the condoms and ripped one off the strip.

Zed closed his eyes. "Don't fucking tell me that."

"Open your eyes."

"I can't keep them open."

"Yeah you can, Mr Eyes Like the Sun."

Zed opened his eyes. Caspian chewed his lip as he carefully rolled on the condom.

"I wish I'd practised this. How long did it take me to get it on? No more than ten minutes surely. That's not bad."

Zed grinned and handed him the lube. "Fingers first, right?"

"Why?"

Zed opened his mouth to tell him, then caught the look in Caspian's eyes. "Ha ha."

"Are you going to be a toppy bottom?"

"Are you?" Zed asked.

"I don't know. Maybe I'll call you sir and beg you to fuck me. It'll be a surprise for both of us."

Caspian gave an exasperated groan when the lube went everywhere except the place it was supposed to land. He used the side of his hand to swipe it down Zed's chest and behind his balls as Zed sniggered.

"We have a limited supply. I'm not wasting it," Caspian said. "Oh look, my entire hand is lubed up. Fingers. Hand. Cock. Not much difference. Why don't I try to put—"

"Don't even think about it." Zed's eyes fluttered shut.

Caspian used his middle finger to work the lube around the entrance to Zed's body, then just inside. Zed's breathing changed pitch. Caspian had tried to hide his anxiety with humour, but he *was* worried about hurting him.

"Shout if it hurts or I do something wrong," Caspian whispered. "I am in the right hole, yeah?"

"There's more than one? I'd never noticed."

"Shut the fuck up." He slid his finger deeper and Zed arched his back.

"Yessss," Zed hissed.

Then Caspian was in up to his knuckle, moving his finger backwards and forwards and Zed was pushing against him, fucking himself on Caspian's hand. It was so hot, Caspian reached for his own balls and pressed down hard. Coming before he got inside Zed was not going to happen. He curled his finger in the tight space, feeling for the bundle of nerves that he'd once upon a time found inside himself, stroked the sensitive gland and Zed just about levitated off the bed.

The sounds coming from him made no sense. Caspian caught his name a couple of times but he was mesmerised by the sight of him, the way Zed spread and lifted his legs and pushed back against him. *He's mine.* No one had ever done this to him before. *No one apart from me will ever do this to him again.* Caspian slid another finger alongside the first and Zed cried out. The feeling of Zed's body grasping at him wound Caspian tighter.

It was getting harder and harder to resist the drag in his belly, the ache in his balls that had him wanting to come *right fucking now.* Were two fingers enough to stretch him? Probably not. He slid in a third and Zed went rigid. So Caspian did too.

"Fuck have I killed you? Can rigor mortis set in that fast?"

Zed's teeth were clenched together. He didn't move. Caspian tried to move, tried to slide his fingers just a little way in and out but Zed was in lockdown.

"Hey, little flamingo, you have to relax." Caspian leaned between Zed's legs and kissed him, swallowed Zed's frantic exhalations.

"Deep breaths," Caspian urged. "Want me to get a brown paper bag for you to breathe into? Or a puppy to cuddle?"

Zed laughed and the hold on Caspian's fingers lessened. But Caspian had slid back toward the edge and was in definite danger of coming before he even got inside Zed. He pulled his fingers out, wiped them on the damp towel Zed had discarded, and squirted the rest of the packet of lube onto his hand and cock.

"That was so good. Was it good for you?" Caspian asked.

"Shut the fuck up and get on with it."

"You are such a deeply romantic guy."

"Do it."

Caspian's confidence slipped. "I'm frightened of hurting you."

Zed opened his eyes. "You will. But I can cope. I read that the first time always hurts."

"I won't let it. I'll be really careful."

He lined up his cock against the tight pucker of Zed's arse and pushed as gently as he could against the resistant muscles.

Tight, tight, tight.

"Fuck, fuck, fuck," Zed gasped.

"I am, I am, I am."

Caspian's response made Zed laugh which relaxed him enough that Caspian could slide a little way in. *Oh shit. So hot. So tight. So fucking good.*

"All the way," Zed blurted.

"I am."

"Liar." Zed clenched around him and Caspian saw stars.

"Okay, okay. Commencing docking procedure…"

"Stop making me laugh. Just do it."

"I want us to remember this forever. Me being highly amusing. You being an arsehole."

"One more word and I'm fucking you instead."

Caspian held his breath as he pushed, felt that perfect moment when Zed's body accepted him. He filled him, slid in until there was no more of him left outside the clench of Zed's muscles. They both stopped moving. Raw pleasure had taken control of Caspian's cock, flooded his veins, stolen the air from his lungs.

The urge to move, to fuck grew until Caspian could no longer resist it. He pulled out as slowly as he could, left just the head of his cock inside, then pushed back.

333

"Yesss," Zed groaned.

He held onto Zed's hips and did it again, harder. He must have hit his prostate because Zed let out a strangled cry and a string of sounds with the word *more* in there somewhere.

All too soon Caspian felt the tell-tale signs of orgasm, the tingle in his balls, the pressure at the back of his skull. *Shit.* He wanted Zed to come first.

"Touch your cock," he told him. "Bring yourself off."

Zed wrapped his hand around his dick. Caspian was going faster and faster, his hips shunting, his back arching, caught in a current that he wouldn't escape until he'd come. Zed came with a cry, cum spurting over his chest in long thick streaks. It seemed almost before he'd finished coming that his hands were reaching for Caspian's and with fingers linked, orgasm ripped through Caspian like a tornado, the world disappearing right in front of his eyes.

He slumped on top of Zed as if he was falling into another dimension, not one muscle under his control, not even his heart. *Oh fuck, that was so good. Thank fuck I didn't know how good that was before now.* But it wouldn't have been that good with anyone other than Zed.

For a long time their hands stayed linked before Caspian finally mustered the energy to withdraw and roll off him. He turned his head to find Zed staring at him.

"That was the best fuck I've ever had," Zed said.

Caspian burst out laughing.

By the time Caspian woke on Monday morning, Zed was up and dressed.

Caspian whined. "Clothes? Really?"

"Yes because otherwise we'd be at it like bunnies when the house clearance guys arrive."

While Caspian showered, Zed loaded the car with his bag and Caspian's belongings so that nothing was taken by accident. Caspian helped him drag down the mattress they'd slept on and they heaved it into the skip along with the duvet, sheets and towels.

"We can't be this extravagant every time we fuck," Caspian said.

Zed chuckled. "It's all old stuff."

After the charity had loaded up their large van and driven off, the house was more or less empty. Zed had kept back the hoover and Caspian volunteered to tackle upstairs while Zed cleaned the kitchen, emptied the fridge and freezer and switched it off. By the time they'd done, the hoover was in the skip and the house looked pretty good. The estate agent arrived at ten, checked Zed's ID and his father's death certificate and took copies of the documents with her phone.

"You'll have to prove ownership but we can start the selling process. I'd suggest £699,000."

Zed almost had to be picked up off the floor.

"I don't think I'll have any problem selling this house," the woman said. "Popular village, close to a high-speed station, it's in a lovely location. I bet you have fond memories of your childhood."

Caspian's hand rested in the middle of Zed's back and he kept quiet. Zed signed the contract and gave her the spare keys and the fob for the gate. Once she'd left there was nothing to keep them there. Zed took the meter readings for the gas and electricity and they set off for Ashford.

Zed's head ached by the time he came out of the bank. He'd been able to provide all the identification needed for both himself and his father but because of the sum of money involved, thousands and thousands in his father's two accounts, and the amount due from life insurance, Zed had to apply for Letters of Administration.

Caspian was sitting on a bench with his face tipped to the sunshine waiting for him when he emerged. *He looks like he belongs on the front page of a magazine and he's mine.* Almost as though Caspian could sense him looking, he opened his eyes and turned to face him. "All done?"

"For the time being." Zed tugged him to his feet. "Time to go home."

Caspian's smile melted his heart.

"What's that look for?" Caspian asked.

"Your smile. It's beautiful."

"Not my most beautiful."

"Really?"

"I'm saving that one. How's your arse?"

"Sore."

Caspian beamed at him. Zed elbowed him in the ribs.

They reached Greenwich just after five. Zed pulled up next to Jonas's car. He was tired, and not just physically. He'd hated his father but it was still draining having to deal with the aftermath of his death. Hard to believe he wasn't there anymore. Would there ever have been a chance of reconciliation? Only if his father had said he was sorry and that was inconceivable.

"This looks...big," Caspian said.

"It's divided into sections but the part they own is pretty big. Let's leave everything in the car and go in and speak to Jonas first. Henry won't be back from work."

"What does he actually do?"

"I don't *actually* know." Zed grinned. "Government stuff."

"The *if I tell you I'll have to kill you* type of stuff?"

Zed nodded. "So don't press him."

Jonas came rushing to the door when he heard them come in. He wrapped his arms around Zed, but when Caspian hung back Jonas didn't try to hug him.

"Good journey?" Jonas asked.

"Terrible traffic. Took us twice as long as it should have done." Partly because he'd been careful not to drive too fast. He was all too aware of Caspian clutching the sides of his seat so tightly that his knuckles were white.

"A drink," Jonas said. "What would you like? Caspian?"

Caspian shrugged. Zed could see him looking round, taking everything in.

"I'd love a glass of white wine," Zed said. "Mr Grumpy will have the same."

Jonas took wine from the fridge and poured their drinks. "Show Caspian around. If you two want to move into the basement, that's fine."

Zed started at the roof terrace and worked his way down. Caspian was too quiet, not himself at all, and Zed wondered what was going through his head. It was pointless saying anything. Caspian had been in a dark place for so long it would take him time to fully emerge and stay out of the darkness.

When Zed pushed open the door to the tunnel-like underground room, he knew this was where they ought to be, where he now wanted to be, but he'd let Caspian decide.

"The band sometimes rehearses down here. Well, if Jonas and Henry are out. It's private. We'd even have our own kitchen. What do you think?"

"That I'm lucky."

"Let's bring everything in and then you can help me move my stuff down here from the bedroom."

By the time they'd sorted everything out, Henry was back. Jonas had cooked.

"Do you always eat together?" Caspian whispered.

"We try to but Henry works crazy hours and Jonas is out a lot of nights playing in concerts. We take it in turns to cook."

"I can't cook," Caspian said.

Jonas laughed. "Neither can Henry."

Zed squeezed Caspian's fingers. "You can learn. I'll teach you."

Zed set the table, showing Caspian where things were kept. He was still far too subdued and Zed was worried.

"Jonas tells me you've moved to the basement," Henry said.

"Thank you for letting me stay here," Caspian blurted. "I'll get a job. Pay rent. I won't tell anyone what you do."

Henry froze momentarily as he helped himself to salad. "And what do I do?"

"I have no idea. That's why I won't tell anyone."

Henry laughed and glanced at Zed. "I work for the government. Not very exciting." He turned to Caspian. "What would you like to do?"

"I can...wash dishes or do garden work or maybe work in a shop."

Zed gaped at him. "What would you *like* to do, not what you think you might have to do and you're not going to wash dishes."

"Except here," Jonas said.

At least that brought a small smile to Caspian's face.

"You like inventing things," Henry said.

"He's come up with hundreds of ideas." Zed glanced at Caspian.

"They're not all original," Caspian muttered.

"Most products that are patented are just improvements on existing ideas," Henry said. "There's an inventors club near the London School of Economics. They have a meeting every month. You could join. You might find people who'd offer help in building prototypes and they'd be able to give you business advice."

"Or tell me my idea is crap."

"Yep, they might." Henry shrugged. "But investors won't put money into something that no one has any faith in. Your idea has to look credible, well thought out and well presented to stand any chance of success. And you need to protect it."

"Patent it. Yeah, I know. Not just in this country too. It costs a lot of money."

"I'll help," Zed said. "Once I get my share of my father's money."

Caspian sighed. "I can't let you do that."

Zed opened his mouth to argue and caught Henry's warning glance.

"Be careful what you say to people," Henry said. "Whatever's special about what you've invented, keep those details a secret. But telling someone you've invented a way to recycle plastic bags or found a new source of green energy is fine because you might just be speaking to someone who works in that field or knows someone who does."

"Okay."

"So are we all set for Cornwall?" Jonas asked.

Henry nodded. "We leave on Wednesday. I've hired surfboards and wetsuits. They'll be waiting for us at the cottage. Can you surf, Caspian?"

"I told you—" Henry's glance shut Zed up.

Caspian turned to Zed. "Have you been abroad, ridden on a roller coaster, climbed a mountain, skied, surfed?"

And Zed knew exactly what was wrong. Caspian had wanted to do those things with him. But it wasn't fair to have expected him to wait. Irritation rose and fell. He'd waited in the most important way.

"I've been to the States with Jonas and Henry. Oregon and then California. I went on a roller coaster with Jonas. Henry is a wimp."

"Hey. Vertigo. Remember?" Henry said.

Jonas laughed. "Right. Of course it is."

"I've surfed with them both. Henry taught me to ski. I've climbed a mountain with them. With *them* not you." He nudged Caspian's foot under the table. "I've not seen the northern lights. I've not stayed in an ice hotel. I haven't biked down a volcano in Hawaii. I've not been to the top of Kilimanjaro to look at the stars. We have a lot of things to do. And I haven't changed my mind about swimming with sharks. You've got a long list of things you want to do with me. We've already done some."

"What were they?" Caspian asked and when Zed saw the look in his eyes he knew he had him back again.

He called Caspian's bluff. "You took me into space. I lost my virginity to you."

Both Henry and Jonas let out a cry of mock-horror and clamped their hands over their ears.

"I still can't believe you said that," Caspian mumbled as he cleaned his teeth next to Zed.

"It was true."

"Yeah but there's sharing and then there's sharing."

Zed spat into the neighbouring basin, then swilled out his mouth.

"Did I really take you into space?" Caspian asked.

"Don't fish for compliments."

"I like space travel. We need to do it again."

"We definitely do." Zed grabbed a towel and wiped his mouth. "We also need to pack for Cornwall. You don't have any swimming trunks. We'll go and buy some tomorrow. I'm meeting the band in the afternoon for a quick practice session. Come with me?"

"Okay."

That was something, Zed thought. He'd worried Caspian would say no.

"What are you going to do about getting in touch with the guy who's probably your birth father?" Caspian asked.

"It can wait until we're back from Cornwall. I need to think about the right thing to do."

Caspian went back into the bedroom and Zed washed his face. As he reached Caspian's side and caught a glimpse of the TV, he froze.

"What's happened?" Zed asked.

"A bomb," Caspian whispered.

A device had gone off in the packed foyer of the Manchester Arena at the end of a pop concert. Hundreds had been wounded and several people killed.

"All those kids." Zed swallowed hard. "How can they think this is the right thing to do? To deliberately target children?"

How could he think playing in a band was more important than helping stop things like this from happening?

Caspian tugged him to the bed and pulled him down, spooning behind him, his arms holding Zed tight. "You can't save everyone," he said quietly.

But I can save some.

"I know what you're thinking, but what can you do?" Caspian kissed his neck. "Don't go back into that world. Please. Please. Remember what you wrote to me? *I want to keep you safe, but I can't. So you have to stay safe. Promise me. Look after yourself. When you get out we'll be together and we'll be happy. That's my promise to you.*"

"You remember what I wrote?"

"I remember every word. You promised we'd be together and be happy."

Zed turned in Caspian's arms and kissed him. "I did. We will." *But I want the world to be safe for you and if that means working for MI5, that's what I'll do.*

Chapter Thirty

Caspian woke the next morning with a smile on his face. A warm, wet, insistent tongue was caressing his cock. He was already hard. Now he went harder.

"Zed, come out of the bathroom," he shouted. "Hey, do Jonas and Henry have a cat? Ouch. Oh no, it's one of those sensory alarm clocks. Ouch."

Caspian flung back the covers and watched as Zed played with him. Each lick, each suck sent flickers of lightning racing down his veins. He ran his fingers over the bulge in Zed's cheek, and as he felt his cock inside Zed's mouth, he groaned.

"I thought *I* might get breakfast in bed but it looks like you're getting it instead." Caspian grinned.

Zed let him free with a soft pop. Caspian's cock was slick with precum and saliva and Zed's lips glistened. When his tongue slipped out to lick his lips, Caspian pulled him up and did some licking of his own. "Oh, I taste good. Maybe not as good as toast and marmalade but pretty good."

"Stand up and fuck my mouth."

Goose bumps raced down Caspian's arms and legs. "Christ, you're bossy in the mornings."

He rolled out of bed and stood. Zed knelt at his feet and wrapped his fingers around the base of Caspian's cock, before feeding it inch by inch into his mouth until it disappeared.

"Oh shit. That is some magic trick," Caspian panted. "Tell me you can make it reappear and not on the other side of the room."

Zed laughed, choked and pulled off. "I can't do it if you make me laugh."

"Oh, it's still there. Thank Christ for that." Caspian ran his hand up his entire length. "All fifteen inches."

"Shut up." Zed licked around the tip, slid his tongue into the slit and Caspian pressed his lips together to trap his whine.

He locked his hands in Zed's hair, held tight and thrust his cock between Zed's lips.

Zed's bright eyes were wide open, watching him. That was such a turn on except Caspian's eyes were glazing over. Zed dropped his hand from the base of Caspian's cock, let *him* take control and his heart melted. How could Zed swallow so much? How could he breathe? How could he do *that thing* with his tongue at the same time as… *Oh fuck.*

Caspian wanted it to last longer but *want* wouldn't make it happen. The strong suction…the tight slide…the sensation of his balls slapping against Zed's chin. Then Zed did something…swallowed against the head of his cock, and as a strangled sound burst from Caspian's throat, he came. He gasped and trembled with each spurt and when Zed licked him clean, the whine of pleasure finally escaped.

"Oh God, that was so good, that felt so fucking fantastic, I can't tell you how sensational it was. Yeah, I can, oh fuck… No, I can't. You… ohhh."

"Shut up," Zed said. "I'm trying to concentrate here."

Caspian looked down to see Zed jerking himself off. Caspian yanked him up, kissed him and wrapped his fingers around Zed's. Zed gasped and warm cum splattered between them. Zed rested his head on Caspian's shoulder as he came down.

"Wow," Zed muttered.

"Is that all I get? Wow?"

"I did most of the work myself."

Caspian dropped to his knees and licked Zed's stomach. "I'm still going to need breakfast."

Breakfast was a subdued affair. Henry had gone into work early and Jonas sat glued to the TV. The pictures of the Manchester bombing were horrifying. Caspian swallowed hard when they interviewed kids and their parents who'd been at the concert. So many innocents killed and wounded by a homemade bomb filled with shrapnel.

"It breaks my heart." Jonas turned from the TV. "What are you two up to today?"

"We were going to go shopping," Zed said. "Caspian needs some swimming trunks. Now I don't feel like we should."

"Life goes on," Jonas said. "They win if you don't do the things you'd normally do."

"I suppose," Zed muttered. "We can get what we need in Greenwich."

"But be careful." Jonas rose to his feet and flung his arms around Zed. "Really careful."

Zed rolled his eyes at Caspian, but he thought Jonas was right. Everyone had to be vigilant.

Zed made shopping fun, though Caspian refused to buy the trunks plastered with pink flamingos and instead chose a pair the colour of Zed's eyes. Caspian hadn't worried when he'd walked into any of the shops. No one knew him. They ate lunch in a café and no one knew him there either. *No more panic attacks,* he told himself. This was the new start he'd wanted and he had the bonus of his life beginning again with Zed when he'd never dared to dream that could happen. Well, he'd dreamed it but known it was only a fantasy.

Dreams can come true.

Though Caspian's anxiety returned at the prospect of meeting Zed's band. After lunch, they'd gone back to collect Zed's guitar and were now on the way to Tower Hamlets.

"Have you told them about me?" Caspian asked.

"No. I've only ever talked about you to Henry, Jonas and Jackson, and not very often, but that's not because I was embarrassed you were in prison but because I didn't want that to define you when you came out. You don't need to tell anyone. No one needs to know. Unless you want them to know."

"Not really. So are they going to ask how we met, how long we've known one another?"

"We can tell them the truth. We met when we were teenagers and we just got back together after my father died."

"And when they ask where I live?"

"We'll say you're staying at my place for a while."

"And if they ask what I do?"

"You're an inventor." Zed smiled. "They're not going to interrogate you. You'll be fine."

Zed brushed his fingers against Caspian's and Caspian grasped his hand.

"You sure you want to hold hands?" Zed asked.

"Don't you?"

"I'd be honoured to hold your hand."

"I should think so," Caspian said. "Anyway, if anyone objects you can hit them with your guitar case."

Zed wrapped his fingers tighter around Caspian's.

The moment they walked into the garage where the band was going to rehearse, and Caspian locked eyes with the guy strumming a guitar, he knew he wasn't welcome.

Fin, he assumed, came straight over to Zed and nodded in Caspian's direction. "You know the rule. No guests. Who is he?"

"My boyfriend. Caspian."

The tall, rake-thin redhead's cheeks twitched before he gave a snort of disbelief. "Boyfriend? Since when?"

"Since I was fourteen."

That shut Fin up but Caspian knew there was a problem. It wasn't just the not wanting strangers to hear them rehearse, Fin fancied Zed.

"Everyone, meet Caspian," Zed said. "Jonesie is the crazy dude on the drums who never shuts up, Akash plays bass and rarely speaks, and the moody one is Fin."

Akash and Jonesie smiled and waved at him. Zed went to the other side of the garage to sort out his guitar leaving Fin alone with Caspian.

Fin glared. "Just get lost for a few hours while we rehearse."

"Are you that bad?" Caspian widened his eyes. "Don't worry. I won't criticise."

"Fucking arsehole," Fin muttered under his breath. "I don't like you."

"Sadly for you, my give-a-fuck is broken."

Caspian watched as Fin decided what to do. Fight or flee. The guy walked away.

"We need to get started," Fin said. "We don't have long. Pete's coming later with some news. He wouldn't tell me what it was."

"Pete Corrigan is our manager," Zed told Caspian.

Zed tuned up and Caspian went to sit on an upturned box in the corner.

"We'll run through *Hurricane, Edge of Town* and then *Heavy Breathing,*" Fin said. "We make a mistake, we start again. Mobiles off. Mine will record. We tuned up? Okay." He pressed a button on his phone and set it aside. "Ready? One, two, three…"

Caspian couldn't take his eyes off Zed. The band's energy was appropriately electrifying, and the breath caught in his throat. *Hurricane* was about the power of love that can draw a couple together, lift them up in joy, then sweep them apart. Fin might have had the solo riff, but it was Zed's voice that gave the song its soul. They were Zed's lyrics, he was sure of it. The song sounded great to Caspian, but Fin made them start again four times and play it through twice more before they moved on to the next.

Edge of Town wasn't as impressive. The lyrics didn't fit the music which was too fast for a song about living on the edge of everything. It felt to Caspian as if it should be slow and soulful when you were singing about loneliness and despair. But then what did he know? He'd sometimes imagined his poems set to music but he wasn't musical enough to compose a melody.

He started when a guy suddenly appeared next to him. He was a short man in his forties with thick white hair, dressed in a flashy blue suit. Caspian assumed this was the manager, Pete Corrigan. When they finished the song, Corrigan made a *carry on* gesture and they played *Heavy Breathing.*

Zed had the lead.

"Promise you won't let them find us
My heart'll break if they do
You breathe too loud and they'll hear us
And you know just what they'll do.
Hiding's all that's left now
If they catch us we are done
At least we'd be together
Climbing to the sun."

Caspian watched Zed's face as he played and it was as if he became a different person. He *was* the music, the music was him. The sound filled Caspian's lungs. The chorus was one of those that was instantly memorable. Caspian found himself tapping his foot. When the song ended, he clapped and Zed caught his eye and smiled.

Fin came over to Corrigan and shook his hand. "Thanks for coming."

"You're sounding good, guys," Corrigan said.

The others came over and shook the manager's hand.

"Sorry about your father, Zed." Corrigan squeezed Zed's shoulder.

Zed nodded.

"And you are?" Corrigan turned to Caspian.

"Zed's boyfriend, Caspian," Fin said.

"My hobby is ventriloquism." Caspian spoke through closed lips.

Corrigan laughed. "And what did you think of them?"

"*Heavy Breathing* was brilliant. *Hurricane* too. Energetic. With *Edge of Town* I wasn't sure the lyrics fit the music."

"Oh fuck off," Fin muttered.

345

Corrigan swivelled to face him. "That going to be your response when a fan says something you don't like? You're going to tell them to fuck off? If it is, you might as well give up now."

"He's not a fan. He's never heard us before." Fin's voice was sullen.

Corrigan glared. "He'll never be a fan if you act like that and I happen to think he's right. The tempo makes you rush those lyrics. They're both good on their own but not together."

"We could slow it down, maybe change the key," Zed said.

"Try it," Corrigan said.

The four of them messed around for a few minutes and then Fin led them in.

Corrigan nodded his head to the beat. "Better?" he asked Caspian.

"Yes."

"Good ear. Do you play?"

"The guitar but not well, apart from *Twinkle Twinkle Little Star*."

Corrigan looked him up and down. "Do you sing?"

"Only rap and opera."

The manager laughed. "Are you squeaky clean?"

Caspian's heart gave a painful thump. "Sorry. I'm filthy."

"Pity."

"Do you think they need a...*look*?" Caspian asked. "I've never seen them play before so I don't know what they usually wear but something that links them together might be good."

"Such as."

"Silver lurex jumpsuits."

"Alternately?"

"Only black and grey clothes? Some distinctive footwear? Hats? They all seem to be very different characters so maybe that would be something to build on."

Corrigan leaned back and crossed his legs. "Go on then."

"I'm not sure I know them well enough."

"Try anyway."

It was so tempting to come up with a persuasive argument for Fin to lose all his hair and have piercings all over his face. "I know nothing about image creation but maybe Fin could wear black with a shark's fin on a black T-shirt. Jonesie is funky. I'd have him in something wild. Akash would look cool in a suit. Zed should be naked, obviously."

Corrigan laughed and turned back to watch the band.

346

When they'd finished the number, they came back to where Caspian and Corrigan were sitting.

"What did you think?" Corrigan asked Fin.

"Yeah, it's much better slower and in a minor key." Fin smiled at Zed but the smile came nowhere near his eyes.

"Right. My news," Corrigan said. "I got you a spot at Glastonbury."

There was a stunned silence before Jonesie exclaimed, "What the fucking fuckity fuck?"

"A pub in Glastonbury, right?" Fin asked.

"No, not a pub. The festival," Corrigan said.

"Next year?" Akash asked.

"There's no festival next year. I'm talking about this year. Twenty-third of June. The Park Stage. One of my bands has had to pull out and I'm giving you the chance instead. You're lucky I have the right connections. Your slot is twelve fifteen to five past one. You need between ten and fifteen numbers ready. You should be able to play at least nine."

"Oh my God, that's unbelievable." Fin was bouncing around hugging everyone.

Fortunately not me.

"Draw up your playlist and send it to me," Corrigan said. "We need to have a think about your image. I'll be in touch."

The band erupted when he'd gone. Zed hugged Caspian and kissed him.

"Congratulations." Caspian put an innocent look on his face. "Can I have your autograph and your boxers? I can see a way to make money on eBay. Or I—"

"We need to arrange more practice sessions," Fin interrupted. "This weekend. Saturday *and* Sunday. Here or at your place, Zed?"

"Tomorrow I'm going to Cornwall for a week."

Fin stared at him in disbelief. "What the hell? You can't."

"Yes, I can. It's all arranged. We know all our stuff really well. Corrigan won't want us to do anything new. It's just a matter of deciding which songs we want to play and in what order. Glastonbury's a month away."

"You're fucking telling me a holiday is more important than playing at Glastonbury?"

"No, but it's equally important to me."

347

"Or to him?" Fin glared at Caspian.

"I'm just going outside for a bit." Caspian left the garage.

Maybe Zed would decide not to go to Cornwall. Caspian wouldn't blame him. *Fuck! Glastonbury! That's huge. And if they make it... I'm a liability.*

Caspian knew he was looking well into the future. It took time for bands to succeed. Though maybe Electric Ice's rise to fame would be meteoric. But what if one of the band members had a boyfriend who had a conviction for causing death by dangerous driving? Corrigan might tell Zed he had to choose between Caspian and the band. *And he'd choose me.*

That was neither a guess nor a hope. Caspian knew Zed would choose him.

The weight of that knowledge pushed him to walk away down the line of garages. *He'd choose me and I can't let him.*

Though maybe it wasn't as bad as he was thinking. There were plenty of rock stars who'd been to jail and he wasn't even in the band. He took a deep breath. If it came to Zed having to make a choice, if that fuckwit Fin found out about Caspian's past and told Corrigan, if the band members wanted Zed out if he stayed with Caspian … *Then I won't stay around for him to have to choose.* But for now, he waited.

Early the next morning, they packed the car for the trip to Cornwall.

"One small bag is all I need," Henry said. "What the hell are the three of you taking?"

"I've got all the clothes that you'll realise you wanted," Jonas said.

Henry muttered under his breath. He'd heaved a sigh when Caspian and Zed had packed their guitars and a small amp. Caspian hadn't wanted to take his but Zed had an adapter cable that would allow them to plug in both instruments and Caspian had given way. Apparently, the cottage where they were staying was isolated so they could make as much noise as they wanted. *While we are out,* Henry had added.

Caspian sat in the back with Zed and Jonas slid onto the front passenger seat with a chuckle. "No more shouting *shotgun*, Zed?"

"Nope. There's plenty to entertain me in the back."

"We have a TV?" Caspian asked. "What button do I press?"
Zed rolled his lovely eyes and Caspian bit back his smile.

"Oh, I forgot to mention I get travel sick on long journeys,"
Caspian said. "I'll try not to throw up."

He tricked them for a moment. Three horrified faces before Henry
laughed. Caspian smiled. Everything was going to be okay. He liked
them and they liked him. There'd be no more panic attacks. He'd join
the inventors club Henry had told him about. He'd work hard. He'd be
a success. No more negative thoughts. No more looking back. If Zed
stayed with the band, they'd make it work. Caspian amazed himself
with his ability to switch so quickly, except he wasn't convinced it was
entirely a good thing. He should be more balanced. But was he hoping
for too much, too soon?

Caspian held onto Zed's hand, rubbing his thumb over Zed's
palm. He stared out of the window watching the world go by as the
three of them talked about Glastonbury. The last thing Fin had smugly
said to Caspian yesterday was that tickets for the festival had sold out
an hour after they'd gone on sale last October, so there was no way
Caspian could go. When Zed had given Henry and Jonas the news,
Jonas had opened champagne while Henry grabbed his phone and left
the room. When he came back, he announced he'd arranged tickets for
the three of them. Was there anything the guy couldn't do?

Even at five in the morning, London traffic was heavy but once
they reached the motorway, it flowed more freely. Henry drove fast but
not over the speed limit. Caspian couldn't help wondering if that was
for his benefit.

"Have you two decided on when and where you're getting
married?" Zed asked.

"Next summer," Jonas said. "Westminster Abbey."

"What?" Zed gasped.

Caspian elbowed him. "Gullible," he mouthed.

"We haven't decided where yet," Henry said.

"We need to decide because of booking a venue for the
reception," Jonas pointed out.

"How many guests?" Zed asked.

"About a hundred," Jonas said as Henry said, "No more than
twenty."

Jonas draped his hand over Henry's shoulder and stroked his ear.
"Eighty."

"Twenty-two."

"Seventy."

"Twenty-three."

Jonas sighed. "Sixty."

"Fine. At my parents' place."

"Okay."

Zed glanced at Caspian and smiled. Caspian liked listening to Jonas and Henry. They argued good-naturedly and if one of them did get annoyed, the other quickly snapped them out of it. He could see why Zed liked them so much. They were kind, generous, fun guys. If he and Zed made it as a couple, he hoped they'd be like the pair sitting in front of them.

He was glad Zed had gone to live with them. He deserved people who'd think about him twenty-four hours a day, who'd worry for his happiness, his future. People who wanted to keep him safe forever, who'd worry about who he'd meet, who'd love him, who'd hurt him. That was the sort of parent Caspian wanted to be, if it ever happened. Someone who cared.

Caspian was impressed with the cottage. Zed had been before and told him it was a lovely place and he was right. Old on the outside, sparkling modern on the inside, it was equipped with everything needed for a holiday. Almost too much, Caspian thought. Shelves laden with books and jigsaws and board games. Lots of original paintings on the walls. It looked like a home though there were no photos.

The cottage sat on a clifftop with stunning sea views and a private pathway to the beach. The sandy cove below was apparently never crowded because there was only a small car park. The fridge was crammed with food Jonas had ordered, and the wetsuits and surf boards were in the garage, along with four bikes, kites, buckets and spades, a paddling pool and water shooters.

"We'll take it in turns to prepare meals," Jonas said. "Plenty of choice of restaurants if we want to eat out. Everywhere will be busier next week because it's half-term, but not as manic as in the summer."

Zed turned to Caspian. "You want to surf, play our guitars, go exploring, or read a book?"

"Is *read a book* a euphemism?" Caspian asked.

"Yes," Zed said, and Henry and Jonas groaned.

"Let's go surfing," Caspian said. "It takes me ages to read a book."

"Not that long." Zed smirked.

"Well, depends how exciting it is."

"I can find you a really exciting one."

"Better than the last one? That was pretty exciting at the end."

"Hey, it was great all the way through."

"Stop it, the pair of you," Jonas said. "Eat first and then we'll all go down to the beach."

Caspian was happy. Yet worry about letting happiness slip from his grasp came into his mind more than he wanted it to. He felt guilty for feeling good about life and even though he knew that was stupid, it made no difference. He had to accept there'd be blips while he adjusted. Maybe forever. He'd cope.

He helped Jonas make tuna sandwiches for their lunch and they ate outside. Jonas and Zed talked about surfing and the size of the waves they'd caught last year. Caspian only half-listened.

"You're quiet," Henry said when Zed and Jonas took the empty plates back in. "Are you okay?"

Caspian nodded.

"It takes a while to get your mind around being free. Give yourself time and space to get used to things. Don't put pressure on yourself or expect too much. Everything changed when you walked out of jail but you don't get your life back immediately in the way you might have thought."

"Talking from experience?" Caspian snapped more sharply than he'd intended.

"Not five years' experience but I was once held captive in Afghanistan for three months."

Caspian's jaw dropped. "What did you do?" *Oh fuck he won't tell me.* "Steal a camel?"

"Something like that." Henry smiled.

Military? SAS? It didn't surprise him.

"I know you're right," Caspian said. "It *is* hard to get my head around everything. Five years of being fed, clothed, given a bed to sleep in with not a single day under my control."

"But you have control now and choice. You can make your own decisions. No doors are locked. You can do what you like, within reason. Take it steady, that's all I'm saying."

351

Caspian nodded.

"Your family did a terrible thing. Your father in particular. But you made it worse than it needed to be by not pleading guilty. It made you look arrogant and uncaring and I know that's not true."

"Would you have pleaded guilty if you'd been in my position?"

Henry smiled. "No. I'm just as obstinate as you."

"My brother's changed. I almost like him."

"I understand he's working with disadvantaged youngsters and works for a LGBTQ charity. He's well thought of. Committed. Determined."

"How do you know?"

Henry smiled. "I also know that your father is not going to head the committee he's been angling for. His political aspirations are going to come to a grinding halt."

Caspian's heart stuttered. "Am I bad for Zed? Am I going to hold him back?"

But the return of Jonas and Zed stopped Henry from answering. They were wearing wetsuits and Jonas had a camera dangling from his wrist.

"I didn't want you to split your sides in hysterics at me getting into this," Jonas said. "I'm still haunted by how hard you laughed last year."

"I did apologise." Henry pushed to his feet.

"Well, maybe I'll have the last laugh. The other suit is tighter and you're bigger than me."

"Bastard." Henry growled.

When the sea washed over his bare feet, Caspian winced. Even wearing a full wetsuit, the water was chilly. But conditions were great for surfing, good sized breakers were rolling in and the sun was out. He waded in, securely attached to his board by his ankle, and as soon as he was waist deep, he climbed on, lay flat and paddled out. *Nope. Not thinking about how many years since I did this.*

Caspian had been good at surfing. Better than Lachlan but he wasn't sure if he could stand up straight away. Maybe he'd bodyboard the first time. Then he thought again. The old him would have just gone for it and risked a wipe-out and kept trying until he rode to the shallows standing all the way.

"Okay?" Zed called.

"Great." Caspian sat on his board, his legs dangling either side, the sun in his face.

That was one thing about surfing, you left everything behind when you were out on the water. You could sit quietly, wait for the right wave and think about nothing or everything. Caspian chose nothing. Only he couldn't help thinking about what Henry had said. Was his father at last getting what he deserved? The kick that Caspian couldn't give him?

Henry was the first to grab a wave and he stood up right to the beach. Then Jonas and Zed went for the same wave, Jonas fell, then Zed did too. Caspian's heart jumped. He watched until he saw Zed climbing back on his board before he let himself relax. He tipped his face to the sky and closed his eyes, content to let himself rise and fall for a while. He licked salt from his lips and sighed. *Thank fuck I didn't kill myself or I'd have never done this again.* Though maybe killing himself was going to happen now instead.

As the other three paddled back towards him, Caspian spotted a larger wall of white water rolling his way and he pointed his board toward the beach. Flat on his stomach, he waited, then paddled fast. He felt the back of his board rise up and then he was gliding. *Do it. Do it.* He put his hands in a push-up position, shoved himself up in one movement and firmly planted his feet. Front foot forward, back foot sideways. *Stay crouched until you're stable.*

Once he was sure he was balanced, he turned the board across the wave and rode it parallel to the beach. He heard Zed whooping somewhere behind him. *Oh shit. I can do it. This is fun.*

Then suddenly it wasn't. He was tumbling, sucked down, his mouth full of the sea until he fought his way back to the surface and spat it out. *Fuck.* Another wave broke over him and dragged him toward the shore. He crawled onto the sand with such an overwhelming sense of relief that he expected to sink into it and put out roots. *I'm not going out there again.*

But he got his breath back, pulled himself up, picked up his board and waded back out.

"That was spectacular," Jonas shouted. "Before you fell, I mean."

"The fall was spectacular too," Zed called.

Caspian let out a spluttering laugh. He kept trying. He kept falling but he didn't give up. It had turned into a personal battle and he knew he might not win but he wasn't going to stop until he'd managed to ride to the beach.

It was a crazy feeling, paddling out knowing that if you made a mistake you could be driven into the sand. Even for the best surfers there was always danger which was part of the sport's attraction. No two waves were the same. With a combination of the sea, the board and your body, all of them moving, surfing a wave was a different experience every time.

He kept wiping out. He was tired but he wouldn't stop. It was a matter of balance. He needed his feet in a different place.

"We're going in now," Zed called. "Lifeguards have packed up. Last run."

Caspian watched Jonas and Zed ride to the beach. Henry was still out on his board close to Caspian.

"An inch further back with your front foot and you'll do it," Henry said. "Look behind you. This wave's yours."

It *was* his wave. Caspian paddled hard, pushed himself up and he knew this time he'd make it. He turned across the wave and heard Henry's whoop as he rode home. Caspian's smile was born of exhilaration and pride. The wave took him all the way in.

As he walked through the shallows with his board, Henry joined him. "Well done."

"Thank you. You were right about my foot."

Zed came splashing up. "Yay! You did it."

Caspian's sun-touched face glowed as they made the long uphill trek back to the cottage. He was exhausted, still half-pumped with adrenaline but filled with a huge sense of satisfaction. He had a sudden feeling that this holiday and the surfing had been arranged for him.

"Thank you for bringing me here," he said to Henry.

"We do try to come every year."

"Still, thank you."

"You're welcome. Enjoy yourself?"

"It was brilliant."

"Like riding a bike, yeah? You'll get the hang of everything you missed."

Chapter Thirty-One

Zed cooked that night and Caspian helped. Barbequed shrimp, vegetable kebabs and an Iranian salad. The difference in Caspian brought a lump to Zed's throat. He was happy, chatty, smiley—back to the boy Zed remembered he'd first met. His face had caught the sun and he'd lost his prison pallor. Pointless trying to deny that he loved him because he did. But he wouldn't say it, wouldn't add more pressure to Caspian's life. He could wait.

It was too chilly to eat outside so they sat at the table in the conservatory and after they'd finished the meal, opened another bottle of wine and watched the setting sun. The sky was painted in shades of gold, orange, purple and red. It was a long time since Zed had seen a sunset like it.

"Wow," Caspian muttered. "That's spectacular."

Something else he'd not been able to do in prison. Zed caught hold of his hand and squeezed his fingers.

Jonas took a few pictures with his camera of the sky and of them. "We're going to St Ives tomorrow," he said. "Want to come?"

"What are you going to do?" Zed asked.

"Walk along the coast from Perranuthnoe to Marazion."

"We'll stay here," Zed said. "Unless you want to go?" He turned to Caspian. "I was thinking we could rehearse."

"Okay." Caspian yawned. He pushed to his feet and carried the plates into the kitchen.

"Go to bed. I'll load the dishwasher," Zed said.

"I can't believe how tired I am."

"Bed." Zed gave him a gentle nudge toward the room they were in.

Henry and Jonas brought in the rest of the dishes and the glasses.

"Look after him," Henry whispered. "I'm worried he'll push himself too hard."

Zed nodded, then flung his arms around Henry and hugged him, then he hugged Jonas. "Thank you for everything. You've done so much for me."

"You've done just as much for us." Jonas let him go. "Off to bed."

Zed smiled. "Keep the noise down."

"You cheeky…" But Henry laughed as he said it.

When Zed slipped into the bedroom, Caspian was fast asleep. He wasn't pretending. He didn't even stir when Zed got in beside him. Moments after Zed's head hit the pillow, he was out for the count.

He woke with a start to find it was morning with no Caspian next to him. When he saw the time, he gaped. Nine thirty? He never slept that late. He pulled on a pair of boxers and left the bedroom. There was no sign of Henry or Jonas. The car had gone. When he couldn't find Caspian in the house, Zed felt a fluttering of panic. He checked the garage and all four boards were there, so he felt better but where the hell had he gone?

Zed went back into the house and picked up his phone. There was a message from Fin—*stuff that*—and one from Caspian.

Skinny dipping in the garden. Join me?

He tossed his phone onto the bed and went back outside. Caspian lounged in a children's paddling pool on the lawn at the side of the house. He was naked. Zed laughed.

"Get in here with me and we can tick another one off our list," Caspian said. "I didn't fancy doing this in the sea. Too cold and too many things that might show interest in parts of my anatomy that I only want one person to find fascinating."

Zed stripped out of his boxers and stepped into the water. "Ooh, it's warm."

"While you were sleeping, I've been filling buckets with hot water." He reached up and pulled Zed down on top of him, water slopping over the inflated sides.

Zed groaned into Caspian's mouth, the kiss instantly intoxicating. They were both hard, squirming against each other, hands all over each other. Then Zed was under Caspian and all he could feel were Caspian's hands and mouth and cock. Caspian licked across his stomach, swirling his tongue in Zed's navel before sucking a path to his nipple. He bit it and Zed almost bucked him out of the pool.

When his mouth reached the hollow of Zed's neck, Zed turned as liquid as the water. Caspian held him down with his body, rocking against him, their cocks kissing and sliding. Then Caspian wriggled around so that his cock was close to Zed's mouth and as Zed wrapped his lips around him, Caspian did the same to him. Zed didn't have the strength to lift his hips. He sucked and licked and everything he did, Caspian copied until all that was left was to come.

356

They exploded within seconds of each other and Caspian rolled off him panting.

"Fuck," Caspian gasped.

He wriggled round until he was lying alongside Zed, their lower legs hanging over the side of the pool. Zed slid his arm under Caspian's neck and pulled him close.

Caspian held up his hand. "I'm shaking."

"Me too."

"Are we putting that down to hot sex or should we be worried we're sickening for something?"

"I'm definitely coming down with something."

Caspian laughed, then rolled so his chin rested on Zed's chest. "I like you naked. Don't put clothes on again. We can fuck all day. Jonas said they won't be back until late afternoon. In between bouts of me licking you all over, you can play your guitar."

"We can both play."

Caspian groaned. "I'm crap."

They eventually put on clothes and set up the guitars and the amp. When Zed checked the message from Fin, he'd sent him a slightly different order of play. Corrigan had tweaked it. Zed didn't mind what the order was.

"I'll go through our playlist for the festival and you join in when you can. I'll do each song at least a couple of times. Okay?"

When Caspian picked up his guitar and started to play, the sounds he made were so awful, Zed froze. Caspian attacked the song, if it *was* a song, as if it had personally insulted him. The discordant chords, the ear-splitting feedback set Zed's teeth on edge. *Oh shit. He really can't play.*

Caspian gave a final hard strum and beamed at him. "Hey, what do you know? I *can* play."

Zed couldn't think of anything positive to say.

"What did you think?" Caspian looked so hopeful, Zed crumpled.

"What was it called?" Zed hoped he wasn't supposed to have recognised it.

"Gay Werewolf Rhapsody in Blue." Caspian howled and Zed threw a cushion at him.

"You shit."

Caspian grinned. "I'll tone it down a bit."

He wasn't bad, Zed was relieved to find. The more Zed played the same song, the better Caspian got, but there was no way he was good enough to play with the band. Though he wasn't being fair when Caspian had hardly played an electric guitar for five years and didn't know the songs.

Zed started one that had been on the MP3 player he'd sent Caspian, Hozier's *Take Me To Church* and Caspian stopped playing and sang instead. *Oh fuck, his voice.* It was sweet, it was soulful, strong and individual. When he sang the words *our gentle sin* he stared straight at Zed with his big, dark eyes and Zed swallowed hard. Caspian's voice gave him chills in the best possible way.

The last guitar chord faded away and Zed set his guitar aside. He pulled Caspian into his arms and whispered, "Bed."

"I'm not tired."

"Good."

Zed dragged him to the bedroom, kicked the door closed and shoved Caspian up against it, kissing him, mauling him, pulling at his clothes, stripping him out of his T-shirt, then his jeans and boxers before yanking off his own clothes. They stumbled across the room to the bed and fell on it. Zed reached into the drawer for the condoms and lube and then froze.

Too fast? Was Caspian ready? Am I?

"Yes," Caspian said. "My safe word is angle grinder."

"That's two words. A plain *Stop* is fine."

"I like angle grinder."

"Fine. Okay. If I hear you say that, I'll stop."

"Don't stop on angle, wait for grinder."

Zed laughed. He was as careful as he could be considering the level of his desperation. *Plenty of lube, stretch him first, find that spot, oh yeah, his low groan—or was that me?— don't be too rough, don't hurt him, slow, slow.* Caspian lay on his back, his legs up and Zed was pushing into him, willing him to help, begging those tight muscles to cede *right now* because his cock was doing an excellent impersonation of a heat-seeking missile, locked on target and relentless. Caspian gasped, pushed back and Zed slid into him, kept sliding—*how much of there is me?* —until he was buried inside the guy he loved.

Don't rush this.

He rushed it.

He tried not to, but he failed. His hips weren't listening. He drove in and out of Caspian's body on an endorphin high, fizzing as if he'd eaten a large bar of chocolate, the sugar rush overpowering. Caspian's arse was like a glove around his cock. Every time Caspian arched his back, Zed's body reacted. Joined like magnets, Zed couldn't move far before he had to be back inside him. Caspian reached back to hold onto the headboard and Zed slid forward to kiss him, but he didn't stop moving.

When Caspian rocked up into him, there was nothing left in the world but the push and shove of their bodies, as they cantered, galloped, catapulted into orgasm. Zed's balls drew up, his spine tingled and he came in a shower of sparks, cum shooting from his cock, jet after jet, and he wished there was nothing between them, no condom because he wanted Caspian full with all of him.

Breathe!

Oh yeah.

Caspian cried out as he came, his hand squeezing, jerking, then slowing on his cock and Zed collapsed on top of him, his head on Caspian's chest. Caspian stroked his hair. Caspian's heart was beating hard under his ear. A strong heart was a good thing because they were going risk heart attacks every time they fucked.

"Want to hear a poem?" Caspian asked.

"You make it up?"

"Yeah."

"I didn't know you wrote poetry."

"I didn't want you to think I was a weird shit."

Zed laughed. "I *know* you're a weird shit."

Caspian took a deep breath.

"My dreams have no place to go
This journey will end
But I don't know
When that will be
What I will be
And when I'm free
There's no place to hide
Unless you're by my side
We'll run till we fall
We can have it all
Strange roads

Dark days
Our path is right before us
If we dare risk it
All we need to do is fly
The world is ours
Stay close to me
Listen to me call
Only you can make me feel
Like we can have it all
Make me believe
We can have it all."

Zed rolled to one side and looked into Caspian's face. "I love you. I'll never love anyone as much as you." *What are you going to say to that?*

"What about if we get a dog?" Caspian asked. "You'd have to love a dog as much as me."

Zed laughed. That hadn't been what he'd expected. "Ah damn. That's true."

Caspian smiled. "Let's go surfing."

"Too rough."

"It'll be exciting. The waves are huge."

"Too huge. The wind is blowing onshore. That's not good for surfing."

Particularly for someone who'd wiped out so many times yesterday, someone whose body bore the bruises. Caspian had to be aching.

"Kites then," Caspian suggested.

"Okay." That was nice and safe.

They picked up the two bags labelled *kites* from the garage and walked down to the beach which was deserted. Red flags flying. No lifeguards on duty. Zed unzipped the bag and winced. There looked a lot of material for a simple kite, so it wasn't a simple kite.

"Not sure about this," Zed said, but Caspian was already attaching cuffs around his wrists.

"They're power kites." He grinned at Zed. "It's fine. I've done this before."

"I haven't. I'll watch." *And make sure you don't get into trouble.*

360

To be fair to Caspian, he *did* look as if he knew what he was doing but when wind filled the red and blue kite and turned it into a large C-shaped wing, Zed groaned.

"You need to keep clear," Caspian said. "If the kite sweeps down and across, you don't want to be in the way. The lines are dangerous."

"You're fucking dangerous. I don't like the look of this."

The kite went up and Caspian planted his feet and tugged hard on the handles.

"What if it drags you into the air?" Zed called.

"That's the whole point."

Oh shit. "What if it drags you into the sea?"

"I can depower in an instant by letting go of the handles. The kite will just fall from the sky, but I won't lose it because it'll stay attached."

"I'm not worried about the kite falling or getting lost. I'm worried about you."

"I'll be fine."

Zed retreated to the back of the beach and watched Caspian wrestling with the kite, his only protection a pair of gloves. Zed's heart leapt into his mouth when Caspian became airborne, and again when he crashed onto the sand and was dragged for several feet. *Fuck.* But Caspian stood up and tried once more. He ought to be wearing a helmet. How high could—*fucking hell!* That was too high. Zed started to walk toward him, but when he heard Caspian laughing, he went back to where he'd been standing.

There was a kind of manic energy in what Caspian was doing, not dissimilar to the way he'd been yesterday when he was determined to ride a wave all the way to the beach standing up. Zed didn't think he was trying to kill himself, but he was careless of his own safety and Zed worried he was going to get hurt. He called out twice to try and get him to stop but Caspian had said no. Zed assumed he'd tire eventually. Or he'd decide he was hungry. Zed could tempt him to stop with the offer of lunch. Or sex. *And* sex.

The wind suddenly gusted and the kite flew back toward the cliff. Zed leapt to his feet.

"Let go," he screamed.

Caspian ended up lying on the sand at the base of the rockface, the kite plastered high above him.

Zed ran to his side. "Fuck! Are you okay?"

"Yep." His eyes were shining.

"You st…" Zed swallowed his comment.

Caspian stood and tugged at the kite to free it, but it wouldn't move. "Shit. It's caught on something."

"Leave it. We'll buy them another."

"Don't be daft." Caspian took off the cuffs and gloves and handed them and the handles to Zed. "Keep hold and I'll climb up and free it."

"No. Leave it," Zed snapped. "It's got to be thirty foot up. It's too dangerous."

"I can climb that. No problem."

"Please don't."

Caspian ignored him. Zed was filled with a combination of fury and fear. To start with there was more fury than fear but the higher Caspian climbed, the more anxious Zed became. When Caspian slipped and slithered down a few feet, dislodging a few pieces of rock before grabbing hold again, Zed had to look away, but he couldn't bear not watching either. If Caspian fell now, he could die. *Please, please, please be careful.* Zed chewed the inside of his cheek so fiercely, he tasted blood.

Then the kite was falling free. Zed yanked it back down to the sand, then stood on it. Caspian slipped on the descent and for a moment hung on with only one hand. But he stabilised and climbed the rest of the way down, jumping the last five feet. He had the widest smile on his face, full of joy and pride and Zed wanted to thump him.

"You're a fucking idiot," Zed snapped.

He stepped off the kite and dropped the cuffs and handles. Once he'd retrieved the bag he'd brought down, he set off up the path toward the cottage.

"Hey, wait for me," Caspian called.

No, I'm fucking not. He strode off. If Caspian couldn't work out why he was so pissed off with him… *If he's going to kill himself, he can't expect me to watch.* When his phone vibrated in his pocket, he pulled it out, hoping Caspian was saying sorry but it was a text from a number he didn't recognise.

I'm coming back for you, little brother.

Zed almost dropped his phone. *Fahid.* How did he know the number? Zed thought for a moment, then called Jackson as he continued up the path.

"Hi," Jackson said.

"I just had a text. *I'm coming back for you, little brother.*"

"Ah. Who do you think it's from?"

"Fahid used to call me *little brother.* Tamaz too sometimes. But I think this is Fahid. If it was Tamaz saying he was coming home to help me sort out our father's affairs, I don't think those words would be the ones he'd use. I think it's a threat from Fahid."

"Possibly, but there's a chance that whoever sent it *does* mean it in a pleasant way. Fahid feeling guilty for leaving you in the lurch, running and not taking you? Your brother preparing to return to the UK for your sake?"

Maybe. "How did they get my number?"

"Presumably you've given it to several organisations over the last week or so in connection with your father's death."

"Yes."

"But not your actual address."

"No. I used the one on the driver's licence. Does it exist?"

"It's an empty house. If whoever sent that text checked it out, they'd know you weren't living there." Jackson sighed. "Text them back. Try to anyway. Put *Masha' Alla* and see if they respond."

Whatever Allah wants? His heart thumped. "Okay."

"When are you back from Cornwall?"

"Next Wednesday."

"I'll have someone keep an eye on you once you return. Have you told Henry?"

"No. They're out."

"Tell him when he gets back. I'll return your father's phone. There's nothing of significance on there but it's the number Tamaz knows so you should always have it on you."

Caspian folded the kite and put everything back into the bag. He'd got such a buzz from jumping into the air with the kite. For a couple of seconds, he'd been weightless, able to fly and all he'd been able to think about was doing it again, going higher and higher.

Then when he'd climbed the cliff, something had woken inside him, some memory of what he used to be like. The higher he climbed, the greater the adrenaline rush, the more focused he became on getting the kite. There had a been a few stomach-in-the-mouth moments, but he'd done it! But back on the beach, his sense of pride and satisfaction had been wrecked by Zed's reaction. All the fun of that morning had gone leaving him sliding down into a dark place. He trudged up the path and put the kite in the garage. Zed was in the kitchen holding a mug of coffee and still looked furious which made Caspian angry not apologetic.

"I can climb. I wasn't in any danger," he snapped.

"Oh, there were climbing walls in prison, were there? You've been practising for the last five years? You didn't need to scale that rock. You don't have anything to prove."

"I wanted to jump with the kite. I wanted to climb. You can't wrap me in cotton wool. I want to be like I was. I *can* be like that, but I don't need your disapproving face fixed on me every time I try to have some fun."

Zed slammed his coffee down so hard that liquid sloshed over the brim. "Do you have any idea what it was like to see you freeclimbing up a sheer rock face thinking that you could fall at any second and I'd be able to do nothing to save you?"

"I wasn't going to fall."

"You nearly did a couple of times," Zed yelled. "You selfish fucker. You didn't think about me at all, did you? I fucking told you this morning that I loved you. The first time I've said it and you made a joke about it and then you try and fucking kill yourself."

Caspian's belligerence vanished. He wasn't tackling the *love* comment. "I didn't try to kill myself," he whispered.

"Really? What are you going to do next? Base jumping? Canyoning? Russian roulette?"

"I l—"

"Don't you dare tell me you love me. Don't you fucking dare. Just fuck off and leave me alone."

Caspian walked out of the cottage and kept walking. Not down to the beach but along the cliff top. His heart was pounding even before he started to run. He'd been *enjoying* himself. Zed had no idea what it had been like to spend five years locked up. The chance to do something exciting, exhilarating had been too much to resist. *I am fucking alive!* Why didn't Zed understand?

The run turned into a sprint, Caspian trying to outrun some truth he didn't want to hear, a concern he didn't want to contemplate. He didn't want to be pinned down, held down, made to conform. He wanted to fly. But when he stumbled on a rock and fell, he stayed down, rolled onto his back on the grass. His chest heaved as he fought to drag air into his lungs. He wasn't sure he could get up even if he'd wanted to.

The panic attack rolled over him like a rogue wave, crushing, suffocating. It was as if someone had wrapped their hands around his throat and he couldn't even lift his arms to pull them off. His body was tingling. It was a cool day and he was burning up. He knew he was hyperventilating but he couldn't control his breathing.

Caspian kept trying to reassure himself he was okay, that he'd been through this before and survived. Fuck, he'd survived prison, he could deal with this. Panicking over nothing was just his brain playing tricks. But the tricks continued to the point that he wondered if he really was dying, that this time, it actually *was* a heart attack because it hurt so much. He was on his own. Zed had sent him away. No one knew where he was. He wasn't on a path. He lay only a few yards from the edge of a cliff. If he rolled, he'd go over the edge, but in a twist of fate, he was safe from that because he couldn't *fucking* move.

The fear eventually began to subside, and his breathing eased, the noisy gasps quietening. *Was it minutes, hours?* He had no idea. But thinking once again became possible. His body slipped back under his control and he pushed himself to a sitting position. Exhaustion and dizziness swamped him. He patted his pockets but he'd not got his phone. Oh yeah, he hadn't taken it to the beach that morning. But who did he have to call? Zed was angry, and Caspian was still pissed off with him. Getting to his feet was a step too far. He lay down again, curled up and fell asleep.

He woke shivering with cold. Dark clouds skittered overhead obscuring the sun. That one looked like a dragon. Caspian gave a heavy sigh as he pushed himself to his feet. He staggered back to the cottage still feeling tired to the bone. There was no car outside so Jonas and Henry weren't home. He wasn't sure he had the energy to talk to Zed. His head throbbed. As he approached the door, Henry pulled into the drive. Coward that he was, Caspian waited so he could go in behind them. Jonas was chattering about what a great day they'd had, spotting minke whales and a basking shark.

Caspian slipped past them to the bedroom, tossed his clothes on the floor and slid into bed. He knew he ought to talk to Zed but he was too tired.

Chapter Thirty-Two

Zed heard the car on the drive and wondered how he was going to explain Caspian's absence to Jonas and Henry.

Jonas was first into the living room. "What happened while we were gone?"

"Why?"

"Caspian followed us in and slunk to the bedroom looking as if he was having trouble putting one foot in front of the other," Henry said.

"And you're too pale." Jonas pushed Zed's feet off the couch and sat down.

"I had a text," Zed said, relieved Caspian was back and that he could put off talking about him for a while.

"What text?" Henry said.

Zed told them and what Jackson had said to do.

"Have you had a response?" Henry asked.

"No."

Henry put the kettle on. "What are your instincts telling you?"

"That it's from Fahid. He knows I betrayed him and he's coming to get me."

Jonas put his arm around him. "Oh Zed. We won't let that happen."

Henry sat on the arm of the chair. "Anything to support that?"

"Only that he's gone to the trouble of uncovering my phone number."

"But to hear nothing until now… Why wait so long?" Henry pinned him with his gaze.

"Until my father died, and I called Tamaz and started to have to give my address out—obviously not our address—maybe he hadn't been able to trace me."

"You need to lie low," Jonas said. "Maybe rethink the band and Glastonbury."

Zed groaned. "I can't do that. I don't *want* to do that."

"You'd be a sitting—standing target," Jonas said. "Up there on that stage."

"The security will be tight and it's been stepped up this year," Henry said. "Every person, vehicle and bag will be searched."

"Even so…" Jonas muttered.

Zed picked at the edge of the couch. "I think maybe Jackson likes the idea of luring Fahid and or my brother back."

Henry hmphed. "You do what keeps you safe, not necessarily what Jackson wants."

"I'm not worried about Glastonbury. I want to play there. It's the chance of a lifetime."

"Have you thought further than that?" Henry asked. "About the effect on Caspian of you continuing with the band? He can't follow you around when you're touring, not even in this country. Five more years under licence. I can't find a way around that."

"I don't think he wants to follow me anywhere," Zed mumbled.

"What else happened while we were gone?" Jonas asked.

"We took those kite bags down to the beach, but they turned out to be power kites. I left mine in the bag. Caspian let himself get lifted into the air. A lot. And high. It freaked me out, though not as much as when the kite got caught on the cliff and he climbed up to get it. He freeclimbed about thirty feet and he almost fell and…" Zed shuddered.

Jonas squeezed his shoulders. "And?"

"I yelled at him. Told him he was being selfish. Asked if he wanted to kill himself." He tried to swallow away the lump in his throat. "He said no. I told him to fuck off and he did. He's been gone for hours."

"You didn't go and look for him?" Jonas asked.

"Yes, but I couldn't find him. I walked all the way along the beach, did the cliff top walk. This morning I told him… I told him I loved him and now it's all spoiled."

Jonas hugged him, then held him by his shoulders and looked him straight in the face. "You should have stopped him leaving. Talked to him. Showed him you were worried. Explained."

"He's not well, Zed," Henry said. "He's spent the last five years doing everything he could to merely survive, pretending he doesn't care, following the rules day after day, constantly watching his back. Prison crushes confidence, diminishes self-worth. How many guys like him do you think were in that Young Offender Institution? The moment he opened his mouth, he'd get picked on. I'd guess in all the time he was inside, he never met anyone who was remotely like him."

"He hasn't talked much about it." Zed sighed.

"But you can imagine," Henry said. "Think what it must be like to have no space to call your own, no choice of who to be with or what to eat. Unable to trust anyone. Kindness is rarely encountered. You couldn't have faith in it even if you came across it because everyone is doing the same as you. Doing whatever they can to survive. Even worse for Caspian, he didn't do what he'd been found guilty of. Those who've been to prison emerge as harder individuals. Different." Henry paused. "Have you asked Caspian to tell you about it?"

Zed shook his head. "I didn't want to upset him."

"Maybe he doesn't want to talk about it, but you should ask him. He's struggling. Everything he did to keep himself controlled and balanced has gone now he's been released. The panic attacks he's been having show how badly he's been affected. He might need to speak to someone to help him get his head straight. Counselling might work. In the meantime, don't expect too much. Let him find his feet."

"Let him climb a cliff and risk falling?" Zed didn't try to keep the bitterness out of his voice.

Henry shrugged. "You want to wrap him up and stop him getting hurt? You can't."

Zed jumped to his feet. "I thought I was going to lose him when I watched him scrambling up that rockface. You saw what he was like when we were surfing. Manic. He wanted to keep going and going. He wanted to surf today but at least I managed to talk him out of that."

"Well that shows he *does* listen to you," Jonas said.

"But he's frightening me. I don't know what he's going to throw himself at next."

"Be there for him. That's the advice I'd give." Henry glanced at Jonas. "He needs someone on his side, someone to rein him in at times. Ten years ago, I was held in the cellar of a house in Afghanistan for three months. I still have flashbacks. Jonas is my rock. Be Caspian's rock."

Zed chewed his lip and nodded. Jonas stood and pulled Henry into his arms and kissed him.

"And if he tries to do something stupid again," Henry said, "you tell him you'll do it first. He won't let you, hopefully, but maybe that way you'll make him understand."

Jonas rolled his eyes. "This is where Henry's advice gets a bit shaky. He wanted to go ice swimming. I didn't want to and I didn't want him to. So I said if he did it, I'd do it too. He knows I have a phobia about getting stuck under the ice, but he stood back and said *fine, you go first.* I thought I'd be so freaked out, he'd not want to do it.

368

But after I was hauled out, unable to even speak because my tongue was frozen, he checked I was breathing and fucking jumped in. The complete bastard."

Henry rolled his eyes. "Your tongue wasn't frozen."

"It nearly was."

Henry smiled and turned to Zed. "An hour before dinner. Caspian needs to eat. Try to persuade him."

Caspian was asleep when Zed went into the bedroom. His clothes were strewn on the floor. Zed stripped and pulled back the covers to climb in behind him. He wrapped his arms around Caspian and pulled him to his chest. Caspian was still wearing boxers, Zed wasn't. His cock hardened. He doubted that would ever change when he was in bed with Caspian. He was incapable of not wanting him.

"Wake up." Zed leaned over to breathe into his ear.

"What for?"

"I need to say I'm sorry and I can't do that if you're asleep." He licked around Caspian's ear.

"Aaaah. Don't stop doing that to start talking. Talking is overrated. Sending me wild with desire, isn't."

Zed smiled, relief flooding his veins that Caspian wasn't angry. "I have things I need to say." He took Caspian's entire ear into his mouth.

Caspian vibrated. "Make it quick. You say sorry. I say sorry and we fuck."

"Sorry," Zed whispered.

"Good."

Zed tried not to laugh but he couldn't help it. "And?"

"And what?"

Zed nipped his ear.

"Sorry." Caspian groaned into the pillow.

Zed pushed back the covers and trailed his tongue slowly down the bumps of Caspian's spine, rubbing his chin against them, then licking the places he'd abraded. As he reached his lower back, Caspian dragged down his boxers and gave a frantic wriggle to get them off his feet before dragging them back up the bed and stuffing them under his belly.

"Oh God, you stopped driving me wild with desire," Caspian whined. "I was trying to remove all obstacles."

Zed pushed Caspian face down on the bed and started again from his neck.

"Fuck. I'm sinking into the bed." Caspian's breathing turned ragged.

The sensation of pressing his teeth into Caspian's neck was a bigger turn on than Zed could have imagined. He didn't want to hurt him but it was a display of dominance, knowing that he could hurt him.

"Keep doing that and I'll come. God," Caspian panted.

Zed alternately kissed and licked down the centre of his back until his face was pressed against Caspian's arse, his fingers digging into Caspian's hips. Zed licked down the seam, pausing to flutter his tongue over the hole.

"You found it," Caspian said. "I was worried about your sense of direction."

Zed reached between Caspian's legs, took hold of his cock and eased it back so he could flutter his tongue along it, then over Caspian's balls and up the seam of his backside.

He did it over and over while Caspian shook and whined and groaned, pleading with him, begging him, and every sound and every movement wound Zed tighter, sending goose bumps flashing into life all over his body. His cock leaked precum over the back of Caspian's thighs. His balls were tight and aching. Zed wrapped his hands around Caspian's hips and hauled him onto his knees. When he spread his arse cheeks wide and exposed the puckered entrance to his body, Zed's heart stuttered. *Oh fuck.*

"Put on condom, apply lube, insert seven-inch battering ram. In that order."

"Right." Zed's fingers shook as he prepped himself.

"God, I really want you to fuck me," Caspian moaned. "Could you manage that before you start the waterboarding?"

"Oh shut up."

"Hey, I'm nervous. I talk when I'm nervous. You go quiet. That makes me sound noisier than I am."

Zed positioned his cock against the ring of nerve-rich muscle and rubbed over it a few times. Wasn't it going to hurt if he didn't stretch him first?

"I need you. I need this. Now," Caspian gasped. He pulled his cock back under his body and began to jack himself off. "Yeah, yeah, yeah."

Zed pushed the head of his cock more firmly against the hole, the urge to ram himself home lighting up his balls. *Steady, steady.* But as

370

Caspian's muscles gave way, along with his voice, Zed slid in and kept sliding until he'd bottomed out. They both froze for a long moment.

"Forgotten what to do?" Caspian gasped. "I missed out that part. Withdraw battering ram, then re-insert. Continue until you break me."

Zed pulled back, then thrust so hard that Caspian slumped and Zed collapsed on top of him.

"Yep, I'm broken," Caspian grunted.

Zed grabbed the pillow Caspian was shoving toward him and pushed it under Caspian's hips before he began to move again. Each drive into that warm, tight channel was bliss. Every withdrawal the same. Watching himself do this did something to his insides. Made them melt, made them burn.

He couldn't stop moving now—a living machine, pile driver, jackhammer, electric drill. His body was aligned to Caspian's. His hands pressing on his shoulder blades, his legs rubbing on Caspian's, his hips rolling on and on, thrusting his cock all the way in then out until only the very tip was left inside before he shoved back again.

"Harder," Caspian gasped. "Slower, softer, faster, harder, twist and turn and shake it all about. Oh fuck do what the hell you like. Just keep doing it."

How can you make me laugh so much when I'm doing this? Zed's movements grew faster and choppier as the need to come galloped through every cell in his body. His brain fogged to everything but that. Caspian was bucking up into him as Zed drove down and Caspian gave a long wail as he came. Moments later, lightning zipped down Zed's spine and he was exploding. As long, hard spurts of cum filled the condom, he plastered himself against Caspian's back.

It was a while before either of them could move. The only sound in the room was their frantic breathing which took a while to slow. When Zed regained muscle control, he tugged Caspian to the bathroom and they showered together in the cramped space.

Back in the bedroom, they dressed and Zed pulled Caspian back onto the bed. "You scared me," he whispered, pulling his fingers through Caspian's wet hair. "You are my reason for living, for breathing, for everything. I care about you above anything else. If you'd fallen... My life would be over."

"I didn't mean to scare you."

"If you'd have been wearing a helmet and a harness I'd have been fine, but one slip..."

371

"I'm sorry."

"And then I said something stupid."

"You called me a fucking idiot."

"You *are* a fucking idiot. It wasn't that. It was when I told you to fuck off. Because you did and I couldn't find you. All I could do was sit and hope you'd come back." Zed choked back a sob.

"I didn't even know if I could climb it. I started and thought—yes I can. Scared but determined. When I actually got back to the sand, I was on such a high. By sheer willpower and determination, I'd done something I didn't think I could do. And I wanted you to be thrilled for me and you weren't."

"But you understand why."

"Yes, I do but maybe I'm going to do more crazy stuff. Maybe I can't help myself. When I was inside, I felt…as if I was in water and having to swim all the time except I kept getting pulled under the surface. I'd always swim up again but… sometimes the temptation to let myself sink, to disappear, sleep without dreams… Yeah, well it was always there, always tempting because it was the only way out that I could manage all on my own. My pad mate told me that just about everyone works out how to kill themselves, usually by hanging. Not that most of them would ever want to, but it was the comfort of knowing they could that they liked. And I understood."

Zed held him tighter.

"I'm not trying to tempt fate now I'm out. I don't want to die. I want to live, but I want to live a full life, one where I can conquer my fears and do what the fuck I like… As long as you're with me."

"I'm still not going diving with sharks. And I don't want a piercing either. I read where a guy had the skin of his cock ripped off when clothing caught on his piercing. People have choked on piercings, chipped their teeth or got one trapped between their teeth and the person with them has had to call 9-9-9. So can we skip that too?"

"I love you."

Zed jolted, then smiled. "*Now* you choose to tell me?"

Caspian grinned. "My first ten times I'm going for memorable occasions. Then you'll always remember."

"Hmm."

"And I'm fine with no piercings. I want us to have our cocks tattooed."

Shit. "You first then."

"That wasn't what Henry said you had to do."

Zed's jaw dropped. "You were listening? You little… I am *not* having my cock tattooed. If you want to, go ahead. It won't kill you. I'm fine with that."

"What do you like to eat?"

"Why? Oh." Zed laughed. "Brussels sprouts."

"Damn it. I don't want those on my cock. Okay no tattoos there."

"Let's go and see the northern lights. That sounds fairly safe."

Caspian kissed him. "Base jumping in Dubai."

"I'd rather bike down a volcano in Hawaii."

"While it's erupting?"

"No. Are you crazy?"

"Of course I am."

The rest of the holiday was just about as perfect as Zed could have hoped for. A mixture of surfing, sex, walking, sex, flying the kites…oh hell, even *he* had jumped and understood where Caspian was coming from. They'd eaten out, eaten in. They'd played board games with Henry and Jonas. The weather had been perfect. Enough to give them all a bit of a tan. Caspian had told him he loved him while he was taking a piss in the bathroom, and then he burped *I love you.* Zed hadn't been able to stop the laugh from bursting out.

"Are you counting?" Caspian asked.

"That was three."

Four was yelled out at the top of a cliff scattering a flock of birds and freaking out a couple out walking.

Five was written in the sand along with *I love your arse.* Zed had to kick that part out.

Six was laid out in stones and shells along with *I love your cock.* He had to kick that out too.

Seven was when Zed was trying to persuade a traffic warden not to give him a ticket when they'd gone to Newquay. Though Caspian had told the traffic warden he loved him too, several times and in the end the guy had laughed and let them off.

Eight was muttered into Zed's arse.

Nine was said at the checkout in the supermarket when Caspain had put five packets of condoms on the conveyor belt.

Apparently Caspian was saving ten.

Zed was sorry when it was time to go home.

Even more sorry when they'd packed up the car and he'd had another text from a different number. *I'll see you soon, little brother.* He called Jackson and told him before they set off. Then texted back. *Are you Fahid or Tamaz? Either way, I look forward to seeing you.*

There was no reply.

Another text came the following day and the one after that. Same message. On Jackson's advice, Zed didn't respond.

The following Saturday, Caspian went to a meeting of the inventors club while Zed was rehearsing in Tower Hamlets. They'd arranged to meet up afterwards so they could go home together. Jonas was rehearsing at the Barbican for a concert with Michael Tilson Thomas due to take place the following evening and Henry said he was looking forward to a few hours of peace and quiet.

Zed waited for Caspian at the far end of London Bridge and waved when he saw him coming.

"Had fun?" Zed asked.

"Not as much fun as I had this morning."

Zed laughed. "I should hope not."

They set off across the bridge.

"So how did it go? Did you talk to anyone?"

"Everyone was really friendly. I discussed the basics of a few of my ideas and had some encouraging comments. Well, if you count—that's interesting—as encouraging. I even managed to make some suggestions of my own on an idea a woman had about baby changing mats. I know zip about babies but the restraining system she was proposing was similar to the one I'd imagined for something else. Then I had a call from my new SO, just checking in now Glenn has handed me over. Great timing but at least the biscuits were delicious."

Zed chuckled. They checked the road and began to cross. "Want to go for a drink in Borough?"

"No, let's go home. I'm tired."

"Okay." They headed into the station.

"Fin still being a pain in the arse?" Caspian asked as they stood on the down escalator.

"He's a perfectionist but he doesn't go about getting perfection in the right way. We sound good. Fin thinks we can sound better but he's never satisfied."

374

There was a muffled noise behind them that sounded like a car crash then a scream. *What the hell?*

"Should we go and see if we can help?" Caspian asked.

Zed was torn but hey were already at the bottom of the escalator. "There's a lot of people around. We don't have medical skills. We're more likely to get in the way."

When they were on the overground train and it was moving, Zed had a call on his phone.

"Hi Henry."

"Where are you?"

"On the train. We just left London Bridge."

"A van's been driven into pedestrians on London Bridge."

"Shit. Is Jonas back?"

"No. He's not answering his phone."

"He has to turn it off when they're rehearsing."

"Yes, but he should be on his way home. Oh fuck. I'm going to try him again. Don't block his line."

Zed slipped the phone back into his pocket.

"What the hell's happened?"

Around them in the carriage, people began to talk.

"That noise we heard… A van's been driven into people on London Bridge." Zed took a shaky breath. "Jonas isn't back and he sometimes walks across the bridge instead of using the Tube."

"And Henry can't get in touch with him?"

Zed shook his head. Caspian wrapped his arm around him and Zed began to search for news on his phone.

By the time they got off the train in Greenwich, they knew that the crash they heard was being treated as terrorism. The attackers had abandoned the van and moved into the Borough Market area where they'd stabbed people.

"I should have—" Zed began.

"No. What could we have done?"

When Zed's phone rang, he pulled it from his pocket and put it on speaker.

"He's okay," Henry said.

Caspian pulled Zed into his arms and hugged him. Zed started to cry.

"He's on his way back on the Tube. Where are you?"

"Cutty Sark station. We'll wait for him."

375

"I'm on my way."

By the time they went to bed, the details of the attack were still unfolding. Seven were dead but the total might rise, and three attackers had been shot dead. It wasn't a surprise when the attackers were later named as Islamic radicals. Forty-eight people had been injured and eight innocent lives lost.

Henry was subdued. He left for work early in the morning and came back late at night. Caspian was in bed asleep but Zed wanted to speak to Henry, wanted to know if MI5 had missed something, missed some opportunity to stop this before it happened. But Henry wouldn't talk about it. Though he did hand over Zed's father's phone.

"I don't like the idea of you being used as bait but…"

"I'll be careful."

Henry sighed. "Be more than careful."

The security service was already under criticism for missing clues before the Westminster attack last March when a guy had driven a car into pedestrians on Westminster Bridge and crashed into the gates outside the Palace of Westminster. Four had been killed and more than fifty injured before he jumped out of the vehicle and fatally stabbed a policeman.

"How do you cope with all this?" Zed asked.

"If I don't leave it behind before I step through the door, it wouldn't just be me who was worrying." Henry ruffled Zed's hair. "It's something to think about before you decide on Jackson's offer. The cost of working to ensure the safety of others is high and while success brings great satisfaction, failure is hard to deal with. Your music can bring joy and pleasure to many. Don't feel guilty for wanting that."

"Which is more important?"

"Ah, well that's your decision to make, not mine. But you know I'm as musical as a weasel. People would pay to *not* hear me."

A week later, Jackson came to the house to see Zed. Zed hoped he wasn't going to ask him if he'd made his mind up about the job, because he hadn't. Jackson asked him to walk in the garden.

"Is it Tamaz?" Zed asked, his heart thumping.

"No. Fahid was killed two days ago in an American drone attack in a remote area of Afghanistan's eastern Kunar province."

Zed exhaled. "You're sure?"

"Yes."

"Was he the target?"

"Yes and no. It was a meeting that he happened to be attending of Isis commanders who were planning a terrorist attack. Those texts to your phone helped locate him. The Americans confirmed he was one of the casualties."

"So it was Fahid and not Tamaz who texted me." Zed wanted to be relieved but he was still worried about Tamaz. "What now?"

"We wait to see if your brother surfaces."

Chapter Thirty-Three

Jonas stared at Caspian in disbelief. "I can't believe you mended that. It's been broken for ages. I meant to throw it away."

It was an ancient music system, so old it had a cassette player as part of the stacked tower. Caspian had enjoyed taking it apart and putting it back together. He'd bought a couple of new circuit boards and other parts online and now it worked.

"Do you want it?" Jonas asked him.

"No thanks. I listen to music on my phone or live." He gave a dramatic groan.

Jonas chuckled. "You're not the only one fed up of hearing the same songs played over and over again. I think it's different when you're playing them yourself, but to listen…"

Caspian shrugged. "The band wants to be perfect for Glastonbury next weekend. I get that though I'm pretty sure the crowd isn't going to spot one duff note."

Zed was currently out playing a gig in a bar in Borough. Something that hadn't made any of them very happy, including Zed, but Caspian knew once you changed what you did because of fear of what might happen, the terrorists had won. But when he'd said he'd go and meet Zed there, Zed had asked him not to *this time*. Caspian couldn't help but wonder when the right time would be. They didn't talk about lightning not striking the same place twice because both of them knew it could.

"You have any idea what Zed is going to decide to do?" Jonas put a cup of coffee in front of Caspian and sat opposite him at the kitchen table.

"No, but he's told me he doesn't want to say anything until after Glastonbury which makes me think he's not going to continue with the band. Otherwise, why not just announce he's chosen music? The number of terrorist attacks this year have put pressure on him to make him think he ought to be helping with the fight against Muslim extremists."

"Even though Fahid is now dead?"

"There are a lot more fanatics out there. Maybe his brother is one of them. I think Zed needs to know one way or the other about Tamaz. It preys on his mind. Maybe he thinks he can find out the truth if he works for MI5. But he comes alive when he's playing his guitar or the piano, well, whatever the instrument. Music's his drug. You understand that."

Jonas nodded. "I do but it was never a matter of choice for me. Music is all I've ever been good at. Zed has a brilliant mind. Between you and me, what would you like to him to choose?"

Caspian shrugged.

"You must have thought about it."

All the time. "Do you worry about Henry?"

"All the time. He's not a frontline guy but even so…"

"I suppose Zed's safer working for MI5 provided he stays behind a desk and doesn't even think about going out into the field. I know he's clever. Brilliant with computers. Plus he speaks Farsi and some Arabic. The job would mean largely regular hours. But I don't trust Jackson. If he thought he could use Zed in some op, he would."

"Not if Henry caught wind of it."

"Henry doesn't know everything even though he thinks he does."

Jonas laughed. "You're not going to catch him out."

"I'm going to keep trying." Caspian had taken over Zed's game with Henry and looked up random facts to test Henry's knowledge of trivia. He hadn't caught him out yet.

"What do you see happening if Zed goes for the music option?" Jonas asked.

"I guess whether the band makes it or not, it will be all-consuming. Years of playing all over the place trying to make it or maybe instant success after Glastonbury and they'll be catapulted to fame. If that happens, then life moves out of his control. The schedule will be relentless, not just playing music but talking about it too and Zed's not so keen on that side of it."

Jonas nodded. "You're right. If the band makes it, it will be one concert after another all over the country and even abroad, long journeys on buses, nights in hotels, appearances on TV and radio, meetings with publicists, sponsors, interviews with the press, working with photographers. It'll be as if he's climbed on a train that never stops. Exciting but exhausting."

"He'd have to yank me on board when it occasionally slowed down in the neighbourhood. If it was just him and not the band, maybe he'd have more say and it wouldn't be so punishing. But if he decides against the band, he's letting at least three people down very badly."

379

Caspian paused. That was more than he'd said in a long while on a subject that should stay private. But Zed never wanted to talk about it and now Caspian had started, he didn't want to stop.

"You have a punishing schedule too. You do masterclasses, teach at a conservatory and play in that chamber group, but the orchestra has to come first. I remember you telling me that the LSO had landed a week of film sessions that would pay really well but then it was postponed and didn't fit in the schedule anymore. You and Henry had cancelled a holiday so that you could do the work, only to find it wasn't going to happen. You even have to rush back from Glastonbury on Sunday because you have a concert at seven that night."

"It *is* all-consuming. I'm lucky Henry understands."

"I'd be a problem for Zed too," Caspian muttered. "What does he say if the press ask about me? Can't be anything other than the truth because they'll catch him out if he lies. *Electric Ice's guitarist is going out with a guy whose dangerous driving killed three young girls.* I don't want to be responsible for making Zed's life difficult. All I want is for him to be happy."

"Are you planning to leave him? You think that will make him happy?"

"I've thought about it, but I can't leave him. I physically cannot walk away. I know what that would do to him because I know what it would do to me. I have to wait and see if he walks away from me. But I don't want him to choose MI5 because he thinks that's the way we can stay together. If he makes that choice, it has to be because of something other than me. He won't talk about any of this. Please don't tell him we've discussed it."

"I won't. Has he mentioned his birth father?"

"He's read everything he could find about him. He told me he didn't want to write or email him in case a member of his family saw it. I think he wants to give him a chance to react to him privately but he's not sure how to arrange that. I'm not sure that leaping out of a box and saying *Surprise, I'm your son* is the right way to go. I think Zed is desperate that the guy likes him and wants to get to know him."

"Gulshan's coming to the UK next week."

"What?"

"He's been invited to be a guest conductor at a charity concert we're playing on Monday night for the victims of the London Bridge and Westminster attacks."

Caspian widened his eyes. "How did you manage that?"

Jonas shrugged. "I suggested it to our musical director and he agreed. Gulshan was only too delighted to accept. I think having a Muslim conducting us is a good thing as well."

"When are you going to tell Zed that a guy who's probably his birth father is coming to the UK?"

"I was wondering if he already knows."

"He's not said anything to me and that's not a topic that's out of bounds."

"I'll wait and tell him after Glastonbury. I don't want to make him anxious. Plus I've arranged for him to play his cello at the concert. I have tickets for you and Henry."

"You do know he'll kill you?"

Jonas laughed.

"You also have to know how much Zed loves the pair of you. And for what you have done for him, I will love you forever."

Jonas choked up and put his hand to his mouth. "And you said the L word without doing anything objectionable."

Caspian laughed. "He told you about that?"

"Yes. You are the perfect guy for him. He didn't need to tell me that. I can see it." Jonas took a deep breath. "Not to destroy the moment, but how are you? Do you think the panic attacks are a thing of the past or are you worried the possibility of having one is still lurking? I guess I'm asking if you'd like to speak to someone."

"I think maybe the possibility of having a panic attack will always be there. I'm not counting how long passes between them. But though I know how terrifying they can be, I also know that I can come out of them. I feel better as a person now. My life is more than good. That makes a difference. I won't give in to them. My life is mine, not theirs. When they happen, it's fucking scary, but they end and I don't have to end with them."

"If you ever need to talk..."

Caspian nodded.

Zed left for Glastonbury with his manager and the rest of the band in a van on Saturday afternoon, though not without grumbling because Henry had chartered a helicopter to get there on Sunday with Caspian and Jonas.

381

"You can come back with us," Henry said.

Caspian gave Zed a lingering kiss goodbye then watched until the van was out of sight. It was his mother's charity ball today. She'd texted to remind him. He'd texted her back. *Sorry. Can't make it.* Everyone would have a better time without him around.

Henry and Jonas were drinking Pimm's in the kitchen when Caspian went back into the house.

Jonas poured him a glass. "Ever been in a helicopter?"

Caspian nodded. "Once in Switzerland. Zed hasn't. He's not happy."

Henry laughed. "Life on the road isn't pleasant. Motorway food. Motorway bathrooms. Long boring journeys."

"Did you charter a helicopter to prove a point?" Caspian asked.

"Jonas needs to get back fast tomorrow and it takes too long by car or train though it won't hurt Zed to see what he's letting himself in for."

"Want anything to eat?" Jonas asked.

"Cheese and biscuits would be good." Henry smiled at him.

"Ever eaten *casu marzu*?" Caspian asked.

"No," Jonas said. "Should I look for it in Sainsbury's?"

Henry laughed. "It's banned."

Caspian's shoulders slumped. "Don't tell me you've eaten it."

"No way." Henry shuddered.

"What the hell is it?" Jonas asked.

"Sardinian cheese that contains live maggots. The maggots can jump up to five inches out of the cheese while you're eating it." Henry pinned his gaze on Caspian. "You'll have to do better than that."

Caspian laughed.

"So how's the inventing going?" Henry asked.

"I've got an investor interested in my idea for battery powered irons using the waste energy from washer and driers. I'm pitching the idea next week. The problem I have is that the more I know, the more I realise how stupid my ideas are. For instance, I thought there should be some way to use the heat that comes out of the back of fridges but apparently, there's not enough heat to be of any use. Maybe that's going to be true for washers and driers. Or I find out that someone has already invented what I thought was something original. I'm going to start looking for a job if this investor isn't interested. And if… If it looks like mega-stardom is beckoning Zed, I'll find somewhere to live. You won't want me—"

"Stop," Henry said. "You can stay here as long as you want, as long as you need to."

"Thank you." *As long as I'm still with Zed.* Caspian took a gulp of Pimm's and almost choked on the slice of cucumber.

Glastonbury was immense, colourful and noisy. Caspian found it overpowering, the crowds too much to cope with. He worried it was the sort of thing that could trigger a panic attack, so he kept his head down, fixed his gaze on Henry's trim jean-clad backside and followed him and Jonas to The Park Stage where *Electric Ice* was due to start playing at twelve fifteen. *She Drew The Gun* were currently on stage.

"A lot of people here already." Jonas slung his arm over Caspian's shoulder. "Want to get nearer?"

"Let's stay here," Henry said. "If Zed can see anything, he'll spot us if we're out of the crowd."

"This act is good," Caspian said. "Zed told me they won the Emerging Talent prize last year."

"Maybe that's a good omen." Jonas hugged him.

Or bad omen.

Then Zed and the others were on. The guys were dressed in blue and silver which Caspian thought looked too forced. Fin introduced them all and made a joke about the weather. Caspian knew how they played their first song would determine whether people hung around to listen or went off to have a piss or get something to eat.

"*House of Knives* is the first one," Caspian mumbled.

Jonas and Henry laughed. "We know," they said at the same time. Of course they did.

The song was loud, helped by the enormous speakers. It had a compulsive beat and the lyrics were brilliant and quirky, about a relationship in trouble and how everything could go wrong in an instant. Fin was strutting around the stage as if he owned it, but Caspian couldn't take his eyes off Zed, who was singing his heart out. Caspian's foot was tapping. He'd sung this song so many times with Zed. The chorus was brilliant, instantly memorable, and when he did manage to drag his gaze from the stage he could see people were dancing. The song ended and the applause was loud. Caspian put his fingers in his mouth and whistled.

Zed looked up. He couldn't have heard him but he stared straight at Caspian and smiled.

They were a huge success. By the time they'd finished playing, the crowd had doubled. Not long after they'd left the stage, Caspian's phone vibrated.

"Hi, brilliant one," Caspian said. "Though you did cock up a few notes in *Hurricane.*"

Zed laughed. "Stay where you are and I'll come to you."

"We have to stay here," Caspian said to Jonas and Henry.

The next group were halfway through their set before Zed appeared carrying his guitar case. He was wearing eyeliner and he looked gorgeous, except Caspian had wanted them to wear it at the same time. He plastered a smile on his face as Zed headed toward them. No way could he have every first with Zed. *Be reasonable.*

Caspian flung his arms around him. "You were so good."

"Well done," Henry said.

"Our very own star." Jonas smiled.

"Hmm," Zed said.

"What does that mean?" Caspian stared at him.

"I'll tell you when we get back. Where's my helicopter? Where's my champagne and caviar?"

Jonas groaned. "See, Henry? You've created a monster."

Zed was wide-eyed with delight as they flew back to London. "The journey there was crap. The only good thing about going down yesterday was that we got to see *The Foo Fighters* last night. Pete had arranged a caravan for us to sleep in and Jonesie snores worse than you."

Caspian smiled. He was distracted by what it was that Zed wanted to tell them. Was it better for Jonas to give him the news about Gulshan Pasdar before he said whatever it was he was going to say?

Nothing was said on the way back to the house. Jonas had an hour before he needed to leave. Henry opened champagne but as they held up their glasses, Zed put his down and sighed.

"I've left the band."

Caspian's lungs locked. *Don't tell me you've done it for me.*

384

Zed turned to Caspian. "Fin is an arsehole. I don't want to be in a band with him. He found out who you were. Not difficult when we'd told him we met as teenagers. Even without knowing your surname, he put two and two together and got the right answer. Last night he told Pete what you're supposed to have done."

Caspian pressed his lips together.

"I think Fin thought I'd dump you if it was risking the success of the band. He's a fucking idiot. I didn't say a word until after we'd played and then I told Pete I couldn't play with Fin anymore, that I was done."

"Oh fuck," Caspian muttered. "I worried something like that might happen. I'm sorry."

"Don't you dare say you're sorry. This is *not* because of you, it's because of Fin. Every time I see him, he gets more and more on my nerves. There is no way we'd have made it beyond a few more months without me killing him. So I will drink the champagne except not to *Electric Ice* but to all of us—family."

"To family," Jonas and Henry chorused.

"And talking of family…" Jonas put three tickets on the table. "Gulshan Pasdar is conducting the LSO tomorrow night in a charity concert for the victims of terror attacks. I thought you might like to play the cello with us."

Zed upended his glass.

Jonas grabbed the kitchen roll and mopped up the liquid. "The Swan. You could play it in your sleep. Three minutes, more or less. Okay?"

"With the LSO?"

"Yes and with the pianist. On this occasion—that pianist would be me. We can practise tomorrow. And you can decide how to approach Gulshan. After you've played would be better."

Zed felt as if his whole world had been turned on its head. He *had* left the band and would have after Fin's fucking treachery, but Pete had asked Zed to leave because of Caspian. It didn't fit with the band's image to have one of the members involved with a guy who'd been to prison for killing three young girls. Zed had gritted his teeth and made it clear there was no choice to be made between the band and Caspian. He would always choose Caspian. Fin and the others had been shocked when Zed had told them he was done. Zed hadn't told them that Pete had also suggested once Zed and Caspian were over, he'd love to represent Zed in a solo career.

Fuck you. Words he'd thought and not said. The only thing keeping him anchored was Caspian and yet Zed knew he had to tread carefully not to dislodge that anchor, because while Zed's life was full of possibilities, Caspian's was still full of restrictions and disappointments.

So far all Caspian's ideas and inventions had been met with a distinct lack of enthusiasm. No one wanted to invest in him. Caspian had laughed it off but Zed knew he was hurt. He'd told Zed that if the meeting this week about his idea to power a battery to run an iron, using the wasted heat from a tumble drier and washing machine, was greeted with laughter, he was going to look for a job. Zed didn't think it was his imagination that Caspian seemed too bright and cheerful. Zed had tried to reassure him that nothing had changed between them, but he could feel that it had. No matter how many times he said he'd left the band because Fin was a dick, he didn't feel Caspian believed him.

The following day Zed made Jonas practise the Saint-Saens with him until they were both sick of it. Caspian was holed up in Henry's office working on a 'secret project' and had left strict instructions he wasn't to be disturbed.

By the time they all set off for the Barbican in Henry's car, Zed was hyper. "What if he tells me to fuck off? What if says he doesn't want to have anything to do with me? What if he denies he's my father?"

"He might not be your father," Henry said.

Though Zed was sure he was.

"I suppose there could be another Gulshan Pasdar who clears fatbergs out of the sewers for Thames Water," Caspian said. "Or maybe a Gulshan Pasdar who cleans up bird shit."

"Thanks." Zed rolled his eyes.

"You're welcome. I'll love you even if Gulshan Pasdar is a barnyard masturbator. And that makes ten." He grinned.

"What?" Henry asked.

"Caspian's first ten *I love you's* have not been said in the most romantic situations." Zed elbowed him.

"The first one—" Caspian began.

Zed put his hand over Caspian's mouth.

"Please don't tell us," Jonas said.

"Please do," Henry said with a laugh.

"No," Zed said.

"You could ask Pasdar to do a paternity test," Henry said.

Jonas turned to look over his shoulder at Zed. "When you see him, I think you'll know."

"Zed. I. Am. Your. Father," Caspian intoned.

"You know Darth Vader never said *Luke, I am your father,*" Henry said. "It's one of the most misquoted lines from films."

"He definitely didn't say, *Zed, I am your father.*" Caspian laughed.

Zed groaned. "So I walk on stage, we take one look at each other and fall to pieces in front of four hundred people?"

"You should both be so focused on the music you don't see anything," Jonas said. "I meant when you see him afterwards."

Henry dropped Jonas and Zed off outside the orchestra entrance and went to park the car.

"We're first up," Jonas said.

"Shit. You didn't tell me that!"

Jonas laughed. "Because I knew you'd freak out. I'm only playing the piano for your piece and then I'll be on the violin. You can go and sit with Caspian and Henry for the rest of the performance and then come to the Green Room in St Luke's."

"Okay."

"Take a deep breath."

"That didn't help."

But when Zed walked onto the stage with the rest of the orchestra who almost to a man and woman had told him to break a leg, a calmness came over him. This was a chance in a million. To play with the LSO. To play in front of a man who was most likely his birth father. He wasn't going to fuck it up.

The orchestra was ready, waiting for the conductor and when Zed saw the silver-haired, silver-bearded guy walk out, his heart completed the journey into his throat. *Oh fuck. His eyes are the same colour as mine.* Zed nodded his head to acknowledge the conductor and then looked down at his cello. *Do not shake, fingers. Stop pounding, heart.*

A hush swept over the auditorium and Zed looked from the conductor to Jonas who nodded and began playing. Zed joined in at exactly the right point and from then controlled the pace. Within a few sweeps of his bow he was transported to the surface of a lake, his

387

smooth notes on the cello showing the graceful swan gliding across the water. The piano sounded like rippling water and Zed's bird moved majestically, king of the lake, before taking flight.

Zed lost himself in the music. It was an emotional piece known and loved by almost everyone. There were a lot of shifts, bow changes that had to be immaculate plus tricky string crossings. Not necessarily difficult to play, but to do it well, to feel it, that was the key. He'd practised until he was as perfect as he could get. His hands knew exactly what to do. Zed could see the lake stretching out ahead of him. He was the swan.

Slow now. Take your time. One final long fading note which was probably the hardest one of the piece because he had to sustain it as long as he could until the swan disappeared into the distance.

Hold the note until it dies.

And it was done.

Oh wow, did I even breathe in that?

Jonas was urging him to his feet to accept the applause. Zed somehow managed to smile when he wanted to cry. He scanned the audience and saw Caspian on his feet, Henry next to him. He didn't even look at the conductor. He couldn't.

Zed had to wait until the end of the next piece before he could slip into the seat next to Caspian.

Caspian squeezed his fingers and whispered in his ear, "Well done, birdie. You made the hairs on my arms stand on end."

Zed could hardly concentrate on the rest of the music. He was rerunning the Saint-Saens wondering if it had been as good as he'd wanted it to be, then rehearsing what he was going to say to Gulshan Pasdar. What was he supposed to call him? Mr Pasdar? Sir? Maybe sir was the best option. That's what they did in the States.

When the last piece of the evening was over and Zed wasn't sure he could have told anyone what had been played, the applause faded and they pushed to their feet. Caspian took a badly wrapped parcel from under his seat and handed it to Zed.

"This is what I was working on today."

Zed unwrapped it. It was the book of him. The letter his mother had written. Copies of photographs he'd found in his mother's box, his school reports, drawings he'd done as a child, certificates for swimming and music. There was a gap after his mother had died but then there were more photos that Henry or Jonas or Caspian had taken.

A copy of his degree certificate and the final picture, one of Zed on stage at Glastonbury.

"Good thing Henry and Jonas have a top-quality printer," Caspian said. "It's for you to give your father. I made one for Jonas and Henry too."

Zed flung his arms around him. "I love you so much. Promise never to leave me."

Caspian hugged him back. "I'm yours as long as you want me."

Once they were in the Green Room, Zed lost his voice and his nerve. The room was milling with people. Maybe this was the wrong place to approach the guy. He didn't want to cause a scene. Someone pushed a glass of champagne into his hand and he put it down. He couldn't drink. His throat had closed up.

"Go and talk to him," Caspian whispered.

"*Ungghh.*"

"Just say hello and see what he says."

"*Anuugh.*"

"Try to come out with actual words or he'll think you're mentally ill or from outer space or both."

"I've gone through so many versions of what my first sentence should be and decided on none of them."

"*I like your shirt* is a good opener. Or *Where did you get your baton?* That's my favourite.*"

Zed laughed and as Caspian moved away, suddenly the conductor was standing in front of him. It was so weird looking into the face of someone with eyes just like his. It had to the right guy, didn't it?

"You played the Saint-Saens beautifully."

Speak to him! Zed couldn't manage one word. He opened the book to the page with his mother's letter, the envelope addressed to Gulshan Pasdar on the opposite page and held it out. Zed knew the words off by heart. *My dearest one, you have a son. I've named him Hvarechaeshman...*

When the guy looked up, Zed got his voice back. "I'm sorry if this is springing it on you. I know it's a lot to take in. I don't know anything other than what it says in this letter and I only found it a short time ago. You might be the wrong Gulshan Pasdar." *Of course, now you can't shut up?* "If it is you, you might not even believe what it says. You might not want to know me. You might not want me to disrupt your life

389

because you have a family and I understand that and I'm sorry. And I don't know what to call you assuming you are my birth father, but you are, aren't you?" *Shut up, right now.*

Zed held his breath.

"I…"

Looked like he wasn't the only one who wasn't sure what to say but unlike the man standing in front of him, Zed couldn't stop talking.

"We look like each other, well I don't have silver hair or a beard but there's something in your face I see in mine when I look in the mirror. Apart from our eyes which are so similar… I *will* shut up now. Sorry. Sorry."

"I…I… You have too many words and I have none."

"Are you him? Is it you?" Zed whispered, his heart in his throat.

"Yes. I can manage one word." He smiled. He took hold of Zed's hand and lifted it. "My son. Unbelievable, yet undeniable. You have a musician's fingers. Agile, perceptive, sensitive. I see your mother in your face. I didn't know. I'm…stunned, shocked, astounded. Happy. Yes, I'm happy. I'd never have left her if I'd known. How is she?"

Zed groaned. "She died ten years ago when I was eleven."

"Ah." He let Zed's hand go as he sucked in a breath, for a moment his face creased in anguish. "I did as she wanted. I took the job in Boston and I tried not to think of her again. What of your father, your brother?"

"My father died this summer. That was when I found the letter, hidden in the house. Tamaz is… abroad. I live with Jonas and Henry. Jonas played the piano with me. I have a boyfriend. I'm gay. He made this book for me to give you."

I am a blathering idiot.

"What a kind thing to do."

"Jonas and Henry took me in when life became…difficult for me."

"Difficult?"

Zed sagged.

"We have a lot to tell each other," his birth father said. "You have brothers and sisters. All younger than you. Your mother… She was my love and I perhaps should have fought harder for her. You say life became difficult but were you happy? Was your life mostly good?"

His birth father stared at him as if he couldn't believe he was there. Zed felt the same.

"I...I..." How could he answer that? Well, he could but it was too much for this moment. "If you want to see me, we could meet and talk. I don't expect anything from you. You don't have to see me ever again, I just wanted to meet you and now I have, I'm glad. I hope you are too."

"I am. I fly back the day after tomorrow. Can you come to my hotel tomorrow morning?" He took Zed's hand again and squeezed his fingers. "I'm staying at the St James's Hotel and Club in Mayfair. Ten o'clock in the lobby. Okay?"

Zed nodded.

"I need to mingle. I'll see you tomorrow. Call me...Gul. And thank you for this book. Thank your boyfriend. I feel a lucky man."

SUMMER NINE

Chapter Thirty-Four

2018

Caspian stood impatiently with his sign in the arrivals hall at Heathrow's Terminal 5. He was waiting for Zed who'd been to Boston for two weeks to stay with Gul and his family. It was the second time Zed had gone over since they'd met last summer. On this occasion Zed had taken his cello and played in his father's orchestra. Caspian wished he'd been there to see him.

When a flurry of passengers began to emerge, Caspian held up his sign.

WELCOME TO MANCHESTER
VERY SEXY BLUE-EYED ROCK STAR

A few people read it and smiled, a couple did a double take, presumably at the word Manchester or maybe at the rock star bit. Caspian had missed Zed. Life seemed empty without him, even when the guy was deep in the zone composing with a focused ferocity that was almost frightening.

Zed was his family.

Zed was his everything.

Caspian had very little contact with his parents or sisters—the occasional phone call from his mother or sisters to ask how he was. Nothing from his father who had taken early retirement and fallen into obscurity. Lachlan rarely spoke to their father either but had told Caspian that now he wasn't working, he was driving their mother mad. *Good.* Part of Caspian wished his father knew exactly why he'd fallen from grace but Henry had told him to let it go.

Lachlan now had a son and Caspian had been to see him. Though he'd been invited to the christening, he hadn't gone, but sent a present. He'd read articles online about his brother being praised for his work for the LGBTQ charity and Caspian hoped Lachlan wasn't just doing it to try and make up for what he'd done. Same with his brother's work with young offenders. The door wasn't closed between them and maybe one day it would be fully open.

He and Zed were still living with Jonas and Henry, the four of them eating together when they could. They'd looked for somewhere of their own but nowhere they could afford had been anywhere near as nice, and when Jonas and Henry insisted they didn't want them to leave, Zed and Caspian had taken them at their word. Though they were paying rent and covering their share of the bills.

Zed had agreed to work part-time for MI5 so he could pursue a solo music career. *Electric Ice* were still playing with a replacement guitarist and Corrigan as their manager but hadn't yet made it. Caspian felt mean for being glad. Corrigan was still trying to persuade Zed to sign with him as a solo artist, but Zed wouldn't. Caspian hoped it had nothing to do with him. Zed said he didn't want the pressure of being with a label, though was that the truth?

When Zed emerged through the doors, rolling a suitcase, his blue cello case on his back and a messenger bag looped over his chest, Caspian's heart did a few cartwheels and somersaults. He hid his face behind his sign and waved it.

He knew the moment Zed had moved to within a couple of feet of him.

Caspian lowered the sign, glanced at him, then looked past him. "Would you mind moving out of the way, please? I'm waiting for a very sexy, blue-eyed rock star."

Zed laughed. "What about a quite sexy, blue-eyed musician?"

"Er...no."

"Well, I have some bad news. You're at the wrong airport."

"Shit! In that case, you *will* do." Caspian reached out, let his fingers drift over Zed's face and leaned to whisper in his ear. "I've spent the last hour wondering if that cello case will fit in a bathroom stall."

Zed's mouth quirked in a grin. "Not with us and my case in there too."

"Who said I wanted you and your case in there as well?"

Zed laughed out loud then.

"Seriously, I think we should check," Caspian whispered. "My mouth has a long-standing date with your cock."

"I'm not letting it out on a date until I've showered."

"Come on then, hurry. Jonas and Henry won't be back until late and I've set the timer on the hot tub."

Caspian dropped his sign in a waste bin and took the case from Zed.

"Anything exciting happen while I was away?" Zed asked.

393

"Not since yesterday. We've skyped every day you were gone."

"Yeah, but we didn't have a lot of intelligent conversation. You were too distracting."

"Was I? Actually, I've been wondering if I should go for a career in the adult entertainment industry."

Zed raised his eyebrows. "I learnt my lesson about not answering a video call from you in front of anyone after that first time. Everyone wanted to see my boyfriend, and my sisters saw far too much of you. I slammed my phone down so fast, I thought I'd broken it."

"Were they impressed?"

"Caspian!"

He handed Zed a ticket and they went through the barrier.

"So you had a good time?" Caspian knew he had. He just didn't want him to have too much of a good time.

"Everyone was really kind. I think my brothers are warming up to me now. Well not think. They are. Isaac is going to Julliard in the fall. He's a brilliant pianist. We played a few duets. One evening, we all performed together in a concert for their friends. Me on the cello, Isaac on the piano, Saul and Bella on the violin, Dessie on the flute, Mira on the viola and Dad on percussion made from a variety of stuff out of the kitchen."

"I bet you could have done with me on the triangle." Caspian was trying hard not to be jealous.

"The one thing missing. Everyone commented on it. *If only we'd had someone to play the triangle.* I wish you could come to the States with me."

"Me too." Henry had tried again to find a way around the conditions of Caspian's release but hadn't had any success.

Caspian's current supervising officer, a woman called Hatty Marks, had seemed to take pleasure in telling him he'd never be able to go the States because of his criminal record. Caspian didn't like her but at least she only required him to go for an interview every three months.

"We went surfing at the Hamptons. Even the girls came. Dad had hired a house for a weekend and it was right on the beach."

Zed hadn't told him about that.

"I'd love to live somewhere like that." Zed sighed.

Me too.

The train pulled in and they climbed on, choosing seats that let them keep an eye on Zed's cello.

Once they were settled, Zed took hold of Caspian's hand. "I missed you."

"I should think so." Caspian squeezed his fingers.

"Ouch."

"Sorry."

"No, you're not," Zed whispered.

"You can punish me when we get home."

"I will."

"Promises, promises."

"I'll gag you."

Caspian's cock unfurled. A little kink of his they'd discovered. Not enough to stop him breathing but... He shuddered.

"My father asked me to stay." Zed kept a tight hold of Caspian's fingers as if he knew Caspian was going to try and pull away.

He didn't try, but it was a close-run thing. His cock deflated.

"Stay? For how long?" *My voice sounded okay, didn't it? Not squeaky or panicked?*

"Forever. He said he could get me a job with the orchestra or I could try and break into the US rock scene. Because I'm his son, I'm a US citizen, though it's not quite that straightforward because I was born out of wedlock *and* found out after I was eighteen, or something like that. I'd have to get a lawyer to sort it out."

Caspian's heart stuttered and stopped.

"But I told him I didn't want to live in the States."

Please let it not be me that stopped him saying yes.

Please let me be the reason he said no.

Shit.

"I guess Jackson wouldn't be too pleased," Caspian mumbled.

"You know that's not why I said no."

"Is it because you don't like mac and cheese? Though I'd have thought that would be enough to bar you from entry."

"Don't." Zed mock-gagged. "I don't know how anyone can eat that. I said no because I want to be with you, live with you."

"Even though I'm a fuck-up?" Caspian smiled but he meant it.

Hidden by the table, Zed slid his hand onto Caspian's lap and stroked his cock.

Caspian groaned. "Though it kills me to say it—don't."

395

Zed did it again.

"You do know that if you carry on, we'll have to drag the cello into the train toilet?"

Zed laughed and leaned in to lick Caspian's ear.

"Stop making me want to fuck you," Caspian whispered. "All I can think about is stripping you naked and I'll be the one arrested."

Zed moved his hand. "Distract me. Tell me about the stag-do you've arranged for Henry."

"No because he'll worm the truth out of you."

"He'll kill you if you don't give him what he asked for. We sat and discussed it. No drag artist make-up course, no naked butlers, no strip clubs, no dressing up in silly outfits. He's written a comprehensive list."

Caspian laughed. "Anyone would think he didn't trust me. Hey, Saturday will be the cultural day he requested. We're going to a museum then we're going for a meal."

"What museum?" Zed gave him a suspicious look.

"Not telling."

"He's not going to like it. You do realise he's got work colleagues coming?"

"Yep and I've talked to all of them. They're fine with what I've arranged and sworn to secrecy."

"But you're not going to tell me?"

"No."

Zed smiled. "Well, I guess I can't get blamed if I knew nothing."

"There you go."

"Jonas is much easier to please. Afternoon tea at Fortnum and Mason and a trip to the theatre. I was torn between *Paw Patrol—The Great Pirate Adventure* or *King Lear*."

Caspian snorted with laughter. "Is that what you're actually going to do?"

"I'm not going to tell you."

"Maybe we should all meet up at a club afterwards. Get the grooms together for a while."

"What club though?" Zed asked.

"Maybe a boat on the Thames instead? That could be fun."

"Good idea. I'll look into it. If I book for twenty-five we should be fine. So what have you been up to? Heard from any of your family?"

"What do you think?"

"No."

"And you'd be right."

Zed winced. "How's work?"

"It's okay."

His meeting last year to pitch one of his ideas to an investor had turned into a discussion about what else he'd thought about, that in turn morphed into a job offer, three days in the office, two working from home. His boss, Steve Greenaway, invested in new technology companies, and Caspian was learning from the bottom up. Every time Steve said that Caspian had a hard time not laughing.

"Steve's given me responsibility for researching the limb support business. You remember I had the idea of 3D printing supports to help children with walking difficulties? Well, there are a few companies already doing it, including helmets for skull deformities. Plus there are leg and foot supports made from low temperature thermoplastics that can be altered at home with a hairdryer if they don't quite fit. *And* there's a company who want to do 3D printing for animals' limbs."

"You don't sound enthusiastic."

"I am but yeah well, I'm not quick at reading as you know. I like thinking things up and I suppose I should be pleased a lot of my ideas are already in production, but I still want to come up with something no one else has yet thought of. Steve would like me to do an Open University degree in engineering but I can't cope with the thought of struggling for three or four years. He says there are a few universities that specialise in helping dyslexic students. I don't know if I want to be a dyslexic student."

Caspian wished he hadn't said any of that. Zed was soaring and he was climbing a long ladder rung by rung, and had been for some time.

"Written any new songs?" Caspian changed the subject.

"A couple. I'll play them to you later."

Zed hadn't signed with a label but made full use of modern technology to go it alone, albeit with help from a recording studio and advice from people in the business. He'd created a website, posted the lyrics to his songs, made regular blog posts, let people download for free and ended up on playlists for Spotify and Apple Music among others. Caspian had even played the guitar on a few tracks and he and Zed had written some songs together. Zed had tens of millions of streams of his music though the royalties were small, but at least it was something. He'd also sold lyrics and made money from that. Zed said

397

he was content to stick to what he was doing and maybe do a few live performances, in clubs, parks and festivals, but Caspian wasn't convinced that was true.

Zed yawned as they walked up to the house from Maze Hill station. He ached.

"Did you sleep on the plane?" Caspian asked.

"A bit. But I was sandwiched between a guy who kept laughing at the film he was watching and a kid who wriggled the whole time."

"Anything new on the Tamaz front?"

"No. I don't know whether that's a good thing or bad."

After Letters of Administration were granted, Zed, with help from Jackson and Henry, had sorted out his father's affairs. All the money was now in the bank in Zed's account. He and Tamaz had almost three-quarters of a million pounds each after splitting their father's assets and from the sale of the house. Jackson had Zed call Tamaz to try and persuade him to come back to the UK. Tamaz had said no, and not hidden his anger when Zed refused to transfer the money to him.

Tamaz had ranted about Zed's selfishness, told him to google the El-Shariz orphanage because it was those children he was hurting. Zed wished he could believe his brother was involved in the orphanage but to his bitter disappointment, Tamaz had been identified with a group of Isis soldiers on footage shot by a drone. Tamaz hadn't been dressed like them but he was with them and nowhere near the El-Shariz children's home. Jackson didn't want a million pounds going to support terrorism. Nor did Zed.

Now they were playing a waiting game. Would Tamaz come back to the UK or not?

Caspian opened the door and pulled the suitcase inside.

"It's good to be home." Zed yawned as he carried his cello to the music room.

"You need a hand showering?"

"Not if you want us to make it up to the hot tub."

Caspian smiled. "Have a cold shower and wake up. I'll make sure the hot tub's at the right temperature."

Zed was *not* going to have a cold shower. But he was quick, checked his father's phone to see if Tamaz had sent him a message—no—then put his phone on charge, pulled on his trunks, wrapped a towel around his waist and headed up the stairs to the roof. Caspian was already in the steaming, bubbling water—naked. Zed shucked off his trunks, let them drop with the towel and climbed in.

"Shiiiiit," he yelped. "You trying to cook me?"

Zed sat on the edge, reached back for the towel and draped it over his lap but his cock tented the material.

"Worried about passing planes?" Caspian slid over to him.

"Now I know just how much drones can see, and how we can't even trust that insects are actually insects, I'm being cautious."

Caspian rose up on his knees, pressed his lips to Zed's and Zed melted against him. His tongue surged into Zed's mouth and he grabbed Caspian's arse to keep him close. Caspian groaned as he sucked on his tongue and somehow, in a magician's trick, the towel disappeared from between them and Caspian pulled him down into the water. *Hot, hot* but Zed didn't want to move. Wrapped around each other, he had one hand threaded in Caspian's hair and the other plastered to his back, while Caspian clung to Zed's neck with both hands. The kiss continued.

Zed adored kissing Caspian, loved the way the kiss lit up his body, ramped up need, made his heart pound and his toes curl. Caspian angled Zed's mouth so he could plunge his tongue deeper and gentle nibbling turned greedy, noisy and desperate. Zed sat with his legs over Caspian's, their chests pressed together, cocks sandwiched between them. Every movement, every rock, every brush that Caspian made against him sent bolts of lust spiralling to Zed's groin, winding him up like a clockwork toy.

Finally, Caspian pulled back, breathing heavily, his eyes glazed, his lips kiss-swollen.

"You do remember Henry's rules about the hot tub?" Zed panted.

"No glass. No peeing. No adding your own bubbles. No soap. No diving. No front crawl, no back crawl. No hanky panky—whatever that means. No eating. He didn't say *No eating Zed.*"

Zed laughed.

"So eating Zed is top of my list along with breaststroke." He tweaked Zed's nipple. "I'm not going to spill a drop of you. Just don't let me drown. Move a bit higher in case I need to surface fast."

Zed sat on the seat and Caspian knelt in front of him, leaning in to lick around Zed's nipple. Zed arched into him and wrapped his hand around the back of Caspian's head to hold him in place.

"Oh Christ." Zed's breathing was shaky.

Caspian nipped and licked and sucked each nipple in turn before he licked down the centre of Zed's chest. He fluttered his tongue in and around his navel, looked up at him while he did it and Zed felt the pull in his balls.

"I think we should make the water flavoured," Caspian said.

"Too many chemicals in it. How long can you hold your breath?"

"Long enough to make you come." Caspian smacked his lips and Zed groaned.

"Ten minutes?"

"Ha ha."

Caspian dipped below the surface, wrapped his mouth around Zed's cock and sucked. Zed's hips jerked so strongly, he propelled Caspian out of the water and caused a small tidal wave. Caspian fell back, went under and came up spluttering.

"Sorry," Zed blurted.

"Shall we try that again? I'll hold on with one hand and wave my hat in the air at the same time. Time me."

Zed stretched out his arms and grabbed the sides of the tub. He held tight and closed his eyes. Maybe not looking would help.

Caspian's hands slid under his backside and lifted him. The top of his cock was out of the water, his balls still submerged. If someone could see them…he didn't care. Caspian blew across the tip of his shaft and Zed caught his breath. The slide of Caspian's slick, talented tongue along and into the narrow slit, kickstarted his lungs. Then Caspian set him back on the seat so that his cock was underwater and took almost all of him into his mouth. Zed *had* to open his eyes to watch.

He couldn't see much more than Caspian's dark head bobbing in his lap but when he brought a hand down to Caspian's cheek and felt the head of his cock surging in his mouth, his balls tingled. He loved the feel of himself under Caspian's skin.

Every time he thought he might come, Caspian changed what he was doing, pressed down at the base of his cock, bit the inside of his thighs, or gently sucked his balls before he went back to his cock. Didn't he need to breathe?

Caspian deepthroated him and Zed groaned. "Fuuuuck."

Then everything was suddenly speed and pressure and intensity in a rhythm that ensured orgasm bounded toward him. He slammed his hand to his mouth to muffle his cry as he exploded into Caspian's mouth, his body jerking with the force of each spasm.

When he'd finally done and Caspian let him free, he still didn't emerge and Zed had a moment of panic before Caspian shot up like a champagne cork and gasped. "Personal best—twenty seconds."

Zed pushed him down again.

They spent the rest of the day in bed together, each other's body a personal adventure playground. While Caspian slept, Zed found a party boat company and booked twenty-five places for Saturday night, though when he put the phone down, he realised he'd used his father's phone by mistake. *Bloody jet lag.*

Jonas and Henry bought home an Indian takeaway and Zed set the table.

"Did you have fun in the States?" Jonas asked.

"Yep, I did. I bought Mira some flowers before I left and when she burst into tears, I almost did too. Out of all of them, it was her reaction I'd been worried about but she's been nothing but kind. The only difficulty was being asked about Tamaz. I couldn't tell them the truth so I had to repeat his lie about the orphanage. It pisses me off they think he's a good guy."

"He might be," Jonas said.

Zed shrugged. "I wish that was true."

"Is everything arranged for Saturday?" Henry asked. "Am I going to be happy?"

Caspian smiled. "You'll be ecstatic."

"Oh fuck," Henry muttered.

Jonas laughed.

"Did you go for option one or two on the theatre?" Caspian asked Zed.

"One."

"Good." Caspian grinned at Jonas.

"Oh shit," Jonas said. "You're not going to handcuff me in a train and send me to Aberdeen?"

"That's a good idea," Zed said. "But no."

"Nor kidnap me, drive me out into the countryside and force me to cycle home wearing nothing but a mankini?"

The three of them gaped at Jonas.

"I've been googling," he said. "Please don't shave off all my hair, paint me blue, pretend to have me arrested or leave me anywhere naked."

Zed smiled. "You're both getting what you asked for."

"Maybe not quite what you asked for but nearly," Caspian added.

"How about the actual wedding. No hiccups?" Zed asked.

"No," Henry said. "My mother and sister are quietly panicking but would deny it if asked. My father is still quietly hoping I'll change my mind and marry a woman. When the registrar asks if there is any lawful impediment to the marriage taking place, we all better cross our fingers."

Zed liked Henry's father. He didn't really think he was a homophobe. He just liked winding Henry up. Jonas and Henry were getting married in the family castle. Zed had gaped when he'd first seen it. It had battlements and a moat, though when you looked closely, much of it was falling apart. Henry had been to boarding school like Caspian though he seemed to have had a much happier time. Maybe because he'd been a brilliant sportsman, but he said no one had ever picked on him twice.

If it hadn't been for the nagging worry about Tamaz, Zed had never been happier.

Chapter Thirty-Five

Caspian nudged Henry towards Jonas. "I suggest a long, lingering goodbye."

Henry pulled Jonas into his arms. "Letting these two organise our stag events was your worst idea ever."

"Hey, you agreed with me. You said we could trust them better than any of our colleagues."

"I was a fucking idiot."

Jonas laughed. "Have fun. See you later."

Henry turned to Caspian and frowned. "Where are we going?"

"It's a surprise."

"I don't like surprises."

"I know." Caspian grinned.

The cab was waiting for them and all the way into London, Henry pressed him, threatened him, bribed him to reveal what had been arranged and Caspian refused to budge.

"Good thing you don't have access to water," Caspian said.

"Why?"

"Because you'd have resorted to waterboarding. It's going to be fun. Stop worrying."

"I'll stop worrying when I'm in bed tonight with Jonas and we're both still intact. I bet Zed's stuck to what Jonas wanted and has cream tea organised at some swanky hotel, and an evening at the theatre."

"And would you have liked that too?"

"No."

"Shut up then."

Henry snorted.

Eight of Henry's friends and colleagues, including Jackson, were waiting in front of the Brandon Museum. It didn't look much from the outside, more like a quirky old-fashioned shop than anything else but Caspian had been inside and the place was a Tardis. It went on and on and up and up. And down for that matter.

"Have you been here before?" Caspian crossed his fingers.

"No."

Henry's friends clapped him on the back or hugged him and they went into the museum. Kurt Brandon waited inside. He was a stocky,

403

eccentric figure with wild grey hair barely trapped under a black fez and he wore what looked to Caspian like a dressing gown. He guessed it was supposed to be a smoking jacket but the Disney characters all over it said not.

"How wonderful to see you all," Brandon said. "Welcome to my world of the beautiful, the bizarre and the ugly. There is no organisation, no categorisation, no attempt to educate or explain. There has been no hiding away of a large percentage of discoveries that the public will never see. No neat labelling of drawer after drawer of specimens of the same thing that serves little purpose unless you are an expert in that particular field. Instead, I display in this world of mine everything and anything that has caught my eye over my life and continues to catch my eye. It is all here for your entertainment. Feel free to touch. Don't break." He winked—unnervingly—at Caspian. "Embark, explore and enjoy."

Caspian was instantly captivated by the exhibits and almost forgot to check that Henry was enjoying himself. He went to look for him and found Henry examining a guillotine blade.

"Not for my neck, I hope," Caspian said.

"Let's see what the day holds." He turned the blade in his hands. "I wonder how authentic this is?"

"Very," Brandon said at his shoulder. "That mark—blood."

Caspian slipped away again. He wanted to bring Zed here. There were dodo bones, a two-headed monkey in a jar, three lots of mummified genitalia—one of which looked distinctly human, McDonald's Happy Meal toys, a snake skeleton that wrapped around the room twice above their heads, sketches by Da Vinci alongside drawings done by inmates of mental asylums and a fantastic cityscape by an autistic teenager. Everywhere he went, every place he looked, there was something to marvel at.

When the bell rang to alert them it was time for lunch, Caspian had barely seen half of the exhibits. Henry and his friends joined Caspian in the lobby.

"This place is great," Jackson said.

"Thank you," said Brandon.

"However did you find out about it?" Henry asked Caspian.

"I googled *penis trivia* and discovered there were mummified ones here. Did you know that King Tutankhamun's penis was mummified erect?"

404

"Heaven help us," Henry muttered. "Everyone prepare themselves for everything you didn't want to know about male genitalia."

"We're eating upstairs," Caspian said. "But it's a sensory experience. Complete darkness. No one's allergic to anything and you've already told me your preference for meat, fish or vegetarian. You won't be able to see what's on your plate but it will be what you asked for."

"*Meat* covers a lot of options," Henry said.

"Which was why I went for vegetarian." Caspian winked. No way was he putting anything in his mouth he couldn't identify. "You can put these bib things on in case you spill anything." He handed them round. "We'll be led in and taken to our seats. There'll be another group in there eating with us who are doing the museum tour after lunch. If you panic or you need to leave the room say the word *cock* and someone will help you out."

"I believe the word is *out*," Brandon said with a laugh.

They were taken to another room in a conga line, right hand on the right shoulder of the person in front. Everyone was strangely silent as they were led in pitch darkness to their seats. It was more unnerving than Caspian had anticipated.

"Your cutlery is reasonably blunt," said a male voice. "We don't want to have to clean up blood—yours or anyone else's. All your serving staff are visually impaired so please be respectful."

Caspian was surprised how reluctant he was to speak. It made him realise how much he relied on people's expressions and body language for clues as to how to behave and respond. But no one was saying anything. The silence grew awkward.

"Hi there everyone. My name's Brad Pitt," Caspian said in his best American accent.

A woman gasped and a man laughed. Henry.

"I'm James Bond," Henry said.

"I'm M," Jackson added.

From there it went downhill conversation-wise but it was fun. Drinking from a wine glass wasn't easy when you couldn't even find it and Caspian had to guess at the food by smell but the two groups—the other was a hen party—got on really well. Lying about what they did for a living probably helped because none of Henry's friends could admit to working at MI5 so they made up outlandish occupations— fighter pilot, winkle picker, statue cleaner.

405

After they'd eaten surprisingly good food, they went up another flight of stairs to a studio where they were going to sculpt models from clay and take turns to use a potter's wheel. Everything would be fired and Caspian could collect the pieces in a week's time. Henry looked as thrilled as if Caspian had offered him a chance to drive a Ferrari. *Seriously!* Who would have guessed? Caspian had thought he'd roll his eyes, but Henry was first in the line for the potter's wheel. They put on overalls to protect their clothes and then the model walked in. A naked guy in his thirties who was—*fucking hell*—well hung. Henry looked at Caspian and glared. *Tough.*

That afternoon, Caspian found something else he was no good at. Neither hand sculpting nor throwing a pot. He gave up trying to do the whole figure and just did the cock. Life size with the curved head and veins. Though his looked like a tree covered in ivy. The cock was the part everyone else had avoided. Henry threw a set of fucking perfect soup bowls in the time he was allotted. Caspian managed one very wonky bowl with a hole in it.

He put it alongside Henry's. "There. Now you have an extra one." Henry laughed.

They left the museum in the late afternoon, went for a drink, then had a meal at Tower 42 with fantastic views over London. Followed by a pub quiz Caspian had arranged.

"What's angel lust?" Caspian asked.

Of course Henry knew. An erection a guy might get if killed by hanging. *And* Henry knew the average speed of ejaculation. Twenty-eight miles per hour. When he also knew the average number of erections a man has in the night was nine, and that thirty to forty men in the UK break their erect penis in a year, he realised Caspian had set him up as the only one who'd know any answer because over the last month, Caspian had *fed* him the answers.

"You little…" He grabbed Caspian and rubbed his knuckles in his hair.

All his friends were laughing.

They emerged from the pub at eight slightly drunk.

"We going home yet?" Henry asked.

"Not yet." Caspian looked around the group. "I've arranged tickets on a party boat."

"If anyone wants to drop out, feel free," Henry said.

"We're meeting Jonas and his group of friends," Caspian told him. "Your last chance to bump and grind before you're married."

"Ha."

Jonas and co were on the boat when they got there. All Henry's friends had stayed with him.

Henry pulled Jonas into his arms. "You're still alive! And have all your hair. It's a miracle."

Jonas laughed. "We had to sit through *Paw Patrol—The Great Pirate Adventure.* What did you get up to?"

"I handled three cocks, threw us a set of soup bowls, ate in the dark and won a quiz about male genitals. The cocks weren't attached to their owners just in case you're wondering."

Jonas grimaced. "Not sure if that makes it better or worse."

"Apparently this is our last chance to bump and grind before we're married." Henry glanced at Caspian.

"You can bump and grind? Come and show me."

Jonas dragged Henry off and Caspian pulled Zed into his arms and kissed him.

"I can't believe you made them go to that *Paw Patrol* thing," Caspian said.

"They laughed. We only stayed until the interval. I was surprised they let us in. A group of guys with no kids. We got some funny looks. I hadn't thought that through. What did you do?"

"Visited a museum of oddities which was where Henry saw the cocks, lunched in the dark, sculpted from life and had a go on a potter's wheel. Then a meal at Tower 42, followed by a pub quiz and then this."

"We went glass blowing. I was crap."

"Well you're used to sucking and you're so good at that."

"Ha ha."

"We can relax now," Caspian said. "Duty done. I wonder if the bathroom is big enough to fuck in."

Zed chuckled. "Let's have a dance instead."

"I knew you'd get fed up of me."

The area where people were dancing was bigger than Caspian had expected. There was a DJ, the music was loud, the beat strong and the lighting flashed through the entire spectrum so fast that Caspian felt dizzy. Or maybe that was the amount of champagne he'd drunk.

Zed danced like he had no bones. He was all sinuous movement, at one with the music. Caspian felt like an elephant in comparison. But Zed pulled him into his arms, held him close and Caspian let Zed take charge. At least it was dark enough that no one would spot the state of his cock.

Halfway through the second dance, Zed put his mouth to his ear and said, "I'm too hot."

"Not for me." Caspian mock-leered but allowed Zed to tug him outside.

The two of them leaned against the side of the boat and stared out over the dark river.

"God, I'm tired," Zed moaned.

"You're not allowed to be tired until we've checked out the bathroom."

Zed turned to him and laughed, but as Caspian watched his face, the smile disappeared.

"Shit," Zed muttered. "It's Tamaz."

Caspian turned and saw Zed's brother dressed in the white jacket of a waiter. He was staring straight at them. It took Caspian a moment, but even as *why would Zed's brother be serving drinks on a boat* lurched into his head, he took in the way the white jacket looked too big for a slender guy and that he had his hand wrapped around something. *Oh God. Let me be wrong.*

Zed gasped as if he couldn't believe what he was seeing. Had he noticed his brother's jacket looked wrong?

"Hello, little brother." Tamaz took a step toward them.

"What are you doing here?" Zed whispered.

"I've come to take you home."

No, no, not going to happen. I can't let this happen. Caspian was choked with shock and fear.

"Come here," Tamaz said. "Let me hug you."

Caspian stepped to block Zed's way. "Zed, go and tell Henry."

Zed glanced at him, a puzzled expression on his face and Caspian knew he didn't realise what Tamaz was planning.

"Stay right where you are," Tamaz called.

Caspian had no time to think through the consequences. He ran at Tamaz, wrapped his arms around him and hauled him over the side.

A split second of stunned disbelief before Zed found his voice and yelled for help but the music was too loud for him to be heard. He stared into the water but there was no sign of Caspian or Tamaz. Then he rushed to the bridge and flung open the door.

The guy behind the wheel gaped at him. "What—?"

"There are two men overboard. I think… I think one of them has a bomb. Turn toward the shore now."

He ran down again and as he reached the bottom of the steps, and looked out over the river, he thought he caught a glimpse of Tamaz's white jacket before there was a massive explosion and a ball of fire erupted over the water. He was thrown to the deck as the boat rocked violently. He could hear screaming. The music stopped and the screaming continued. Zed pushed to his feet. He had blood on his hands. *What…? Where's Caspian?* He leaned on the railing and yelled his name over and over.

He was still yelling it when Henry and Jonas reached him. The boat was listing but had almost reached a quay.

"We have to go back. Caspian's in the water."

"What the hell's happened?" Henry asked.

"Tamaz. He was dressed as a waiter. He must have been wearing a suicide vest. He told me he wanted to hug me and Caspian ran at him and dragged him overboard."

Zed collapsed sobbing into Jonas's arms. Henry pulled out his phone.

"Wapping police, Wapping police. This is an emergency. A bomb has detonated close to a party boat near St Katharine's Pier. Two persons in the water. Boat damaged. Immediate assistance required."

"We have to help him." But then Zed caught the look that passed between Henry and Jonas, and felt his world begin to crumble. "We need a boat. We need to rescue him."

"Zed." Henry put his hand on Zed's shoulder. "You know the physics of this. You know what happens if devices explode underwater. The shockwaves—"

"No. It wasn't underwater, not really. There's a chance he's okay. We have to look for him."

"We will." Henry went back on his phone.

Everyone was being helped off the boat. Jackson was taking charge. The air was filled with the sound of sirens. A few people were limping. Many were smeared with blood.

Zed was frantic. "We need a boat. We have to get on the river."

"You need medical attention," Jonas said. "You're bleeding."

"I don't care. I need Caspian. I need him. I need him."

Jonas wrapped his arms around him on the dock and held him tight. "We'll find him."

"Jonas—" Henry began.

"We'll find him."

Maybe Henry reacted to the determination in Jonas's voice because suddenly he was in charge, ordering people to do stuff, making calls, but nothing was happening fast enough. The explosion hadn't come the moment they'd hit the water. Zed wanted Caspian to have swum off as fast as he could. Maybe he'd found somewhere to shelter. *In the middle of the river?*

But a nagging voice inside Zed's head was telling him that if the bomb *had* detonated below the water, Caspian couldn't have escaped unharmed. Zed wanted him back whatever injuries he had. He'd look after him forever. *He saved my life. He gave his life to save mine. I love him.*

If he's dead, I want to be dead too.

He couldn't stop shaking. It had suddenly struck him that his brother had tried to kill him. *Oh fuck. Tamaz!* Everything was circling around him as if he were drunk, but he wasn't. His heart was racing and he wasn't dragging enough air into his lungs. Jonas sat him down and called over a paramedic. Zed's mind was somehow both blank and overwhelmed at the same time. The paramedic was talking to him, cleaning blood from his face and head and hands, saying something about *hospital.*

"Not leaving here until I know Caspian is safe."

Jonas wrapped the blanket they'd been given around Zed and pulled Zed's face into the crook of his shoulder.

"It's my fault," Zed whispered. "I used the wrong phone to book the boat. My father's phone. I made a mistake. Tamaz must have tracked my call. Fuck, fuck."

"It's not your fault." Jonas hugged him.

But Zed knew it was.

Jonas's friends came over and Jonas told them to go home, that he'd call them when he had any news. Same with Henry's group. They were mostly uninjured. A few bumps and bruises. All of them on their phones.

410

Zed kept repeating the same thing over and over in his head. *Let Caspian be alive.*

When he saw two policemen heading towards them, Zed whimpered.

"Say nothing before you speak to Henry or Jackson," Jonas whispered.

One of the policemen dropped to his haunches beside them. "I presume you two were on the boat?"

"Yes," Jonas said.

"Names?"

"Jonas and Zayne Mallinson. Zayne's my nephew."

"Did you see what happened?"

"No." Jonas shook his head. "I was dancing, there was a loud blast, and the boat suddenly keeled to one side before surging upright. Everyone fell."

"What about you?" The policeman looked at Zed.

"He's in shock. Head injury," Jonas said.

"Better get him looked at in hospital."

"Yes. We're just waiting for transport."

The policemen went off to speak to others around them. Zed wondered if anyone apart from him had seen what Caspian had done. Caspian had acted before Zed could even think what to do. If Tamaz had detonated the device on the boat, how many would have died or been injured? *Fuck it, Tamaz! You fucking, fucking bastard.* Zed assumed his brother was dead and he was glad.

How does this help your cause, brother? And grief for Caspian turned to rage at Tamaz.

There was no sign of Henry. All the passengers were off the boat, which sat at a crazy angle but hadn't sunk. Paramedics were moving among the injured. Armed police swarmed everywhere. Phones flashed as people took pictures. It sickened Zed that anyone would want to do that, preserving images of fear and pain and confusion. He burrowed closer into Jonas's embrace. Jonas kept whispering *it'll be okay, it'll be okay.* How could he know?

Every minute that ticked by was a nail in Caspian's coffin. The Thames was cold, fast flowing, deep and dirty. If Caspian had been injured, knocked unconscious, he could easily have drowned. *My fault. My brother. I should be the one in the water.* Tears rolled down Zed's cheeks. Several smaller boats were on the river, moving slowly, shining lights back and forth over the water. *What if they hit him?*

Zed couldn't bear to look.

When he felt Jonas's phone vibrate, he froze. Jonas stood up and moved away to answer it.

No, no, no. Zed pushed to his feet. *I won't let him be dead.* When Jonas turned to face him, Zed held his breath.

"They found him. Pulled him out of the water unconscious. He's on his way to the Royal London hospital. Henry's with him."

Zed took one step and his knees buckled.

He came around in the ambulance with Jonas beside him. "Caspian!"

"I've heard nothing," Jonas said. "Lie still."

"You're in shock and concussed." A paramedic checked his blood pressure. "You'll be fine."

No, I won't. Not unless Caspian is okay.

Jonas took Zed's hand and rubbed his thumb over his knuckles. "We're heading for the same hospital."

Zed sighed and closed his eyes.

Caspian's hand rested against something soft and silky. Felt like…hair? When he tried to move, he couldn't. Nor could he open his eyes. It was too much trouble to make more effort.

Then he remembered. *Oh fuck.*

He forced his eyes open. Zed's hair. Zed's head rested next to Caspian's hand. *I'm in hospital. Zed is sitting in a chair beside me with his head by my hand. Why does my throat hurt? Why can't I breathe? Fuck!* There was something in his mouth and a pain in his chest. Caspian lifted his hand to his face. Tried to. It didn't move.

Zed's face was suddenly in front of his. "Caspian!"

I am fucking panicking. What's happening?

A nurse appeared at Zed's side. *Oh Jesus, that pain in my chest again.* It kept coming.

"Caspian, you've got a tube in your throat that's helping you breathe," the nurse said.

Take it out. I know how to breathe. Except he was drowning.

412

But she threaded a length of narrow plastic tube down whatever was in his throat and as soon as it touched his windpipe, he gagged but the drowning sensation faded.

Fuck. Won't I be able to deepthroat Zed anymore?

"I'm suctioning liquid out," she said.

I want to cough. I want you to fucking stop. The sensation of not breathing was freaking him out. He could feel air being pushed into his lungs but the awareness of his inability to expel it was frightening.

Zed, tell them to stop. Please. I'm fine. Please. You can hear me, can't you? Talk to me!

Caspian went back underwater.

Whenever he came to the surface and felt the strange pressure in his chest, he panicked for a short while before he submerged again.

He came up convinced he'd spoken to Zed. They'd had a long conversation about eating in the dark, and a discussion about an idea he'd had to collect polystyrene for recycling.

Eventually, he surfaced and the tube was out. He could breathe. He could cough! *Arggh don't cough. It hurts.* Before his eyes fluttered closed, he saw Zed standing with Jonas and Henry. *They're all safe. Thank fuck for that. Unless they're ghosts. Shit!*

"He's getting better," Zed said. "Now he's breathing on his own, he'll stay awake longer, won't he?"

I heard that. Caspian was trying to stay awake. He didn't want to go back in the river.

"He has to wake up properly," Zed said.

"Be patient." That was Jonas.

"Believe you can." Zed was close to him, whispering in his ear. Caspian could smell his coconut shampoo. He'd kiss him—if he could move.

"You made me believe I could do anything," Zed said. "We *could do anything.* People talk about what they're going to be in life, what they'll achieve, where they're going to go but they lie on the couch and watch TV, wait for something to happen and wonder why their lives are boring. You're not like that. Life with you is never boring. Will never *be* boring. You're a believer. You can do anything. Come back to me."

Caspian made a monumental effort to open his eyes and stared at Zed.

"You're giving me a headache," Caspian croaked.

413

He had no idea why Zed was crying. It was him who had the headache.

Caspian began to feel stronger. His body gradually came back under his control. IVs and drains were removed. He hadn't even been able to piss normally for a while. He'd been battered by the explosion, his skull fractured, he'd punctured a lung, had a bleed on the brain and his kidneys had stopped working for a while. There was a whole list of injuries but nothing he couldn't recover from.

Zed slept on the bed next to him when he could get away with it, cuddled up close and told him he loved him. Henry and Jonas came a lot as well. By the time the police were allowed to speak to him, Caspian had been given his story to tell.

He and Zed had been on deck looking at the river. Caspian had seen the waiter, spotted the suicide vest and acted instinctively in knocking him overboard. He'd never met the guy before. The name Aazim Bashir meant nothing to him. He didn't think the man had targeted them in particular. They were just in the wrong place at the wrong time. The fall had broken Bashir and Caspian apart. Caspian had kicked to the surface and swum as fast as he could toward the middle of the river. That was all he remembered. Apparently, Henry had dived into the water to get him.

The press was fed another part of the story, created by Jackson. Bashir was a lone wolf terrorist, not thought to be part of a bigger network. A radicalised Brit, who hated liberal UK culture. He'd gotten ideas after the London Bridge terrorist attack, wanting to attack London's social scene again because people assume lightning never strikes twice and he wanted to hit Londoners where it hurt. A note had been found in his digs.

Tamaz's name didn't appear in the press but Caspian's did. Zed hadn't let him see a paper and when Caspian asked to see an old copy of the *Metro* another patient had discarded, he wondered if he'd have been better not reading it. The headline was *From Zero To Hero*. Details of the dangerous driving conviction were in there. There was a comment from the father of one of the girls. *Nothing will make up for losing my daughter. But Caspian Tarleton saved lives when he pushed the terrorist into the river and I'm glad that there are mothers and fathers who still get to see their sons and daughters because of what he did.*

414

And also a comment from Caspian's father. *I'd expect nothing less of my son. We're very proud of him.* If he'd said anything about Caspian making up for his mistakes, Caspian would have never spoken to him again—not that he was currently speaking to him—but he didn't. His parents and siblings had come one time while Zed had gone to get something to eat. Only three allowed at a bedside. His sisters were first. Talked at him for five minutes, told him they thought he was brave, and left. His parents were next. His mother cried. Caspian didn't. He didn't want to hear that they were proud of him for what he'd done. They should have been proud of him anyway.

As his father left, he asked Caspian to keep in touch for his mother's sake.

Maybe.

Lachlan was in last. *What can I do?* his brother asked. *Shall I tell the truth?*

What was the point now? All that time in prison for nothing? But Caspian wouldn't help Lachlan's conscience by telling him to keep quiet. Deep down, he knew part of him wanted Lachlan to admit to what he'd done. But the other part of him didn't. That part was steadily growing. Lachlan had changed and Caspian was grateful for that.

Zed was with him when Jackson came to the hospital. He told Caspian that Tamaz had entered the UK a few weeks earlier using a genuine passport. Aazim Bashir was a recently deceased Pakistani who looked very similar to Tamaz and was the same age. Tamaz had told an immigration officer he'd come to the UK for his brother's funeral. That had chilled Caspian. He knew Zed had lost his brother years ago, but he could see how much it hurt knowing Tamaz had deliberately targeted him.

"There was a will in his hotel room," Jackson said. "He left everything to a guy in Syria, an academic who's already on our radar. Needless to say, we'll deny all knowledge of the will if challenged. Tamaz's false identity will be released to the press tomorrow. It'll keep you safe. We'll sort everything out. You'll inherit everything. Not much consolation I know but…"

The day Caspian left hospital was bright and sunny. A heatwave gripped the country. The grass was patchy and parched. Zed had talked about going away on holiday but Caspian didn't feel up to that yet. In any case, they had a wedding to go to at the weekend. Just as well that

415

the wedding hadn't immediately followed the stag nights. Henry had said it hadn't been because he didn't trust the pair of them but he'd wanted to make sure he and Jonas still had all four limbs and full heads of hair. Words that had almost come back to haunt them.

Zed drove him back to Greenwich in Jonas's car. Caspian hadn't written his best man's speech yet. He might have to get Zed to help him.

Caspian stared out of the passenger window. "Everything looks different."

"Scorched grass, sunburnt faces, sunglasses, sundresses. Rare sights."

"Yeah." But it was more than that. "Did I nearly die?"

Zed made a choked noise in his throat. "Not when you were in the hospital but the moment you threw yourself at a suicide bomber, ycah, you nearly died."

"I'm sorry about Tamaz."

"Don't be." Zed reached to grip his fingers for a moment. "I'm sad when I remember the kind things he did for me when I was a little boy but not when I think about what he became. No more heroics though, okay? I want a quiet life. In bed by seven every night."

Caspian laughed. "You remember when we first met?"

Zed gaped at him. "Of course I do. I remember every little thing. How you pretended to be stuck up a tree. How you made a den with me even though you had a fantastic treehouse yards away."

"I remember how lonely I was. How lonely you were. That was the beginning of our story."

"And it will go on forever."

Caspian smiled. "Forever."

416

Chapter Thirty-Six

Zed stared out of the window of Henry's old bedroom at Jedstone Castle. The building sat on a chalk hilltop, the sea that once upon a time had been within walking distance, now a distant line of blue.

He turned away from the window and looked at Henry, lounging in an uncomfortable chair in a white shirt, blue tie and silver waistcoat, his grey trouser-clad legs stretched out, crossed at the ankles. He held a glass of champagne and looked deceptively relaxed.

"Are you happy?" Zed asked.

Henry glanced at him in surprise. "You're not asking me if I'm nervous? Yeah, I'm happy. I'm the luckiest man alive. Happy doesn't come near it. I don't really care about all this…palaver, but I knew Jonas wanted it. I'd do anything for him."

Henry's sisters had been responsible for all the arrangements. Getting the licence to hold a wedding in the great hall, the hiring of the marquee, the catering, flowers, cake, photography, entertainment. Henry had asked the pair not to go overboard but had given in when he'd seen how much the idea of going overboard had pleased Jonas. There were fireworks planned too.

"How's Caspian, do you think?" Henry asked.

"He's doing okay. Just occasionally, I see a look on his face as if he's gone away somewhere inside his head. He still limps sometimes and his hands shake if he gets overtired, but he's getting better." In bed, well, he was great in bed. "He told me to tell you that if you asked about him I was to inform you that over a period of two weeks a single man can produce enough sperm to impregnate every woman on earth."

Henry laughed. "Glad he hasn't saved that for his speech. Do you know what he's going to say?"

"Sorry, I have no idea."

"Hmm. You're a terrible liar." Henry emptied his glass and pushed to his feet. "We'll go down now."

Zed grabbed Henry's jacket and held it out for him to put on before he slipped into his own. They had white roses in their buttonholes and he straightened Henry's.

"Do I look okay?" Henry asked.

"I know you only asked that because you think I need to feel I've been supportive. You don't care because you know you look more than okay."

Henry laughed.

They emerged from their room and Zed knocked on the door opposite.

Caspian opened it. "He's changed his mind."

"Don't say that," Jonas called. "I changed my socks not my mind."

"Ready?" Zed asked.

They were sharing best man duties and had each spent time with the other that morning.

"You look very handsome," Henry said to Jonas.

"Thank you." Caspian twirled a finger in his hair and cocked his head on one side.

Henry rolled his eyes.

"So do you," Jonas said. "Even when you're rolling your eyes. This morning has passed so slowly. Caspian's not stopped talking for the last hour."

"Hey, I did my job," Caspian said indignantly. "Told you jokes. Gave you drinks. Helped you get dressed. Repeatedly told you that you were too good for Henry. And stopped you bolting."

"And he's still in one piece for which I thank you." Henry turned to Jonas and held out his hand. "Ready?"

Caspian and Zed went downstairs first and once they were sure everyone was in place in the Great Hall, they signalled to the musicians then beckoned Henry and Jonas. Caspian and Zed walked in together, past the seated guests and took up positions either side of the old refectory table set across the end of the room. The male registrar who stood behind the table, smiled at them. Zed turned to look over his shoulder as Henry and Jonas walked down the centre of the room towards them. Henry looked straight ahead but Jonas was smiling at guests on either side. Zed's heart was so full of love, he almost cried. He wanted this day to be perfect for them.

The ceremony was short and formal, merely the legal requirements. Henry hadn't wanted to open his heart in front of everyone with personal vows and Jonas accepted that. Though Zed wondered what the pair would say in their speeches. Zed and Caspian handed over the rings. Caspian had been warned not to mess around and he didn't. Then the register was signed and Henry kissed Jonas. Not just a quick peck either. *Oh wow!* He'd opened his heart in his own way and the room burst into applause. The pair left holding hands and Zed took hold of Caspian's as they followed.

"That was lovely," Zed said.

"Are you going to cry?" Caspian smiled.

"I might."

Caspian let go of his hand and hugged him instead.

Guests were milling around in the sunshine on the lawn in front of the marquee. It was a huge structure, a triple-peaked tipi with a couple of catering tents behind. Henry's father had said he'd thrown open the curtains a few days ago and thought a whole tribe of Native Americans had set up camp. The tipi sides were open and it looked fantastic inside, flowers everywhere, beautifully laid tables with gleaming glasses and cutlery. Henry's sisters had done a brilliant job.

Trays of canapés were being carried among the guests by black-clad teenagers.

"Fig and goat's cheese puff?"

"Beef tataki roll?"

"Seared scallops with sweet chili sauce?"

"Parma ham, artichoke and parmesan bruschetta?"

"They're well trained in canapé-speak," Caspian whispered and accepted another glass of champagne.

"Don't get drunk before we have to do our speech." Zed really didn't want to do it on his own.

The wedding breakfast was delicious. Zed and Caspian sat at a table with Jonas, Henry, Henry's parents, Jonas's mother, Henry's sisters and Jonas's brother. *My family.* The thought choked Zed and he felt Caspian's hand on his knee as if he'd known what had gone through his mind.

After the main course, Henry's father made a touching speech about Henry. What he'd been like as a boy and what he was like as a man. Jonas's brother did the same. Zed had been surprised to hear what a rebel Henry had been, while Jonas had lived, breathed, eaten music.

The grooms spoke after the dessert. Zed saw a different Henry, one who for once *was* prepared to wear his heart on his sleeve and he guessed this was the Henry that Jonas had in the bedroom. At one point, when Henry was talking about Jonas, he choked up, and Jonas reached for his hand and rubbed his thumb over his knuckles.

"You just blew your hard man reputation," someone shouted.

419

"And you're fired," Henry called back.

Then it was Zed's and Caspian's turn. They stood up together.

"A double act?" Henry asked.

"We know we're joined at the hip," Caspian told him. "More than the hip, in fact—"

"Don't," Henry warned.

Zed began. "I think everyone here knows how Jonas and Henry gave me a home when I was sixteen years old. For several years up to that point, my life had been difficult. I wasn't loved. I wasn't treated well. Then through a series of unusual circumstances, I was offered a new home in Greenwich with two of the kindest men I've ever met and my life began again. Jonas and Henry have been far more than I could have ever hoped for. They balanced their roles of guardian and friend, were supportive, encouraging, strict when necessary but always caring. Apart from the guy standing by my side, they are the most important people in my world. I owe them everything. I love them."

Oh dammit. Don't cry.

Caspian squeezed his fingers, then cleared his throat. "Not many guys would offer their home to a strange boy. I mean a stranger. Zed's not strange. Well not very strange. But Henry and Jonas had no idea about Zed's horrible habits when they took him in."

"Hey, where's this part come from?" Zed asked.

There was a ripple of laughter.

"I'm improvising," Caspian said.

Zed groaned.

"Even fewer would have invited someone like me to live with them too." Caspian let out a shaky breath. "They're probably regretting it now because they can't get rid of us. We know too much." He gave a knowing nod. "I promised not to say anything about Henry's collection of rubber ducks, so I won't. Nor about Jonas's DIY skills because we don't let him near hammer and nails since the shelves collapsed and broke Henry's glass model of a polar bear."

Zed put his hand over Caspian's mouth. "They asked us to be their best men because they could trust us to keep their secrets."

Caspian pulled Zed's hand away. "And we will." Caspian grinned. "Most of them."

Henry groaned.

"We googled what best men are supposed to say," Zed said.

420

Caspian widened his eyes. "And we found some really good stuff before we remembered we were supposed to be writing a speech."

"You got distracted, not me." Zed glared at him.

"Firstly, we should praise the bridesmaids and say how lovely they look even if they don't." Caspian looked round and frowned. "Er…"

Everyone laughed.

"Secondly, we assure the bride that she is a saint and tell her how lovely she looks." Zed looked from Jonas to Henry and scratched his head. "You both look lovely and you are both saints."

"Can we come up with any childhood anecdotes or work-related ones?"

"Maybe a few," Zed said.

"But remember we promised not to tell about how Jonas got stuck in his wetsuit and Henry had to cut him out of it with nail scissors and he took a picture. For a fifty-pound donation to a charity of Jonas's choice, I'll show it anyone who asks."

Jonas put his head in his hands.

"And we're not supposed to tell anyone about the time Jonas lost his grip on his bow when he was playing Beethoven's Fifth and how the bow went flying about five rows into the audience. Jonas had to climb down, make his way through the rows to get it, only to find when he got back to the stage he couldn't climb up. A member of the audience helped him and Jonas sat down and carried on playing to huge applause."

"There's lots to say about Jonas," Caspian said, "but Henry is a dark horse. Someone told me he once climbed on a horse and fell straight over the other side and pretended he'd meant to do it."

"He sniggers every time his sat nav tells him to go straight."

"He once vacuumed the whole house wearing his headphones and didn't realise the vacuum wasn't plugged in." Caspian smiled.

Now Henry was the one with his head in his hands.

By the time Zed and Caspian had finished, everyone was in stitches. Henry and Jonas stood to hug them.

"I will get even," Henry whispered.

"But I'm perfect," Caspian said.

There was no cake. Henry had put his foot down about that. But there was an ice cream machine and a chocolate fountain.

"I'm too full to eat another thing." Zed groaned.

421

"Oh no." Caspian pouted. "That's ruined my plans."

"Okay, just one chocolate strawberry."

Zed chuckled and slung his arm over Caspian's shoulder. "It's been great, hasn't it?"

"They haven't heard us play yet."

"Hey, we're good. Don't worry."

"You're good. I'm average."

As Cap

Henry tapped Caspian on the shoulder as he and Zed were heading for the bar.

"We've been looking for you two."

Jonas took Zed's hand. "Come outside."

Caspian followed the three of them to a tree that had been draped with fairy lights that hung in strings.

"We want to thank you," Jonas said. We feel like the luckiest guys alive. We took a risk when we opened our house to Zed but it turned out to be the best thing we ever did. We never really told you why we had you come and live with us."

"I thought Jackson asked you," Zed said.

"He did." Henry cleared his throat. "I had… I had a younger brother. His name was Edward. He got involved with drugs when he was a teenager and overdosed aged seventeen. He was a friend of Jackson's at boarding school. Jackson was the one who found him in the grounds of the school. I was twenty-one. Jackson felt he'd failed Edward. But I never blamed him. Edward was bent on self-destruction. I think Jackson saw a way for us both to help you."

"You were the light in our home," Jonas said. "You brought Henry and I closer together. And along came Caspian and our family was complete. We have loved having you live with us. There's not been one moment when we've regretted it."

"This is for you." Jonas handed Zed an envelope.

Zed opened it, gasped and turned to Caspian. "Tickets for a holiday in Hawaii next year."

What? "I hope you have a lovely time," Caspian said. "Take pictures."

"For you too, you idiot." Zed elbowed him.

Caspian opened his mouth to remind him he couldn't go to the States and then closed it again.

"This one is more personal, but it does benefit you both." Henry turned to Caspian. "Your criminal record has been removed from the Police National Computer. An exception has been made because of your heroic action on the Thames. You're no longer on licence. All restrictions have been lifted. You'll be able to travel wherever you want. There'll be no bar to you adopting children if that's what you'd like to do. The families of the girls who died have been told your record has been expunged, and whilst not…happy, accepted you deserved another chance. You have your life back."

Caspian had sort of heard what Henry said but couldn't take it in.

"You've also been put forward for the George Medal for an act of conspicuous bravery." Henry smiled at him.

"I can go to Hawaii with Zed?" Caspian mumbled.

Henry laughed. "Yes."

Zed sighed. "Did you hear what Henry said?"

I heard. Fuck, I heard. "Yeah, we can go to Hawaii. We can bike down a volcano." He turned to Henry and Jonas. "Thank you."

Henry dragged him into his arms and held him tight. "You saved everyone on the boat that night from death or serious injury. If Zed had been killed, we'd have fallen apart. If you'd not survived, how could we have convinced Zed to carry on? If you'd both died, our hearts would have broken. If I'd lost Jonas…"

"I wasn't thinking," Caspian mumbled.

"Yeah you were. You knew what would happen if Tamaz detonated that bomb. You knew that you and Zed would probably die along with many others. You chose Zed's life over your own. What you did was insanely brave."

Henry clung to him so tightly, Caspian struggled to breathe.

"I wondered," Henry said, "if you'd do me the very great honour of taking my surname as yours. You don't have to tell me now. Think about it. I won't be offended if you say no."

"I don't need to think about it. I'd love to be Caspian Steele. Even though it does sound like I've been cast in steel. Caspian, Man of Steel. I'll shut up now."

Caspian was nervous about performing. He'd joined Zed in the recording studio a few times, but never played in front of an actual

423

audience. He had his lucky marble in his pocket, though once they'd started, he forgot there was anyone watching at all. They played old favourites by Queen, Bruce Springsteen, Take That, and a couple that he and Zed had written together. Everyone was dancing. Carried on a rush of adrenaline, Caspian knew he'd never played this well before. Definitely time to stop before something went wrong.

"You tired?" Zed asked.

"Yeah."

"Come on. Let's go back to our room. You can lie down."

"And you can lie on top of me."

Zed laughed as he tugged Caspian back into the castle. "I thought you were tired."

"I'm never *that* tired. I'm going to make you see stars."

"Is that a promise?"

"Absolutely. If I'm willing to give you the stars and the moon, I reckon you should be willing to sacrifice Uranus."

Zed groaned. "That is a terrible joke. Definitely time to leave."

They were hard long before they were naked, shedding their shoes, then clothes along the corridor on the way to their room, leaving a trail to the bed. Caspian allowed Zed to propel him there, but it was Zed beneath him now, pinned down by Caspian. Zed writhed and groaned as Caspian landed kisses on the delicate skin below his ear.

"Any stars yet?" Caspian breathed the words into his ear before he licked Zed's neck and worked his way slowly down his body.

"Not yet."

He drew on Zed's flat stomach with his tongue, then blew over the places he'd licked while Zed shuddered and clenched the sheet in his fists. Caspian curled his tongue over Zed's angular hip bone, nipped it, then pressed his face into his groin, rubbing him with his chin before turning his face to his cock.

A pearl of moisture beaded at the tip. Caspian ran his finger along a vein then scooped up the precum and sucked his finger, his mouth watering with the salty tang that was so uniquely Zed.

"I'm full now," Caspian said.

Zed laughed, his fingers dipping, diving and pulling at Caspian's hair. "You can't manage just a little more?"

"Maybe." Caspian slid the rough flat of his tongue from Zed's balls up to the rounded crest and licked over it before reversing the journey. When he nibbled Zed's hip, Zed let out a strangled groan.

424

"Don't muddle up where you're biting," Zed panted.

"I'll try not to."

"If you do, you'll be the one seeing stars because I'll buck you off the bed."

Caspian wrapped his hand around the base of Zed's cock and fed it into his mouth while he looked up at him. Short, fasts sucks had Zed lifting his hips to get him to take more. Long, deep sucks had Zed running his fingers over the hollows in Caspian's cheeks. Everything they did primed Caspian's lust, sending shivers and goose bumps racing over his skin. Every touch of Zed's skin, cock, balls, wound his *own* body tighter.

"I love you, I love you, I love you." Zed whispered the words over and over again.

"Only three *love you's*? I was hoping for four."

"Don't push your luck."

Caspian fumbled for the lube, found it pressed into his hand and while he still kissed and licked Zed's cock, he pressed a lube-coated finger against the entrance to Zed's body, circling the puckered hole, pushing, pressing until the muscles relaxed and let him in.

"I love you too," Caspian whispered. "I love sticking my fingers up your arse."

Zed's body shook as he laughed. "How many *love you's* said at inappropriate times is that?"

"I've lost count."

When Caspian found the spongy gland that made Zed arch his back in ecstasy, the thrill was almost as strong for Caspian. The giving of pleasure, making Zed happy, making him smile was a flame burning inside Caspian. He thought he couldn't love Zed more than he did, and then something would happen that showed him he could. He couldn't imagine life without him. He didn't want to. When they died, Caspian wanted them to die together.

Not yet though.

Zed's words became incoherent as Caspian slowly brought him off. He pulled back, sped up, let Zed take charge and fuck his mouth, thrusting deep enough to bruise his tonsils before Caspian regained control. He pulled off with a soft pop, then wrapped his lips around Zed's balls. Pressure from his tongue, quick flicks, gentle rolls would drive Zed towards his breaking point.

"Please," Zed whispered. "I need to come. Now."

Caspian let him out of his mouth but kept pushing into him with his finger, then two fingers, pumping them in and out. "Not until I'm inside you."

Zed opened his eyes. "You're joking."

"No, and you're on top. I'm tired."

Zed chuckled.

Caspian reached for a condom and Zed caught his wrist. "We don't need it."

Fuck. Caspian wanted to ask if he was sure, but no words emerged from his mouth.

"I want to feel you come inside me. I want to feel your cum inside me, then dripping out of me."

Caspian whimpered.

"What's wrong?"

"I was hoping to last ages, drive you insane with need, but now you'll have to make do with thirty minutes of fabulous, furious fucking."

"Shut up and lie on your back."

Caspian did as he was told. Zed squirted lube onto his hand and rubbed it up then down Caspian's cock. When he started to do it again, Caspian grabbed his hand.

"No more. My brain is telling me you're giving me a hand job. I'll be spurting all over your chest not inside you."

Zed came up on his knees and reached behind him to push his fingers into his own arsehole. "I figure the more stretching and more lube the better, right?" He bit his lip and stared at Caspian the whole time.

Caspian swallowed his whimper. "Need a hand? A finger? Two? Three? Four?"

"Stop before you offer your entire arm. That's not going to happen."

Zed straddled him on his knees, then lowered himself down, reaching for Caspian's cock to hold it in place. It was such a *fucking* turn on watching him do this that Caspian forgot to breathe. Zed pushed down slowly and kept pushing until Caspian's cock was buried completely inside him.

Caspian let out a long groan.

"It feels different," Zed panted.

"More like a Lamborghini than a Ferrari?"

426

"You always feel good but you're hotter, warmer, tighter around me."

Zed clenched his anal muscles, Caspian sucked in a breath, then leaned up and kissed him. "You are so beautiful," he whispered into Zed's neck.

Zed came back onto his knees and began to move. How he could undulate his hips in the perfect rhythm, jerk himself off and breathe at the same time was beyond Caspian. Then Caspian began to move too, driving his cock up into Zed faster and faster. They were both moaning, gasping. Caspian caught hold of Zed's hip with one hand while the other made a fist around Zed's hand where he held his own cock. *Maybe I can multitask too.*

They were caught up in a maelstrom, hair sticking up, lips swollen, pupils blown. Caspian wasn't sure they'd ever moved this fast when they were fucking but the sounds Zed was making were his power source. Inside Caspian, every cell bubbled and fizzed with excitement. The rhythm was frantic and Caspian could feel orgasm racing toward him. Electricity arced down his spine and set fire to his balls.

Zed came with a loud gasp and Caspian followed. At that moment of release, the fireworks exploded outside, the dark sky lighting up with colour. Everything seemed to stretch as if a rocket had been fired up and didn't stop ascending. Orgasm went on and on through a series of bangs and hissing and crackling, splattering the sky with red and green and blue.

"I promised I'd make you see stars," Caspian said.

The two of them collapsed laughing into each other's arms.

SUMMER TEN

Epilogue

May

Young inventor Caspian Steele scoops award for devising a way to harness surplus energy from household appliances, enough to produce a third of the electricity used daily by an average household.

June

Young part-time composer Zed Mallinson wins a BAFTA for the soundtrack of the latest Bond film. Is he Oscar-bound?

July

Henry picked up the postcard from the mat. "From Zed and Caspian," he told Jonas.

"What does it say?"

"Read it with me." He pulled Jonas closer. "A line from each of them."

Today we biked down the volcano, Zed had written.

Zed is a wuss, wrote Caspian.

At least I arrived intact.

But I got there first and I only had to have ten stitches.

I shouldn't have hit him so hard, wrote Zed.

Henry laughed. "Oh God, if I didn't know that Zed was reining him in…"

"Keep reading!"

I asked Zed to marry me.

I'm making him wait, Zed had written.

How long?

The answer is yes, wrote Zed

xxxx

The End

About the Author

Barbara Elsborg lives in Kent in the south of England. She always wanted to be a spy, but having confessed to everyone without them even resorting to torture, she decided it was not for her. Volcanology scorched her feet. A morbid fear of sharks put paid to marine biology. So instead, she spent several years successfully selling cyanide.

After dragging up two rotten, ungrateful children and frustrating her sexy, devoted, wonderful husband (who can now stop twisting her arm) she finally has time to conduct an affair with an electrifying plugged-in male, her laptop.

She writes stories about two guys, two guys and one woman, and one guy and one woman in most genres—contemporary, paranormal, sci fi, suspense, urban fantasy. Her books feature bad boys and quirky heroines, and she hopes they are as much fun to read as they are to write.

She loves hearing from readers and can be contacted at bjelsborg@gmail.com If you'd like to hear about future releases please ask to be put on her mailing list.

Other books by Barbara Elsborg

There are a few linked books in my list but all can be read as standalones.

Contemporary MMs
The Story of Us
Edge of Forever
Cowboys Down
With or Without Him
Give Yourself Away
Every Move He Makes
Falling (Fall and Break book 1)
Breaking (Fall and Break book 2)
Drawn In

Paranormal MMs

Dirty Angel
Bloodline (Norwood book 2)
The Demon You Know (Norwood book 3)
Archangel's Assassin

Short Stories (MM)
Zeke's Wood

Contemporary MFs
Strangers
Summer Girl Winter Boy
Kiss a Falling Star
An Ordinary Girl
Perfect Timing (Bedlington book 1)
Something About Polly (Bedlington book 2)
Doing the Right Thing (Mansell brothers book 1)
Finding the Right One (Mansell brothers book 2)
Digging Deeper
The Princess and the Prepper (novella)
Snow Play (novella)
On the Right Track (novella)

Contemporary MMFs
Anna in the Middle
Susie's Choice
Girl Most Likely to
Talking Trouble
Just What She Wants (novella)
Starting Over (novella)

Paranormal MFs and MMFs
Perfect Trouble MF
Power of Love MF
Kiss Interrupted MF
Jumping in Puddles MF (Norwood book 1)
Rocked MMF
The Small Print MMF
Worlds Apart MMF
The Consolation Prize MF (Trueblood book 1)
Falling for You MF (Trueblood book 2)
Lightning in a Bottle MF ((Trueblood book 3)

The Misfits MMF(Trueblood book 4)
Fight to Remember MMF(Trueblood book 5)
Lucy in the Sky MF (sci fi)
Taking Stock MMF (sci fi)
Just One Bite MF (novella)

Short Stories (MF)

Saying Yes
The Bad Widow
The Gift
Dragon Race
Two Birds, One Stone

Romantic Suspense (MF)
Chosen
Crossing the Line

Made in the
USA
Middletown, DE